The Defector

DANIEL SILVA

PENGUIN BOOKS

PENGUIN BOOKS

Published by the Penguin Group

Penguin Books Ltd, 80 Strand, London WC2R ORL, England

Penguin Group (USA) Inc., 375 Hudson Street, New York, New York 10014, USA

Penguin Group (Canada), 90 Eglinton Avenue East, Suite 700, Toronto, Ontario, Canada M4P 2Y3
(a division of Pearson Penguin Canada Inc.)

Penguin Ireland, 25 St Stephen's Green, Dublin 2, Ireland (a division of Penguin Books Ltd)

Penguin Group (Australia), 250 Camberwell Road, Camberwell, Victoria 3124, Australia
(a division of Pearson Australia Group Pty Ltd)

Penguin Books India Pvt Ltd, 11 Community Centre, Panchsheel Park, New Delhi – 110 017, India

Penguin Group (NZ), 67 Apollo Drive, Rosedale, North Shore 0632, New Zealand
(a division of Pearson New Zealand Ltd)

Penguin Books (South Africa) (Pty) Ltd, 24 Sturdee Avenue, Rosebank, Johannesburg 2196, South Africa

Penguin Books Ltd, Registered Offices: 80 Strand, London WC2R ORL, England

www.penguin.com

First published in the United States of America by G.P. Putnam's Sons 2009
First published in Great Britain by Michael Joseph 2009
Published in Penguin Books 2010

1

Set in Garamond MT 12.5/14.75pt
Printed in England by Clays Ltd, St Ives plc

ISBN: 978-0-141-04276-3

www.greenpenguin.co.uk

Penguin Books is committed to a sustainable future
for our business, our readers and our planet.
The book in your hands is made from paper
certified by the Forest Stewardship Council.

For Marilyn Ducksworth,
for many years of friendship,
support, and laughter.

And as always, for my wife, Jamie,
and my children, Nicholas and Lily.

If an injury has to be done to a man it should be so severe that his vengeance need not be feared.

Machiavelli

PART ONE
Opening Moves

1. Vladimirskaya Oblast, Russia

Pyotr Luzhkov was about to be killed, and for that he was grateful.

It was late October, but autumn was already a memory. It had been brief and unsightly, an old babushka hurriedly removing a threadbare frock. Now this: leaden skies, arctic cold, windblown snow. The opening shot of Russia's winter without end.

Pyotr Luzhkov, shirtless, barefoot, hands bound behind his back, was scarcely aware of the cold. In fact, at that moment he would have been hard-pressed to recall his name. He believed he was being led by two men through a birch forest but could not be certain. It made sense they were in a forest. That was the place Russians liked to do their blood work. *Kurapaty, Bykivnia, Katyn, Butovo* . . . Always in the forests. Luzhkov was about to join a great Russian tradition. Luzhkov was about to be granted a death in the trees.

There was another Russian custom when it came to killing: the intentional infliction of pain. Pyotr Luzhkov had been forced to scale mountains of pain. They had broken his fingers and his thumbs. They had broken his arms and his ribs. They had broken his nose and his jaw. They had beaten him even when he was unconscious. They had beaten him because they had been told to. They had beaten him because they were Russians. The only time they had

3

stopped was when they were drinking vodka. When the vodka was gone, they had beaten him even harder.

Now he was on the final leg of his journey, the long walk to a grave with no marker. Russians had a term for it: *vyshaya mera*, the highest form of punishment. Usually, it was reserved for traitors, but Pyotr Luzhkov had betrayed no one. He had been duped by his master's wife, and his master had lost everything because of it. Someone had to pay. Eventually, everyone would pay.

He could see his master now, standing alone amid the matchstick trunks of the birch trees. Black leather coat, silver hair, head like a tank turret. He was looking down at the large-caliber pistol in his hand. Luzhkov had to give him credit. There weren't many oligarchs who had the stomach to do their own killing. But then there weren't many oligarchs like him.

The grave had already been dug. Luzhkov's master was inspecting it carefully, as if calculating whether it was big enough to hold a body. As Luzhkov was forced to kneel, he could smell the distinctive cologne. Sandalwood and smoke. The smell of power. The smell of the devil.

The devil gave him one more blow to the side of his face. Luzhkov didn't feel it. Then the devil placed the gun to the back of Luzhkov's head and bade him a pleasant evening. Luzhkov saw a pink flash of his own blood. Then darkness. He was finally dead. And for that he was grateful.

2. London: January

The murder of Pyotr Luzhkov went largely unnoticed. No one mourned him; no women wore black for him. No Russian police officers investigated his death, and no Russian newspapers bothered to report it. Not in Moscow. Not in St Petersburg. And surely not in the Russian city sometimes referred to as London. Had word of Luzhkov's demise reached Bristol Mews, home of Colonel Grigori Bulganov, the Russian defector and dissident, he would not have been surprised, though he would have felt a pang of guilt. If Grigori hadn't locked poor Pyotr in Ivan Kharkov's personal safe, the bodyguard might still be alive.

Among the lords of Thames House and Vauxhall Cross, the riverfront headquarters of MI5 and MI6, Grigori Bulganov had always been a source of much fascination and considerable debate. Opinion was diverse, but then it usually was when the two services were forced to take positions on the same issue. He was a gift from the gods, sang his backers. He was a mixed bag at best, muttered his detractors. One wit from the top floor of Thames House famously described him as the defector Downing Street needed like a leaky roof — as if London, now home to more than a quarter million Russian citizens, had a spare room for another malcontent bent on making trouble for the Kremlin. The MI5 man had gone on the record with his prophecy that one day they would all regret the decision to grant Grigori Bulganov asylum and a British passport. But even he was surprised by the speed with which that day came.

A former colonel in the counterintelligence division of the Russian Federal Security Service, better known as the FSB, Grigori Bulganov had washed ashore late the previous summer, the unexpected by-product of a multinational intelligence operation against one Ivan Kharkov, Russian oligarch and international arms dealer. Only a handful of British officials were told the true extent of Grigori's involvement in the case. Fewer still knew that, if not for his actions, an entire team of Israeli operatives might have been killed on Russian soil. Like the KGB defectors who came before him, Grigori vanished for a time into a world of safe houses and isolated country estates. A joint Anglo-American team hammered at him day and night, first on the structure of Ivan's arms-trafficking network, for which Grigori had shamefully worked as a paid agent, then on the tradecraft of his former service. The British interrogators found him charming; the Americans less so. They insisted on fluttering him, which in Agencyspeak meant subjecting him to a lie-detector test. He passed with flying colors.

When the debriefers had had their fill, and it came time to decide just what to do with him, the bloodhounds of internal security conducted highly secret reviews and issued their recommendations, also in secret. In the end, it was deemed that Grigori, though reviled by his former comrades, faced no serious threat. Even the once-feared Ivan Kharkov, who was licking his wounds in Russia, was deemed incapable of concerted action. The defector made three requests: he wanted to keep his name, to reside in

London, and to have no overt security. Hiding in plain sight, he argued, would give him the most protection from his enemies. MI5 readily agreed to his demands, especially the third. Security details required money, and the human resources could be put to better use elsewhere, namely against Britain's homegrown jihadist extremists. They bought him a lovely mews cottage in a backwater of Maida Vale, arranged a generous monthly stipend, and made a onetime deposit in a City bank that would surely have caused a scandal if the amount ever became public. An MI5 lawyer quietly negotiated a book deal with a respected London publisher. The size of the advance raised eyebrows among the senior staff of both services, most of whom were working on books of their own – in secret, of course.

For a time it seemed Grigori would turn out to be the rarest of birds in the intelligence world: a case without complications. Fluent in English, he took to life in London like a freed prisoner trying to make up for lost time. He frequented the theater and toured the museums. Poetry readings, ballet, chamber music: he did them all. He settled into work on his book and once a week lunched with his editor, who happened to be a porcelain-skinned beauty of thirty-two. The only thing missing in his life was chess. His MI5 minder suggested he join the Central London Chess Club, a venerable institution founded by a group of civil servants during the First World War. His application form was a masterpiece of ambiguity. It supplied no address, no home telephone, no mobile, and no e-mail. His occupation was described as 'translation services,' his employer as 'self.' Asked to list any hobbies or outside interests, he had written 'chess.'

But no high-profile case is ever entirely free of controversy – and the old hands warned they had never met a defector, especially a Russian defector, who didn't lose a wheel from time to time. Grigori's came off the day the British prime minister announced a major terrorist plot had been disrupted. It seemed al-Qaeda had planned to simultaneously shoot down several jet-liners using Russian-made antiaircraft missiles – missiles they had acquired from Grigori's former patron, Ivan Kharkov. Within twenty-four hours, Grigori was seated before the cameras of the BBC, claiming he had played a major role in the affair. In the days and weeks that followed, he would remain a fixture on television, in Britain and elsewhere. His celebrity status now cemented, he began to move in Russian émigré circles and cavort with Russian dissidents of every stripe. Seduced by the sudden attention, he used his newfound fame as a platform to make wild accusations against his old service and against the Russian president, whom he characterized as a Hitler in the making. When the Kremlin responded with uncomfortable noises about Russians plotting a coup on British soil, Grigori's minder suggested he tone things down. So, too, did his editor, who wanted to save something for the book.

Grudgingly, the defector lowered his profile, but only by a little. Rather than pick fights with the Kremlin, he focused his considerable energy on his forthcoming book and on his chess. That winter he entered the annual club tournament and moved effortlessly through his bracket – like a Russian tank through the streets of Prague, grumbled one of his victims. In the semifinals, he defeated the defending champion without breaking a sweat. Victory in the finals appeared inevitable.

On the afternoon of the championship, he lunched in Soho with a reporter from *Vanity Fair* magazine. Returning to Maida Vale, he purchased a house plant from the Clifton Nurseries and collected a parcel of shirts from his laundry in Elgin Avenue. After a brief nap, a prematch ritual, he showered and dressed for battle, departing his mews cottage a few minutes before six.

All of which explains why Grigori Bulganov, defector and dissident, was walking along London's Harrow Road at 6:12 p.m., on the second Tuesday of January. For reasons that would be made clear later, he was moving at a faster pace than normal. As for chess, it was by then the last thing on his mind.

The match was scheduled for half past six at the club's usual venue, the Lower Vestry House of St George's Church in Bloomsbury. Simon Finch, Grigori's opponent, arrived at a quarter past. Shaking the rainwater from his oilskin coat, he squinted at a trio of notices tacked to the bulletin board in the foyer. One forbade smoking, another warned against blocking the corridor in case of fire, and a third, hung by Finch himself, pleaded with all those who used the premises to recycle their rubbish. In the words of George Mercer, club captain and six-time club champion, Finch was 'a Camden Town crusty,' bedecked with all the required political convictions of his tribe. Free Palestine. Free Tibet. Stop the Genocide in Darfur. End the War in Iraq. Recycle or Die. The only cause Finch didn't seem to believe in was work. He described himself as 'a social activist and freelance journalist,' which Clive Atherton, the club's reactionary treasurer, accurately translated as 'layabout and sponge.' But even Clive was the first to admit that Finch possessed the loveliest of games: flowing, artistic, instinctive, and ruthless as a snake. 'Simon's costly education wasn't a total waste,' Clive was fond of saying. 'Just misapplied.'

His surname was a misnomer, for Finch was long and languid, with limp brown hair that hung nearly to his shoulders and wire-rimmed spectacles that magnified the resolute gaze of a revolutionary. To the bulletin board he added a fourth item now – a fawning letter from the Regent Hall Church thanking the club for hosting the first annual Salvation Army chess tournament for the homeless – then he drifted down the narrow corridor to the makeshift cloakroom, where he hung his coat on the rollaway rack. In the kitchenette, he deposited twenty pence in a giant piggy bank and drew a cup of tepid coffee from a silver canister marked CHESS CLUB. Young Tom Blakemore – a misnomer as well, for Young Tom was eighty-five in the shade – bumped into him as he was coming out. Finch seemed not to notice. Interviewed later by a man from MI5, Young Tom said he had taken no offense. After all, not a single member of the club gave Finch even an outside chance of winning the cup. 'He looked like a man being led to the gallows,' said Young Tom. 'The only thing missing was the black hood.'

Finch entered the storage cabinet and from a row of sagging shelves collected a board, a box of pieces, an analog tournament clock, and a score sheet. Coffee in one hand, match supplies carefully balanced in the other, he entered the vestry's main room. It had walls the color of mustard and four grimy windows: three peering onto the pavements of Little Russell Street and a fourth squinting into the courtyard. On one wall, below a small crucifix, was the tournament bracket. One match remained to be played: S. FINCH VS. G. BULGANOV.

Finch turned and surveyed the room. Six trestle tables had been erected for the evening's play, one reserved for the championship, the rest for ordinary matches – 'friendlies,' in the parlance of the club. A devout atheist, Finch chose the spot farthest from the crucifix and methodically prepared for the contest. He checked the tip of his pencil and wrote the date and the board number on the score sheet. He closed his eyes and saw the match as he hoped it would unfold. Then, fifteen minutes after taking his seat, he looked up at the clock: *6:42*. Grigori was late. *Odd*, thought Finch. The Russian was never late.

Finch began moving pieces in his mind – saw a king lying on its side in resignation, saw Grigori hanging his head in shame – and he watched the relentless march of the clock. *6:45 . . . 6:51 . . . 6:58 . . .*

Where are you, Grigori? he thought. *Where the hell are you?*

Ultimately, Finch's role would be minor and, in the opinion of all involved, mercifully brief. There were some who wanted to have a closer look at a few of his more deplorable political associations. There were others who refused to touch him, having rightly judged Finch to be a man who would relish nothing more than a good public spat with the security services. In the end, however, it would be determined his only crime was one of sportsmanship. Because at precisely 7:05 p.m. – the time recorded in his own hand on the official score sheet – he exercised his right to claim victory by forfeiture, thus becoming the first player in club history to win the championship without moving a single piece. It was a dubious honor, one the chess players of British intelligence would never quite forgive.

Ari Shamron, the legendary Israeli spymaster, would later say that never before had so much blood flowed from so humble a beginning. But even Shamron, who was guilty of the occasional rhetorical flourish, knew the remark was far from accurate. For the events that followed had their true origins not in Grigori's disappearance but in a feud of Shamron's own making. Grigori, he would confide to his most devoted acolytes, was but a shot over our complacent bow. A signal fire on a distant watchtower. And the bait used to lure Gabriel into the open.

By the following evening, the score sheet was in the possession of MI5, along with the entire tournament logbook. The Americans were informed of Grigori's disappearance twenty-four hours later, but, for reasons never fully explained, British intelligence waited four long days before getting around to telling the Israelis. Shamron, who had fought in Israel's war of independence and loathed the British to this day, found the delay predictable. Within minutes he was on the phone to Uzi Navot giving him marching orders. Navot reluctantly obeyed. It was what Navot did best.

3. Umbria, Italy

Guido Reni was a peculiar man, even for an artist. He was prone to bouts of anxiety, riddled with guilt over his repressed homosexuality, and so insecure about his talents he worked only behind the protective shroud of a mantle. He harbored an unusually intense devotion to the Virgin Mary but loathed women so thoroughly he would not allow them to touch his laundry. He believed witches were stalking him. His cheeks would flush with embarrassment at the mere sound of an obscenity.

Had he followed his father's advice, Reni would have played the harpsichord. Instead, at the age of nine, he entered the studio of the Flemish master Denys Calvaert and embarked on a career as a painter. His apprenticeship complete, he left his home in Bologna in 1601 and traveled to Rome, where he quickly won a commission from the pope's nephew to produce an altarpiece, *Crucifixion of St Peter*, for the Church of San Paolo alle Tre Fontane. At the request of his influential patron, Reni took his inspiration from a work hanging in the Church of Santa Maria del Popolo. Its creator, a controversial and erratic painter known as Caravaggio, was not flattered by Reni's imitation and vowed to kill him if it ever happened again.

Before beginning work on Reni's panel, the restorer had gone to Rome to view the Caravaggio again. Reni had obviously borrowed from his competitor – most strikingly, his technique of using chiaroscuro to infuse his figures with life and lift them dramatically from the background – but there were many differences between the paintings, too. Where Caravaggio had placed the inverted cross diagonally through the scene, Reni positioned it vertically and in the center. Where Caravaggio had shown the agonized face of Peter, Reni deftly concealed it. What struck the restorer most was Reni's depiction of Peter's hands. In Caravaggio's altarpiece, they were already fastened to the cross. But in Reni's portrayal, the hands were free, with the right stretched toward the apex. Was Peter reaching toward the nail about to be driven into his feet? Or was he pleading with God to be delivered from so terrible a death?

The restorer had been working on the painting for more than a month. Having removed the yellowed varnish, he was now engaged in the final and most important part of the restoration: retouching those portions damaged by time and stress. The altarpiece had suffered substantial losses in the four centuries since Reni had painted it – indeed, the mid-restoration photos had sent the owners into a blue period of hysteria and recrimination. Under normal circumstances, the restorer might have spared them the shock of seeing the painting stripped to its true state, but these were hardly normal circumstances. The Reni was now in the possession of the Vatican. Because the restorer was considered one of the finest in the world – and because he was a personal friend of the pope and his powerful private secretary – he was allowed to work for the Holy See on a freelance basis and to select his own assignments. He was even permitted to conduct his restorations not in the Vatican's state-of-the-art conservation lab but at a secluded estate in southern Umbria.

Known as Villa dei Fiori, it lay fifty miles north of Rome, on a plateau between the Tiber and Nera rivers. There was a large cattle operation and an equestrian center that bred some of the finest jumpers in all of Italy. There were pigs no one ate, goats kept solely for entertainment value, and, in summer, fields filled with sunflowers. The villa itself stood at the end of a long gravel drive lined with towering umbrella pine. In the eleventh century it had been a monastery. There was still a small chapel and the remains of an oven where the monks had baked their daily bread. At the base of the house was a large swimming pool and a trellised garden where rosemary and lavender grew along walls of Etruscan stone. Everywhere there were dogs: a quartet of hounds that roamed the pastures, devouring fox and rabbit, and a pair of neurotic terriers that patrolled the perimeter of the stables with the fervor of holy warriors.

Though the villa was owned by a faded Italian nobleman named Count Gasparri, its day-to-day operations were overseen by a staff of four: Margherita, the young housekeeper; Anna, the gifted cook; Isabella, the ethereal half Swede who tended to the horses; and Carlos, an Argentine cowboy who tended the cattle, the crops, and the small vineyard. The restorer and the staff existed in something resembling a cold peace. They had been told he was an Italian named Alessio Vianelli, the son of an Italian diplomat who had lived abroad for much of his life. The restorer's name was not Alessio Vianelli, nor was he the son of a diplomat, or even an Italian. His real name was Gabriel Allon, and he came from the Valley of Jezreel in Israel.

He was below average in height, perhaps five-eight, and

had the spare physique of a cyclist. His face was high at the forehead and narrow at the chin, and his long bony nose looked as though it had been carved from wood. His eyes were a shocking shade of emerald green; his short dark hair was shot with gray at the temples. Entirely ambidextrous, he could paint equally well with either hand. At the moment, he was using his left. Glancing at his wristwatch, he saw it was nearly midnight. He debated whether to continue working. One more hour, he reckoned, and the background would be complete. Better to finish it now. The director of the Vatican Picture Gallery was keen to have the Reni on exhibit again by Holy Week, the annual springtime siege of pilgrims and tourists. Gabriel had pledged to do his utmost to meet the deadline but had made no firm promises. He was a perfectionist who viewed each assignment as a defense of his reputation. Known for the lightness of his touch, he believed a restorer should be a passing spirit, that he should come and go leaving no trace, only a painting returned to its original glory, the damage of the centuries undone.

His studio occupied what should have been the villa's formal sitting room. Emptied of its furnishings, it contained nothing now but his supplies, a pair of powerful halogen lamps, and a small portable stereo. *La Bohème* issued from its speakers, the volume lowered to the level of a whisper. He was a man with many enemies, and, unlike Guido Reni, they were not figments of his imagination. It was why he listened to his music softly – and why he always carried a loaded Beretta 9mm pistol. The grip was stained with paint: a dab of Titian, a bit of Bellini, a drop of Raphael and Veronese.

Despite the hour, he worked with energy and focus and managed to complete his work as the final notes of the opera faded into silence. He cleaned his brushes and palette, then reduced the power on the lamps. In the half-light, the background receded into darkness and the four figures glowed softly. Standing before the painting, one hand pressed to his chin, head tilted to one side, he planned his next session. In the morning he would begin work on the uppermost henchman, a figure in a red cap holding a spike in one hand and a mallet in the other. He felt a certain grim kinship with the executioner. In other lifetimes, concealed by other names, he had performed a similar service for his masters in Tel Aviv.

He switched off the lamps and climbed the stone steps to his room. The bed was empty; Chiara, his wife, had been in Venice for the last three days visiting her parents. They had endured long separations because of work, but this was the first of their own choosing. A loner by nature and obsessive in his work habits, Gabriel had expected her brief absence would be easy to bear. In truth, he had been miserable without her. He took a peculiar comfort in these feelings. It was *normal* for a happily married man to miss his wife. For Gabriel Allon – a child of Holocaust survivors, a gifted artist and restorer, an assassin and spy – life had been anything but normal.

He sat down on Chiara's side of the bed and picked through the stack of reading material on her nightstand. Fashion magazines, journals on interior design, Italian editions of popular American murder mysteries, a book on child rearing – intriguing, he thought, since they were childless and, as far as he knew, weren't expecting one.

Chiara had begun carefully to broach the topic. Gabriel feared it would soon become a point of contention in their marriage. The decision to remarry had been torturous enough. The idea of having another child, even with a woman he loved as much as Chiara, was for the moment incomprehensible. His only son had been killed by a terrorist bomb in Vienna and was buried on the Mount of Olives in Jerusalem. Leah, his first wife, had survived the explosion and resided now in a psychiatric hospital atop Mount Herzl, locked in a prison of memory and a body ravaged by fire. It was because of Gabriel's work that his loved ones had suffered this fate. He had vowed he would never bring into the world another child who could be targeted by his enemies.

He slipped off his sandals and crossed the stone floor to the writing desk. An icon shaped like an envelope winked at him from the screen of the laptop computer. The message had arrived several hours ago. Gabriel had been doing his best not to think about it because he knew it could have come from only one place. Ignoring it forever, however, was not an option. Better to get it over with. Reluctantly, he clicked on the icon, and a line of gibberish appeared on the screen. Typing a password into the proper window, the encryption melted away, leaving a few words in clear text:

MALACHI REQUESTS MEETING. PRIORITY RESH.

Gabriel frowned. Malachi was the code word for the chief of Special Operations. Priority Resh was reserved for time-sensitive situations, usually those involving questions of life and death. He hesitated, then typed in a reply. It took just ninety seconds for the response to arrive:

MALACHI LOOKS FORWARD TO SEEING YOU.

Gabriel switched off the computer and climbed into the empty bed. *Malachi looks forward to seeing you* . . . He doubted that was the case, since he and Malachi were not exactly on speaking terms. Closing his eyes, he saw a hand reaching toward an iron spike. He tapped a brush against his palette and painted until he drifted into sleep. Then he painted some more.

4. Amelia, Umbria

To traverse the road from the Villa dei Fiori to the hill town of Amelia is to see Italy in all its ancient glory and, Gabriel thought sadly, all its modern distress. He had resided in Italy for much of his adult life and had witnessed the country's slow but methodical march toward oblivion. Evidence of decay was all around: governing institutions rife with corruption and incompetence; an economy too feeble to provide enough work for the young; once-glorious coastlines fouled by pollution and sewage. Somehow, these facts escaped the notice of the world's travel writers, who churned out countless words each year extolling the virtue and beauty of Italian life. As for the Italians themselves, they had responded to their deteriorating state of affairs by marrying late, if at all, and having fewer children. Italy's birthrate was among the lowest in Western Europe, and more Italians were over the age of sixty than under twenty, a demographic milestone in human history. Italy was already a country of elderly people and was aging rapidly. If trends continued unabated, it would experience a decline in population not seen since the Great Plague.

Amelia, the oldest of Umbria's cities, had seen the last outbreak of Black Death and, in all likelihood, every one before it. Founded by Umbrian tribesmen long before the dawn of the Common Era, it had been conquered by Etruscans, Romans, Goths, and Lombards before finally being placed under the dominion of the popes. Its dun-colored walls were more than ten feet thick, and many of its ancient streets were navigable only on foot. Few Amelians sought refuge behind the safety of the walls any longer. Most resided in the new town, a graceless maze of drab apartment blocks and concrete shopping malls that spilled down the hill south of the city.

Its main street, Via Rimembranze, was the place where most Amelians passed their ample amounts of free time. In late afternoon, they strolled the pavements and congregated on street corners, trading in gossip and watching the traffic heading down the valley toward Orvieto. The mysterious tenant from the Villa dei Fiori was among their favorite topics of conversation. An outsider who conducted his affairs politely but with an air of standoffishness, he was the subject of substantial mistrust and no small amount of envy. Rumors about his presence at the villa were stoked by the fact that the staff refused to discuss the nature of his work. *He's involved in the arts*, they would respond evasively under questioning. *He prefers to be left alone.* A few of the old women believed him to be an evil spirit who had to be cast out of Amelia before it was too late. Some of the younger ones were secretly in love with the emerald-eyed stranger and flirted with him shamelessly on those rare occasions when he ventured into town.

Among his most ardent admirers was the girl who presided over the gleaming glass counter of Pasticceria Massimo. She wore the cateye spectacles of a librarian and a permanent smile of mild rebuke. Gabriel ordered a cappuccino and a selection of pastries and walked over to a table at the far end of the room. It was already occupied by a man with strawberry blond hair and the heavy shoulders of a wrestler. He was pretending to read a local newspaper – pretending, Gabriel knew, because Italian was not one of his languages.

'Anything interesting, Uzi?' Gabriel asked in German.

Uzi Navot glared at Gabriel for a few seconds before resuming his appraisal of the paper. 'If I'm not mistaken, there seems to be some sort of political crisis in Rome,' he responded in the same language.

Gabriel sat in the empty seat. 'The prime minister is involved in a rather messy financial scandal at the moment.'

'Another one?'

'Something to do with kickbacks on several large construction projects up north. Predictably, the opposition is demanding his resignation. He's vowing to stay in office and fight it out.'

'Maybe it would be better if the Church were still running the place.'

'Are you proposing a reconstitution of the Papal States?'

'Better a pope than a playboy prime minister with shoe-polish hair. He's raised corruption to an art form.'

'Our last prime minister had serious ethical shortcomings of his own.'

'That's true. But fortunately, he isn't the one protecting the country from its enemies. That job still belongs to King Saul Boulevard.'

King Saul Boulevard was the address of Israel's foreign intelligence service. The service had a long and deliberately misleading name that had very little to do with the true nature of its work. Those who worked there referred to it as 'the Office' and nothing else.

The girl placed the cappuccino in front of Gabriel and a plate of pastries in the center of the table. Navot grimaced.

'What's wrong, Uzi? Don't tell me Bella has you on a diet again?'

'What makes you think I was ever off it?'

'Your expanding waistline.'

'We all can't be blessed with your trim physique and high metabolism, Gabriel. My ancestors were plump Austrian Jews.'

'So why fight nature? Have one, Uzi – for the sake of your cover, if nothing else.'

Navot's selection, a trumpet-shaped pastry filled with cream, disappeared in two bites. He hesitated, then chose one filled with sweet almond paste. It vanished in the time it took Gabriel to pour a packet of sugar into his coffee.

'I didn't get a chance to eat on the plane,' Navot said sheepishly. 'Order me a coffee.'

Gabriel asked for another cappuccino, then looked at Navot. He was staring at the pastries again.

'Go ahead, Uzi. Bella will never know.'

'That's what you think. Bella knows everything.'

Bella had worked as an analyst on the Office's Syria Desk before taking a professorship in Levantine history at Ben-Gurion University. Navot, a veteran agent-runner and covert operative schooled in the art of manipulation, was incapable of deceiving her.

'Is the rumor true?' Gabriel asked.

'What rumor is that?'

'The one about you and Bella getting married. The one about a quiet wedding by the sea in Caesarea with only a handful of close friends and family in attendance. And the

Old Man, of course. There's no way the chief of Special Ops could get married without Shamron's blessing.'

Special Ops was the dark side of a dark service. It carried out the assignments no one else wanted, or dared, to do. Its operatives were executioners and kidnappers; buggers and blackmailers; men of intellect and ingenuity with a criminal streak wider than the criminals themselves; multi-linguists and chameleons who were at home in the finest hotels and salons in Europe or the worst back alleys of Beirut and Baghdad. Navot had never managed to get over the fact he had been given command of the unit because Gabriel had turned it down. He was competence to Gabriel's brilliance, caution to Gabriel's occasional recklessness. In any other service, in any other land, he would have been a star. But the Office had always valued operatives like Gabriel, men of creativity unbound by orthodoxy. Navot was the first to admit he was a mere field hand, and he had spent his entire career toiling in Gabriel's shadow.

'Bella wanted the Office personnel kept to a minimum.' Navot's voice had little conviction. 'She didn't want the reception to look like a gathering of spies.'

'Is that why I wasn't invited?'

Navot devoted several seconds to the task of brushing a few crumbs into a tiny hillock. Gabriel made a mental note of it. Office behaviorists referred to such obvious delaying tactics as displacement activity.

'Go ahead, Uzi. You won't hurt my feelings.'

Navot swept the crumbs onto the floor with the back of his hand and looked at Gabriel for a moment in silence. 'You weren't invited to my wedding because I didn't *want* you at my wedding. Not after that stunt you pulled in Moscow.'

The girl placed the coffee in front of Navot and, sensing tension, retreated behind her glass barricade. Gabriel peered out the window at a trio of old men moving slowly along the pavement, heavily bundled against the sharp chill. His thoughts, however, were of a rainy August evening in Moscow. He was standing in the tired little square opposite the looming Stalinist apartment block known as the House on the Embankment. Navot was squeezing the life out of his arm and speaking quietly into his ear. He was saying that the operation to steal the private files of Russian arms dealer Ivan Kharkov was blown. That Ari Shamron, their mentor and master, had ordered them to retreat to Sheremetyevo Airport and board a waiting flight to Tel Aviv. That Gabriel had no choice but to leave behind his agent, Ivan's wife, to face a certain death.

'I had to stay, Uzi. It was the only way to get Elena back alive.'

'You disobeyed a direct order from Shamron and from *me*, your direct, if nominal, superior officer. And you put the lives of the entire team in danger, including your wife's. How do you think that made me look to the rest of the division?'

'Like a sensible chief who kept his head while an operation was going down the tubes.'

'No, Gabriel. It made me look like a coward who was willing to let an agent die rather than risk his own neck and career.' Navot poured three packets of sugar into his coffee and gave it a single angry stir with a tiny silver spoon. 'And you know something? They would be right to say that. Everything but the part about being a coward. I'm not a coward.'

'No one would ever accuse you of running from a fight, Uzi.'

'But I do admit to having well-honed survival instincts. One has to in this line of work, not only in the field but at King Saul Boulevard, too. Not all of us are blessed with your gifts. Some of us actually need a job. Some of us even have our sights set on a promotion.'

Navot tapped the spoon against the rim of his cup and placed it in the saucer. 'I walked into a real storm when I got back to Tel Aviv that night. They scooped us up at the airport and drove us straight to King Saul Boulevard. By the time we arrived, you'd already been missing for several hours. The Prime Minister's Office was calling every few minutes for updates, and Shamron was positively homicidal. It's a good thing he was in London; otherwise, he would have killed me with his bare hands. The working assumption was that you were dead. And I was the one who had allowed it to happen. We sat there for hours and waited for word. It was a bad night, Gabriel. I never want to go through another one like it.'

'Neither do I, Uzi.'

'I don't doubt it.' Navot looked at the scar near Gabriel's right eye. 'By dawn, we'd all but written you off. Then a communications clerk burst into the Operations Room and said you'd just called in on the flash line – from Ukraine, of all places. When we heard your voice for the first time, it was pandemonium. Not only had you made it out of Russia alive with Ivan Kharkov's darkest secrets, but you'd brought along a carload of defectors, including Colonel Grigori Bulganov, the highest-ranking FSB officer to ever come across the wire. Not bad for an evening's work.

Moscow was among your finest hours. But for me, it will be a permanent stain on an otherwise clean record. And you put it there, Gabriel. *That's* why you weren't invited to my wedding.'

'I'm sorry, Uzi.'

'Sorry for what?'

'For putting you in a difficult position.'

'But not for refusing a direct order?'

Gabriel was silent. Navot shook his head slowly.

'You're a smug bastard, Gabriel. I should have broken your arm in Moscow and dragged you to the car.'

'What do you want me to say, Uzi?'

'I want you to tell me it will never happen again.'

'And if it does?'

'First I'll break your arm. Then I'll resign as chief of Special Ops, which will leave them with no other option but to give you the job. And I know how much you want that.'

Gabriel raised his right hand. 'Never again, Uzi – in the field, or anywhere else.'

'Say it.'

'I'm sorry for what transpired between us in Moscow. And I swear I'll never disobey another direct order from you.'

Navot appeared instantly mollified. Personal confrontation had never been his strong suit.

'That's it, Uzi? You came all the way to Umbria because you wanted an apology?'

'And a promise, Gabriel. Don't forget the promise.'

'I haven't forgotten.'

'Good.' Navot placed his elbows on the table and leaned

forward. 'Because I want you to listen to me very carefully. We're going to go back to your villa of flowers, and you're going to pack your bags. Then we're going to Rome to spend the night inside the embassy. Tomorrow morning, when the ten o'clock flight takes off from Fiumicino Airport for Tel Aviv, we're going to be on it, second row of first class, side by side.'

'Why would we do that?'

'Because Colonel Grigori Bulganov is gone.'

'What do you mean *gone*?'

'I mean *gone*, Gabriel. No longer among us. Vanished into thin air. *Gone*.'

5. Amelia, Umbria

How long has he been missing?'

'About a week now.'

'Be specific, Uzi.'

'Colonel Grigori Bulganov was last spotted climbing into the back of a Mercedes sedan on Harrow Road at 6:12 p.m. on Tuesday evening.'

They were walking through the dying twilight, along a narrow cobblestone street in Amelia's ancient center. Trailing a few paces behind was a pair of fawn-eyed bodyguards. It was a troubling sign. Navot usually traveled with only a *bat leveyha*, a female escort officer, for protection. The fact he had brought along two trained killers indicated he took the threat to Gabriel's life seriously.

'When did the British get around to telling us?'

'They placed a quiet call to London Station on Saturday afternoon, four days after the fact. Because it was Shabbat, the duty officer was a kid who didn't quite understand the significance of what he'd just been told. The kid tapped out a cable and sent it off to King Saul Boulevard at low priority. Fortunately, the duty officer on the European Desk *did* understand and immediately placed a courtesy call to Shamron.'

Gabriel shook his head. It had been years now since Shamron had done his last tour as chief, yet the Office was still very much his private fiefdom. It was filled with officers like Gabriel and Navot, men who had been recruited and groomed by Shamron, men who operated by a creed, even spoke a language, written by him. In Israel, Shamron was known as the Memuneh, the one in charge, and he would remain so until the day he finally decided the country was safe enough for him to die.

'And I assume Shamron then called *you*,' Gabriel said.

'He did, though it was distinctly lacking in courtesy of any kind. He told me to send you a message. Then he told me to grab a couple of boys and get on a plane. This seems to be my lot in life – the dutiful younger son who is dispatched into the wilderness every few months to track down his wayward older brother.'

'Was Grigori under surveillance when he got into the car?'

'Apparently not.'

'So how are the British so certain about what happened?'

'Their little electronic helpers were watching.'

Navot was referring to CCTV, the ubiquitous network of ten thousand closed-circuit television cameras that gave London's Metropolitan Police the ability to monitor activity, criminal or otherwise, on virtually every street in the British capital. A recent government study had concluded that the system had failed in its primary objective: deterring crime and apprehending criminals. Only three percent of street robberies were solved using CCTV technology, and crime rates in London were soaring. Embarrassed police officials explained away the failure by pointing out that the criminals had accounted for the cameras by adjusting their tactics, such as wearing masks and hats to conceal their identities. Apparently, no one in charge had considered that possibility before spending hundreds of millions of pounds and invading the public's privacy on an unprecedented scale. The subjects of the United Kingdom, birthplace of Western democracy, now resided in an Orwellian world where their every movement was watched over by the eyes of the state.

'When did the British discover he was gone?' Gabriel asked.

'Not until the following morning. He was supposed to check in by telephone each night at ten. When he didn't call on Tuesday, his minder wasn't overly concerned. Grigori played chess every Tuesday night at a little club in Bloomsbury. Last Tuesday was the championship of his club's annual tournament. Grigori was expected to win easily.'

'I never knew he played.'

'I guess he never had a chance to mention it during that evening you spent together in the interrogation rooms of Lubyanka. He was too busy trying to figure out how a midlevel functionary from the Israeli Ministry of Culture had managed to disarm and kill a pair of Chechen assassins.'

'As I recall, Uzi, I wouldn't have been in the stairwell if it wasn't for you and Shamron. It was one of those little in-and-out jobs you two are always dreaming up. The kind that are supposed to go smoothly. The kind where no one is supposed to get hurt. But it never seems to work out that way.'

'Some men are born great. Others just get all the great assignments from King Saul Boulevard.'

'Assignments that get them thrown into the cells in the

31

basement of Lubyanka. And if it wasn't for Colonel Grigori Bulganov, I would have never walked out of that place alive. He saved my life, Uzi. *Twice.*'

'I remember,' Navot said sardonically. 'We *all* remember.'

'Why didn't the British tell us sooner?'

'They thought it was possible Grigori had simply strayed off the reservation. Or that he was shacked up with some girl in a little seaside hotel. They wanted to be certain he was missing before pulling the fire alarm. He's gone, Gabriel. And the last place on earth they can account for him is that car. It's as if it was a portal to oblivion.'

'I'm sure it was. Do they have a theory yet?'

'They do. And I'm afraid you're not going to like it. You see, Gabriel, the mandarins of British intelligence have concluded that Colonel Grigori Bulganov has redefected.'

'*Redefected?* You can't be serious.'

'I am. What's more, they've convinced themselves he was a double agent all along. They believe he came to the West to spoon-feed us a load of Russian crap and to gather information on the Russian dissident community in London. And now, having succeeded, he's flown the coop and returned home to a hero's welcome. And guess whom they blame for this catastrophe?'

'The person who brought Grigori to the West in the first place.'

'That's correct. They blame *you.*'

'How convenient. But Grigori Bulganov is no more a Russian double agent than I am. The British have concocted this ludicrous theory in order to shift the blame for his disappearance from their shoulders, where it belongs, to mine. He should never have been allowed to live openly in

London. I couldn't turn on the BBC or CNN International last fall without seeing his face.'

'So what do you think happened to him?'

'He was killed, Uzi. Or worse.'

'What could be worse than being taken out by a Russian hit team?'

'Being kidnapped by Ivan Kharkov.' Gabriel stopped walking and turned to face Navot in the empty street. 'But then you already know that, Uzi. You wouldn't be here otherwise.'

6. Amelia, Umbria

They climbed the winding streets to the piazza at the highest point of the city and looked down at the lights glowing like bits of topaz and garnet on the valley floor. The two bodyguards waited on the opposite side of the square, well out of earshot. One held a cell phone to his ear; the other, a lighter to a cigarette. When Gabriel glimpsed the flame, an image flashed in his memory. He was riding through the misty plains of western Russia at dawn in the front passenger seat of a Volga sedan, his head throbbing, his right eye blinded by a crude dressing. Two beautiful women slept like small children in the backseat. One was Olga Sukhova, Russia's most famous opposition journalist. The other was Elena Kharkov, wife of Ivan Borisovich Kharkov: oligarch, arms dealer, murderer. Seated behind the wheel, a cigarette burning between his thumb and forefinger, was Grigori Bulganov. He was speaking softly so as not to wake the women, his eyes fixed on a Russian road without end.

Do you know what we do with traitors, Gabriel? We take them into a small room and make them kneel. Then we shoot them in the back of the head with a large-caliber handgun. We make certain the round exits the face so there's nothing left for the family to see. Then we throw the body in an unmarked grave. Many things have changed in Russia since the fall of Communism. But the punishment for betrayal remains the same. Promise me one thing, Gabriel. Promise me I won't end up in an unmarked grave.

Gabriel heard a sudden rustle of wings and, looking up, saw a squadron of warring rooks wheeling around the piazza's Romanesque campanile. The next voice he heard was Uzi Navot's.

'You can be sure of one thing, Gabriel. The only person Ivan Kharkov wants dead more than Grigori is *you*. And who could blame him? First you stole his secrets. Then you stole his wife and children.'

'I didn't *steal* anything. Elena offered to defect. I just helped her.'

'I doubt Ivan sees it that way. And neither does the Memuneh. The Memuneh believes Ivan is back in business. The Memuneh believes Ivan has made his first move.'

Gabriel was silent. Navot turned up the collar of his overcoat.

'You may recall that we were picking up reports last autumn about a special unit Ivan had created within his personal security service. That unit was given a simple assignment. Find Elena, get back his children, and kill everyone who participated in the operation against him. We allowed ourselves to be lulled into thinking that Ivan had cooled off. Grigori's disappearance suggests otherwise.'

'Ivan will never find me, Uzi. Not here.'

'Are you willing to bet your life on that?'

'Five people know I'm in the country: the Italian prime minister, the chiefs of his intelligence and security services, the pope, and the pope's private secretary.'

'That's five people too many.' Navot laid a large hand on Gabriel's shoulder. 'I want you to listen to me very carefully. Whether Grigori Bulganov left London voluntarily or at the point of a Russian pistol is of little or no consequence.

You're compromised, Gabriel. And you're leaving here tonight.'

'I've been compromised before. Besides, Grigori has no knowledge of my cover or where I'm living. He can't betray me, and Shamron knows it. He's using Grigori's disappearance as his latest excuse to get me back to Israel. Once I'm there, he'll lock me away in solitary confinement. And I'm sure when my defenses are at their weakest, he'll offer me a way out. I'll be the director, and you'll be in charge of Special Ops. And Shamron will be able to finally die in peace, knowing that his two favorite sons are finally in control of his beloved Office.'

'That might be Shamron's overall strategy, but for the moment he's only concerned about your safety. He has no ulterior motives.'

'Shamron is ulterior motives personified, Uzi. And so are you.'

Navot removed his hand from Gabriel's shoulder. 'I'm afraid this isn't a debate, Gabriel. You might be the boss one day, but for now I'm ordering you to leave Italy and come home. You're not going to disobey another order, are you?'

Gabriel made no reply.

'You have too many enemies to be alone in the world, Gabriel. You might think your friend the pope will look after you, but you're wrong. You need us as much as we need you. Besides, we're the only family you've got.'

Navot gave a shrewd smile. The countless hours he had spent in the executive conference rooms of King Saul Boulevard had significantly sharpened his debating skills. He was now a formidable opponent, one who had to be handled with care.

'I'm working on a painting,' Gabriel said. 'I can't leave until it's finished.'

'How long?' Navot asked.

Three months, thought Gabriel. Then he said, 'Three days.'

Navot sighed. He oversaw a unit consisting of several hundred highly skilled operatives but only one whose movements were dictated by the fickle rhythms of restoring Old Master paintings.

'I take it your wife is still in Venice?'

'She's coming back tonight.'

'She should have told me she was going to Venice *before* she left. You might be a private contractor, Gabriel, but your wife is a full-time employee of Special Ops. As such, she is required to keep her supervisor, *me*, abreast of all her movements, personal and professional. Perhaps you would be good enough to remind her of that fact.'

'I'll try, Uzi, but she never listens to a thing I say.'

Navot glared at his wristwatch. A large stainless steel device, it did everything except keep accurate time. It was a newer version of the one worn by Shamron, which is why Navot had bought it in the first place.

'I have some business in Paris and Brussels. I'll be back here in three days to pick up you and Chiara. We'll go back to Israel together.'

'I'm sure we can find the airport by ourselves, Uzi. We're both well trained.'

'That's what concerns me.' Navot turned around and looked at the bodyguards. 'And by the way, they're staying here with you. Think of them as heavily armed house-guests.'

'I don't need them.'

'You don't have a choice,' Navot said.

'I assume they don't speak Italian.'

'They're settler boys from Judea and Samaria. They barely speak English.'

'So how am I supposed to explain them to the staff?'

'That's not my problem.' Navot held a trio of thick fingers in front of Gabriel's face. 'You have three days to finish that damn painting. Three days. Then you and your wife are going home.'

7. Villa dei Fiori, Umbria

Gabriel's studio was in semidarkness, the altarpiece shrouded by gloom. He attempted to walk past it but could not – as always, the pull of a work in progress was far too strong. Switching on a single halogen lamp, he gazed at the pale hand reaching toward the apex of the panel. For an instant, it belonged not to Saint Peter but to Grigori Bulganov. And it was reaching not toward God but toward Gabriel.

Promise me one thing, Gabriel. Promise me I won't end up in an unmarked grave.

The vision was disturbed by the sound of singing. Gabriel switched off the lamp and climbed the stone steps to his room. The bed, unmade when he left, now looked as if it had been prepared for a photo shoot by a professional stylist. Chiara was executing one final adjustment to a pair of decorative pillows, two useless disks trimmed in white lace that Gabriel always hurled on the floor before climbing between the sheets. An overnight bag lay at the foot, along with a Beretta 9mm. Gabriel placed the weapon in the top drawer of the nightstand and lowered the volume on the radio.

Chiara looked up, as if surprised by his presence. She was wearing faded blue jeans, a beige sweater, and suede boots that added two inches to her tall frame. Her riotous dark hair was constrained by a clasp at the nape of her neck and pulled forward over one shoulder. Her caramel-colored eyes were a shade darker than normal. It was not a good sign. Chiara's eyes were a reliable barometer of her mood.

'I didn't hear you drive up.'

'Maybe you shouldn't play the radio so loudly.'

'Why didn't Margherita make the bed?'

'I told her not to come in here while you were away.'

'And of course you couldn't be bothered.'

'I couldn't find the instructions.'

She gave him a slow shake of the head to show her disappointment. 'If you can restore Old Master paintings, Gabriel, you can make a bed. What did you do when you were a boy?'

'My mother tried to force me.'

'And?'

'I slept on top of the bedding.'

'No wonder Shamron recruited you.'

'Actually, the Office psychologists found it revelatory. They said it displayed a spirit of independence and the ability to solve problems.'

'So is that why you refuse to make it now? Because you want to demonstrate your independence?'

Gabriel answered her with a kiss. Her lips were very warm.

'How was Venice?'

'Almost bearable. When the weather is cold and rainy, it's almost possible to imagine Venice is still a real city. The Piazza di San Marco is overrun with tourists, of course. They drink their ten-euro cups of cappuccino and pose for photographs with those awful pigeons. Tell me, Gabriel, what kind of holiday is that?'

'I thought the mayor drove the birdseed vendors out of business.'

'The tourists feed them anyway. If they love the pigeons so much, maybe they should take them home as souvenirs. Do you know how many tourists came to Venice this year?'

'Twenty million.'

'That's right. If each person took just one of those filthy birds, the problem would be solved within a few months.'

It was odd to hear Chiara speak so harshly of Venice. Indeed, there was a time, not so long ago, when she would have never imagined a life outside the picturesque canals and narrow alleyways of her native city. The daughter of the city's chief rabbi, she had spent her childhood in the insular world of the ancient ghetto, leaving just long enough to earn a master's degree in history from the University of Padua. She returned to Venice after graduation and took a job at the small Jewish museum in the Campo del Ghetto Nuovo, and there she might have remained forever had she not been noticed by an Office talent spotter during a visit to Israel. The talent spotter introduced himself in a Tel Aviv coffeehouse and asked Chiara whether she was interested in doing more for the Jewish people than working in a museum in a dying ghetto. Chiara said she was and vanished into the secretive training program of the Office.

A year later she resumed her old life, this time as an undercover agent of Israeli intelligence. Among her first assignments was to covertly watch the back of a wayward Office assassin named Gabriel Allon, who had come to Venice to restore Bellini's San Zaccaria altarpiece. She revealed herself to him a short time later in Rome, after an incident involving gunplay and the Italian police. Trapped alone with Chiara in a safe flat, Gabriel had wanted desperately to touch her. He had waited until the case was resolved and they had returned to Venice. There, in a canal house in Cannaregio, they made love for the first time, in a bed prepared with fresh linen. It was like making love to a figure painted by the hand of Veronese. Now that same figure frowned as he removed his leather jacket and tossed it over the back of a chair. She made a vast show of hanging it in the closet, then unzipped her overnight bag and began removing the contents. All the clothing was clean and painstakingly folded.

'My mother insisted on doing my laundry before I left.'

'She doesn't think we have a washing machine?'

'She's a Venetian, Gabriel. She doesn't believe it's proper for a girl to live on a farm. Pastures and livestock make her nervous.' Chiara began placing the clean clothing in her dresser drawers. 'So why weren't you here when I arrived?'

'I had a meeting.'

'A *meeting*? In Amelia? With whom?'

Gabriel told her.

'I thought you two weren't speaking.'

'We've agreed to let bygones be bygones.'

'How lovely,' Chiara said coldly. 'Did my name come up?'

'Uzi's miffed at you for failing to tell the desk that you were going to Venice.'

'It was private.'

'You know there's no such thing as private when you work for the Office.'

'Why are you taking his side?'

'I'm not taking anyone's side. It was a simple statement of fact.'

'Since when have you ever given a damn about Office rules and regulations? You do whatever you want, whenever you want, and no one dares to lay a finger on you.'

'And Uzi gives you plenty of preferential treatment because you're married to me.'

'I'm still angry with him for leaving you behind in Moscow.'

'It wasn't Uzi's fault, Chiara. He tried to make me leave, but I wouldn't listen.'

'And you almost got yourself killed as a result. You *would* have been killed if it wasn't for Grigori.' She lapsed into silence for a moment while she refolded two items of clothing. 'Did you two have something to eat?'

'Uzi devoured about a hundred pastries at Massimo. I had coffee.'

'How's his weight?'

'He seems to be carrying some postnuptial happy pounds.'

'You never gained any weight after we were married.'

'I suppose that means I'm deeply unhappy.'

'Are you?'

'Don't be silly, Chiara.'

She slipped a thumb inside the waistband of her blue jeans. 'I think I'm gaining weight.'

'You look beautiful.'

She frowned. 'You're not supposed to say I look *beautiful*. You're supposed to reassure me that I'm not gaining weight.'

'Your shirt *is* fitting you a little more tightly than normal.'

'It's Anna's cooking. If I keep eating like this, I'm going to look like one of those old ladies in town. Maybe I should just buy a black frock now and get it over with.'

'I gave her the night off. I thought it might be nice to be alone for a change.'

'Thank God. I'll make you something to eat. You're too thin.' Chiara closed the dresser drawer. 'So what brought Uzi to town?'

'He's making his semiannual tour of European assets. Patting backs. Showing the flag.'

'Do I detect a slight bit of resentment in your voice?'

'Why on earth would I be resentful?'

'Because you should be the one making the grand tour of our European assets instead of Uzi.'

'Traveling isn't what it once was, Chiara. Besides, I didn't want the job.'

'But you've never been comfortable with the fact that they gave it to Uzi when you turned it down. You don't think he has the intellect or the creativity for it.'

'Shamron and his acolytes at King Saul Boulevard disagree. And if I were you, Chiara, I'd stay on Uzi's good side. He's likely to be the director one day.'

'Not after Moscow. According to the rumor mill, Uzi was lucky to keep his job.' She sat at the edge of the bed and made a halfhearted effort to remove her right boot. 'Help me,' she said, extending her foot toward Gabriel. 'It won't budge.'

Gabriel took hold of the boot by the toe and the heel and it slid easily off her foot. 'Maybe you should try pulling on it next time.'

'You're much stronger than I am.' She raised her other leg. 'So how long are you planning to make me wait this time, Gabriel?'

'Before what?'

44

'Before telling me why Uzi came all the way to Umbria to see you. And why two Office bodyguards followed you home.'

'I thought you didn't hear me arrive.'

'I was lying.'

Gabriel slipped off Chiara's second boot.

'Don't ever lie to me, Chiara. Bad things happen when lovers tell lies.'

8. Villa dei Fiori, Umbria

Maybe the British are right. Maybe Grigori did redefect.'

'And maybe Guido Reni will show up here later tonight to help me finish his altarpiece.'

Chiara plucked an egg from its carton and expertly broke it one-handed into a glass mixing bowl. She was standing at an island in the center of the villa's rustic kitchen. Gabriel was opposite, perched atop a wooden stool, a glass of Umbrian Merlot in his hand.

'You're going to kill me with those eggs, Chiara.'

'Drink your wine. If you drink wine, you can eat as many as you like.'

'That's nonsense.'

'It's true. Why do you think we Italians live forever?'

Gabriel did as she suggested and drank some of his wine. Chiara cracked another egg against the side of the bowl, but this time a fragment of shell lodged in the yoke. Annoyed, she delicately removed it with the tip of her fingernail and flicked it into the rubbish bin.

'What are you making, anyway?'

'Frittata with potato and onion and *spaghetti alla carbonara di zucchine*.'

She turned her attention to the trio of pots and pans spattering and bubbling on the antiquated range. Blessed with a Venetian's natural sense of aesthetics, she brought artistry to all things, especially food. Her meals, like her beds, seemed too perfect to disturb. Gabriel often wondered why she had ever been attracted to a scarred and broken relic like him. Perhaps she viewed him as a tired room in need of redecoration.

'Anna could have left us something to eat other than eggs and cheese.'

'You think she's trying to kill you by clogging your arteries with cholesterol?'

'I wouldn't put it past her. She detests me.'

'Try being nice to her.'

A strand of stray hair had escaped the restraint of Chiara's clasp and fallen against her cheekbone. She tucked it behind her ear and treated Gabriel to a puckish smile.

'It seems to me you have a choice,' she said. 'A choice about your future. A choice about your life.'

'I'm not good at making decisions about life.'

'Yes, I've noticed that. I remember a certain afternoon in Jerusalem not long ago. I'd grown weary of waiting for you to marry me, and so I'd finally worked up the nerve to leave you. When I got into that car outside your apartment, I kept waiting for you to chase after me and beg me to stay. But you didn't. You were probably relieved I was the one walking out. It was easier that way.'

'I was a fool, Chiara, but that's ancient history.'

She speared a piece of potato from the frying pan, tasted it, then added a bit more salt. 'I knew it was Leah, of course. You were still married to her.' Chiara paused, then added softly, 'And you were still in love with her.'

'What does any of this have to do with the situation at hand?'

'You are a man who takes vows seriously, Gabriel. You

47

took a vow to Leah and you couldn't break it, even though she no longer lived in the present. You took an oath to the Office as well. And you can't seem to break that one, either.'

'I've given them more than half my life.'

'So what are you going to do? Give them the rest of it? Do you want to end up like Shamron? He's eighty years old, and he can't sleep at night because he's worried about the security of the State. He sits on his terrace at night on the Sea of Galilee staring off to the east, watching his enemies.'

'There wouldn't be an Israel if it weren't for men like Shamron. He was there at the creation. And he doesn't want to see his life's work destroyed.'

'There are plenty of qualified men and women who can look after Israel's security.'

'Try telling that to Shamron.'

'Trust me, Gabriel. I have.'

'So what are you suggesting?'

'Leave them – for good this time. Restore paintings. Live your life.'

'Where?'

She raised her arms to indicate that the present surroundings would do nicely indeed.

'This is a temporary arrangement. Eventually, the count is going to want his villa back again.'

'We'll find a new one. Or we'll move to Rome so you can be closer to the Vatican. The Italians will let you live wherever you like, so long as you don't abuse that passport and new identity they generously gave you for saving the pope's life.'

'Uzi says I'll never have the nerve to walk away for good. He says the Office is the only family I've got.'

'Start a new family, Gabriel.' Chiara paused. 'With me.'

She tasted a piece of zucchini and switched off the burner. Turning around, she saw Gabriel gazing at her intently with one hand pressed thoughtfully to his chin.

'Why are you looking at me like that?'

'Like what, Chiara?'

'Like I'm one of your paintings.'

'I'm just wondering why you left that book about child rearing in our room where you knew I would see it. And why you haven't taken a single sip of the wine I poured for you.'

'I have.'

'You haven't, Chiara. I've been watching.'

'You just didn't see me.'

'Take one now.'

'Gabriel! What's got into you?' She lifted the glass to her lips and took a sip. 'Are you satisfied?'

He wasn't. 'Are you pregnant, Chiara?'

'No, Gabriel, I'm not pregnant. But I would like to be at some point in the near future.' She took hold of his hand. 'I know you're afraid because of what happened to Dani. But the best way to honor his memory is to have another child. We're Jews, Gabriel. That's what we do. We mourn the dead and keep them in our hearts. But we live our lives.'

'With names that are not our own, stalked by men who wish to kill us.'

Chiara gave an exasperated sigh and cracked another egg against the side of the mixing bowl. This time, the shell broke to pieces in her hand.

'*Now* look what you've made me do.' She mopped up the egg with a paper towel. 'You have three days until Uzi comes back. What do you intend to do?'

'I need to go to London to find out what really happened to Grigori Bulganov.'

'Grigori isn't your problem. Let the British handle it.'

'The British have bigger problems than one missing defector. They've swept Grigori under the rug. They've moved on.'

'And so should you.' Chiara added one more egg to the bowl and began beating. 'Russians have long memories, Gabriel – almost as long as the Arabs. Ivan lost everything after Elena defected: his homes in England and France and all those bank accounts in London and Zurich filled with his dirty money. He's the subject of an Interpol Red Notice and can't set foot outside of Russia. He has nothing else to do except plot your death. And if you go to London and start poking around, there's a good chance he'll find out about it.'

'So I'll do it quietly, then I'll come home. And we'll get on with our lives.'

Chiara's arm went still. 'You tell lies for a living, Gabriel. I hope you're not lying to me now.'

'I've never lied to you, Chiara. And I never will.'

'What are you going to do about the bodyguards?'

'They'll stay here with you.'

'Uzi's not going to be happy.'

Gabriel held his wine to the light. 'Uzi's never happy.'

9. Villa dei Fiori • London

The Office had a motto: By way of deception, thou shalt do war. The deception was usually visited upon Israel's enemies. Occasionally, it was necessary to deceive one's own. Gabriel was sorry for them; they were good boys, with bright futures. They had just drawn the wrong assignment at the wrong time.

Their names were Lior and Motti – Lior being the older and more experienced of the pair, Motti a youthful probationer barely a year out of the Academy. Both boys had studied the exploits of the legend and had leapt at the opportunity to escort him safely back to Israel. Unlike Uzi Navot, they viewed the three additional days of duty at the beautiful villa in Umbria as a windfall. And when Chiara asked them to tread lightly so that Gabriel might finish his painting before returning home, they agreed without protest. They were simply honored to be in his presence. They would stand a distant post.

They spent that night in the drafty little guest cottage, sleeping in shifts and keeping a careful watch on the window of his studio, which was aglow with a searing white light. If they listened carefully, they could just make out the faint sound of music – first *Tosca*, then *Madame Butterfly*, and finally, as dawn was breaking over the estate, *La Bohème*. As the villa stirred to life around eight, they wandered up to the kitchen and found three women – Chiara, Anna,

Margherita – sharing breakfast around the island. The door to the sitting room was tightly closed, and two vigilant hounds were curled on the floor before it. Accepting a bowl of steaming coffee, Lior wondered whether it might be possible to have a look at him. 'I wouldn't recommend it,' Chiara said sotto voce. 'He tends to get a bit grouchy when he's on deadline.' Lior, the child of a writer, understood completely.

The bodyguards spent the remainder of that day trying to keep themselves occupied. They went out on the odd reconnaissance mission and had a pleasant lunch with the staff, but for the most part they remained prisoners of their little stucco bunker. Every few hours, they would poke their heads inside the main villa to see if they could catch just a glimpse of the legend. Instead, they saw only the closed doors, watched over by the hounds. 'He's working at a feverish pace,' Chiara explained late that afternoon, when Lior again screwed up the courage to request permission to enter the studio. 'There's no telling what will happen if you disturb him. Trust me, it's not for the faint of heart.'

And so they returned to their outpost like good soldiers and sat outside on the little veranda as night began to fall. And they stared despondently at the white light and listened to the faint sound of music. And they waited for the legend to emerge from his cave. At six o'clock, having seen no evidence of him since the previous evening, they reached the conclusion that they had been duped. They didn't dare enter his studio to confirm their suspicions. Instead, they spent several minutes quarreling over who should break the news to Uzi Navot. In the end, it was Lior, the older and more experienced of the two, who placed the call. He was a good boy with a bright future. He had just drawn the wrong assignment at the wrong time.

There were far worse places for a grounded defector to spend his final days than Bristol Mews. It was reached by a passageway off Bristol Gardens, flanked on one side by a Pilates exercise studio that promised to strengthen and empower its clients and on the other by a disconsolate little restaurant called D Place. Its courtyard was long and rectangular, paved with gray cobblestone and trimmed in red brick. The spire of St Saviour Church peered into it from the north, the windows of a large terrace house from the east. The door of the tidy little cottage at No. 8, like its neighbor at No. 7, was painted a cheerful shade of bright yellow. The shades were drawn in the ground-floor window. Even so, Gabriel could see a light burning from within.

He had arrived in London in midafternoon, having flown to the British capital directly from Rome using a false Italian passport and a ticket purchased for him by a friend at the Vatican. After performing a routine check for surveillance, he had entered a phone box near Oxford Circus and dialed from memory a number that rang inside Thames House, headquarters of MI5. As instructed, he had called back thirty minutes later and had been given an address, No. 8 Bristol Mews, along with a time: 7 p.m. It was now approaching 7:30. His tardiness was intentional. Gabriel Allon never arrived anywhere at the time he was expected.

Gabriel reached for the bell, but before he could press it, the door retreated. Standing in the entrance hall was Graham Seymour, MI5's deputy director. He wore a perfectly fitted suit of charcoal gray and a burgundy necktie. His face was fine boned and even featured, and his hair had a rich silvery cast to it that made him look like a male model one sees in ads for costly but needless trinkets — the sort who wears expensive wristwatches, writes with expensive fountain pens, and spends his summers sailing the Greek islands aboard a custom-made yacht filled with younger women. Everything about Seymour spoke of confidence and composure. Even his handshake was a weapon designed to demonstrate to its recipient that he had met his match. It said Seymour had gone to the better schools, belonged to the better clubs, and was still a force to be reckoned with on the tennis court. It said he was not to be taken lightly. And it had the added benefit of being true. All but the tennis. In recent years, a back injury had diminished his skills. Though still quite good, Seymour had decided he was not good enough and had retired his racquet. Besides, the demands of his job were such that he had little time for recreation. Graham Seymour had the unenviable task of keeping the United Kingdom safe in a dangerous world. It was not a job Gabriel would want. The sun may have set on the British Empire long ago, but the world's revolutionaries, exiles, and outcasts still seemed to find their way to London.

'You're late,' Seymour said.

'The traffic was miserable.'

'You don't say.'

Seymour snapped the dead bolt into place and led Gabriel into the kitchen. Small but recently renovated, it had sparkling German appliances and Italian marble counters. Gabriel had seen many like it in the home-design magazines Chiara was always reading. 'Lovely,' he said, looking around theatrically. 'Makes one wonder why Grigori would want to leave all this to go back to dreary Moscow.'

Gabriel opened the refrigerator and looked inside. The contents left little doubt that the owner was a man of middle age who did not entertain often, especially not women. On one shelf was a tin of salted herring and an open jar of tomato sauce; on another, a lump of pâté and a wedge of very ripe Camembert cheese. The freezer contained only vodka. Gabriel closed the door and looked at Seymour, who was peering into the filter basket of the coffeemaker, his nose wrinkled in disgust. 'I suppose we really should get someone in here to clean up.' He emptied the coffee filter into the rubbish bin and gestured toward the small café-style table. 'I'd like to show you something. It should put to rest any questions you have about Grigori and his allegiances.'

The table was empty except for an attaché case with combination locks. Seymour manipulated the tumblers with his thumbs and simultaneously popped the latches. From inside he removed two items: a portable DVD player of Japanese manufacture and a single disk in a clear plastic case. He powered on the device and loaded the disk into the drawer. Fifteen seconds later, an image appeared on the screen: Grigori Bulganov, sheltering from a gentle rain at the entranceway of Bristol Mews.

In the bottom left of the image was the location of the CCTV camera that had captured the image: BRISTOL GARDENS. In the top right was the date, the tenth of January, and beneath the date was the time: 17:47:39 and counting. Grigori was now lighting a cigarette, cupping the flame in his left hand. Returning the lighter to his pocket, he scanned the street in both directions. Apparently satisfied there was no danger, he dropped the cigarette to the ground and started walking.

With the cameras tracking his every move, he made his way to the end of Formosa Street and crossed the Grand Union Canal over a metal footbridge lined with spherical white lamps. Four youths in hooded sweatshirts were loitering in the darkness on the opposite bank; he slipped past them without a glance and walked past the colony of dour council flats lining Delamere Terrace. It was a few seconds after six when he descended a flight of stone steps to the boat basin known as Browning's Pool. There, he entered the Waterside Café, emerging precisely two minutes and fifteen seconds later, holding a paper cup covered by a plastic lid. He stood outside the café for a little more than a minute, then dropped the cup in a rubbish bin and walked along the quay to another flight of steps, this one leading to Warwick Crescent. He paused briefly in the quiet street to light another cigarette and smoked it during the walk to Harrow Road Bridge. His pace now visibly quicker, he continued along Harrow Road, where, at precisely 18:12:32, he stopped suddenly and turned toward the oncoming traffic. A black Mercedes sedan immediately pulled to the curb and the door swung open. Grigori climbed into the rear compartment, and the car lurched forward out of frame. Five seconds later, a man passed through the shot, tapping the tip of his umbrella against the pavement as he moved. Then, from the opposite direction, came a young woman. She wore a car-length leather coat, carried no umbrella, and was hatless in the rain.

10. Maida Vale, London

The image dissolved into a blizzard of gray and white. Graham Seymour pressed the STOP button.

'As you can see, Grigori willingly got into that car. No hesitation. No sign of distress or fear.'

'He's a pro, Graham. He was trained never to show fear, even if he was frightened half to death.'

'He was *definitely* a pro. He fooled us all. He even managed to fool you, Gabriel. And from what I hear, you've got quite an eye for forgeries.'

Gabriel refused to rise to the bait. 'Were you able to trace the car's movements with CCTV?'

'It turned left into Edgware Road, then made a right at St John's Wood Road. Eventually, it entered an underground parking garage in Primrose Hill, where it remained for fifty-seven minutes. When it reemerged, the passenger compartment appeared to be empty.'

'No cameras in the garage?'

Seymour shook his head.

'Any other vehicles leave before the Mercedes?'

'Four sedans and a single Ford Transit van. The sedans all checked out. The van had the markings of a carpet-cleaning service based in Battersea. The owner said he had no jobs in the area that evening. Furthermore, the registration number didn't match any of those leased by his firm.'

'So Grigori left in the back of the Ford?'

'That's our working assumption. After leaving the garage, it headed northeast to Brentwood, a suburb just outside the M25. At which point, it slipped out of CCTV range and disappeared from sight.'

'What about the Mercedes?'

'Southeast. We lost sight of it near Shooter's Hill. The next day a burned-out car was discovered along the Thames Estuary east of Gravesend. Whoever set it afire hadn't bothered to remove the serial numbers. They matched the numbers of a car purchased two weeks ago by someone with a Russian name and a vague address. Needless to say, all attempts to locate this person have proven fruitless.'

'The door of that car was clearly opened from the inside. It looked to me as if there was at least one person in the back.'

'Actually, there were *two*.'

Seymour produced an eight-by-ten close-up of the car. Though grainy and heavily shadowed, it showed two figures in the backseat. Gabriel was most intrigued by the one nearest the driver's-side window. It was a woman.

'I don't suppose you were able to get a picture of them *before* they got into the car?'

'Unfortunately not. The Russians deliberately ran it through a gap in the cameras a couple of miles from Heathrow Airport. We never saw anyone enter *or* leave it. They appeared to vanish into thin air, just like Grigori.'

Gabriel stared at the image a moment longer. 'It's a lot of preparation for something that could have been handled far more simply. If Grigori was planning to redefect, why not slip him a passport, an airline ticket, and a change of appearance? He could have left London in the morning and been back home in time for his borscht and chicken Kiev.'

Seymour had an answer ready. 'The Russians would assume we had Grigori under watch. From their point of view, they had to create a scenario that would look completely innocent to the CCTV cameras.' Seymour raised a long pale hand toward the now-blank screen. 'You saw it yourself, Gabriel. He was clearly checking for watchers. When he was certain we weren't following him, he sent a signal of some sort. Then his old comrades scooped him up.'

'Moscow Rules?'

'Exactly.'

'I assume you checked Grigori's route for chalk marks, tape marks, or other signs of impersonal communication.'

'We did.'

'And?'

'Nothing. But as a professional field operative, you know there are any number of ways of sending a signal. Hat, no hat. Cigarette, no cigarette. Wristwatch on the left hand, wristwatch on the right.'

'Grigori was right-handed. And he was wearing his watch, as usual, on his left wrist. Also, it was a different watch than the one he was wearing in Russia last autumn.'

'You *do* have a keen eye.'

'I do. And when I look at those CCTV images, I see something different. I see a man who's frightened of something and trying damn hard not to show it. Something made Grigori stop suddenly in his tracks. And something made him get inside that car. It wasn't a redefection, Graham. It was an abduction. The Russians stole him right from under your nose.'

'Thames House doesn't see it that way. Neither do our colleagues on the other bank of the river. As for Downing Street and the Foreign Office, they're inclined to accept our findings. The prime minister is in no mood for another high-stakes confrontation with the Russians. Not after the Litvinenko affair. And not with a G-8 summit just around the corner.'

Confronted by the global financial meltdown, the leaders of the Group of Eight industrialized nations had just agreed to hold emergency talks in February to coordinate their fiscal and monetary stimulus policies. Much to the consternation of the many bureaucrats and reporters who would also be in attendance, the summit would take place in Moscow. Gabriel was not concerned about the pending G-8 summit. He was thinking of Alexander Litvinenko, the former FSB man who was poisoned with a dose of radioactive polonium-210.

'Your conduct after Litvinenko's murder probably convinced the Russians they could pull a stunt like this and get away with it. After all, the Russians carried out what amounted to an act of nuclear terrorism in the heart of London, and you responded with a diplomatic slap on the wrist.'

Seymour placed a finger thoughtfully against his lips. 'That's an interesting theory. But I'm afraid our response to Litvinenko's murder, however feeble in your opinion, had no bearing on Grigori's case.'

Gabriel knew that to belabor the point was futile. Graham Seymour was a trusted counterpart and occasional ally, but his first allegiance would always be to his service and his country. The same was true for Gabriel. Such were the rules of the game.

'Do I have to remind you that Grigori helped you and the Americans track down Ivan's missiles? If it weren't for him, several commercial airliners might have been blown out of the sky on a single day.'

'Actually, all the information we needed was contained in the records you and Elena stole from Ivan's office. In fact, the prime minister had to be talked into giving Grigori asylum and a British passport. London is already home to several prominent Russian dissidents, including a handful of billionaires who ran afoul of the regime. He was reluctant to stick another finger in Moscow's eye.'

'What changed his mind?'

'We told him it was the proper thing to do. After all, the Americans had agreed to take Elena and her children. We felt we had to do our bit. Grigori promised to be a good boy and to keep his head down. Which he did.' Seymour paused, then added, 'For a while.'

'Until he became a celebrity defector and dissident.'

Seymour nodded his head in agreement.

'You should have locked him away in a little cottage in the countryside somewhere and thrown away the key.'

'Grigori insisted on London. The Russians *love* London.'

'So this worked out rather nicely for you. You never wanted Grigori, and now the Russians have been kind enough to take him off your hands.'

'We don't see it that way.'

'How *do* you see it?'

Seymour made a show of deliberation. 'As you might expect, Grigori's motivations are now the subject of rather intense debate. As you also might expect, opinion is divided. There are those who believe he was bad from the start.

There are others who think he simply had a change of heart.'

'A change of heart?'

'Rather like that Yurchenko chap who came over to the Americans back in the eighties. You remember Vitaly Yurchenko? A few months after he defected, he was dining at a dreadful little French restaurant in Georgetown when he told his CIA minder that he was going out for a walk. He never came back.'

'Grigori was homesick?' Gabriel shook his head. 'He couldn't get out of Russia fast enough. There's no way he would willingly go back.'

'His own words would suggest otherwise.' Seymour removed a plain buff envelope from the attaché and held it aloft between two fingers. 'You might want to listen to this before attaching your star to a man like Grigori. He's not exactly the marrying kind.'

11. Maida Vale, London

The letter was dated January the twelfth and addressed to the cover name of Grigori's MI5 minder. The text was brief, five sentences in length, and written in English, which Grigori spoke quite well – well enough, Gabriel recalled, to conduct a rather terrifying interrogation in the cellars of Lubyanka. Graham Seymour read the letter aloud. Then he handed it to Gabriel, who read it silently.

> *Sorry I didn't tell you about my plans to return home, Monty, but I'm sure you can understand why I kept them to myself. I hope my actions don't leave a permanent stain on your record. You are far too decent to be working in a business like this. I enjoyed our time together, especially the chess. You almost made London bearable.*
>
> *Regards, G*

'It was mailed from Zurich to an MI5 postbox in Camden Town. That address was known to only a handful of senior people, Grigori's minder, and Grigori himself. Shall I go on?'

'Please do.'

'Our experts have linked the original A4 stationery to a German paper company based in Hamburg. Oddly enough, the envelope was manufactured by the same company but was of a slightly different style. Our experts have also conclusively attributed the handwriting, along with several latent fingerprints found on the surface of the paper, to Grigori Bulganov.'

'Handwriting can be forged, Graham. Just like paintings.'

'What about the fingerprints?'

Gabriel lifted Seymour's hand by the wrist and placed it against the paper. 'We're talking about Russians, Graham. They don't play by Marquis of Queensberry rules.'

Seymour freed his hand from Gabriel's grasp. 'It's clear from the letter that Grigori was cooperating. It was addressed to the correct cover name of his minder and mailed to the proper address.'

'Perhaps they tortured him. Or perhaps torture wasn't necessary because Grigori knew full well what would happen if he didn't cooperate. He was one of them, Graham. He knew their methods. He used them from time to time. I should know. I saw him in his element.'

'If Grigori was kidnapped, why bother with the charade of a letter?'

'The Russians committed a serious crime on your soil. It's only natural they might try to cover their tracks with a stunt like this. No kidnapping, no crime.'

Seymour regarded Gabriel with his granite-colored eyes. Like his handshake, they were an unfair weapon. 'Two men stand before an abstract painting. One sees clouds over a wheat field, the other sees a pair of blue whales mating. Who's correct? Does it matter? Do you see my point, Gabriel?'

'I'm trying very hard, Graham.'

'Your defector is gone. And nothing we say now is going to change that.'

'*My* defector?'

'You brought him here.'

'And *you* agreed to protect him. Downing Street should have lodged an official protest with the Russian ambassador an hour after Grigori missed his first check-in.'

'An official protest?' Seymour shook his head slowly. 'Perhaps you're not aware of the fact that the United Kingdom has more money invested in Russia than any other Western country. The prime minister has no intention of endangering those investments by starting another blazing row with the Kremlin.'

'"When we hang the capitalists, they will sell us the rope."'

'Stalin, right? And the old boy had a point. Capitalism is the West's greatest strength, and its greatest weakness.'

Gabriel placed the letter on the table and changed the subject. 'As I recall, Grigori was working on a book.'

Seymour handed Gabriel a stack of paper. It was approximately one inch thick and bound by a pair of black metal clasps. Gabriel looked at the first page: KILLER IN THE KREMLIN BY GRIGORI BULGANOV.

'I thought it was rather catchy,' Seymour said.

'I doubt the Russians would agree. I assume you've read it?'

Seymour nodded his head. 'He's rather hard on the Kremlin and not terribly kind to his old service. He accuses the FSB of all manner of sins, including murder, extortion, and links to organized crime and the oligarchs. He also makes a very persuasive case that the FSB was involved in those apartment-house bombings in Moscow, the ones the Russian president used as justification for sending the Red

Army back into Chechnya. Grigori claims he personally knew the officers involved in the operation and identifies two by name.'

'Any mention of me?'

'There *is* a chapter in the book about the Kharkov affair, but it's not terribly accurate. As far as Grigori is concerned, *he* was the one who single-handedly tracked down the missiles Ivan sold to al-Qaeda. There's no mention of you or any Israeli connection in the manuscript.'

'What about his handwritten notes or computer files?'

'We searched them all. As far as Grigori was concerned, you do not exist.'

Gabriel leafed through the pages of the manuscript. On the sixth page was a margin note, written in English. He read it, then looked at Seymour for an explanation.

'It's from Grigori's editor at Buckley and Hobbes. I suppose, at some point, we're going to have to tell them that they're not going to get a book anytime soon.'

'You read her notes.'

'We read *every*thing.'

Gabriel turned several more pages, then stopped again to examine another margin note. Unlike the first, it was written in Russian. 'It must have been written by Grigori,' Seymour said.

'It doesn't match the handwriting in the letter.'

'The letter was written in Roman. The note is Cyrillic.'

'Trust me, Graham. They weren't written by the same person.'

Gabriel leafed quickly through the remaining pages and found several more notations written by the same hand. When he looked up again, Seymour was removing the disk from the DVD player. He returned it to the clear plastic case and handed it to Gabriel. The message was clear. The briefing was over. If there was any doubt about Seymour's intent, it was put to rest by a ponderous examination of his wristwatch. Gabriel made one final request. He wanted to see the rest of the house. Seymour rose slowly to his feet. 'But we're not going to be pulling up any floorboards or peeling back the wallpaper,' he said. 'I have a dinner date. And I'm already ten minutes late.'

12. Maida Vale, London

Gabriel followed Seymour up two flights of narrow stairs to the bedroom. On the night table to the right of the double bed was an ashtray filled with crushed cigarettes. They were all the same brand: Sobranie White Russians, the kind Grigori had smoked during Gabriel's interrogation at Lubyanka and during their escape from Russia. Piled beneath the brass reading lamp were several books: Tolstoy, Dostoyevsky, Agatha Christie, P. D. James. 'He loved English murder mysteries,' Seymour said. 'He thought that reading P. D. James would help him become more like us, though why anyone would want to become more like us is beyond me.'

At the foot of the bed was a white box printed with the logo of a dry-cleaning and laundry service located in Elgin Avenue. Lifting the lid, Gabriel saw a half dozen shirts, neatly pressed and folded and wrapped in tissue paper. Resting atop the shirts was a cash register receipt. The date on the receipt matched the date of Grigori's disappearance. The time of the transaction was recorded as 3:42 p.m.

'We assume his controllers wanted his last day in London to be as normal as possible,' Seymour said.

Gabriel found the explanation dubious at best. He entered the bathroom and opened the medicine cabinet. Scattered among the various lotions, creams, and grooming devices were three bottles of prescription medication: one for sleep, one for anxiety, and one for migraine headaches.

'Who prescribed these?'

'A doctor who works for us.'

'Grigori never struck me as the anxious type.'

'He said it was the pressure of writing a book on dead-line.'

Gabriel removed a bottle of indigestion medication and turned the label toward Seymour.

'He had a fickle stomach,' Seymour said.

'He should have eaten something other than salted herring and pasta sauce.'

Gabriel closed the cabinet and lifted the lid of the hamper. It was empty.

'Where's his dirty laundry?'

'He dropped it off the afternoon he vanished.'

'That's exactly what I would do if I were preparing to redefect.'

Gabriel switched off the bathroom lights and followed Seymour down a flight of steps to the sitting room. The coffee table was scattered with newspapers, a few from London, the rest from Russia: *Izvestia, Kommersant, Komsomolskaya Pravda, Moskovskaya Gazeta*. On one corner of the table stood a Russian-style tea glass, its contents long evaporated. Next to the glass was another ashtray filled with cigarette butts. Gabriel picked through them with the tip of a pen. They were all the same: Sobranie White Russians. Just then, he heard the sound of laughter outside in the mews. Parting the blinds in the front window, he watched a pair of lovers pass arm in arm beneath his feet.

'I assume you have a camera somewhere in the court-yard?'

Seymour pointed to a downspout near the passageway.

'Any Russians dropping by for a peek?'

'No one that we've been able to link to the local *rezidentura.*'

Rezidentura was the word used by the SVR, the Russian foreign intelligence service, to describe their operations inside local embassies. The *rezident* was the station chief, the *rezidentura* the station itself. It was a holdover from the days of the KGB. Most things about the SVR were.

'What happens when someone comes into the mews?'

'If they live here, nothing happens. If we don't recognize them, they get a tail and a background check. Thus far, everyone's checked out.'

'And no one's tried to enter the cottage itself?'

Seymour shook his head. Gabriel released the blinds and walked over to Grigori's cluttered desk. In the center was a darkened notebook computer. Next to the computer was a telephone with a built-in answering machine. A red message light blinked softly.

'Those must be new,' Seymour said.

'Do you mind?'

Without waiting for a response, Gabriel reached down and pressed the PLAYBACK button. A high-pitched tone sounded, then a robotic male voice announced there were three new messages. The first was from Sparkle Clean Laundry and Dry-Cleaning, requesting that Mr. Bulganov collect his belongings. The second was from a producer at the BBC's *Panorama* program who wished to book Mr. Bulganov for an upcoming documentary on the resurgence of Russia.

The last message was from a woman who spoke with a pronounced Russian accent. Her voice had the quality of a minor scale. *C minor*, thought Gabriel. Key of concentration in solemnity. Key of philosophical introspection. The woman said she had just finished reading the newest pages of the manuscript and wished to discuss them at Grigori's convenience. She left no callback number, nor did she mention her name. For Gabriel, it wasn't necessary. The sound of her voice had been echoing in his memory from the moment of their first encounter. *How do you do*, she had said that evening in Moscow. *My name is Olga Sukhova.*

'I suppose we now know who wrote those notes in Grigori's manuscript.'

'I suppose we do.'

'I want to see her, Graham.'

'I'm afraid that's not going to be possible.' Seymour switched off the answering machine. 'Rome has spoken. The case is closed.'

13. Maida Vale, London

The blocks of council flats looming over Delamere Terrace looked like something the Soviets might have thrown up during the halcyon days of 'developed Socialism.' Artlessly designed and poorly constructed, each building bore a very English-sounding name suggesting a peaceful countryside existence within, along with a yellow sign warning that the area was under continuous surveillance. Grigori had walked past the flats a few minutes before his disappearance. Gabriel, retracing the Russian's steps, did so now. Though he hated to admit it, Seymour's briefing had shaken his absolute faith in Grigori's innocence. Did he redefect? Or was he abducted? Gabriel was certain the answer could be found here, on the streets of Maida Vale.

Show me how they did it, Grigori. Show me how they got you into that car.

He walked to Browning's Pool and stood outside the Waterside Café, now closed and shuttered. In his mind, he replayed the video. At precisely 18:03:37, it appeared Grigori had taken note of a couple crossing Westbourne Terrace Road Bridge from Blomfield Road. The man was wearing a belted raincoat and a waxed hat and holding an open umbrella in his left hand. The woman was pressed affectionately to his shoulder. She wore a woolen coat with a fur collar and was reading something – a street map, thought Gabriel, or perhaps a guidebook of some sort.

Gabriel turned now, as Grigori had turned, and walked along the edge of Browning's Pool to the steps leading to Warwick Crescent. At the top of the steps he paused, as Grigori had paused, though he lit no cigarette. Instead, he made his way to Harrow Road, where Grigori had seen something – or some*one* – that made him quicken his pace. Gabriel did the same and continued on along the empty pavements for another two hundred meters.

Despite the hour, traffic along the busy four-lane thoroughfare was still thunderous. He stopped briefly near St Mary's Church, walked a few paces farther, and stopped again. *It was here*, he thought. This was the spot where Grigori had become too frightened to continue. The spot where he had frozen in his tracks and turned impulsively toward the oncoming traffic. In the recording, it had appeared as if Grigori had briefly considered attempting to cross the busy road. Then, as now, it almost certainly would have meant death by other means.

Gabriel looked to his left and saw a brick wall, six feet tall and covered in graffiti. Then he looked to his right and saw the river of steel and glass flowing along Harrow Road. Why did he stop here? And why, when a car appeared without being summoned, did he get in without hesitation? Was it a prearranged bolt-hole? Or a perfectly sprung trap?

Help me, Grigori. Did they send an old enemy to frighten you into coming home? Or did they send a friend to take you gently by the hand?

Gabriel gazed into the glare of the oncoming headlamps. And for an instant he glimpsed a small, well-dressed figure advancing toward him along the pavement, tapping his umbrella. Then he saw the woman. A woman in a car-length leather coat who carried no umbrella. A woman who was hatless in the rain. She brushed past him now, as if late for an appointment, and hurried off along Harrow Road. Gabriel tried to recall the features of her face but could not. They were ghostlike and fragmentary, like the first faint lines of an unfinished sketch. And so he stood there alone, London's rush hour roaring in his ears, and watched her disappear into the darkness.

14. West London

It had been more than thirty-six hours since Gabriel had slept, and he was bone-weary with exhaustion. Under normal circumstances, he would have contacted the local station and requested use of a safe flat. That was not an option, since assets from the local station were probably engaged in a frantic search for him at that very moment. He would have to stay in a hotel. And not a nice hotel with computerized registration that could be searched by sophisticated data-mining software. It would have to be the sort of hotel that accepted cash and laughed at requests for amenities like room service, telephones that functioned, and clean towels.

The Grand Hotel Berkshire was just such a place. It stood at the end of a terrace of flaking Edwardian houses in West Cromwell Road. The night manager, a tired man in a tired gray sweater, expressed little surprise when Gabriel said he had no reservation and even less when he announced he would pay the bill for his stay – three nights, perhaps two if his business went well – entirely in cash. He then handed the manager a pair of crisp twenty-pound notes and said he was expecting no visitors of any kind, nor did he want to be disturbed by telephone calls or maid service. The night manager slipped the money into his pocket and promised Gabriel's stay would be both private and secure. Gabriel bade him a pleasant evening and saw himself upstairs to his room.

Located on the third floor overlooking the busy street, it stank of loneliness and the last occupant's appalling cologne. Closing the door behind him, Gabriel found himself overcome by a sudden wave of depression. How many nights had he spent in rooms just like it? Perhaps Chiara was right. Perhaps it was time to finally leave the Office and allow the fighting to be done by other men. He would take to the hills of Umbria and give his new wife the child she so desperately wanted, the child Gabriel had denied himself because of what had happened on a snowy night in Vienna in another lifetime. He had not chosen that life. It had been chosen for him by others. It had been chosen by Yasir Arafat and a band of Palestinian terrorists known as Black September. And it had been chosen by Ari Shamron.

Shamron had come for him on a brilliant afternoon in Jerusalem in September 1972. Gabriel was a promising young painter who had forsaken a post in an elite military unit to pursue his formal training at the Bezalel Academy of Art and Design. Shamron had just been given command of Operation Wrath of God, the secret Israeli intelligence operation to hunt down and assassinate the perpetrators of the Munich Olympics massacre. He required an instrument of vengeance, and Gabriel was exactly the sort of young man for whom he was searching: brash but intelligent, loyal but independent, emotionally cold but inherently decent. He also spoke fluent German with the Berlin accent of his mother and had traveled extensively in Europe as a child.

After a month of intense training, Shamron dispatched him to Rome, where he killed a man named Wadal Abdel

Zwaiter in the foyer of an apartment building in the Piazza Annibaliano. He and his team of operatives then spent the next three years stalking their prey across Western Europe, killing at night and in broad daylight, living in fear that, at any moment, they would be arrested by European police and charged as murderers.

When finally Gabriel returned home again, his temples were the color of ash and his face was that of a man twenty years his senior. Leah, whom he had married shortly before leaving Israel, scarcely recognized him when he entered their apartment. A gifted artist in her own right, she asked him to sit for a portrait. Rendered in the style of Egon Schiele, it showed a haunted young man, aged prematurely by the shadow of death. The canvas was among the finest Leah ever produced. Gabriel had always hated it, for it portrayed with brutal honesty the toll Wrath of God had taken on him.

Physically exhausted and stripped of his desire to paint, he sought refuge in Venice, where he studied the craft of restoration under the renowned Umberto Conti. When his apprenticeship was complete, Shamron summoned him back to active duty. Working undercover as a professional art restorer, Gabriel eliminated Israel's most dangerous foes and carried out a series of quiet investigations that earned him important friends in Washington, the Vatican, and London. But he had powerful adversaries as well. He could not walk a street without the nagging fear that he was being stalked by one of his enemies. Nor could he sleep in a hotel room without first barricading the door with a chair, which he did now.

He loaded the disk of the CCTV footage into the

in-room DVD player, then, after removing only his shoes, climbed into the bed. For the next several hours he watched the surveillance video over and over, trying to blend what he could see on the screen with what he had experienced on the streets of Maida Vale. Unable to find the connection, he switched off the television. As his eyes adjusted to the gloom, the images of Grigori's final moments appeared like photographs on an overhead projector. Grigori entering a car on Harrow Road. A well-dressed man with an umbrella. A woman in a leather coat, hatless in the rain. The last image dissolved into a painting, darkened by a layer of dirty varnish. Gabriel closed his eyes, dipped a swab in solvent, and twirled it gently against the surface.

The answer came to him an hour before dawn. He groped in the gloom for the remote and pointed it at the screen. A few seconds later, it flickered to life. It was 17:47 last Tuesday. Grigori Bulganov was standing in the passageway of Bristol Mews. At 17:48, he dropped his cigarette and started walking.

He followed the now-familiar route to the Waterside Café. At 18:03:37, the young couple appeared precisely on schedule, belted raincoat for the man, woolen coat with fur collar for the woman. Gabriel reversed the image and watched the scene again, then a third time. Then he pressed PAUSE. According to the time code, it was 18:04:25 when the couple reached the end of the Westbourne Terrace Road Bridge. If the operation had been well planned – and all evidence suggested it had – there was plenty of time.

Gabriel advanced the video to the final thirty seconds

and watched one last time as Grigori entered the back of the Mercedes. As the car slid from view, a small, well-dressed man entered from the left. Then, a few seconds later, came the woman in the car-length leather coat. No umbrella. Hatless in the rain.

Gabriel froze the image and looked at her shoes.

15. Westminster, London

It was bitterly cold in Parliament Square, but not cold enough to keep the protesters at bay. There was the inevitable demonstration against the crimes of Israel, another calling for the Americans to leave Iraq, and still another that predicted the south of England would soon be turned to desert by global warming. Gabriel walked to the other side of the square and sat on an empty bench, opposite the North Tower of Westminster Abbey. It was the same bench where he had once waited for the daughter of the American ambassador to be delivered to the abbey by two jihadist suicide bombers. He wondered whether Graham Seymour had chosen the spot intentionally or if the unpleasantness of that morning had simply slipped his mind.

A chauffeured Jaguar limousine eased to the edge of the square shortly after three. Seymour emerged from the back, wearing a chesterfield coat. He waited until the car had sped off down Victoria Street before walking over to the bench. This time, it was Seymour who was late.

'Sorry, Gabriel, my meeting with the prime minister went longer than expected.'

'How is he?'

'Given the fact he's the most unpopular British leader in a generation, he put on a rather good show. And for a change we were actually able to bring him a bit of good news.'

'What's that?'

'Nice try.'

'Come on, Graham.' Gabriel glanced toward the façade of the abbey. 'We have a history, you and I.'

Seymour said nothing for a moment. 'Bloody awful day, wasn't it? I'm not sure I'll ever be able to get that image out of my mind, the image of you—'

'I remember it, Graham. I was there.'

Seymour tucked the ends of his woolen scarf under the lapel of his overcoat. 'As we speak, officers of the Metropolitan Police are conducting raids across East London.'

'East London? I guess they're not arresting Russians.'

'It's an al-Qaeda cell we've been watching for some time. They're the real thing. They were in the final stages of a plan to attack several financial and tourist targets. The loss of life would have been significant.'

'When are you going to announce the arrests?'

'The prime minister plans to issue a public statement later this evening, just in time for the *News at Ten*. His handlers are hoping for a much-needed bump in the opinion polls.' Seymour stood. 'I need to get back to Thames House. Walk with me.'

The two men rose in unison and headed across the square toward the Houses of Parliament. They were an incongruous pair, Gabriel in his jeans and leather jacket, Seymour in his tailored suit and overcoat.

'Honor is due, Gabriel. At your suggestion, we dug a little deeper and pulled up some new CCTV images from the surrounding streets. The couple who crossed West-bourne Terrace Road Bridge at three minutes past six climbed into a waiting car in a quiet side street. It brought them to Edgware Road, where the woman emerged alone. She'd changed her coat along the way.' Seymour cast an admiring glance toward Gabriel. 'May I ask what made you suspicious of her?'

'Her umbrella.'

'But she didn't have one.'

'Precisely. There was a light rain falling, but the woman wasn't carrying an umbrella. She needed her hands free.' Gabriel gave Seymour a sideways glance. 'People like me don't carry umbrellas, Graham.'

'Assassins, you mean?'

Gabriel didn't respond directly. 'If Grigori hadn't climbed into that car on his own, the woman would have probably killed him on the spot. I suppose he decided it was better to take his chances. Better to be a missing defector than a dead one.'

'What else did you notice about her?'

'She never bothered to change her shoes. I suppose there wasn't time.'

'What I wouldn't do for your eye.'

'It's a professional affliction.'

'Which profession?'

Gabriel only smiled. They had reached the southern end of the Houses of Parliament and were walking now along the Victoria Tower Gardens. Ahead of them loomed the heavy gray façade of Thames House. Seymour suddenly appeared in no hurry to get back to the office.

'Your discovery presents me with an obvious dilemma. If I bring this to the attention of my director-general, it will ignite a battle royal within the Security Service. I'll be branded a heretic. And you know what we do with heretics.'

'I don't want you to say a thing, Graham.' Gabriel paused, then added, 'Not until I've had a chance to talk to Olga.'

'I'm afraid that's out of the question. My DG would have my head on a stick if he knew how much access I've already given you. Your involvement in this affair is now over. In fact, if you hurry, you can pack your bags and catch the last Eurostar to Paris. It leaves at 7:39 on the dot.'

'I need to talk to her, Graham. Just for a few minutes.'

Seymour stopped walking and stared at the lights burning on the top floor of Thames House. 'Why do I know I'm going to regret this?' He turned toward Gabriel. 'You have twenty-four hours. Then I want you out of the country.'

Gabriel ran a finger over his heart twice.

'She's hiding out in Oxford on the dodgy side of Magdalen Bridge. Number 24 Rectory Road. Goes by the name Marina Chesnikova. We got her a job tutoring Russian-language students at the university.'

'What's her security like?'

'Same as Grigori's. She had it for the first couple of months, then asked us to back off. She has a minder and a daily check-in call. We monitor her phones and follow her from time to time to make sure she's not under surveillance and that she's behaving herself.'

'I would appreciate it if you didn't follow her tomorrow. Or me.'

'*You're* not even here. As for Ms. Chesnikova, I'll tell her to expect you. Don't disappointment me.' He gave Gabriel an admonitory pat on the shoulder and started across Horseferry Road alone.

'What kind of car was it?'

Seymour turned. 'Which car?'

'The car that took the woman from Maida Vale to Edgware.'

'It was a Vauxhall Insignia.'

'Color?'

'I believe they call it Metro Blue.'

'Hatchback?'

'Saloon, actually. And don't forget. I want you on the last train to Paris tomorrow night.'

'Seven thirty-nine. On the dot.'

16. Oxford

The wind swept in from the northwest, over the Vale of Evesham and down the slopes of the Cotswold Hills. It whipped past the shops in Cornmarket Street, chased round the Peckwater Quad of Christ Church, and laid siege to the flotilla of punts lashed together beneath Magdalen Bridge. Gabriel paused to gaze upon this emblematic image of an England that died long ago, then struck out across the Plain to Cowley Road.

Oxford, he remembered from his last visit, was not one city but two: an academic citadel of limestone colleges and spires on the western bank of the river Cherwell, a redbrick industrial town to the east. It was in the district of Cowley that a young bicycle maker named William Morris built his first automobile factory in 1913, instantly transforming Oxford into a major center of British manufacturing. Though the neighborhood remained true to its English working-class heritage, it had been remade into a bohemian quarter of colorful shops, cafés, and nightclubs. Students and dons from the university found lodgings in the cramped houses, along with immigrants from Pakistan, China, the Caribbean, and Africa. The district was also home to a substantial population of recent arrivals from the former Communist lands of Eastern Europe. Indeed, as Gabriel passed an organic grocer, he heard two women debating in Russian as they picked through a pile of tomatoes.

At the corner of Jeune Street an elderly woman was engaged in an altogether futile effort to sweep the dust from the forecourt of a Methodist church, the ends of her scarf fluttering like banners in the wind. Next to the entrance was a blue-and-white sign that read: EARTH IS THE LORD'S: IT IS OURS TO ENJOY, OURS TO FARM AND DEFEND. Gabriel walked another block to Rectory Road and rounded the corner.

The road fell away and bent slightly to the left, just enough so that he could not see to the other end. Gabriel walked the entire length once, searching for evidence of watchers. Finding none, he doubled back to the house at No. 24. Along the edge of the sidewalk was a short brick wall with weeds sprouting from the mortar. Behind the wall, in a tiny patch of white gravel, stood a large green trash receptacle. Leaning against it was a bicycle, its front wheel missing, its saddle covered in a plastic shopping bag. The walkway was perhaps a meter in length. It led to a flaking wood door set within an alcove. Apparently, the bell no longer functioned because nothing happened when Gabriel placed his thumb against the button. He gave the door three firm raps and heard the *tap-tap-tap* of female footsteps in the foyer. Then the sound of a voice, a woman speaking English with a distinct Russian accent.

'Who is there, please?'

'It's Natan Golani. We sat next to one another at dinner last summer at the Israeli ambassador's residence. We chatted briefly on the terrace when you went out for a cigarette. You told me that Russians cannot live as normal people and never will.'

Gabriel heard the rattle of a chain and watched the door

swing slowly open. The woman standing in the tiny entranceway was clutching a Siamese cat with luminous blue eyes that matched hers to perfection. She wore a tight-fitting black sweater, charcoal-gray trousers, and smart black boots. Her hair, once long and flaxen, was now short and dark. Her face, however, was unchanged. It was one of the most beautiful Gabriel had ever seen: heroic, vulnerable, virtuous. The face of a Russian icon come to life. The face of Russia itself.

Until six months ago, Olga Sukhova had been a practitioner of one of the world's most dangerous trades: Russian journalism. From her post at *Moskovskaya Gazeta*, a crusading weekly, she had exposed the atrocities of the Red Army in Chechnya, unearthed corruption at the highest levels of the Kremlin, and been an unflinching critic of the Russian president's assault on democracy. Her reporting had left her with a dim view of her country and its future, though nothing could have prepared her for the most important discovery of her career: a Russian oligarch and arms dealer named Ivan Kharkov was preparing to sell some of Russia's most sophisticated weapons to al-Qaeda terrorists. Though never published by the *Gazeta*, the story resulted in the murder of two of Olga's colleagues. The first, Aleksandr Lubin, was stabbed to death in a hotel room in the French ski resort of Courchevel. The second, an editor named Boris Ostrovsky, died in Gabriel's arms on the floor of St Peter's Basilica, the victim of a poisoning. Were it not for Gabriel and Grigori Bulganov, Olga Sukhova would surely have been murdered as well.

The dangerous nature of Olga's work and the constant threats against her life had left her with the finely tuned tradecraft of a seasoned spy. Like Gabriel, she assumed all rooms, even the rooms of her own home, were bugged. Important conversations were best conducted in public places. Which explained why five minutes after Gabriel's arrival, they were walking along the windswept pavements of St Clement's Street. Gabriel listened to the clatter of her boots against the pavement and thought of a cloudy afternoon in Moscow when they had walked among the dead in Novodevichy Cemetery, shadowed by rotating teams of Russian watchers. *Perhaps you should kiss me now, Mr. Golani. It is better if the FSB is under the impression we intend to become lovers.*

'Do you miss it?' he asked.

'Moscow?' She smiled sadly. 'I miss it terribly. The noise. The smells. The horrendous traffic. Sometimes I even find myself missing the snow. January is nearly over, and not a single flake. The woman on the BBC called this a cold snap. In Moscow, we call it springtime.' She looked at him. 'Does it ever snow in Oxford?'

'If it does, it won't be anything like home.'

'Nothing is like home. Oxford is a lovely city, but I must confess I find it rather dull. Moscow has many problems, but at least it is never dull. You might find this hard to understand, but I desperately miss being a Russian journalist.'

'A very wise and beautiful woman once told me there is no journalism in Russia – not real journalism, at least.'

'It's true. The regime has managed to silence its critics in the press, not by overt censorship but with murder, intimidation, and forced changes of ownership. The *Gazeta* is now nothing but a tabloid scandal sheet, filled with stories about pop stars, men from outer space, and werewolves living in the forests outside Moscow. You'll be happy to know circulation is higher than ever.'

'At least no one is getting killed.'

'That's true. Poor Boris was the last to die.'

She gave Gabriel's arm a melancholy squeeze. 'I *did* notice a story about Ivan on the *Gazeta*'s website last month. He was attending the opening-night party for a new restaurant in Moscow. His new wife, Yekaterina, was ravishing as usual. Ivan looked quite well himself. In fact, he was sporting a suntan.' She furrowed her brow into an affected frown. 'Where do you suppose Ivan was able to get a suntan in Russia in the middle of winter? In one of those tanning beds? No, I don't think so. Ivan's not the sort to radiate his skin with lights. Ivan used to get his tan in Saint-Tropez. Perhaps he slipped into Courchevel with a false passport for a bit of skiing at Christmastime. Or perhaps he paid a visit to one of his old haunts in Africa.'

'We've been picking up reports that he's rebuilding his old networks.'

'You don't say.'

'Have you heard similar things?'

'To be honest, I try not to think about Ivan. I have a blog. It's quite popular here in Britain as well as Moscow. The FSB has launched repeated cyberattacks against it.' She gave a fleeting smile. 'It gives me inordinate pleasure to know I can annoy the Kremlin, even from a cottage in Cowley.'

'Perhaps it would be wiser for you to—'

'To what?' she interrupted. 'To keep quiet? The people of Russia have been silent for too long. The regime has used that silence as justification for crushing any semblance of democracy and imposing a form of soft totalitarianism. Someone has to speak up. If it has to be me, then so be it. I've done it before.'

They had reached the other side of Magdalen Bridge: the side of spires and limestone and great thoughts. Olga stopped in the High Street and pretended to read the notice board.

'I must confess I wasn't surprised when Graham Seymour called last night to tell me you were coming. I assume this concerns Grigori. He's missing, isn't he?'

Gabriel nodded.

'I was afraid of that when he didn't return my call. He's never done that before.' She paused, then asked, 'How did you travel from London to Oxford?'

'The train from Paddington.'

'Did the British follow you?'

'No.'

'You're sure?'

'As sure as one can be.'

'And what about Russians? Were you followed by Russians?'

'Thus far, they seem unaware of my presence here.'

'I doubt they will be for long.' She looked across the street toward the entrance of the Oxford Botanic Gardens. 'Let's talk there, shall we? I've always enjoyed gardens in winter.'

17. Oxford

'My God,' she whispered. 'When will it end? When will it ever end?'

'Is it possible, Olga? Is there any way Grigori would go home on his own?'

She brushed away tears and looked around the gardens. 'Have you been here before?'

It seemed an odd question, given what he had just told her. But he knew Olga well enough to understand it was not without purpose.

'This is my first visit.'

'A hundred and fifty years ago, a mathematician from Christ Church used to come here with a young girl and her two sisters. The mathematician was Charles Lutwidge Dodgson. The girl was Alice Liddell. Their visits served as the inspiration for a book Dodgson would write under the pen name Lewis Carroll – *Alice's Adventures in Wonderland*, of course. Fitting, don't you think?'

'How so?'

'Because the British theory about Grigori is a tale worthy of Lewis Carroll. His hatred of the regime and his old service was real. The idea he would willingly return to Russia is absurd.'

They sat on a wooden bench in the center of the garden next to a fountain. Gabriel did not tell Olga he had reached the same conclusion or that he had photographic evidence to support it.

'You were working with him on his book.'

'I was.'

'You spent time with him?'

'More than the British probably realized.'

'How often did you see him?'

Olga searched the sky for an answer. 'Every couple of weeks.'

'Where did you meet?'

'Usually, here in Oxford. I went to London two or three times when I needed a change of scenery.'

'How did you arrange the meetings?'

'By telephone.'

'You spoke openly on the phone?'

'We used a rather crude code. Grigori said the eavesdropping capability of the Russian services wasn't what it once was but still good enough to warrant reasonable precautions.'

'How did Grigori travel here?'

'Like you. The train from Paddington.'

'He was careful?'

'So he said.'

'Did he come to your house?'

'Sometimes.'

'And others?'

'We would meet for lunch in the city center. Or for coffee.' She pointed toward the spire of Magdalen College. 'There's a lovely coffeehouse across the street called the Queen's Lane. Grigori was quite fond of it.'

Gabriel knew it. The Queen's Lane was the oldest

coffeehouse in Oxford. For the moment, though, his thoughts were elsewhere. Two women of late middle age had just entered the garden. One was wrestling with a brochure in the wind; the other was tying a scarf beneath her chin. Gabriel scrutinized them for a moment, then resumed his questioning.

'And in London?'

'A dreadful little sandwich shop near the Notting Hill Gate tube stop. He liked it because it was close to the Russian Embassy. He took a perverse pleasure walking by it from time to time, just for fun.'

The Russian Embassy, a white wedding-cake structure surrounded by a high-security fence, stood at the northern end of Kensington Palace Gardens. Gabriel had walked past it himself the previous afternoon while killing time before his meeting with Graham Seymour.

'Did you ever go to his place?'

'No, but his description made me a bit jealous. Too bad I wasn't a thug from the FSB. I would have liked a nice London house along with my new British passport.'

'How long did Grigori usually stay when he came here?'

'Two or three hours, sometimes a bit longer.'

'Did he ever spend the night?'

'Are you asking if we were lovers?'

'I'm just asking.'

'No, he never spent the night.'

'And were you lovers?'

'No, we were not lovers. I could never make love to a man who looked so much like Lenin.'

'Is that the only reason?'

'He was FSB once. Those bastards turned a blind eye

while many of my friends were murdered. Besides, Grigori wasn't interested in me. He was still in love with his wife.'

'Irina? To hear Grigori tell it, they nearly killed each other before they finally got a divorce.'

'His views must have changed with a bit of time and space. He said he'd been a fool. That he'd been too wrapped up in his work. She was seeing another man but hadn't agreed to marry him yet. Grigori thought he could pry her away and bring her to England. He wanted Irina to know what an important person he'd become. He thought she would fall in love with him all over again if she could see him in his new element and in his smart new London mews house.'

'Was he in contact with her?'

Olga nodded.

'Did she respond to his overtures?'

'Apparently so, but Grigori never went into the details.'

'If I remember correctly, she's a travel agent.'

'She works for a company called Galaxy Travel on Tver-skaya Street in Moscow. She arranges flights and accommodations for Russians traveling to Western Europe. Galaxy caters to a high-end clientele. *New* Russians,' she added with a distinct note of disdain. 'The kind of Russian who likes to spend winters in Courchevel and summers in Saint-Tropez.'

Olga dug a pack of cigarettes from her coat pocket. 'I suspect business is rather slow at the moment for Galaxy Travel. The global recession has hit Russia extremely hard.' She made no attempt to conceal her pleasure at this development. 'But that was predictable. Economies that depend on natural resources are always vulnerable to the inevitable cycle of boom and bust. One wonders how the regime will react to this new paradigm.'

Olga removed a cigarette from the pack and slipped it between her lips. When Gabriel reminded her that smoking was not permitted in the garden, she responded by lighting the cigarette anyway.

'I might have a British passport now, but I'm still a Russian. No Smoking signs mean nothing to us.'

'And you wonder why Russians die when they're fifty-eight.'

'Only the men. We women live much longer.'

Olga exhaled a cloud of smoke, which the wind carried directly into Gabriel's face. She apologized and switched places with him.

'I remember the night we all left together – the four of us crammed into that little Volga, pounding over the godforsaken roads of Russia. Grigori and I were smoking like fiends. You were leaning against the window with that bandage over your eye, begging us to stop. We couldn't stop. We were terrified. But we were also thrilled about what lay ahead. We had such high hopes, Grigori and I. We were going to change Russia. Elena's hopes were more modest. She just wanted to see her children again.' She blew smoke over her shoulder and looked at him. 'Have you seen her?'

'Elena?' He shook his head.

'Spoken to her?'

'Not a word.'

'No contact at all?'

'She wrote me a letter. I painted her a painting.'

Gabriel appealed to her to put out the cigarette. As she

buried the butt in the gravel at her feet, he watched a group of four tourists enter the garden.

'What did you think when Grigori became the celebrity defector and dissident?'

'I admired his courage. But I thought he was a fool for leading such a public life. I told him to lower his profile. I warned him that he was going to get into trouble. He wouldn't listen. He was under Viktor's spell.'

'Viktor?'

'Viktor Orlov.'

Gabriel recognized the name, of course. Viktor Orlov was one of the original Russian oligarchs, the small band of capitalist daredevils who gobbled up the valuable assets of the old Soviet state and made billions in the process. While ordinary Russians were struggling for survival, Viktor earned a king's ransom in oil and steel. Eventually, he ran afoul of the post-Yeltsin regime and fled to Britain one step ahead of an arrest warrant. He was now one of the regime's most vocal, if unreliable, critics. Orlov rarely allowed trivial things like facts to get in the way of the salacious charges he leveled regularly against the Russian president and his cronies in the Kremlin.

'Ever had any dealings with him?' Gabriel asked.

'Viktor?' Olga gave a guarded smile. 'Once, a hundred years ago, in Moscow. It was just after Yeltsin left office. The new masters of the Kremlin wanted Viktor to *voluntarily* sell his businesses back to the state – at bargain-basement prices, of course. For understandable reasons, Viktor wasn't interested. It got nasty – but then it always does. The Kremlin started talking about raids and seizures. That's what the Kremlin does when it wants something. It brings to bear the power of the state.'

'And Viktor thought you could help?'

'He asked me to lunch. He said he had an exclusive for me: a man whose job was to procure young women for the president's personal entertainment. Very young women, Gabriel. When I told him that I wouldn't touch the story, he got angry. A month later, he fled the country. Officially, the Russians want him back to face tax and fraud charges.'

'And unofficially?'

'The Kremlin wants Viktor to surrender his majority stake in Ruzoil, the giant Siberian energy company. It's worth many *billions* of dollars.'

'What did Viktor want with Grigori?'

'Viktor's motives for opposing the Kremlin were hopelessly transparent and hardly noble. Grigori gave him something he never had before.'

'Respectability.'

'Correct. What's more, Grigori knew some of the regime's darkest secrets. Secrets Viktor could wield as a weapon. Grigori was the answer to Viktor's prayers and Viktor took advantage of him. That's what Viktor does. He uses people. And when they're of no value to him, he throws them to the wolves.'

'Did you say any of this to Grigori?'

'Of course. But it didn't go over terribly well. Grigori thought he could take care of himself and didn't like being told by a journalist to watch his step. He was like an older man in love with a pretty girl. He wasn't thinking straight. He liked being around Viktor, the cars, the parties, the houses, the expensive wine. It was like a drug. Grigori was hooked.'

'When was the last time you saw him?'

'Two weeks ago. He was very excited. Apparently, Irina was thinking seriously about coming to London. But he was also nervous.'

'About Irina?'

'No, his security. He was convinced he was being watched.'

'By whom?'

'He didn't go into specifics. He gave me the newest pages of his manuscript. Then he gave me a letter for safekeeping. He told me that if anything ever happened to him, a friend would look for him. He was confident this man would eventually make his way to Oxford to see me. Grigori liked this man and respected him very much. Apparently, they made some sort of pact during a long drive through the Russian countryside.' She slipped the letter into Gabriel's hand and lit another cigarette. 'I have to admit, I don't remember hearing it. I must have been asleep at the time.'

18. Oxford

'You've never read it?' Gabriel asked.

'No, never.'

'I find that hard to believe.'

'Why?'

'Because you were once the most famous investigative reporter in Russia.'

'And?'

'Investigative reporters are natural snoops.'

'Like spies?'

'Yes, like spies.'

'I don't read other people's mail. It's unseemly.'

They were seated in the Queen's Lane coffee house against a latticed window. Gabriel was facing the street; Olga, the busy interior. She was holding the letter in one hand and a mug of tea in the other.

'I think it puts to rest the debate over whether Grigori redefected or was abducted.'

'Rather conclusively.'

Coincidentally, the letter was five sentences in length, though unlike the forged letter announcing Grigori's redefection, it had been produced on a word processor, not written by hand. It bore no salutation, for a salutation would have been insecure. Gabriel took it back from Olga and read it again:

IF THIS IS IN YOUR POSSESSION, IVAN HAS TAKEN ME. I HAVE NO ONE TO BLAME BUT MYSELF, SO PLEASE DO NOT FEEL OBLIGATED TO KEEP THE PROMISE YOU MADE THAT NIGHT IN RUSSIA. I DO HAVE ONE FAVOR TO ASK; I AM AFRAID MY DESIRE TO REUNITE WITH MY FORMER WIFE MAY HAVE PLACED HER IN DANGER. IF YOUR OFFICERS IN MOSCOW WOULD CHECK IN ON HER FROM TIME TO TIME, I WOULD BE GRATEFUL. FINALLY, IF I MAY OFFER ONE PIECE OF ADVICE FROM THE GRAVE, IT IS THIS: TREAD CAREFULLY.

Attached to the letter with a paper clip was a three-by-five photo. It showed Grigori and his former wife seated before a vodka-laden table in happier times. Irina Bulganova was an attractive woman with short blond hair and a compact body that suggested an athletic youth. Gabriel had never seen her before. Still, he found something remotely familiar in her face.

'Do you believe it?' Olga asked.

'Which part?'

'The part about Ivan. Could he really have pulled off an operation as complex as this?'

'Ivan is KGB to the bone. His arms-trafficking network was the most sophisticated the world had ever seen. It employed dozens of former and current intelligence officers, including Grigori himself. Grigori took Ivan's money. And then he betrayed him. In Russia, the price of betrayal is still the same.'

'*Vyshaya mera*,' Olga said softly.

'The highest measure of punishment.'

'Do you think he's dead?'

'It's possible.' Gabriel paused, then said, 'But I doubt it.'

'But he disappeared a week ago.'

'It might sound like a long time, but it isn't. Ivan will want information, everything Grigori told the British and the Americans about his network. Then I suspect the boys from Lubyanka will want a crack at him. The Russians are very patient when it comes to hostile interrogations. They refer to it as sucking a source dry.'

'How charming.'

'These are the successors of Dzerzhinsky, Yezhov, and Beria. They're not a charming lot, especially when it comes to someone who spilled family secrets to the British and the Americans.'

'I take it you've done this sort of thing yourself?'

'Interrogations?' Gabriel shook his head. 'To be honest, they were never my specialty.'

'How long does it take to do it right?'

'That depends.'

'On what?'

'On whether the subject is cooperating or not. Even if he is, it can take weeks or months to make sure he's told the interrogators everything they want to know. Just ask the detainees at Guantánamo Bay. Some of them have been interrogated relentlessly for years.'

'Poor Grigori. Poor foolish Grigori.'

'He *was* foolish. He should have never lived so openly. He also should have kept his mouth shut. He was just asking for trouble.'

'Is there any possible way to get him back?'

'It's not out of the question. But for now my concern is you.'

Gabriel looked out the window. The sun had slipped

below the tops of the colleges and the High Street was now in shadow. An Oxford city bus rumbled past, followed by a procession of students on bicycles.

'You were in contact with him, Olga. He knows everything about you. Your cover name. Your address. We have to assume Ivan now knows that, too.'

'I have a telephone number to call in case of an emergency. The British say they can collect me in a matter of minutes.'

'As you might expect, I'm not terribly impressed with British security these days.'

'Is it your intention to move me from Oxford without telling them?'

'By force, if necessary. Where's that new British passport of yours?'

'Top drawer of my bedside table.'

'You're going to need it, along with a change of clothing and anything else you don't want to leave behind.'

'I need my computer and my papers. And Cassandra. I'm not going without Cassandra.'

'Who's Cassandra?'

'My cat.'

'We'll leave it plenty of food and water. I'll send someone to collect it tomorrow.'

'Cassandra is a girl, Gabriel, not an *it*.'

'Unless she's a seeing-eye cat, she's not allowed on the Eurostar.'

'The Eurostar?'

'We're going to Paris. And we have to hurry if we're going to make the last train.'

'What time does it leave?'

Seven thirty-nine, he thought. On the dot.

19. Oxford

The Oxford City 5 bus runs from the train station, through the shopping district of Templars Square, and over Magdalen Bridge to the distant council estate of Blackbird Leys. Gabriel and Olga boarded outside All Souls College and disembarked at the first stop in Cowley Road. Five other passengers left with them. Four went their separate ways. The fifth, a middle-aged man, walked behind them for a short time before entering the church at the corner of Jeune Street. From inside came the sound of voices raised in prayer.

'They have evening services every Wednesday.'

'Wait inside while I get your things.'

'I want to say good-bye to Cassandra and make sure she's all right.'

'You don't trust me to feed her?'

'I can tell you don't like animals.'

'Actually, it's the other way around. And I have the scars to prove it.'

They turned into Rectory Road and made their way directly to Olga's door. Her bicycle was still leaning against the rubbish bin behind the tiny brick wall. Hanging from the door latch was a lime-green flyer advertising a new Indian takeaway. Olga removed it before inserting her key into the lock, but the key refused to turn. Then, somewhere along the darkened street, a car engine turned over. And Gabriel felt the back of his neck turn to fire.

To a normal person, the two consecutive events would probably have meant very little. But to a man like Gabriel Allon, they were the equivalent of a flashing neon sign warning of danger. Twisting his head quickly to the right, he saw the car approaching at high speed from the direction of St Clement's Street, headlamps doused. The driver had wide shoulders and was holding the wheel calmly with both hands. Directly behind him, protruding from the open rear window, Gabriel noticed a shape that was instantly familiar: a semiautomatic pistol fitted with a suppressor.

They were trapped, just as Grigori had been trapped before them. But this was not to be an abduction. This was a killing operation. To survive the next ten seconds would require Gabriel to play defense, something that violated decades of experience and training. Unfortunately, he had no other choice. He had come to Oxford unarmed.

He took a step back and gave the door a thunderous kick. Solid as a bulkhead, it refused to budge. Glancing to his left, he saw the tiny front garden of white gravel. As the first shots slammed into the front of the house, he seized Olga by the arm and forced her to the ground behind the stubby brick wall.

The gunfire lasted no more than five seconds – a single magazine's worth, thought Gabriel – and the driver didn't stop for the gunman to reload or switch weapons. Gabriel raised his head as the car rounded the slight bend in the road. He was able to confirm the make and model.

Vauxhall Insignia.

Saloon model.

Dark blue.

I believe they call it Metro Blue . . .

'You're crushing me.'

'Are you all right?'

'I think so. But remind me never to let you walk me home again.'

Gabriel stayed on the ground a moment longer, then got to his feet and gave the door another kick, this one fueled by adrenaline and anger. The dead bolt gave way, and the door flew inward as if it had been hit by a blast wave. Stepping cautiously into the entrance hall, he noticed a pair of feline eyes regarding him calmly from the base of the stairs. Olga scooped up the cat and held it tightly to her breast.

'I'm not leaving here without her.'

'Just hurry, Miss Chesnikova. I'd like to be on our way before the people with the gun come back to finish the job.'

PART TWO
Anatoly

20. The Marais, Paris

The quarter of Paris known as the Marais lies on the right bank of the Seine and spreads across portions of the 3rd and 4th arrondissements. Once a marshland, it had been a fashionable address during the monarchy, a working-class slum after the Revolution, and, in the twentieth century, the city's most vibrant Jewish neighborhood. Scene of a nightmarish Nazi roundup during the Second World War, it had fallen into a state of ruin by the 1960s, when the government launched a concerted effort to bring it back to life. Now among the most fashionable districts in Paris, the Marais was filled with exclusive shops, art museums, and trendy restaurants. It was in one such restaurant, on rue des Archives, that Uzi Navot waited late the following afternoon. He wore a roll-necked sweater that left the unflattering impression his head was bolted directly onto his thick shoulders. He scarcely lifted his eyes as Gabriel and Olga sat down.

They had arrived in Paris shortly after ten the previous evening and checked into a dreary little transit hotel across the street from the Gare du Nord. The journey had been uneventful; there had been no more attacks by Russian assassins, and Olga's cat had behaved as well as could be expected during the train ride from Oxford to Paddington Station. Due to the Eurostar's ban on pets, Gabriel had had no choice but to find lodging for the cat in London.

He had taken it to an art gallery in St James's owned by a man named Julian Isherwood. Over the years Isherwood had suffered many indignities because of his secret association with the Office, but to have a stranger's cat thrust upon him without warning was, he said, the final insult. His mood, however, changed dramatically upon seeing Olga for the first time. But then Gabriel had known it would. Julian Isherwood had a weakness for three things: Italian paintings, French wine, and beautiful women. Especially Russian women. And like Uzi Navot, he was easily appeased.

'I don't know why we had to come to this place,' Navot said now. 'You know how much I love the potted chicken at Jo Goldenberg.'

'It's closed, Uzi. Haven't you heard?'

'I know. But I still can't quite believe it. What's the Marais without Jo Goldenberg?'

For more than half a century, the kosher delicatessen had occupied a prominent corner at 7 rue des Rosiers. Jews from around the world had crowded into the restaurant's worn red banquettes and gorged themselves on caviar, chopped liver, brisket, and potato latkes. So had French film stars, government ministers, and famous writers and journalists. But the prominence of Jo Goldenberg made it an inviting target for extremists and terrorists, and in August 1982 six patrons were killed in a grenade and machine-gun attack carried out by the Palestinian terrorist group Abu Nidal. In the end, though, it was not terrorism that brought down the Paris landmark but soaring rents and repeated citations for poor sanitary conditions.

'You're lucky that chicken didn't kill you, Uzi. God knows

how long it had been lying around before they tossed it in a bowl and served it to you.'

'It was excellent. And so was the borscht. You loved the borscht at Jo Goldenberg.'

'I hate borscht. I've always hated borscht.'

'Then why did you order it?'

'You ordered it for me. And then you ate it for me, too.'

'I don't remember it that way.'

'Whatever you say, Uzi.'

They had been speaking to one another in rapid French. Navot turned to Olga and in English asked, 'Wouldn't you have enjoyed a good bowl of borscht, Miss Sukhova?'

'I'm Russian. Why on earth would I come to Paris and order borscht?'

Navot looked at Gabriel again. 'Is she always so friendly?' he asked in Hebrew.

'Russians have a somewhat dark sense of humor.'

'I'll say.' Navot glanced out the window into the narrow street. 'This place has changed since I left Paris. I used to come here whenever I had a few hours to kill. It was like a little slice of Tel Aviv, right in the center of Paris. Now . . .' He shook his head slowly. 'It's just another place to buy a handbag or expensive jewelry. You can't even get good falafel here anymore.'

'That's exactly the way the mayor wants it. Neat and tidy with lots of chic stores paying big rents and big tax bills. They even tried to put in a McDonald's a few months back, but the neighborhood rose up in rebellion. Poor Jo Goldenberg couldn't make a go of it anymore. At the end, his rent was three hundred thousand euros a year.'

'No wonder the kitchen was a mess.'

Navot looked down at his menu. When he spoke again, his tone was decidedly less cordial.

'Let me see if I understand this correctly. I come to Italy and order you to return to Israel because we believe your life may be in danger. You tell me that you need three days to finish a painting, and I foolishly agree. Then, within twenty-four hours, I learn that you've slipped away from the bodyguards and traveled to London to investigate the disappearance of one Grigori Bulganov, missing Russian defector. And this morning I receive a message saying you've arrived in Paris, accompanied by Russian defector number *two*, Olga Sukhova. Have I left anything out?'

'We had to leave Olga's cat behind at Julian's gallery. You need to send someone from London Station to collect it. Otherwise, Julian's liable to let it loose in Green Park.'

Gabriel removed Grigori's letter from his coat pocket and dealt it onto the table. Navot read it silently, his face an inscrutable mask, then looked up again.

'I want to know everything you did while you were in England, Gabriel. No shortcuts, deletions, edits, or abridgments. Do you understand me?'

Gabriel gave Navot a complete account, beginning with his first meeting with Graham Seymour and ending with the assassination attempt on Olga's doorstep.

'They disabled the lock?' Navot asked.

'It was a nice touch.'

'It's a shame the shooter didn't realize you were unarmed. He could have simply climbed out of the car and killed you.'

'You don't really mean that, Uzi.'

'No, but it makes me feel better to say it. Rather sloppy for a Russian hit team, don't you think?'

'It's not so easy to kill someone from a moving vehicle.'

'Unless you're Gabriel Allon. When *we* set our sights on someone, he dies. The Russians are usually like that, too. They're fanatics when it comes to planning and preparation.'

Gabriel nodded in agreement.

'So why send a couple of amateurs to Oxford?'

'Because they assumed it would be easy. They probably thought the second string could handle it.'

'You're assuming Olga was the target and not you?'

'That's correct.'

'What makes you so sure?'

'I'd only been in the country three days. Even *we* would be hard-pressed to organize a hit that quickly.'

'So why didn't they call it off when they saw she wasn't alone?'

'It's possible they simply mistook me for Olga's boyfriend or one of her students, not someone who knows to hit the deck when a lock suddenly stops working.'

A waiter approached the table. Navot sent him away with a subtle gesture of his hand.

'It might have been wiser if you'd shared some of these observations with Graham Seymour. He allowed you to conduct your own review of Grigori's disappearance. And how did you repay him? By sneaking out of the country with another one of his defectors.' Navot gave a humorless smile. 'Graham and I could form our own little club. Men who have placed their trust in you, only to be burned.'

Navot looked at Olga and switched from Hebrew to English.

'Your neighbors didn't notice the bullet holes and the broken front door until about eight o'clock. When they couldn't find you, they called the Thames Valley Police.'

'I'm afraid I know what happened next,' she said. 'Because my address had a special security flag on it, the dispatch officer immediately contacted the chief constable.'

'And guess what the chief constable did?'

'I suspect he called the Home Office in London. And then the Home Office contacted Graham Seymour.'

Navot's gaze shifted from Olga to Gabriel. 'And what do you think Graham Seymour did?'

'He called our London Station chief.'

'Who'd been quietly scouring the city for you for the past three days,' Navot added. 'And when Graham got the station chief on the telephone, he read him the riot act. Congratulations, Gabriel. You've managed to bring relations between the British and the Office to a new low. They want a full explanation of what happened in Oxford last night. And they'd also like their defector back. Graham Seymour is expecting us in London tomorrow morning, bright and early.'

'Us?'

'You, me, and Olga.' Then, almost as an afterthought, Navot added, 'And the Old Man, too.'

'How did Shamron manage to get himself involved in this?'

'The same way he always does. Shamron abhors a vacuum. He sees an empty space and he fills it.'

'Tell him to stay in Tiberias. Tell him we can handle it.'

'Please, Gabriel. As far as Shamron is concerned, we're still a couple of kids trying to learn how to ride a bicycle, and he can't quite bring himself to let go of the seat. Besides, it's too late. He's already here.'

'Where is he?'

'A safe flat up in Montmartre. Olga and I will stay here and get better acquainted. Shamron would like a word with you. In private.'

'About what?'

'He didn't tell me. After all, I'm only the chief of Special Ops.'

Navot looked down at his menu and frowned.

'No potted chicken. You know how much I loved the potted chicken at Jo Goldenberg. The only thing better than the potted chicken was the borscht.'

21. Montmartre, Paris

The apartment house stood in the eastern fringes of Montmartre, next to the cemetery. It had a tidy interior courtyard and an elegant staircase covered by a well-worn runner. The flat was on the third floor; from the window of the comfortably furnished sitting room, it might have been possible to see the white dome of Sacré-Coeur had Shamron not been blocking the view. Hearing the sound of the door, he turned round slowly and stared at Gabriel for a long moment, as if debating whether to have him shot or thrown to the wild dogs. He was wearing a gray pin-striped suit and a costly silk necktie the color of polished silver. It made him look like an aging Middle European businessman who made money in shady ways and never lost at baccarat.

'We missed you at lunch, Ari.'

'I don't eat lunch.'

'Not even when you're in Paris?'

'I loathe Paris. Especially in winter.'

He fished a cigarette case from the breast pocket of his jacket and thumbed open the lid.

'I thought you'd finally given up smoking.'

'And I thought you were in Italy finishing a painting.' Shamron removed a cigarette, tapped the end three times on the lid, and slipped it between his lips. 'And you wonder why I won't retire.'

His lighter flared. It was not the battered old Zippo he

carried at home but a sleek silver device that, at Shamron's command, produced a blue finger of flame. The cigarette, however, was his usual brand. Unfiltered and Turkish, it emitted an acrid odor that was as uniquc to Shamron as his trademark walk and his unyielding will to crush anyone foolish enough to oppose him.

To describe the influence of Ari Shamron on the defense and security of the State of Israel was tantamount to explaining the role played by water in the formation and maintenance of life on earth. In many respects, Ari Shamron *was* the State of Israel. He had fought in the war that led to Israel's reconstitution and had spent the subsequent sixty years protecting the country from a host of enemies bent on its destruction. His star had burned brightest in times of war and crisis. He was named director of the Office for the first time not long after the disaster of the 1973 Yom Kippur War and served longer than any chief before or after him. When a series of public scandals dragged the reputation of the Office down to the lowest point in its history, he was called out of retirement and, with Gabriel's help, restored the Office to its former glory. His second retirement, like his first, was involuntary. In some quarters, it was likened to the destruction of the Second Temple.

Shamron's role now was that of an éminence grise. Though he no longer had a formal position or title, he remained the hidden hand that guided Israel's security policies. It was not unusual to enter his home at midnight and find several men crowded around the kitchen table in their shirtsleeves, shouting at one another through a dense cloud of cigarette smoke – and poor Gilah, his long-suffering wife, sitting in the next room with her needlepoint and her Mozart, waiting for the boys to leave so that she could see to the dishes.

'You've managed to create quite a row on the other side of the English Channel, my son. But then, that's become your specialty.' Shamron exhaled a stream of smoke toward the ceiling, where it swirled in the half-light like gathering storm clouds. 'Your friend Graham Seymour is apparently fighting for his job. *Mazel tov*, Gabriel. Not bad for three days' work.'

'Graham will survive. He always does.'

'At what cost?' Shamron asked of no one but himself. 'Downing Street and the top ranks of MI5 and MI6 are in an uproar over your actions. They're making unpleasant noises about suspending cooperation with us on a broad range of sensitive issues. We need them right now, Gabriel. And so do you.'

'Why me?'

'Perhaps it's escaped your notice, but the mullahs in Tehran are about to complete their nuclear weapon. Our new prime minister and I share a similar philosophy. We don't believe in sitting around while others plot our destruction. And when people talk about wiping us off the face of the earth, we choose to take them at their word. We both lost our families in the first Holocaust, and we're not going to lose our country to a second – at least, not without a fight.'

Shamron removed his eyeglasses and inspected the lenses for impurity. 'If we are forced to attack Iran, we can expect a ferocious response from their proxy army in Lebanon: Hezbollah. You should know that a delegation from

Hezbollah made a secret trip to Moscow recently to do a bit of shopping. And they weren't looking for nesting dolls and fur hats. They went to see your old friend Ivan Kharkov. Word is, Ivan sold them three thousand Kornet vehicle mounted antitank weapons, along with several thousand RPG 32s. Apparently, he also gave them a nice discount since he knew they'd be using the weapons against us.'

'We're sure it was Ivan?'

'We heard his name mentioned in several intercepts.' Shamron put on his eyeglasses again and scrutinized Gabriel for a moment. 'With adversaries like Iran, Hezbollah, and Ivan Kharkov, we need friends wherever we can find them, Gabriel. That's why we need good relations with the British.' Shamron paused. 'And it's why I need you to end your honeymoon without end and come home.'

Gabriel could see where this was headed. He decided not to make Shamron's task any easier by posing a leading question. Shamron, visibly annoyed by the calculated silence, stabbed out his cigarette in an ashtray on the coffee table.

'Our new prime minister has been an admirer of yours for many years. The same cannot be said of his feelings toward the current director of the Office. He and Amos served briefly together in AMAN, Israel's military intelligence service. Their hatred was mutual and persists to this day. Amos will not survive long. Last week, over a private dinner, the prime minister asked me who I wanted to be the next chief of the Office. I gave him your name, of course.'

'I've made it abundantly clear I'm not interested in the job.'

'I've heard this speech before. It's tiresome. More to the point, it does not reflect current realities. The State of Israel is facing a threat unlike any in its history. If you haven't noticed, we're not very popular right now. And the Iranian threat means even greater instability and potential violence across the region. What do you intend to do, Gabriel? Sit on your farm in Italy and restore paintings for the pope?'

'Yes.'

'That's not realistic.'

'Perhaps not to you, Ari, but it's what I intend to do. I've given my life to the Office. I've lost my son. I've lost one wife. I've shed the blood of other men and my own blood. I'm finished. Tell the prime minister to choose someone else.'

'He needs you. The country needs you.'

'You're being a bit hyperbolic, don't you think?'

'No, just honest. The country has lost faith in its political leaders. Our society is beginning to fray. The people need someone they can believe in. Someone they can trust. Someone beyond reproach.'

'I was an assassin. I'm hardly beyond reproach.'

'You were a soldier on the secret battlefield. You gave justice to those who could not seek it themselves.'

'And I lost everything in the process. I almost lost myself.'

'But your life has been restored, just like one of your paintings. You have Chiara. Who knows? Perhaps soon you'll have another child.'

'Is there something I should know, Ari?'

Shamron's lighter flared again. His next words were spoken not to Gabriel but the floodlit dome of Sacré-Coeur. 'Come home, Gabriel. Take control of the Office.

It is what you were born to do. Your future was determined when your mother named you Gabriel.'

'That was the same thing you said when you recruited me for Operation Wrath of God.'

'Was it?' Shamron gave a faint smile of remembrance. 'No wonder you said yes to me then.'

Shamron had been hinting at a scenario like this for years, but never before had he stated it so unequivocally. Gabriel, were he foolish enough to accept the offer, knew only too well how he would spend the rest of his life. Indeed, he had to look no further than the man standing before him. Running the Office had ruined Shamron's health and wreaked havoc with his family. The country regarded him as a national treasure, but as far as his children were concerned, Shamron was the father who had never been there. The father who had missed birthdays and anniversaries. The father who traveled in armored cars, surrounded by men with guns. It was not the life Gabriel wanted, nor did he intend to inflict it on his loved ones. To say those words to Shamron now was not an option. Better to hold out a glimmer of hope and use the situation to his advantage. Shamron would understand that. It was exactly the way he would have played it if the roles were reversed.

'How long before I would have to take control?'

'Does that mean you'll take the job?'

'No, it means I'll consider the offer – on two conditions.'

'I don't like ultimatums. The PLO learned that lesson the hard way.'

'Do you want to hear my terms?'

'If you insist.'

'Number one, I get to finish my painting.'

Shamron closed his eyes and nodded. 'And the second?'

'I'm going to get Grigori Bulganov out of Russia before Ivan kills him.'

'I was afraid you were going to say that.' Shamron took a final pull at his cigarette and ground it out slowly in the ashtray. 'See if there's some coffee in this place. You know I'm incapable of discussing an operation without coffee.'

22. Montmartre, Paris

Gabriel spooned coffee into the French press and briefed Shamron while waiting for the water to boil. Shamron sat motionless at the small table in his shirtsleeves, his liver-spotted hands bunched thoughtfully beneath his chin. He moved for the first time to read the letter Grigori had left with Olga Sukhova in Oxford, then a moment later to accept his first cup of coffee. He was pouring sugar into it when he announced his verdict.

'It's clear Ivan is planning to hunt down and kill everyone who was involved in the operation against him. First he went after Grigori. Then Olga. But the person he really wants is *you*.'

'So what do you want me to do? Spend the rest of my life hiding?' Gabriel shook his head. 'To quote the great Ari Shamron, I don't believe in sitting around while others plot my destruction. It seems to me we have a choice. We can live in fear. Or we can fight back.'

'And how do you suggest we do that?'

'By treating Ivan and his operators as though they are terrorists. By putting them out of business before they can go after anyone else. And if we're lucky, we might be able to get Grigori back.'

'Where do you plan to start?'

Gabriel unzipped the side compartment of his overnight bag and withdrew an enlarged photograph of a

Mercedes sedan with two people in the backseat. Shamron slipped on a pair of battered half-moon reading glasses and examined the image. Then Gabriel placed another photograph before him: the photo that had been attached to the letter in Oxford. *Grigori and Irina in happier times . . .*

'I suppose we know how they got him into the car so quietly,' Shamron said. 'Did you share this with your British friends?'

'It might have slipped my mind while I was fleeing the country one step ahead of a Russian hit squad.'

'Accompanied by Graham Seymour's defector.' Shamron spent a moment scrutinizing the photograph. 'Tell me what you have in mind, my son.'

'I made a promise to Grigori the night he saved my life. I intend to keep that promise.'

'Grigori Bulganov has a British passport. That makes him a British problem.'

'Graham Seymour made one thing abundantly clear to me in London, Ari. As far as the British are concerned, Grigori is *my* defector, not theirs. And if I don't try to get him back, no one will.'

Shamron tapped the photograph. 'And you think she can help you?'

'She saw their faces. Heard their voices. If we can get to her, she can help us.'

'And what if she's not willing to help you? What if she willingly took part in the operation?'

'I suppose anything is possible . . .'

'But?'

'I doubt it very seriously. Based on what Grigori told me,

Irina hated the FSB and everything it stood for. It was one of the reasons their marriage came apart.'

'Were there any other reasons?'

'She was ashamed of Grigori for taking money from Ivan Kharkov. She called it blood money. She wouldn't touch it.'

'Perhaps Irina had a change of heart. Russians can be very persuasive, Gabriel. And if there's one thing I've learned in this life, it's that everyone has a price.'

'You might be right, Ari. But we won't know for sure until we ask her.'

'A conversation? Is that what you're suggesting?'

'Something like that.'

'What makes you think they haven't killed her?'

'I called her office this morning. She answered the phone.'

Shamron drank some of his coffee and pondered the implications of Gabriel's statement. 'Let me make one thing clear from the outset. Under no circumstances are you or anyone else from the original operation against Ivan going back to Moscow. *Ever.*'

'I have no intention of going back.'

'So how are you going to arrange a meeting with her?'

Gabriel gave the rough outlines of his plan. Shamron twirled his lighter between his fingertips while he listened: two turns to the right, two turns to the left.

'It has one flaw. You're assuming she'll cooperate.'

'I'm assuming nothing.'

'She'll have to be handled carefully until you're certain of her true loyalties.'

'And after that as well.'

'I suppose you'd like to use your old team.'

'It saves time having to get acquainted.'

'How much money is this going to cost me?'

Gabriel added coffee to Shamron's cup and smiled. The Old Man had worked for the Office during a time when it counted every shekel, and he still acted as if operational funds came directly from his own pocket.

'A hundred thousand should cover it.'

'A hundred thousand!'

'I was going to ask for two.'

'I'll transfer the funds into your account in Zurich tomorrow morning. As soon as you've established a base of operations, I'll dispatch the team.'

'What are you going to tell Amos?'

'As little as possible.'

'And the British?'

'Leave that to me. I'll brief them about your plans and make it clear we'll share whatever information you discover.' Shamron paused. 'You will share nicely, won't you, Gabriel?'

'Absolutely.'

'To be honest, I'm sure they'll be relieved we're handling it. The last thing Downing Street wants is another confrontation with the Russians – not with the British economy on life support. They're more interested in making sure that Russian money continues to flow into the banks of London.'

'That leaves one problem.'

'Just one?'

'Olga.'

'I'll return her to the British tomorrow and fall on my sword on your behalf. I've brought along a little present for them, some chatter we've been picking up in Lebanon about a possible terror plot in London.'

'You can tell them about the chatter in Lebanon, Ari, but I'm afraid Olga isn't going back to Britain anytime soon.'

'You can't leave her here in Paris.'

'I don't intend to. I'm taking her with me. She's really rather good, you know.'

'Something tells me my stay in London isn't going to be a pleasant one.' Shamron sipped his coffee. 'You'd better have a word with Uzi. Whatever you do, don't mention our conversation about your taking control of the Office. He's not going to be thrilled about the prospect of working for you.'

'I never said I would take the job, Ari. I said I would *consider* it.'

'I heard you the first time. But I know you wouldn't be leading me on, not over something as important as this.'

'I need you to do me one other favor while you're in London.'

'What's that?'

'I had to leave Olga's cat with Julian Isherwood.'

Shamron began turning his lighter again. 'I hate cats. And the only thing I hate worse than cats is being lied to.'

23. Lake Como, Italy

Lake Como lies in the northeastern corner of the region of Lombardy, just a few miles from the Swiss border. Shaped like an inverted Y, it is surrounded by soaring Alpine peaks and dotted with picturesque towns and villages. One of Europe's deepest lakes, it is also, sadly, among its most polluted. In fact, a recent study by an Italian environmental group found that bacteria levels had reached sixty-eight times the limit for safe human bathing. The culprits were antiquated lakeside sewage systems, runoff from nearby farms and vineyards, and a reduction in rainfall and mountain snowpack attributed, rightly or wrongly, to global warming. Under pressure from the local tourism industry, the government had promised dramatic action to prevent the lake from slipping past the point of no return. Most Italians weren't holding their breath. Their government was rather like a charming rogue – good at making promises, not so good at keeping them.

To stand on the terraces of Villa Teresa, however, was to forget that the magnificent waters of Lake Como had been spoiled in any way. Indeed, at certain times of the day and under proper light and weather conditions, one could imagine there was no such thing as global warming, no wars in Iraq and Afghanistan, no worldwide financial crisis, and no possible threat looming anywhere over the ring of protective mountains. Built by a wealthy Milanese trader in the eighteenth century, the villa stood on its own small peninsula. It was three floors in height, tawny orange in color, and accessible only by boat – a fact that Herr Heinrich Kiever, chief operating officer of Matrix Technologies of Zug, Switzerland, found highly appealing.

Herr Kiever, it seemed, was looking for a private retreat where his employees could complete work on a major project free from distractions and in a setting that would inspire greatness. After a brief tour, he declared Villa Teresa perfection itself. The contracts were signed over coffee in the town of Laglio, home of an American movie star whose highly publicized presence in Como was, in the opinion of many longtime habitués, the worst thing to happen to the lake since the invention of the gasoline-powered engine. Herr Kiever paid the entire lease with a certified check drawn on his bank in Zurich. He then informed the rental agent he required complete privacy, meaning no maid service, no cooks, and no follow-up calls from the agency. If there were any problems, he explained, the agent would be the first to know.

Herr Kiever took up residence in the villa that same afternoon along with two women. One was a striking brunette with a face like a Russian icon; the other, an attractive Italian accompanied by a pair of matching bodyguards. Unbeknownst to the rental agency, Herr Kiever and the bodyguards had a brief but heated argument before conducting a meticulous sweep of the property for hidden microphones or other eavesdropping equipment. Satisfied the estate was secure, they settled into their rooms and awaited the arrival of the remaining guests. There were six in all, four men and two women, and they came not from

Zug but from an anonymous-looking office block on King Saul Boulevard in Tel Aviv. They had traveled to Europe separately under false names and with false passports in their pockets. Three landed in Rome and made the drive north; three landed in Zurich and drove south. By some miracle, they arrived at the villa's private landing just five minutes apart. Herr Kiever, who was waiting to greet them, declared it a good omen. The six men and women withheld judgment. They had sailed under Herr Kiever's star before and knew calm waters often gave way to storm-tossed seas with little or no warning.

So, too, did the newest addition to this illustrious band of operatives: Olga Sukhova. They knew her by name and reputation, of course, but none had ever actually met the famed Russian journalist. Gabriel saw to the introductions with a studied evasiveness only a veteran of the secret world could summon. He provided Olga with first names but made no mention of current positions or past professional exploits. As far as Gabriel was concerned, the six individuals were blank slates, tools that had been lent to him by a higher power.

They approached her in pairs and carefully shook her hand. The women, Rimona and Dina, came first. Rimona was in her mid-thirties and had shoulder-length hair the color of Jerusalem limestone. A major in the IDF, she had worked for several years as an analyst for AMAN before transferring to the Office, where she was now part of a special Iran task force. Dina, petite and dark-haired, was an Office terrorism specialist who had personally experienced its horrors. In October 1994 she was standing in Tel Aviv's Dizengoff Square when a Hamas terrorist detonated his suicide belt aboard a No. 5 bus. Twenty-one people were murdered that day, including Dina's mother and two of her sisters. Dina herself had suffered a serious leg wound and still walked with a slight limp.

Next came a pair of men in their forties, Yossi and Yaakov. Tall and balding, Yossi was currently assigned to the Russia Desk of Research, which is how the Office referred to its analytical division. He had read classics at All Souls College at Oxford and spoke with a pronounced English accent. Yaakov, a compact man with black hair and a pockmarked face, looked as if he couldn't be bothered with books and learning. For many years he had served in the Arab Affairs Department of Shin Bet, Israel's internal security service, recruiting spies and informants in the West Bank and Gaza. Like Rimona, he had recently transferred to the Office and was currently running agents into Lebanon.

Next came an oddly mismatched pair who shared one common attribute. Both spoke fluent Russian. The first was Eli Lavon. An elfin figure with wispy gray hair and intelligent brown eyes, Lavon was regarded as the finest street surveillance artist the Office had ever produced. He had worked side by side with Gabriel through countless operations and was the closest thing Gabriel had to a brother. Like Gabriel, Lavon's ties to the Office were somewhat tenuous. A professor of biblical archaeology at Jerusalem's Hebrew University, he could usually be found waist-deep in an excavation trench, sifting through the dust and artifacts of Israel's ancient past. Twice each year, he lectured on surveillance techniques at the Academy, and he was forever being drawn out of retirement by Gabriel, who was never truly comfortable in the field without the legendary Eli Lavon watching his back.

The figure standing at Lavon's side had eyes the color of glacial ice and a fine-boned, bloodless face. Born in Moscow to a pair of dissident Jewish scientists, Mikhail Abramov had come to Israel as a teenager within weeks of the Soviet Union's collapse. Once described by Shamron as 'Gabriel without a conscience,' he had joined the Office after serving in the Sayeret Matkal special forces, where he had assassinated several of the top terrorist masterminds of Hamas and Palestinian Islamic Jihad. His talents were not limited to the gun; the previous summer, in Saint-Tropez, he had infiltrated Ivan Kharkov's entourage, along with a CIA officer named Sarah Bancroft. Of all those gathered at the villa by the lake, only Mikhail had had the distinct displeasure of actually sharing a meal with Ivan. Afterward, he admitted it was the most terrifying experience of his professional life – this coming from a man who had hunted terrorists across the badlands of the Occupied Territories.

Within the corridors and conference rooms of King Saul Boulevard, these six men and women were known by the code name 'Barak' – the Hebrew word for lightning – because of their ability to gather and strike quickly. They had operated together, often under conditions of unbearable stress, on secret battlefields stretching from Moscow to Marseilles to the exclusive Caribbean island of Saint-Barthélemy. Usually, they conducted themselves in a highly professional manner and with few intrusions of egotism or pettiness. Occasionally, a seemingly trivial issue, such as assigning bedrooms, could provoke outbursts of childishness and flashes of ill temper. Unable to resolve the dispute themselves, they turned to Gabriel, the wise ruler, who imposed a settlement by decree and somehow managed to satisfy no one, which, in the end, they regarded as just.

After establishing a secure communications link with King Saul Boulevard, they convened for a working dinner. They ate like a family reunited, which in many respects they were, though their conversation was more circumspect than usual, owing to the presence of an outsider. Gabriel could tell by the inquisitive looks on their faces that they had heard rumors in Tel Aviv. Rumors that Amos was yesterday's man. Rumors that Gabriel would soon be taking his rightful place in the director's suite at King Saul Boulevard. Only Rimona, Shamron's niece by marriage, dared to ask whether it was true. She did so in a whisper and in Hebrew, so that Olga could not understand. When Gabriel pretended not to hear, she gave him a covert kick in the ankle, a retaliatory strike only a relative of Shamron would dare undertake.

They adjourned to the great room after dinner and there, standing before a crackling fire, Gabriel conducted the first formal briefing of the operation. Grigori Bulganov, the Russian defector who had twice saved Gabriel's life, had been abducted by Ivan Kharkov and brought to Russia, where in all likelihood he was undergoing a severe interrogation that would end with his execution. They were going to get him back, Gabriel said, and they were going to put Ivan's operatives out of business. And their quest would begin with an extraction and interrogation of their own.

In another country, in another intelligence service, such

a proposal might have been greeted with expressions of incredulity or even mockery. But not the Office. The Office had a word for such unconventional thinking: meshuggah, Hebrew for crazy or foolish. Inside the Office, no idea was too meshuggah. Sometimes, the more meshuggah, the better. It was a state of mind. It was what made the Office great.

There was something else that set them apart from other services: the freedom felt by lower-ranking officers to make suggestions and even to challenge the assumptions of their superiors. Gabriel took no offense when his team embarked on a rigorous deconstruction of the plan. Though they were an eclectic mix – indeed, most were never meant to be field agents at all – they had carried out some of the most daring and dangerous operations in Office history. They had killed and kidnapped, committed acts of fraud, theft, and forgery. They were Gabriel's second eyes. Gabriel's safety net.

The discussion lasted another hour. Most of it was conducted in English for Olga's benefit, but occasionally they lapsed into Hebrew for reasons of security or because no other language would do. There were occasional flashes of temper or the odd insult, but for the most part the tone remained civil. When the last issue had been resolved, Gabriel brought the session to a close and broke the team into working groups. Yaakov and Yossi would acquire the vehicles and secure the routes. Dina, Rimona, and Chiara would prepare the cover organization and create all necessary websites, brochures, and invitations. The Russian speakers, Mikhail and Eli Lavon, would handle the interrogation itself, with Olga serving as their consultant.

Gabriel had no specific task, other than to supervise and to worry. It was fitting, he thought, for it was a role Shamron had played many times before.

At midnight, when the table had been cleared and the dishes washed, they filed upstairs to their rooms for a few hours of sleep. Gabriel and Chiara, alone in the master suite, made quiet love. Afterward, they lay next to each other in the darkness, Gabriel staring at the ceiling, Chiara tracing her fingertip along his cheek.

'Where are you?' she asked.

'Moscow,' he said.

'What are you doing?'

'Watching Irina.'

'What do you see?'

'I'm not quite sure yet.'

Chiara was silent for a moment. 'You're never happier than when they're around, Gabriel. Maybe Uzi was right. Maybe the Office is the only family you have.'

'*You're* my family, Chiara.'

'Are you sure you want to leave them?'

'I'm sure.'

'I hear Shamron has other plans.'

'He usually does.'

'When are you going to tell him that you're not going to take the job?'

'As soon as I get Grigori back from the Russians.'

'Promise me one thing, Gabriel. Promise me you won't get too close to Ivan.' She kissed his lips. 'Ivan likes to break pretty things.'

24. Bellagio, Italy

The Northern Italian Travel Association, or NITA, occupied a suite of small offices on a narrow pedestrian lane in the town of Bellagio – or so it claimed. Its stated mission was to encourage tourism in northern Italy by aggressively promoting the region's incomparable beauty and lifestyle, especially to booking agents and travel writers in other countries. A website for the association appeared soon after Gabriel's team convened on the opposite side of the lake at Villa Teresa. So, too, did a handsome brochure, printed not in Italy but in Tel Aviv, along with an invitation to the third annual winter seminar and showcase at the Grand Hotel Villa Serbelloni – odd, since no one at the Serbelloni would have recalled a first annual showcase and seminar, or even a second for that matter.

With only seventy-two hours until the start of the conference, the organizers were dismayed to learn of a last-minute cancellation and began searching for a replacement. The name Irina Bulganova of Galaxy Travel, Tverskaya Street, Moscow, came quickly to mind. Were NITA an ordinary travel association, there might have been some question as to whether Ms. Bulganova would be able to come to Italy on such short notice. NITA, however, possessed means and methods unavailable to even the most sophisticated organizations. They hacked into her computer and inspected her appointment calendar. They read her e-mail and listened to her telephone calls. Their colleagues in Moscow followed Ms. Bulganova wherever she went and even had a peek at her passport to make certain it was in order.

Their inquiries revealed much about the tangled state of her personal affairs. They learned, for example, that Ms. Bulganova had recently stopped seeing her lover for the vaguest of reasons. They learned she was having trouble sleeping at night and preferred music to television. They learned she had recently placed a telephone call to FSB Headquarters requesting information as to the whereabouts of her former husband, a question greeted by a curt dismissal. All things considered, they believed a woman in Ms. Bulganova's position might relish the opportunity to make an all-expenses-paid visit to Italy. And what Muscovite wouldn't? On the day the invitation was sent, the weather forecast was calling for heavy snow and temperatures of perhaps twenty below.

It was dispatched via e-mail and signed by none other than Veronica Ricci, NITA's chief executive officer. It began with an apology for the last-minute nature of the offer and concluded with promises of first-class air travel, luxury hotel accommodations, and gourmet Italian cuisine. If Ms. Bulganova chose to attend – and it was NITA's fervent hope that she would – an information packet, airline tickets, and a welcoming gift would follow. The e-mail neglected to say that the aforementioned materials were already in Moscow and would be delivered by a courier company that did not exist. Nor did it mention the fact that Ms. Bulganova would remain under surveillance to make certain she was not being followed by agents of Ivan Kharkov. It made only one request: that she RSVP as quickly as possible so that other arrangements could be made should she be unable to attend.

Fortunately, such a contingency would not prove necessary, for exactly seven hours and twelve minutes after the e-mail was sent, a reply arrived from Moscow. At Villa Teresa, the celebration was boisterous but brief. Irina Bulganova was coming to Italy. And they had much work to do.

In every operation, Shamron was fond of saying, there is a choke point. Navigate it successfully, and the operation can sail easily into open waters. Stray off course, even by a few degrees, and it can become stranded on the shoals or, worse still, smash to pieces on the rocks. For this operation, the choke point was none other than Irina herself. As of that moment, they still did not know whether she was heaven-sent or whether she might bring the devil to their doorstep. Handle her well, and the operation might go down as one of the team's finest. Make one mistake, and there was a chance she might get them all killed.

They rehearsed as if their lives depended on it. Mikhail's Russian was superior to Eli Lavon's, and so it was Mikhail, despite his youth, who would serve as lead inquisitor. Lavon, blessed with a kindly face and unthreatening demeanor, would play the role of benefactor and sage. The only variable, of course, was Irina herself. Olga helped them to prepare for any contingency. At Gabriel's direction, she was terrified one minute, belligerent the next. She cursed them like dogs, collapsed in tears, took a vow of silence, and once flew at them in a blind rage. By the final night, Mikhail and Lavon were confident they were prepared for whatever version of Irina they might encounter. All they needed now was the star of the show.

But was she Ivan's pawn or Ivan's victim? It was the question that had troubled them from the beginning, and it was foremost in their thoughts throughout the last long night of waiting. Gabriel made it clear he believed in Irina, but Gabriel was the first to admit his faith had to be viewed through the prism of his well-known fondness for Russian women. The women, he said over and over, were Russia's only hope. Other members of the team, Yaakov in particular, took a far less optimistic view of what lay ahead. Yaakov had seen mankind at its worst and feared they were about to admit one of Ivan's agents into their midst. The fact she was still alive, he argued, was proof of her perfidy. 'If Irina was good, Ivan would have killed her,' he said. 'That's what Ivan does.'

With the help of their assets in Moscow and King Saul Boulevard, they kept careful watch over Irina's final preparations, searching for evidence of treachery. On the evening before her departure they monitored a pair of telephone calls, one to a childhood friend, the other to her mother. They heard her alarm go off at the ungodly hour of 2:30 a.m. and heard it go off again ten minutes later while she was in the shower. And at five minutes past three, they caught a flash of her temper when she called the limousine company to say her car hadn't arrived. Mikhail, who listened to a recording of the call over the secure link, refused to translate it for the rest of the team. Unless Irina was an award-winning actress, he said, her anger was real.

As it turned out, the car was only fifteen minutes late, something of a coup for late January, and she arrived at

Sheremetyevo Airport at 3:45. Shmuel Peled, a field hand from Moscow Station, caught a glimpse of her as she emerged from the car in an angry blur and headed into the terminal. Her plane, Austrian Airlines Flight 606, departed on time and arrived at Vienna's Schwechat at 6:47 a.m. local time. Dina, who had flown to the Austrian capital the previous day, was waiting when Irina emerged from the Jetway. They walked to the departure gate, separated by a generous gap, and settled into their seats in the third row of the first-class cabin – Irina in 3C along the aisle, Dina in 3A against the window. Upon touching down in Milan, she sent a message to Gabriel. The star had arrived. The show was about to begin.

When the aircraft doors opened, Irina was once more in motion, headed toward passport control at a parade-ground clip, her chin at a defiant angle. Like most Russians, she dreaded encounters with men in uniform and presented her travel documents as if braced for combat. After being admitted to Italy without delay, she made her way toward the arrivals hall, where Chiara was holding a sign that read: NITA WELCOMES IRINA BULGANOVA, GALAXY TRAVEL. Lior and Motti, Chiara's ever-present bodyguards, were loitering at a nearby information kiosk, eyes fixed on their quarry.

No one seemed to take notice of Dina as she headed outside to the passenger pickup area where Gabriel was standing at the door of a rented luxury minibus, dressed in the black suit of a chauffeur and wearing wraparound sunglasses. Two cars back, Yaakov was seated behind the wheel of a Lancia sedan, pretending to read the sports pages of *Corriere della Sera*. Dina climbed into the front passenger seat and watched as Irina boarded the minibus. Gabriel, after quickly scanning her bags for tracking beacons, loaded them into the luggage hold.

The drive was ninety minutes in length. They had rehearsed it several times and by that morning could have done it in their sleep. From the airport, they headed north-east through a series of small towns and villages to the city of Como. Had the Grand Hotel Villa Serbelloni been their true destination, they would have split the inverted Y of the lake and headed straight to Bellagio. Instead, they followed the westernmost shoreline to Tremezzo and stopped at a private dock. A boat waited, Lior at the wheel, Motti at the stern. It bore Chiara and Irina slowly across the flat waters of the inlet to the large tawny-orange villa standing at the end of its own peninsula. In the grand entrance foyer was a man with eyes the color of glacial ice and a fine-boned, bloodless face. 'Welcome to Italy,' he said to Irina in perfect Russian. 'May I see your passport, please?'

25. Lake Como, Italy

There is an audio recording of what transpired next. It is one minute and twelve seconds in length and resides to this day in the archives of King Saul Boulevard, where it is considered required listening for its lessons in tradecraft and, in no small measure, for its pure entertainment value. Gabriel had warned them about Irina's temper, but nothing could have prepared them for the ferocity of her response. Eli Lavon, the biblical archaeologist, would later describe it as one of the epic battles in the history of the Jewish people.

Gabriel was not present for it. At that moment he was coming across the inlet by boat and listening to the proceedings over a miniature earpiece. Hearing a sound he took to be the shattering of a crystal vase, he hurried into the villa and poked his head into the dining room. By then, the skirmish was over, and a temporary cessation of hostilities had been declared. Irina was seated along one side of the rectangular table, breathing heavily from exertion, with Yaakov and Rimona each holding one arm. Yossi was standing to one side, with his shirt torn and four parallel scratch marks along the back of one hand. Dina stood next to him, her left cheek aflame, as if it had been recently slapped, which it had. Mikhail was positioned directly across from Irina, his face expressionless. Lavon was at his side, a better angel, staring down at his tiny hands as though he had found the whole sorry spectacle deeply embarrassing.

Gabriel slipped quietly into the library where Olga Sukhova, former crusading journalist, now a member in good standing of the team, was seated before a video monitor, headphones over her ears. Gabriel sat next to her and slipped on a second pair of headphones, then looked at the video screen. Mikhail was now slowly turning through the pages of Irina's passport with a bureaucratic insolence. He placed the passport on the table and stared at Irina for a moment before finally speaking again in Russian. Gabriel uncovered one ear and listened to Olga's translation as the interrogation commenced.

'You are Irina Iosifovna Bulganova, born in Moscow in December 1965?'

'That is correct.'

'Irina Iosifovna Bulganova, former wife of the defector Grigori Nikolaevich Bulganov, of the Russian Federal Security Service?'

'That is correct.'

'Irina Iosifovna Bulganova, traitor and spy for enemies of the Russian Federation?'

'I don't know what you are talking about.'

'I believe you do. I believe you know exactly what I'm talking about.'

Olga lifted her gaze from the monitor. 'Maybe he shouldn't be so rough with her. The poor woman is frightened to death.'

Gabriel made no response. Eventually, Mikhail might be able to release the pressure. But not now. They needed answers to a few questions first. Was she Ivan's pawn or Ivan's victim? Had she been sent by heaven or did they have an agent of the devil in their midst?

26. Lake Como, Italy

'Who are you?' she asked.

'If you wish to call me a name, you may refer to me as Yevgeny.'

'Whom do you work for?'

'That is not important.'

'You are Russian?'

'Again, that is not important. What *is* important is your passport. As a citizen of the Russian Federation, you are not allowed to enter the United Kingdom without obtaining a visa in advance of your arrival. Please tell me how you were able to enter the country without such a visa in your passport.'

'I've never been to Britain in my life.'

'You're lying, Irina Iosifovna.'

'I'm telling you the truth. You said it yourself. Russians need a visa to visit the United Kingdom. My passport contains no visa. Therefore, it is obvious I have never been there.'

'But you went to London earlier this month to assist in the abduction of your former husband, Colonel Grigori Nikolaevich Bulganov of the Russian Federal Security Service.'

'That is completely ridiculous.'

'You were in contact with your former husband after his defection to the United Kingdom?'

She hesitated, then answered truthfully. 'I was.'

'You were discussing the possibility of rekindling your romance. Of reuniting. Of remarrying, perhaps.'

'This is none of your business.'

'*Every*thing is my business. Now, answer my question. Grigori wanted you to come to London?'

'I never agreed to anything.'

'But you *talked* about it.'

'I listened only.'

'Your husband is a defector, Irina Iosifovna. Having contact with him is an act of state treason.'

'Grigori contacted me. I did nothing wrong.'

She was resisting. Gabriel had prepared for this scenario. Gabriel had prepared for everything. *Give her a crack of the whip,* he thought. *Let her know you mean business.*

Mikhail placed three sheets of paper on the table.

'Where were you on January tenth and eleventh?'

'I was in Moscow.'

'Let me ask you one more time. Think carefully before you answer. Where were you on January tenth and eleventh?'

Irina was silent. Mikhail pointed to the first sheet of paper.

'Your computer calendar contains no entries on any of those dates. No meetings. No luncheons. No scheduled phone calls with clients. Nothing at all.'

'January is always slow. This year, with the recession . . .'

Mikhail cut her off with a curt wave of his hand and tapped on the second sheet of paper.

'Your telephone records show you received more than three dozen calls on your mobile but placed none of your own.'

Greeted by silence, he placed his finger on the third sheet of paper.

'Your e-mail account shows a similar pattern: many e-mails received, none sent. Can you explain this?'

'No.'

Mikhail extracted a manila folder from the attaché case at his feet. Lifting the cover with funereal solemnity, he removed a single photograph: Colonel Grigori Bulganov, climbing into a Mercedes sedan on London's Harrow Road on the evening of January the tenth, at 6:12 p.m. He held it carefully by the edges, as though it were crucial evidence in need of preservation, and turned it so Irina could see. She managed to maintain a stoic silence, but her expression had changed. Gabriel, gazing at her face in the monitor, saw it was fear. A remembered fear, he thought, like the fear of a childhood trauma. One more push, and they would have her. On cue, Mikhail produced a second photograph, an enlargement of the first. It was grainy and heavily shadowed, but left no doubt as to the identity of the woman seated nearest the car window.

'This makes you an accessory to a very serious crime committed on British soil.'

Irina's eyes flickered round the room, as if searching for a way out. Mikhail calmly returned both photos to the attaché case.

'Let us begin again, shall we? And this time you will answer my questions truthfully. You have no entrance visa for the United Kingdom, valid or otherwise, in your passport. How were you able to enter the country?'

Her response was so soft as to be nearly inaudible. Indeed, Mikhail and Lavon were not at all sure of what they had just been told. There was no uncertainty, however, at the listening post in the library, which was receiving a crystal clear signal from a pair of ultrasensitive micro-phones concealed inches from Irina's place at the table. Olga looked at Gabriel and said, 'We've got her.' Mikhail looked at Irina and asked her to speak up.

'I used a different passport,' she said, louder this time.

'By that you mean it was in another name?'

'Correct.'

'Who gave you this passport?'

'They said they were friends of Grigori. They said I had to use a false passport for my own protection.'

'Why didn't you tell me this the first time?'

'They told me that I was never to discuss the matter with anyone. They told me they would kill me.' A single tear spilled onto her cheek. She punched away the tear, as if ashamed by her weakness. 'They threatened to kill my entire family. They are not human, these people. They are animals. Please, you have to believe me.'

It was not Mikhail who responded but the previously silent figure seated to his left. The kindly little soul with flyaway hair and a crumpled suit. The better angel who was now holding a letter in his tiny hands. The letter left by Grigori Bulganov in Oxford two weeks before his disap-pearance. He presented the letter to Irina now, as if handing a folded flag to the wife of a fallen soldier. Her hands trembled as she read it.

I am afraid my desire to reunite with my former wife may have placed her in danger. If your officers in Moscow would check in on her from time to time, I would be grateful.

'We don't think he's dead,' Lavon said. 'Not yet. But we have to work quickly if we're going to get him back.'

'Who are you?'

'We're friends, Irina. You can trust us.'

'What do you want from me?'

'Tell us how they did it. Tell us how they took your husband. And whatever you do, don't leave anything out. You'd be surprised, Irina, but sometimes the smallest details are the most important.'

27. Lake Como, Italy

She requested tea and permission to smoke. Yossi and Dina saw to the tea; Lavon, a heavy smoker himself, joined her in a cigarette. Their bond cemented by shared tobacco, she turned her body a few degrees and raised a hand to the side of her face like a blinder, thus excluding Mikhail from her field of vision. As far as Irina was concerned, Mikhail no longer existed. And therefore Mikhail did not need to know that the man who deceived her into taking part in the abduction of her husband made first contact on December the nineteenth. She could recall the date with certainty because it was her birthday. A birthday she shared with Leonid Brezhnev, which, in her childhood, was a great honor in school.

It was a Monday, she recalled, and her colleagues had insisted on taking her out for champagne and sushi at the O2 Lounge at the Ritz-Carlton Hotel. Given the state of the Russian economy, she had thought it rather a profligate thing to do. But they all needed an excuse to get drunk, and her birthday seemed as good a reason as any. Drunkenness was achieved by eight o'clock, and they sailed on together until ten, at which point they stumbled into Tverskaya Street and went in search of their cars, though none of them, including Irina Iosifovna Bulganova, former wife of the defector Grigori Nikolaevich Bulganov, was in any condition to drive.

She had left her car a few blocks away in a narrow street where the Moscow City Militia, for a reasonable bribe, of course, allowed Muscovites to park all day without fear of a ticket. The militiaman on duty was a pimply child of twenty who looked as though he was frozen solid from the cold. Still feeling the effects of the alcohol, Irina had tried to give him a generous handful of rubles. But the boy stepped away and made a vast show of refusing to accept the money. At first, Irina found the display rather amusing. Then she saw a man standing by her car. She knew the type instantly. He was a member of the *siloviki*, the brotherhood of former or current officers of the Russian security services. Irina knew this because she had been married to such a man for twelve years. They had been the worst years of her life.

Irina considered walking away but knew she was in no shape to take evasive action. And even if she weren't drunk, there was no way she could hide for long. Not in Russia. So she walked over and, with more courage than she was actually feeling at the time, demanded to know what was so damn interesting about her car. The man bade her a pleasant evening – Russian style, first name and patronymic – and apologized for the unorthodox circumstances of their meeting. He said he had an important message concerning her husband. '*Former* husband,' Irina replied. '*Former* husband,' he repeated, correcting himself. And by the way, she could call him Anatoly.

'I don't suppose he showed you any identification?' Lavon wondered in the meekest tone he could manage.

'Of course not.'

'Would you please describe him?'

'Tall, well built, sturdy jaw, blond hair going to gray.'

'Age?'

'Over fifty.'

'Facial hair?'

'No.'

'Eyeglasses?'

'Not then. Later, though.'

Lavon let it go. For now.

'What happened next?'

'He offered to take me to dinner. I told him I didn't make a habit of having dinner with strangers. He said he wasn't a stranger; he was a friend of Grigori's from London. He knew it was my birthday. He said he had a present for me.'

'And you believed him because you'd had contact with Grigori?'

'That's correct.'

'So you went with him?'

'Yes.'

'How did you travel?'

'In my car.'

'Who drove?'

'He did.'

'Where did you go?'

'Café Pushkin. Do you know Café Pushkin?'

Lavon, with an almost imperceptible nod of his head, indicated that he did indeed know the famous Café Pushkin. Despite the financial crisis, it was still nearly impossible to get a reservation. But the man named Anatoly had somehow managed to secure a prized table for two in a secluded corner of the second floor. He ordered champagne, which was the last thing she needed, and made a toast. Then he gave her a jewelry box. Inside was a gold bracelet and a note. He said they were both from Grigori.

'Did the gift box have a name on it?'

'Bulgari. The bracelet must have cost a fortune.'

'And the note? Was it Grigori's handwriting?'

'It certainly looked like his.'

'What did it say?'

'It said he never wanted to spend another birthday apart. It said he wanted me to come to London with the man named Anatoly. It said not to worry about money. Everything would be arranged and paid for by Viktor.'

'No last name?'

'No.'

'But you knew it was Viktor Orlov?'

'I'd read about Grigori and Viktor on the Internet. I even saw a photo of the two of them together.'

'Did Anatoly describe his relationship to Mr. Orlov?'

'He said he worked for him in a security capacity.'

'Those were his exact words?'

'Yes.'

'And the letter? I take it you were moved by it?'

Irina gave an embarrassed nod. 'It all seemed real.'

Of course it had, thought Gabriel, gazing at Irina in the monitor. It had seemed real because Anatoly, like Gabriel, was a professional, well versed in the arts of manipulation and seduction. And so it came as no surprise to Gabriel when Irina said she and Anatoly had spent the rest of that evening in pleasant conversation. They had talked about many things, she said, moving from topic to topic with the ease of old friends. Anatoly had seemed to know a great deal about Irina's marriage, things he couldn't possibly have known unless Grigori had told him – or so Irina believed at the time. Over dessert, almost as an afterthought, he had mentioned that the British government was prepared to grant her asylum if she came to London. Money, he had said, would not be a problem. Viktor would take care of the money. Viktor would take care of everything.

'And you agreed to go?' asked Lavon.

'I agreed to pay a brief visit, but nothing more.'

'And then?'

'We talked about the travel arrangements. He said because of Grigori's circumstances, great care would have to be taken. Otherwise, it was possible the Russian authorities wouldn't allow me to leave the country. He told me not to speak to anyone. That he would be in contact when it was time to go. Then he drove me home. He didn't bother asking my address. He already knew it.'

'Did you tell anyone?'

'Not a soul.'

'When did he make contact with you again?'

'The ninth of January, as I was leaving my office. A man came alongside me on Tverskaya Street and told me to look in my bedroom closet when I got home. There were suitcases and a handbag. The suitcases were neatly packed with clothing, all my size. The handbag had the usual assortment of things, but also a Russian passport, airline tickets to London, and a wallet filled with credit cards and cash. There was also a set of instructions, which I was to burn after reading.'

'You were to depart the next day?'

'Correct.'

'Tell me about the passport.'

'The photograph was mine, but the name was false.'

'What was it?'

'Natalia Primakova.'

'Lovely,' said Lavon.

'Yes,' she said. 'I rather liked it.'

28. Lake Como, Italy

She did not sleep that night. She did not even try. She was too nervous. Too excited. And, yes, maybe a bit too frightened. She paced the rooms of the little apartment she had once shared with Grigori and pondered the most trivial of keepsakes as if she might never see them again. In violation of Anatoly's strict instructions, she telephoned her mother, a family tradition before a trip of any magnitude, and she slipped a few personal items into the suitcases of Natalia Primakova. A bundle of yellowed letters. A locket with her grandmother's photo. A small gold cross her mother had given her after the fall of Communism. Lastly, her wedding band.

'You thought you might be leaving Russia for good?'

'I allowed myself to consider the possibility.'

'Do you recall your flight number?'

'Aeroflot Flight 247, departing Sheremetyevo at 2:35 p.m., arriving London Heathrow at 3:40.'

'Very impressive.'

'It is what I do for a living.'

'What time did you leave your apartment?'

'Ten o'clock. Moscow traffic is terrible that time of day, especially on the Leningradsky Prospekt.'

'How did you travel to the airport?'

'They sent a car.'

'Was there any trouble with your new passport?'

'None whatsoever.'

'Your travel was first class or economy?'

'First class.'

'Did you recognize anyone on the flight?'

'Not a soul.'

'And when you arrived in London? Any problems with the passport there?'

'None. When the customs official asked me to state the purpose of my visit, I said tourism. He stamped my passport right away and told me to have a pleasant stay.'

'And when you came into the arrivals hall?'

'I saw Anatoly waiting along the railing.' A pause, then, 'Actually, he saw me. I didn't recognize him at first.'

'He was wearing eyeglasses?'

'And a fedora.'

'Would you describe his mood, please?'

'Calm, very businesslike. He took one of my bags and led me outside. A car was waiting.'

'Do you recall the make?'

'It was a Mercedes.'

'The model?'

'I'm not good with models. It was big, though.'

'Color?'

'Black, of course. I assumed it was Viktor's. A man like Viktor Orlov would only ride in a black car.'

'What happened next?'

'He said Grigori was waiting at a safe place. But first, for my protection, we had to make certain no one was following us.'

'Did he say who he thought might be following you?'

'No, but it was clear he was referring to Russian intelligence.'

'Did he talk to you?'

'He spent most of the time on the telephone.'

'Did he place calls or receive them?'

'Both.'

'Was he speaking English or Russian?'

'Only Russian. Very colloquial.'

'Did you make any stops?'

'Just one.'

'Do you remember where?'

'It was on a quiet road not far from the airport, next to a pond or reservoir of some sort. The driver got out of the car and did something to the front and back of the car.'

'Could he have been changing the license plates?'

'I couldn't say. It was dark by then. Anatoly acted as though nothing was happening.'

'Do you happen to recall the time?'

'No, but afterward we headed straight into central London. We were driving along the edge of Hyde Park when Anatoly's telephone rang. He spoke a few words in Russian, then looked at me and smiled. He said it was safe to go see Grigori.'

'What happened next?'

'Things moved very quickly. I put on some lipstick and checked my hair. Then I saw something from the corner of my eye. A movement.' She paused. 'There was a gun in Anatoly's hand. It was pointed at my heart. He said if I made a sound, he would kill me.'

She lapsed into silence, as if unwilling to go on. Then,

with a gentle nudge from Lavon, she began speaking again.

'The car stopped very suddenly, and Anatoly opened the door with his other hand. I saw Grigori standing on the sidewalk. I saw my husband.'

'Anatoly spoke to him?'

She nodded, blinking away tears.

'Do you remember what he said?'

'I will never forget his words. He told Grigori to get in the car or I was dead. Grigori obeyed, of course. He had no choice.'

Lavon gave her a moment to compose herself.

'Did Grigori say anything after he got in?'

'He said he would do whatever they wanted. That there was no need to harm or threaten me in any way.' Another pause. 'Anatoly told Grigori to shut his mouth. Otherwise, he was going to splatter my brains all over the inside of the car.'

'Did Grigori ever speak to you?'

'Just once. He told me he was very sorry.'

'And after that?'

'He didn't say a word. He barely looked at me.'

'How long were you together?'

'Just a few minutes. We drove to a parking garage somewhere close. They put Grigori into the back of a van with markings on the side. A cleaning service of some sort.'

'Where did *you* go?'

'Anatoly took me into an adjacent building through an underground passage, and we rode an elevator to the street. A car was waiting nearby. A woman was behind the wheel. Anatoly told me to follow her instructions carefully. He said if I ever spoke to anyone about this, I would be killed. And then my mother would be killed. And then my two brothers would be killed, along with their children.'

A heavy silence fell over the dining room of the villa. Irina treated herself to another cigarette; then, emotionally exhausted, she recounted the remaining details of her ordeal in a detached voice. The long drive to the seacoast town of Harwich. The sleepless night in the Hotel Continental. The stormy crossing to Hoek van Holland aboard the *Stena Britannica* car ferry. And the trip home aboard Aeroflot Flight 418, operated by KLM Royal Dutch Airlines, departing Amsterdam at 8:40 p.m., arriving Sheremetyevo at 2 a.m. the following morning.

'Did you and the woman travel together or separately?'

'Together.'

'Did she ever give you a name?'

'No, but I heard the flight attendant call her Ms. Gromova.'

'And when you arrived in Moscow?'

'A car and driver took me to my apartment. The next morning, I returned to work as if nothing had happened.'

'Was there any other contact?'

'Nothing.'

'Did you have the impression you were under surveillance?'

'If I was, I couldn't see them.'

'And when you received the invitation to attend the conference in Italy, they made no effort to prevent you from attending?'

She shook her head.

'Were you at all reluctant after what you had just been through?'

'The invitation seemed very real. Just like Anatoly's.' A silence, then, 'I don't suppose there really is a conference, is there?'

'No, there isn't.'

'Who are you?' she asked again.

'We truly are friends of your husband. And we're going to do everything we can to get him back for you.'

'What happens now?'

'The same as before. You return to your job at Galaxy Travel and pretend this never happened. After you attend the third annual seminar and showcase of the Northern Italian Travel Association, of course.'

'But you just said it wasn't real.'

'Reality is a state of mind, Irina. Reality can be whatever you want it to be.'

29. Lake Como • London

For the next three days, they put her gently through her paces. They described the sumptuous meals she would not eat, the boozy cocktail parties she would not attend, and the deeply boring seminars that mercifully she would be spared. They took her on a frigid cruise of the lake and a long drive through the mountains. They filled her suitcases with gifts and brochures for her colleagues. And they anxiously awaited the hour of her departure. There was not one among them who doubted her authenticity – and not one who wanted to send her back to Russia. When it came time to leave, she marched onto her plane the way she had come off it three days earlier, with her chin up and at a parade-ground clip. That night, they huddled around the secure communications link, waiting for the flash from Moscow that she had arrived safely. It came, much to their relief, a few minutes after midnight. Shmuel Peled followed her home and pronounced her tail clean as a whistle. The following morning, from her desk at Galaxy Travel, Irina sent an e-mail to Veronica Ricci of NITA, thanking her for the wonderful trip. Signora Ricci asked Ms. Bulganova to stay in touch.

Gabriel was not present in Como to witness the successful end of the operation. Accompanied by Olga Sukhova, he flew to London the morning after the interrogation and was immediately whisked to a safe flat in Victoria. Graham

Seymour was waiting and subjected Gabriel to a ten-minute tirade before finally permitting him to speak. After first insisting that the microphones be switched off, Gabriel described the remarkable debriefing they had just conducted on the shores of Lake Como. Seymour immediately placed a secure call to Thames House and posed a single question: Did a woman bearing a Russian passport in the name of Natalia Primakova arrive at Heathrow Airport aboard Aeroflot Flight 247 on the afternoon of January the tenth? Thames House called back within minutes. The answer was yes.

'I'd like to schedule a meeting with the prime minister and my director-general right away. If you're willing, I think you should be the one to brief them. After all, you proved us all wrong, Gabriel. That gives you the right to rub our noses in it.'

'I have no intention of rubbing your noses in anything. And the last thing I want you to do is mention any of this to your prime minister or director-general.'

'Grigori Bulganov is a British subject and, as such, is owed all the protections offered by the British Crown. We have no choice but to present our evidence to the Russians and insist that they return him at once.'

'Ivan Kharkov went to a great deal of trouble to get Grigori, in all likelihood with the blessing of the FSB and the Kremlin itself. Do you really think he's going to hand him over because the British prime minister *insists* on it? We have to play the game by the same rules as Ivan.'

'Meaning?'

'We have to steal him back.'

Graham Seymour made one more phone call, then pulled on his overcoat.

'Heathrow security is getting us pictures. You and Olga stay here. And do try to keep the gunfire to a minimum. I have enough problems at the moment.'

But Gabriel did not remain in the safe flat for long. Indeed, he slipped out a few minutes after Seymour's departure and headed directly to Cheyne Walk in Chelsea. Once a quiet riverside promenade, this historic London street now overlooked the busy Chelsea Embankment. On some of the grand houses were brass plaques commemorating famous occupants of the past. Turner had lived secretly at No. 119, Rossetti at No. 19. Henry James had spent his final days at No. 21; George Eliot had done the same at No. 4. These days, few artists and writers could afford to live in Cheyne Walk. It had become the preserve of wealthy foreigners, pop stars, and moneymen from the City. It also happened to be the London address of one Viktor Orlov, exiled Russian oligarch and Kremlin critic, who resided at the five-story mansion at No. 43. The same Viktor Orlov who was now the target of a clandestine investigation being conducted by a team of burrowers at King Saul Boulevard.

Gabriel entered the small park across the street and sat down on a bench. Orlov's house was tall and narrow and covered in wisteria. Like the rest of the residences along the graceful terrace, it was set several meters back from the street behind a wrought-iron fence. An armored Bentley limousine stood outside, a chauffeur at the wheel. Directly behind the Bentley was a black Range Rover, occupied by four members of Orlov's security detail, all former members of Britain's elite Special Air Service, the SAS. King Saul Boulevard had discovered that the bodyguards were supplied by Exton Executive Security Services Ltd, of Hill Street, Mayfair. Exton was regarded as the finest private security company in London, no small accomplishment in a city filled with many rich people worried about their safety.

Gabriel was about to leave when he saw three body-guards emerge from the Range Rover. One took up a post at the gate of No. 43, while the other two blocked the sidewalk in either direction. With the perimeter security in place, the front door of the house swung open, and Viktor Orlov stepped outside, flanked by two more bodyguards. Gabriel managed to see little of the famous Russian billion-aire other than a head of spiky gray hair and the flash of a pink necktie bound by an enormous Windsor knot. Orlov ducked into the back of the Bentley, and the doors quickly closed. A few seconds later, the motorcade was speeding along Royal Hospital Road. Gabriel sat on his bench for ten more minutes, then got to his feet and headed back to Victoria.

It took less than an hour for Heathrow security to produce the first batch of photographs of the man known only as Anatoly. Unfortunately, none were terribly helpful. Gabriel was not surprised. Everything about Anatoly suggested he was a professional. And like any good professional, he knew how to move through an airport without getting his picture taken. The fedora had done much to shield his face, but he had done a good deal of the work himself with subtle turns and movements. Still, the cameras made a valiant effort: here a glimpse of a sturdy chin, here a partial profile, here a shot of a tight, uncompromising mouth. Flipping through the printouts in the Victoria safe house, Gabriel had a sinking feeling. Anatoly was a pro's pro. And he was playing the game with Ivan's money.

Both British services ran the photos through their databases of known Russian intelligence officers, but neither held out much hope for a match. Between them, they produced six possible candidates, all of whom were dismissed by Gabriel late that same night. At which point Seymour decided it was probably time to bring the dreaded Americans into the picture. Gabriel volunteered to make the trip himself. There was someone in America he was anxious to see. He hadn't spoken to her in months. She had written him a letter once. And he had painted her a painting.

30. CIA Headquarters, Virginia

Intelligence agencies refer to their spies in different ways. The Office calls them gathering officers, and the department for which they work is referred to as Collections. Spies for the CIA are known as case officers and are employed by the National Clandestine Service. Adrian Carter's tenure as chief of the NCS began when it was still known by its old name: the Directorate of Operations. Regarded as one of the Agency's most accomplished secret warriors, Carter had left his fingerprints on every major American covert operation of the last two generations. He had tinkered with the odd election, toppled the odd democratically elected government, and turned a blind eye to more executions and murders than he cared to remember. 'I did the Lord's work in Poland and propped up the devil's regime in El Salvador in the span of a single year,' he once confessed to Gabriel in a moment of interagency candor. 'And for an encore, I gave weapons to the Muslim holy warriors in Afghanistan, even though I knew that one day they would rain fire and death on me.'

Since the morning of September 11, 2001, Adrian Carter had been focused on primarily one thing: preventing another attack on the American homeland by the forces of global Islamic extremism. To accomplish that end he had used tactics and methods even a battle-hardened covert warrior such as himself sometimes found objectionable.

The black prisons, the renditions, the use of coercive interrogation techniques: it had all been made public, much to Carter's detriment. Well-meaning editorialists and politicians on Capitol Hill had been baying for Carter's blood for years. He should have been on the short list to become the CIA's next director. Instead, he lived in fear that one day he would be prosecuted for his actions in the global war against terrorism. Adrian Carter had kept America safe from its enemies. And for that, he would languish in the fires of hell for all eternity.

He was waiting for Gabriel the following afternoon in a conference room on the seventh floor of CIA Headquarters, the Valhalla of America's sprawling and often dysfunctional intelligence establishment. The antithesis of Graham Seymour in appearance, Carter had tousled thinning hair and a prominent mustache that had gone out of fashion with disco music, Crock-Pots, and the nuclear freeze. Dressed as he was now, in flannel trousers and a burgundy cardigan, he had the air of a professor from a minor university, the sort who championed noble causes and was a constant thorn in the side of his dean. He peered at Gabriel over his reading glasses, as if mildly surprised to see him, and offered his hand. It was cool as marble and dry to the touch.

Gabriel had contacted Carter the previous day before leaving London via a secure cable sent from the CIA station at the American Embassy. The cable had given Carter only the broadest outlines of the affair. Now Gabriel filled in the details. At the conclusion of the briefing, Carter picked through the physical evidence, beginning with the letter Grigori had left in Oxford and ending with the Heathrow

Airport surveillance photos of the man known only as Anatoly.

'In all honesty,' said Carter, 'we never put much stock in the story that Grigori had a change of heart and redefected to the motherland. As you might recall, I actually had a chance to spend some time with him the night you came out of Russia.'

Gabriel did recall, of course. In a logistical feat only the Agency could manage, Carter had put a squadron of Gulfstream executive jets on the ground in Kiev, just a few hours after the car bearing Gabriel and his trio of Russian defectors had crossed the Ukrainian border. Gabriel had returned to Israel, while Grigori and Olga had flown into exile in Britain. Carter had personally brought Elena Kharkov to the United States, where she was granted defector status. Her current circumstances were so closely held that even Gabriel had no idea where the CIA had hidden her.

'We sent a team to debrief Grigori within twenty-four hours of his arrival in England,' Carter resumed. 'No one who took part ever voiced any skepticism about Grigori's authenticity. After his disappearance, I ordered a review of the tapes and transcripts to see if we'd missed something.'

'And?'

'Grigori was as good as gold. Needless to say, we were rather surprised when the British thought otherwise. As far as Langley is concerned, it seemed a rather transparent attempt to foist some of the blame for his disappearance onto you. They have no one to blame but themselves. He should have never been allowed to get mixed up with opposition types floating around London. It was only a matter of time before Ivan got to him.'

'Is Ivan still a target of NSA surveillance?'

'Absolutely.'

'Did you know he just sold several thousand antitank missiles and RPGs to Hezbollah?'

'We've heard rumors to that effect. But for the moment, keeping track of Ivan's business activities is low on our list of priorities. Our main concern is keeping his former wife and children safe from harm.'

'Has he ever made any formal effort to reclaim them?'

'A couple of months ago, the Russian ambassador raised the issue during a routine meeting with the secretary of state. The secretary acted somewhat surprised and said she would look into the matter. She's a good poker player, the secretary. Would have made an excellent case officer. A week later, she told the ambassador that Elena Kharkov and her children were not currently residing in the United States, nor had they ever resided here at any time in the past. The ambassador thanked the secretary profusely for her efforts and never raised the matter again.'

'Ivan must know they're here, Adrian.'

'Of course he knows. But there's nothing he and his friends in the Kremlin can do about it. That operation you ran in Saint-Tropez last summer was a thing of beauty. You plucked the children from Ivan cleanly and with a veneer of legality. Furthermore, when Ivan divorced Elena in a Russian court, he effectively gave up all legal claim to them. The only way he can get them now is to steal them. And that's not going to happen. We take better care of our defectors than the British do.'

'She's somewhere safe, I hope.'

'Very safe. But will you allow me to give you a piece of

advice, as one friend to another? Take Grigori's words to heart. Forget about that promise you made that night in Russia. Besides, I suspect Ivan has already put a bullet in the back of his head. Knowing Ivan, I imagine he did the deed himself. Go home to your wife, and let the British clean up their mess.'

'I like to keep promises. I used to think you did, too, Adrian.'

Carter steepled his fingertips and pressed them to his chin. 'I think your characterization is a tad unfair. But since you put it that way, how can Langley be of service?'

'Give those photos of Anatoly to the Counterintelligence Center. See if they can put a name and a résumé to that face.'

'I'll ask the chief to handle it personally.' Carter gathered up the photos. 'How long are you planning to stay in town?'

'As long as it takes.'

'One of our officers is about to leave on an overseas assignment. She was wondering if you might be free for dinner.'

Gabriel didn't bother to ask the officer's name.

'Where's she going, Adrian?'

'That's classified.'

'I don't suppose I have to remind you that she was involved in the operation against Ivan?'

'No, you don't.'

'So why are you letting her leave the country?'

'Your concern over her safety is touching but completely unnecessary. What should I tell her about dinner?'

Gabriel hesitated. 'I'll take a rain check, Adrian. It's complicated.'

'Why? Because she's dating one of your team?'

'What are you talking about?'

'She and Mikhail are seeing each other. I'm surprised no one told you.'

'How long has it been going on?'

'It started shortly after the Saint-Tropez operation. Since Mikhail is an employee of a foreign intelligence service, she was required to report the relationship to the Office of Personnel. Personnel wasn't pleased about it, but I intervened on their behalf.'

'How thoughtful of you, Adrian. Actually, I will have dinner with her.'

Carter jotted the time and place on a slip of paper. 'Just be nice to her, Gabriel. I think she's happy. It's been a long time since Sarah has been happy.'

31.Georgetown, Washington, D.C.

1789 Restaurant, a Georgetown landmark, is regarded as one of the finest in Washington and is one of the few that still requires gentlemen to wear a jacket. With that admonition, Carter sent Gabriel to Brooks Brothers, where in the span of ten minutes he picked out gabardine trousers, an oxford-cloth shirt, and the requisite blue blazer. He drew the line at a necktie, though. Like most Israelis, he wore them only under duress or for the purposes of cover. Besides, if he wore a tie, Sarah might get the wrong impression. The blazer was going to cause him enough problems.

He arrived a few minutes early and was informed by the hostess that his dinner companion was already seated. He wasn't surprised; he had personally overseen Sarah Bancroft's training and regarded her as one of the finest natural operatives he had ever encountered. Multilingual, well-traveled, and extremely well-educated, she had been working as an assistant curator at the Phillips Collection in Washington when Gabriel recruited her to find a terrorist mastermind lurking in the entourage of Saudi billionaire Zizi al-Bakari. After the operation, Sarah joined the CIA on a full-time basis and was assigned to the Counterterrorism Center. Gabriel had borrowed her again the previous summer and, with the help of a forged painting, had placed her alongside Elena Kharkov. Mikhail had posed as Sarah's Russian-American boyfriend during the operation, and they had spent several nights together in a five-star Saint-Tropez hotel. Gabriel reckoned the attraction had started then.

He was not happy about it for a number of reasons, not least of which because it violated his ban on sexual relationships between members of his team. But his anger went only so far. He knew the unique combination of stress and boredom could sometimes lead to romantic entanglements in the field. In fact, he could speak from experience. Twenty years earlier, while preparing for a major assassination in Tunis, he had an affair with his female escort officer that nearly destroyed his marriage to Leah.

The hostess escorted him through the intimate dining room to a corner table near the fireplace. Sarah was seated along the banquette with her shoulders turned in a way that allowed her to discreetly survey the entire space. She was wearing a black sleeveless dress and a double strand of pearls. Her pale hair hung loosely about her shoulders, and her wide blue eyes shone with the warm light of the candles. One hand was resting on the stem of a Martini glass. The other was placed lightly against her teardrop chin. Her cheek, when kissed, smelled of lilac.

'Can I get you one of these?' she asked, tapping a manicured nail on the base of the glass.

'I'd rather drink your nail polish remover.'

'Would you like that with a twist or just on the rocks?' She looked up at the hostess. 'A glass of champagne, please. Something nice. He's had a long day.'

The hostess withdrew. Sarah smiled and raised the Martini to her lips.

'They say it's bad to drink the night before you fly, Sarah.'

'If I can survive one of your operations, I think I can

survive a transatlantic flight with a bit of gin in my blood-stream.'

'So it's Europe? Is that where Carter is sending you?'

'Adrian warned me to be on my toes around you. You're not going to get it out of me.'

'I think I have a right to know.'

'Really?' She set down her glass and leaned forward over the table. 'You might find this difficult to believe, Gabriel, but I don't actually *work* for the Office. I am employed by the National Clandestine Service of the Central Intelligence Agency, which means Adrian Carter, not you, makes my assignments.'

'Would you like to say that a little louder? I'm not sure the cooks and the dishwashers heard you.'

'Weren't you the one who told me that nearly every important professional conversation you'd ever had was conducted in public places?'

It was true. Safe rooms were only safe if they hadn't been bugged.

'At least rule out a couple of places for me. I'll sleep easier knowing that Langley, in its infinite wisdom, hasn't decided to send you to Saudi Arabia or Moscow.'

'You may sleep in peace because Langley has decided nothing of the sort.'

'So it *is* Europe?'

'Gabriel, really.'

'What kind of work will you be doing?'

She gave an exasperated sigh. 'It's related to my govern-ment's continuing efforts to combat global terrorism.'

'How gallant. And to think that four years ago you were putting together an exhibition called Impressionists in Winter.'

'I hope that was meant as a compliment.'

'It was.'

'You obviously don't approve of my going into the field without you.'

'I've stated my concerns. But Adrian is your boss, not me. And if Adrian thinks it's appropriate, then who am I to question his judgment?'

'You're Gabriel Allon, that's who you are.'

The waiter appeared. He gave them menus and a detailed briefing on the evening's specials. When he was gone, Gabriel perused the entrées and, with as much detachment as he could manage, asked whether Mikhail was aware of Sarah's travel plans. Greeted by silence, he looked up and saw Sarah staring at him, her alabaster cheeks flushed.

'It's a good thing you didn't act like that when you were around Zizi and Ivan,' Gabriel said.

'Did Mikhail tell you?'

'Actually, the chief of the National Clandestine Service let it slip in conversation.'

Sarah made no response.

'So it's true, then? You're actually dating a member of my team?'

'Are you jealous or angry?'

'Why on earth would I be jealous, Sarah?'

'I couldn't carry a torch for you forever. I had to move on.'

'And you couldn't find anyone else other than someone who works for me?'

'Funny how that worked out. I guess there was something about Mikhail that I found familiar.'

'Dating a man who's employed by the intelligence service of a foreign country isn't exactly a wise career move, Sarah.'

'Langley is having trouble retaining bright young talent. They're willing to bend some of the old rules.'

'Maybe I should have a quiet word with Personnel. They might have second thoughts.'

'You wouldn't dare, Gabriel. You also have no right to interfere in my private life.'

Sarah's private life, Gabriel knew, had been largely in ruins since 9:03 on the morning of September 11, 2001, when United Airlines Flight 175 crashed into the South Tower of the World Trade Center. On board the doomed aircraft was a young Harvard-trained lawyer named Ben Callahan. Ben had been able to make one call during the final moments of his life, and it had been to Sarah. Since that time, she had permitted herself to have feelings for only one other man. Unfortunately, that man had been Gabriel.

'You should think long and hard before you get involved with a man who kills people for a living. Mikhail's done a lot of terrible things for the sake of his country.' Gabriel paused, then added, 'Things that might make him difficult to be around sometimes.'

'Sounds like someone I know.'

'This isn't a joke, Sarah. This is your life. Besides, Israeli men are notoriously unreliable. Just ask your average Israeli woman.'

'The Israeli men I know are quite wonderful, actually.'

'That's because we're the best of the best.'

'Mikhail included?'

'He wouldn't be on my team if he wasn't. How much time have you spent with him?'

'He's come here a few times, and we met in Paris once.'

'It's not safe for you to be in Paris alone.'

'I'm not alone. I'm with Mikhail.' A silence, then, 'It's almost like being with you.'

Her words hung between them for a moment. 'Is that what this is about, Sarah?'

'Gabriel, please.'

'Because I'd feel bad if Mikhail got hurt in any way.'

'I'm sure I'm the only one who'll get hurt.'

'Not if I have anything to say about it.'

She smiled for the first time since Mikhail's name had come up. 'I was going to tell you tonight. We were just waiting until we knew it was . . .' Her voice trailed off.

'Until it was *what*?'

'Real.'

'And is it?'

She held his hand. 'Don't be upset, Gabriel. I was hoping this could be a celebration.'

'I'm not upset.'

She looked at his champagne glass. He hadn't touched it.

'Do you want something else?'

'Nail polish remover. On the rocks, with a twist.'

Since Gabriel had come to Washington with the full knowledge of the CIA, Housekeeping had assigned him a not-so-safe flat on Tunlaw Road north of Georgetown. In a somewhat curious twist of fate, the apartment overlooked the rear entrance of the Russian Embassy. As Gabriel was crossing the lobby, his secure mobile vibrated in his coat pocket. It was Adrian Carter.

'Where are you?'

Gabriel told him.

'I have something you need to see right away. We'll pick you up.'

The connection went dead. Fifteen minutes later, Gabriel was climbing into the back of Carter's black sedan on New Mexico Avenue. Carter handed him a single sheet of paper: a transcript of a National Security Agency communications intercept, dated the previous evening Moscow time. The target was Ivan Kharkov. He had been speaking to someone inside FSB Headquarters at Lubyanka Square. Though most of the conversation was conducted in coded colloquial Russian, it was clear Ivan had given something to the FSB and now he wanted it back. That something was Grigori Bulganov.

'You were right, Gabriel. Ivan handed Grigori over to the FSB so they could settle accounts, too. Apparently, the FSB interrogation is going too slowly for Ivan's taste. He spent a great deal of money getting his hands on Grigori, and he's tired of waiting. But the good news is Grigori's alive.'

'Is there any way you can prevail upon the FSB to keep him that way?'

'Not a chance. Our relations with the Russian services are getting worse by the day. There's no way they would tolerate our meddling in a strictly internal matter. And, frankly, if the roles were reversed, neither would we. From their point of view, Grigori is a defector and a traitor. You can be sure they want to kill him just as much as Ivan does.'

'Does the CIC have anything for me?'

'Not yet. Who knows? Maybe your friend Anatoly is a ghost.'

'I don't believe in ghosts, Adrian. If there's one thing we know about Ivan, he wouldn't have entrusted Grigori's kidnapping to someone he didn't know.'

'That's Ivan's way. Everything is personal.'

'So it's possible someone who's spent a considerable amount of time around Ivan might have encountered this man at some point.' Gabriel paused. 'Who knows, Adrian? She might even know his real name.'

Carter told the driver to head back to the safe flat, then looked at Gabriel.

'A car will pick you up at six o'clock tomorrow morning. I'm afraid we'll have to play this one rather close to the vest. You won't know where you're going until you're airborne.'

'How should I dress?'

Carter smiled.

'Warmly. Very warmly.'

32. Upstate New York

The Adirondack Park, a vast wilderness area sprawling over six million acres in northeastern New York, is the largest public land preserve in the contiguous United States. Roughly the size of Vermont, it is larger than seven other American states – so large, in fact, the national parks of Yellowstone, Yosemite, Glacier, the Grand Canyon, and the Great Smoky Mountains could all fit neatly within its boundaries. Gabriel had not known these facts until one hour after takeoff, when his pilot, a veteran of the CIA's rendition program, had finally revealed their destination. The forecast was rather grim: clear skies with a high temperature of perhaps zero. Gabriel assumed the pilot had converted the temperature from Fahrenheit to centigrade for the benefit of his foreign-born passenger. He hadn't.

It was a few minutes after ten when the plane touched down at the Adirondack Regional Airport outside Saranac Lake. Adrian Carter had arranged for a Ford Explorer to be left in the parking lot. By some miracle, the engine managed to start on the first attempt. Gabriel switched the heater to high and spent several deplorable minutes scraping ice from the windows. Climbing behind the wheel again, he could no longer feel his face. The temperature gauge of the Explorer indicated minus eight. Not possible, he thought. Surely it had to be instrument malfunction.

Carter, a cautious soul if ever there was one, had decreed

no one could approach the site with anything that transmitted or received a signal, including GPS navigation systems. Gabriel followed a set of typewritten instructions he had been given on board the plane. Leaving the airport, he turned right and followed Route 186 to Lake Clear. He made another right at Route 30 and headed toward Upper St Regis Lake. Spitfire Lake came next, then Lower St Regis, then the small college town of Paul Smiths. A few yards beyond the entrance of the college was Keese Mills Road, a winding lane that ran eastward into one of the more remote corners of the preserve. Somewhere in this part of the Adirondacks, the Rockefellers had kept an immense summer retreat, complete with its own rail station to accommodate the private family train. Gabriel's destination, though far smaller than the Rockefeller estate, was scarcely less secluded. The entrance was on the left side of the road and, as Carter had warned, it was easy to miss. Gabriel sped past it the first time and had to continue driving another quarter mile before finding a suitable place to execute a U-turn on the icy road.

A narrow track ran straight into the thick woods for approximately a hundred yards before encountering a metal security gate. No other fencing or barriers were visible, but Gabriel knew the grounds were littered with cameras, heat sensors, and motion detectors. Something had taken note of his approach because the gate slid open even before he brought the SUV to a stop. On the other side, he saw a Jeep Grand Cherokee speeding toward him across a clearing. Behind the wheel was a man in his mid-fifties with the bearing of a soldier. His name was Ed Fielding. A former officer in the CIA's Special Operations Group, Fielding was in charge of security.

'We told you the entrance was hard to find,' Fielding said through his open window.

'You were watching?'

Fielding only smiled. 'You remembered to leave your cell phone at home?'

'I remembered.'

'What about your BlackBerry?'

'Can't stand the things.'

'No secret pens or X-ray glasses?'

'The only thing electronic in my possession is my wristwatch, and I'd be happy to pitch it into a nearby lake if that would make you more comfortable.'

'As long as it isn't some secret Israeli device that transmits and receives a signal, you can keep it. Besides, all the lakes are frozen.' Fielding revved his engine. 'We have a bit of driving to do. Stay close. Otherwise, you might get shot by the snipers.'

Fielding accelerated hard across the clearing. By the time they reached the next line of trees, Gabriel had closed the gap. After a half mile, the road turned up a steep hill. Though plowed and sanded earlier that morning, the surface was already frozen solid. Fielding scaled it without incident, but Gabriel struggled to maintain traction. He switched the four-wheel-drive setting from high to low and made a second attempt. This time, the tires bit into the ice, and the SUV muscled its way slowly toward the crest. In the ten seconds it had taken to make the adjustment, Fielding had slipped away. Gabriel found him a moment later, paused at a fork in the road. They headed left and drove another two miles, until they reached a clearing at the highest point of the estate.

A large, traditional Adirondack lodge stood in the center, its soaring roof and sweeping porches facing southeast, toward the faint warmth of the midday sun and the frozen lakes of St Regis. A second lodge stood nearer the edge of the forest, smaller than the main house but still grand in its own right. Between the two structures was a meadow where two heavily bundled children were hard at work on a snow-man, watched over by a tall, dark-haired woman in a shearling coat. Hearing the sound of approaching vehicles, she turned with an animal alertness, then, a few seconds later, lifted her hand dramatically into the air.

Gabriel pulled up behind Fielding and switched off the engine. By the time he had opened the door, the woman was rushing toward him awkwardly through the knee-deep snow. She hurled her arms around his neck and kissed him elaborately on each cheek. 'Welcome to the one place in the world Ivan will never find me,' said Elena Kharkov. 'My God, Gabriel, I can't believe you're really here.'

33. Upstate New York

They had lunch in the large rustic dining room beneath a traditional Adirondack antler chandelier. Elena sat against a soaring window, framed by the distant lakes, Anna to her left, Nikolai to her right. Though Gabriel had carried out what amounted to a legal kidnapping of the Kharkov twins in the south of France the previous summer, he had never before seen them in person. He was struck now, as Sarah Bancroft had been upon meeting them for the first time, by their appearance. Anna, lanky and dark and blessed with a natural elegance, was a smaller version of her mother; Nikolai, fair and compact with a wide forehead and prominent brow, was the very likeness of his notorious father. Indeed, throughout an otherwise pleasant meal Gabriel had the uncomfortable feeling that Ivan Kharkov, his most implacable enemy, was scrutinizing his every move from the other side of the table.

He was struck, too, by the sound of their voices. Their English was perfect and had only the faintest trace of a Russian accent. It was not surprising, he thought. In many respects, the Kharkov children were scarcely Russian at all. They had spent most of their life in a Knightsbridge mansion and had attended an exclusive London school. In winter, they had holidayed in Courchevel; in summer, they trooped south to Villa Soleil, Ivan's palace by the sea in Saint-Tropez. As for Russia, it was a place they had visited a few weeks each year, just to keep in touch with their roots. Anna, the more talkative of the two, spoke of her native country as though it were something she had read about in books. Nikolai said little. He just stared at Gabriel a great deal, as if he suspected the unexplained lunch guest was somehow to blame for the fact he now lived on a mountaintop in the Adirondacks instead of west London and the south of France.

When the meal was concluded, the children kissed their mother's cheek and dutifully carried their dishes into the kitchen. 'It took a little time for them to get used to life without servants,' Elena said when they were gone. 'I think it's better they live like normal children for a while.' She smiled at the absurdity of her statement. 'Well, almost normal.'

'How have they handled the adjustment?'

'As well as one might expect, under the circumstances. Their lives as they knew them ended in the blink of an eye, all because their Russian bodyguards were stopped for speeding while leaving the beach in Saint-Tropez. I suspect they were the *only* people pulled over for speeding in the south of France the entire summer.'

'Gendarmes can be rather unpredictable in their enforcement of traffic regulations.'

'They can also be very kind. They took good care of my children when they were in custody. Nikolai still speaks fondly of the time he spent in the Saint-Tropez gendarmerie. He also enjoyed the monastery in the Alps. As far as the children were concerned, their escape was all a big adventure. And I have you to thank for that, Gabriel. You made it very easy on them.'

'How much do they know about what happened to their father?'

'They know he had some trouble with his business. And they know he divorced me in order to marry his friend, Yekaterina. As for the arms trafficking and the killings . . .' Her voice trailed off. 'They're far too young to understand. I'll wait until they're a bit older before telling them the truth. Then they can come to their own conclusions.'

'Surely they must be curious.'

'Of course they are. They haven't seen or spoken to Ivan for six months. It's been hard on Nikolai. He idolizes his father. I'm sure he blames me for his absence.'

'How do you explain the fact that you live in isolation surrounded by bodyguards?'

'That part is actually not so hard. Anna and Nikolai are the children of a Russian oligarch. They spent their entire lives surrounded by men with guns and radios, so it seems perfectly natural to them. As for the isolation, I tell them it's only temporary. Someday soon, they'll be allowed to have friends and go to school like normal American children. For now, they have a lovely tutor from the CIA. She works with them from nine until three. Then I make sure they go outside and play, regardless of the weather. We have several thousand acres, two lakes, and a river. There's plenty for the children to do. It's heaven. But I would never have been able to afford it if not for you and your helpers.'

Elena was referring to the team of Office cyberspecialists who, in the days after her defection, had raided Ivan's bank accounts in Moscow and Zurich and made off with more than twenty million dollars in cash. The 'unauthorized wire transfers,' as they were euphemistically referred to at King Saul Boulevard, were one of many actions connected to the affair that skirted the edge of legality. In the aftermath, Ivan had been in no position to quibble over the missing money or to question the sequence of events that led to the loss of custody of his two children. He was dealing with charges in the West that he had sold some of Russia's deadliest antiaircraft missiles to the terrorists of al-Qaeda, a sale concluded with the blessing of the Kremlin and the Russian president himself.

'Adrian tells me the CIA agreed to provide protection for you and the children for only two years,' Gabriel said.

'You obviously don't think that's long enough.'

'No, I don't.'

'The American taxpayer can't pay the bill forever. When the CIA men leave, I'll hire my own bodyguards.'

'What happens when the money runs out?'

'I suppose I could always sell that painting you forged for me.' She smiled. 'Would you like to see it?'

She led him into the great room and stopped before a precise copy of *Two Children on a Beach* by Mary Cassatt. It was the second version of the painting Gabriel had produced. The first had been sold to Ivan Kharkov for two and a half million dollars and was now in the possession of French prosecutors.

'I'm not sure it matches the Adirondack décor.'

'I don't care. I'm keeping it right where it is.'

He placed his hand to his chin and tilted his head to one side. 'I think it's better than the first one, don't you?'

'Your brushstrokes were a bit too impasto in the first version. This one is perfect.' She looked at him. 'But I don't suppose you came all this way to talk about my children or to hear me criticize your work.'

Gabriel was silent. Elena gazed at the painting.

'You know, Gabriel, you really should have been an artist. You could have been great. And with a bit of luck, you would have never had the misfortune of meeting my husband.'

More than a hundred intelligence professionals from four countries had been involved in the Kharkov affair, and most were still vexed by a single question: Why had Elena Varlamova, the beautiful and cultured daughter of a Communist Party economic planner from Leningrad, ever married a hood like Ivan in the first place?

He had been working for the notorious Fifth Directorate of the KGB at the time of their wedding and seemed destined for a glittering career. But in the late 1980s, as the Soviet Union lay wheezing on its deathbed, his fortunes took a sudden and unexpected turn. In a desperate bid to breathe life into the moribund Soviet economy, Mikhail Gorbachev had introduced economic reforms that allowed the limited formation of investment capital. With the encouragement of his superiors, Ivan left the KGB and created one of Russia's first privately owned banks. Aided by the hidden hand of his old colleagues, it was soon wildly profitable, and when the Soviet Union finally breathed its last, Ivan was uniquely positioned to snatch up some of its most valuable assets. Among them was a fleet of transport ships and aircraft, which he converted into one of the largest freight-forwarding companies in the world. Before long, Ivan's boats and planes were bound for destinations in

Africa, the Middle East, and Latin America, laden with one of the few products the Russians made well: weapons.

Ivan liked to boast he could lay his hands on anything and ship it anywhere, in some cases overnight. He cared nothing about morality, only money. He would sell to anyone, as long as they could pay. And if they couldn't, he offered to arrange financing through his banking arm. He sold his weapons to dictators and he sold them to rebels. He sold to freedom fighters with legitimate grievances and to genocidal maniacs who slaughtered women and children. He specialized in providing weapons to regimes so beyond the pale they were unable to obtain arms from legal sources. He perfected the practice of selling weapons to both sides of a conflict, judiciously moderating the flow of arms in order to prolong the killing and maximize his profits. He destroyed countries. He destroyed peoples. And he became filthy rich in the process. For years, he had managed to keep his network of death carefully concealed. To the rest of the world, Ivan Kharkov was the very symbol of the New Russia – a shrewd investor and businessman who easily straddled East and West, collecting expensive homes, luxury yachts, and beautiful mistresses. Elena would later admit to Gabriel that she had been an enabler of Ivan's grand deception. She had turned a blind eye to his romantic dalliances, just as she had shrouded herself in a willful ignorance when it came to the true source of his immense wealth.

But lives are sometimes upended in an instant. Gabriel's had changed one evening in Vienna, in the time it took a detonator to ignite a charge of plastic explosive placed beneath his car. For Elena Kharkov, it was the night she overheard a telephone conversation between her husband

and his chief of security, Arkady Medvedev. Confronted with the possibility that thousands of innocent people might die because of her husband's greed, she chose to betray him rather than remain silent. Her actions led her to an isolated villa in the hills above Saint-Tropez, where she offered to help Gabriel steal Ivan's secrets. The operation that followed had nearly ended both of their lives. One image would hang forever in Gabriel's terrible gallery of memory: the image of Elena Kharkov, tied to a chair in her husband's warehouse, with Arkady Medvedev's pistol pressed to the side of her head. Arkady wanted Gabriel to reveal the location of Anna and Nikolai. Elena was prepared to die rather than answer.

You'd better pull the trigger, Arkady. Because Ivan is never getting those children.

Now, seated before a fire in the great room of the Adirondack lodge, Gabriel broke the news that Ivan had succeeded in kidnapping Grigori Bulganov, the man who had saved their lives that night. And that Olga Sukhova, Elena's old friend from Leningrad State, had been the target of an assassination attempt in Oxford. Elena took the news calmly, as though she had been informed of a long-expected death. Then she accepted a photograph: a man standing in the arrivals hall of Heathrow Airport. The sudden darkening of her expression instantly told Gabriel his journey had not been in vain.

'You've seen him before?'

Elena nodded. 'In Moscow, a long time ago. He was a regular visitor to our house in Zhukovka.'

'Did he come alone?'

She shook her head. 'Only with Arkady.'

'Were you ever told his name?'

'I was *never* told their names.'

'And you never happened to overhear one?'

'I'm afraid not.'

Gabriel tried to conceal his disappointment and asked whether Elena could recall anything else. She looked down at the photograph, as if trying to wipe the dust from her memory.

'I remember that Arkady was always quite deferential in his presence. I found it rather odd because Arkady was deferential in front of no one.' She looked up at Gabriel. 'Too bad you killed him. He could have told you the name.'

'The world is a much better place without the likes of Arkady Medvedev.'

'That's true. Sometimes I actually wish I'd killed him myself.' She turned her head and stared across the room toward the painting. 'The question is, has Ivan hired this same man to take my children from me?'

Gabriel took hold of Elena's hand and gave it a reassuring squeeze. 'I've experienced Adrian's security firsthand. There's no way Ivan will ever find you and the children here.'

'I'd feel better knowing you were here.' She looked at him. 'Will you stay with us, Gabriel? Just for a day or two?'

'I'm not sure Grigori has a day or two to spare.'

'Grigori?' She gazed despondently into the fire. 'I know what my husband and his friends from the FSB do to those who betray them. You should forget about Grigori. Better to focus on the living.'

34. Upstate New York

Gabriel agreed to spend the night and return to Washington the next morning. After settling into a second-floor guest room, he went in search of a telephone. As a security precaution, Ed Fielding had removed all the phones from the main lodge. Indeed, only one telephone on the entire property was capable of reaching the outside world. It was located in the second lodge, on the desk in Fielding's office. A small sign warned that all calls, regardless of origin or destination, were monitored and recorded. 'It's no joke,' Fielding said as he handed Gabriel the receiver. 'As one professional to another.'

Fielding stepped outside and closed the door. Unwilling to betray normal Office communication procedures, Gabriel dialed King Saul Boulevard on a business line and asked for Uzi Navot. Their conversation was brief and conducted in a form of Hebrew no NSA supercomputer could ever decipher. In the space of a few seconds, Navot managed to give Gabriel a thorough update. Irina Bulganova was safely on the ground in Moscow, Gabriel's team was headed back to Israel, and Chiara was on her way back to Umbria, accompanied by her bodyguards. In fact, Navot added after checking the time, they were probably there by now.

Gabriel severed the connection and debated whether to ring her. He decided it wasn't safe. Making contact with the

Office on an Agency line was one thing, but calling Chiara at home or on her mobile was quite another. He would have to wait until he was outside the CIA's bubble before trying to reach her. Replacing the receiver, he thought of the words Elena had just spoken. *You should forget about Grigori. Better to focus on the living.* Perhaps she was right. Perhaps he had made a promise he couldn't possibly keep. Perhaps it was time to go home and look after his wife. He opened the door and stepped into the corridor. Ed Fielding was there, leaning against the wall.

'Everything okay?'

'Everything's fine.'

'Feel like taking a ride?'

'Where?'

'I know you're concerned about Elena. I thought I'd put your mind at ease by showing you some of our security measures.'

'Even though I work for a foreign service?'

'Adrian says you're family. That's all I need to know.'

Gabriel followed Fielding into the bitter late-afternoon cold. He had expected the tour to be conducted by Jeep. Instead, Fielding escorted him to an outbuilding where two snowmobiles glistened beneath overhead fluorescent lights. From a metal cabinet, the CIA man produced a pair of helmets, two parkas, two neoprene face masks, and two pairs of wind-stopper gloves. Five minutes later, after a perfunctory lesson on the operation of a snowmobile, Gabriel was hurtling through the woods in Fielding's blizzardlike wake, bound for a distant corner of the estate.

They inspected the westernmost edge of the property first, then the southern border, which was marked by a branch of the St Regis River. Two weeks earlier, a black bear had crossed onto the estate from the other side of the stream and triggered the motion detectors and infrared heat sensors. Fielding had responded to the intrusion by dispatching a pair of guards, who confronted the bear within thirty seconds of its arrival. Faced with the prospect of becoming a rug, the bear had wisely retreated to the other side of the stream and had not been seen since.

'Are there any other wild animals we need to worry about?' asked Gabriel.

'Just deer, bobcats, beavers, and the occasional wolf.'

'Wolves?'

'We had one just the other day. A big one.'

'Are they dangerous?'

'Only if you surprise them.'

Fielding twisted the throttle and vanished in a cloud of white. Gabriel followed him along the winding bank of the streambed to the eastern edge of the property. It was marked by a chain-link fence topped by barbed wire. Every fifty yards or so was a sign warning that the property was private and that anyone foolish enough to attempt a crossing would be prosecuted to the full extent of the law. As they sped side by side along the fence, Gabriel noticed Fielding talking over his radio. By the time they reached the road, it was clear something was wrong. Fielding stopped and motioned for Gabriel to do the same.

'You have a phone call.'

Gabriel didn't have to ask who had placed the call. Only one person knew where he was or how to reach him.

'What's it about?'

'He didn't say. He wants to talk to you right away, though.'

Fielding led Gabriel back to the compound by the shortest route possible. It was dusk when they arrived, and the two Adirondack lodges were little more than silhouettes against the fiery horizon. Elena Kharkov stood on the porch of the main house, her arms folded beneath her breasts, her long dark hair moving in the frigid wind. Gabriel and Fielding swept past her without a word and entered the staff lodge. The telephone in Fielding's office was off the hook. Gabriel raised the receiver swiftly to his ear and heard the voice of Adrian Carter.

If there was indeed a recording of the conversation that followed, it did not exist for long. Carter would never speak of it, except to say that it was among the most difficult of his long career. The only other witness was Ed Fielding. The security man could not hear Carter's words, but could see the terrible toll they were taking. He saw a hand gripping the telephone with such force the knuckles were white. And he saw the eyes. The unusually bright green eyes now burning with a terrifying rage. As Fielding slipped quietly from the room, he realized he had never seen such rage before. He did not know what his friend Adrian Carter was saying to the legendary Israeli assassin. But he was certain of one thing. Blood was going to flow. And men were going to die.

PART THREE
All Even

35. Tiberias, Israel

Ari Shamron had long ago lost the gift of sleep. Like most men, it had been taken from him late in life, but for reasons that were uniquely his. He had told so many lies, spun so many deceptions, he could no longer tell fact from fiction, truth from untruth. Condemned by his work to remain forever awake, Shamron spent nights wandering ceaselessly through the secure file rooms of his past, reliving old cases, walking old battlefields, confronting enemies long since vanquished.

And then there was the telephone. Throughout Shamron's long and turbulent career, it had rung at the most appalling hours, usually with word of death. Because he had devoted his life to safeguarding the State of Israel, and by extension the Jewish people, the calls had been a veritable catalog of horrors. He had been told about acts of war and acts of terror, of hijackings and murderous suicide bombings, of embassies and synagogues reduced to rubble. And once, many years earlier, he had been awakened by the news that a man he adored as a son had just lost his family in a car bombing in Vienna. But the call from Uzi Navot that arrived late that evening was nearly one too many. It caused Shamron to unleash a cry of rage and to seize his chest in anguish. Gilah, who was lying beside him at the time, would later say she feared her husband was having another heart attack. Shamron quickly steadied himself and snapped off a few brisk commands before gently hanging up the phone.

He remained motionless for a long moment, his breathing rapid and shallow. There was a ritual in the Shamron household. At the termination of such telephone calls, Gilah would usually pose a single question: 'How many dead this time?' But Gilah could tell by her husband's reaction that this call was different. So she reached out in the darkness and touched the papery skin of his hollowed cheek. For only the second time in their marriage, she felt tears.

'What is it, Ari? What's happened?'

Hearing his answer, she raised both hands to her face and wept.

'Where is he?'

'America.'

'Does he know yet?'

'He's just been told.'

'Is he coming home?'

'He'll be here by morning.'

'Do we know who did it?'

'We have a good idea.'

'What are you going to do?'

'Amos doesn't want me around. He thinks I'll be a distraction.'

'Who is Amos to tell you what to do? Gabriel is like a son to you. Tell Amos he can to go to hell. Tell him you're coming back to King Saul Boulevard.'

Shamron was silent for a moment. 'Maybe he won't want me there.'

'Who?'

'Gabriel.'

'Why would you say that, Ari?'

'Because if I hadn't . . .' His voice trailed off.

'Because if you hadn't recruited him a long time ago, none of this would have ever happened? Is that what you were going to say?'

Shamron made no response.

'Gabriel is more like you than he realizes. He had no choice but to fight. None of us do.' Gilah wiped the tears from her husband's cheeks. 'Get out of bed, Ari. Go to Tel Aviv. And make sure you're waiting at Ben-Gurion when he arrives. He needs to see a familiar face.' She paused, then said, 'He needs to see his *abba*.'

Shamron sat up and swung his feet slowly to the floor.

'Can I make you some coffee or something to eat?'

'There isn't time.'

'Let me get you some clean clothes.'

Gilah switched on her lamp and climbed out of bed. Shamron snatched up the receiver of his telephone again and placed a call to the guard shack at the foot of his drive. It was answered by Rami, the longtime chief of his permanent security detail.

'Get the car ready,' Shamron said.

'Something wrong, boss?'

'It's Gabriel. You'll know the rest soon enough.'

Shamron hung up the phone and got to his feet. By then Gilah had laid his clothes out at the foot of the bed: pressed khaki trousers, an oxford-cloth shirt, a leather bomber jacket with a tear in the right breast. Shamron reached down and tugged at it gently. *We'll wage one more fight together*, he thought. *One last operation.*

He lit a cigarette and dressed slowly, as if armoring himself for the battle ahead. Pulling on his jacket, he made his way to the kitchen, where Gilah was brewing a pot of coffee.

'I told you there isn't time.'

'It's for me, Ari.'

'You should go back to bed, Gilah.'

'I won't be able to sleep now.' She looked at the cigarette burning between his yellowed fingers but knew better than to scold him. 'Try not to smoke too much. The doctor says—'

'I know what he says.'

She kissed his cheek. 'You'll call me when you can?'

'I'll call.'

Shamron stepped outside. The house faced east, toward the Sea of Galilee and the looming dark mass of the Golan Heights. Shamron had bought it many years ago because it allowed him to keep watch on Israel's enemies. Tonight those enemies were beyond the horizon. By their actions they had just declared war on the Office. And now the Office would make war on them in return.

Shamron's armored limousine was waiting in the drive. Rami helped him into the back before settling into the front passenger seat. As the car lurched forward, the bodyguard shot a glance over his shoulder and asked where they were going.

'King Saul Boulevard.'

Rami gave a terse nod. Shamron reached for his secure phone and pressed a speed-dial button. The voice that answered was young, male, and impertinent. It immediately set Shamron's teeth on edge. Making mincemeat of such voices was one of his favorite pastimes.

'I need to speak to him right away.'

'He's asleep.'

'Not for long.'

'He asked not to be disturbed unless it's a matter of national crisis.'

'Then I suggest you wake him.'

'It better be important.'

The aide placed Shamron on hold, never a good idea. Thirty seconds later, another voice came on the line. Heavy with sleep, it belonged to Israel's prime minister.

'What is it, Ari?'

'We lost two boys in Italy tonight,' Shamron said. 'And Gabriel's wife is missing.'

It was Margherita, the housekeeper, who had made the discovery. Later, under questioning from Italian authorities, she would place the time at perhaps five minutes past ten, though she admitted to not having checked her wristwatch. The time happened to correspond satisfactorily to her mobile-phone records, which showed she placed her first call at 10:07. The time also dovetailed well with her movements that night. Several witnesses would recall seeing her leave a café in Amelia at roughly 9:50 p.m., leaving her plenty of time to make the drive back to Villa dei Fiori aboard her little motor scooter.

The first indication of trouble, she said, was the presence of a car outside the security gate. A Fiat sedan, it was parked at a drunken angle, nose against a tree, headlamps doused. She told the police she assumed it had been abandoned or involved in a minor accident. Rather than approach the car, she had first illuminated it with the beam of her headlamp.

It was then she noticed the broken windows and the bits of safety glass scattered over the ground like crystals. She also realized the car was familiar. It belonged to the two friends of the restorer, the young men with odd names who spoke no known language. She told the police she had never truly believed their story. Her father had been a soldier, she said, and she knew a couple of security guards when she saw them. Dismounting the bike, she had hurried over to the car to see if anyone was injured. What she had found, she said, was clearly no accident. Both men had been shot many times and were drenched in blood.

Though Margherita was the first to be questioned by the police, she had not actually been the one to summon them. Like the other members of the staff, she had been given strict instructions about what to do in the event of any incident involving the restorer or his wife. She was to telephone Count Gasparri, the villa's absentee owner, and inform him first. Which she had done at 10:07. The count had then placed a hasty call to Monsignor Luigi Donati, private secretary to His Holiness Pope Paul VII, and Donati had contacted the Vatican Security Office. Within twenty minutes, units of both the Polizia di Stato and Carabiniere had arrived at the villa's entrance and cordoned off the scene. Unable to locate the keys to the vehicle, the officers had opened the trunk by force. Inside they had found three suitcases, one filled with the belongings of a woman, and a woman's handbag. The commanding officer had quickly surmised that the crime scene represented more than just a double homicide. It appeared there had been a woman in the car. And the woman was now missing.

Unbeknownst to the officers at the scene, a quiet call

had already been placed from the Vatican to the woman's employers in Tel Aviv. The officer who had taken the call immediately telephoned Uzi Navot, who was at that moment heading toward his home in the Tel Aviv suburb of Petah Tikvah. He swung a reckless U-turn and drove dangerously fast back to King Saul Boulevard. Along the way, he placed three calls from his secure phone: one to Adrian Carter at Langley, the next to the director of the Office, and a third to the Memuneh, the one in charge.

As for Gabriel, he was largely unaware of the storm swirling around him. Indeed, at the same moment Shamron was rousing the prime minister from his sleep, he was doing his best to console a distraught Elena Kharkov. Her two children, Anna and Nikolai, were playing quietly in the next room, oblivious as to what had just transpired. Precisely what was said between Gabriel and Elena would never be known. They emerged from the lodge together a short time later, Elena in tears, Gabriel looking stoic, with his overnight bag slung over his shoulder. By the time he arrived at Adirondack Regional Airport, his plane was fueled and cleared for takeoff. It took him directly to Andrews Air Force Base, where a second aircraft, a Gulfstream G500, was on standby to ferry him home. The crew would later report that he took no food or drink during the ten-hour flight and spoke not a single word. He just sat in his seat like a statue, staring out the window, into the blackness.

36. Ben-Gurion Airport, Israel

There is a room at Ben-Gurion Airport known to only a handful of people. It is located to the left of passport control, behind an unmarked door kept locked at all times. Its walls are faux Jerusalem limestone; its furnishings are typical airport fare: black vinyl couches and chairs, modular end tables, cheap modern lamps that cast an unforgiving light. There are two windows, one looking onto the tarmac, the other onto the arrivals hall. Both are fashioned of high-quality one-way glass. Reserved for Office personnel, it is the first stop for operatives returning from secret battle-fields abroad. There is a permanent odor of stale cigarettes, burnt coffee, and male tension. The cleaning staff has tried every product imaginable to expel it, but the smell remains. Like Israel's enemies, it cannot be defeated by conventional means.

Gabriel had entered this room, or versions of it, many times before. He had entered it in triumph and staggered into it in failure. He had been fêted in this room, and once he had been wheeled in with a bullet still lodged in his chest. Now, for the second time in his life, he entered after men of indiscriminate violence had targeted his wife. Only Shamron was there to greet him. Shamron might have said many things. He might have said that none of this would have happened if Gabriel had come home to Israel. Or that Gabriel had been a fool to go chasing after a Russian defector like Grigori. But he didn't. In fact, for a long moment he said nothing at all. He just laid his hand on Gabriel's cheek and stared into the green eyes. They were bloodshot and red-rimmed from anger and exhaustion.

'I don't suppose you managed to sleep?'

The eyes answered for him.

'You didn't eat, either. You have to eat, Gabriel.'

'I'll eat when I get her back.'

'The professional in me wants to say we should let someone else handle this. But I know that isn't an option.' Shamron took hold of Gabriel's elbow. 'Your team is waiting for you. They're anxious to get started. We have a great deal of work to do and very little time.'

Stepping outside, they were greeted by a raw blast of windblown rain. Gabriel looked at the sky: no moon or stars, just leaden clouds stretching from the Coastal Plain to the Judean Hills. 'It's snowing in Jerusalem,' Shamron said. 'Down here, only rain.' He paused. 'And missiles. Last night, Hamas let loose from Gaza with some of their longer-range rockets. Five people were killed in Ashkelon – an entire family wiped out. One of the children was handicapped. Apparently, they couldn't make it into the shelters quickly enough.'

Shamron's limousine was parked curbside in the secure VIP area. Rami stood at the open door, hands at his sides, face grim. As Gabriel slipped into the back, the bodyguard gave his arm a reassuring squeeze but said nothing. A moment later, the car was speeding along the circular airport access road through the driving rain. At the end of the road was a blue-and-white sign. To the right was

Jerusalem, city of believers. To the left was Tel Aviv, city of action. The limousine headed left. Shamron ignited a cigarette and brought Gabriel up to date.

'Shimon Pazner has set up shop inside the headquarters of the Polizia di Stato. He's monitoring the Italian search efforts on a minute-by-minute basis and filing regular updates with the Operations Desk.'

Pazner was the Rome station chief. He and Gabriel had had the odd professional altercation over the years, but Gabriel trusted him with his life. And Chiara's, too.

'Shimon has also conducted quiet conversations with the heads of both the Italian services. They've sent their condolences and pledged to do everything in their power to help.'

'I hope he didn't feel obligated to say anything about my recent visit to Como. Under my agreement with the Italians, I'm barred from operating on Italian soil.'

'He didn't. But I wouldn't worry too much about the Italians. You're not going back there anytime soon.'

'How did he explain the fact that Chiara was traveling with bodyguards?'

'He told them we'd picked up some threats against you. He didn't go into specifics.'

'How did the Italians react?'

'As you might expect, they were somewhat disappointed we hadn't mentioned it earlier. But their first concern is trying to locate your wife. We've told them we believe the Russians are involved. Ivan's name hasn't come up. Not yet.'

'It's important the Italians handle this quietly.'

'They will. The last thing they want is for the world to

discover you've been living on a farm in Umbria restoring paintings for the pope. The Polizia di Stato and Carabiniere officers on the ground believe the victim was an ordinary Italian woman. Higher up the chain of command, they know there's a national security connection of some sort. Only the chiefs and their top aides know the truth.'

'What steps are they taking?'

'They're conducting a search in the area surrounding the villa and have officers at every point of entry and border crossing. They can't search every vehicle, but they're running spot checks and tearing apart anything that looks remotely suspicious. Apparently, the truck traffic heading toward the Swiss tunnels is backed up for more than an hour.'

'Do they know anything about how the operation went down?'

Shamron shook his head. 'No one saw a thing. They think Lior and Motti had been dead for a couple of hours before the housekeeper found them. Whoever did this was good. Lior and Motti never managed to get a shot off.'

'Where are their bodies?'

'They've been moved to Rome. The Italians will release them to us later this morning. They're hoping to do it quietly, but I doubt they'll be able to keep a lid on it much longer. Someone in the press is bound to get wind of it soon.'

'I want them buried as heroes, Ari. They didn't deserve to die like this. If I hadn't—'

'You did what you thought was right, Gabriel. And don't worry. Those boys will be buried with honor on the Mount of Olives.' Shamron hesitated, then said, 'Near your son.'

Gabriel looked out the window. He was grateful for the

Italian effort but feared it was little more than wasted time. He didn't have to voice this sentiment aloud. Shamron, by his dour expression, knew it to be true. He crushed out his cigarette and immediately lit another.

'Have you given any thought to how Ivan found her?'

'I've thought of nothing else, Ari – other than getting her back.'

'Perhaps they followed Irina when you brought her to Italy.'

'It's possible . . .'

'But?'

'Extremely unlikely. Moscow Station watched Irina for several days before she left Russia. She was clean.'

'Could they have had a team waiting at the Milan airport and followed you to the villa?'

'We set up a surveillance-detection route. There's no way we would have missed a Russian tail.'

'Maybe they did it electronically.'

'With a beacon?' Gabriel shook his head. 'We checked her out before we ever left the airport. Her luggage contained no transmitters. We did everything by the book, Ari. I suspect Ivan and his friends in Russian intelligence have known my whereabouts for a long time.'

'So why didn't he just kill you and be done with it?'

'I'm sure we'll know soon enough.'

The limousine headed onto an exit ramp and a moment later was speeding north along Highway 20. To the left lay Tel Aviv and its suburbs. To the right was a towering gray wall separating Israel from the West Bank. There were some in Israel's defense and security establishment who referred to it as the Shamron Fence because he had spent years advocating its construction. The separation barrier had helped to drastically reduce acts of terrorism but had caused much damage to the country's already low standing abroad. Shamron never allowed important decisions to be influenced by international opinion. He operated by a simple maxim: Do what is necessary and worry about cleaning up the mess later. Gabriel would operate by the same doctrine now.

'Have we gone on the record with the Russians yet?'

'We summoned the ambassador to the Foreign Ministry last night and read him the riot act. We told him that we believe Ivan Kharkov is responsible for Chiara's disappearance and made it clear we expect her to be released immediately.'

'How did the ambassador react?'

'He said he was certain we were wrong but promised to look into the matter. The formal denial came this morning.'

'Ivan had nothing to do with it, of course.'

'Of course. But I'm afraid it gets better. The FSB has offered to help locate Chiara.'

'Oh, really? And what would they like in return?'

'All information pertaining to her disappearance, plus the names of everyone who took part in the operation against Ivan in Moscow last summer.'

'That means Ivan is acting with the Kremlin's blessing.'

'Without question. It also means we'll have to treat the Russian services as adversaries. Fortunately, you have friends in London and Washington. Graham Seymour says the British services will do whatever they can to help. And Adrian Carter has already sent a cable to all his stations and bases regarding Chiara's abduction. He'll pass along anything the CIA happens to pick up.'

'I need complete coverage of all of Ivan's communications.'

'You've already got it. All relevant NSA intercepts will be turned over to our station chief in Washington.' Shamron paused. 'The question is, what does Ivan want? And when are we going to hear from him?'

The car exited Highway 20 and spiraled down onto a rain-swept avenue in north Tel Aviv. Shamron placed a hand on Gabriel's arm.

'This is not the way I wanted you to come back here, my son, but welcome home.'

Gabriel looked out the window at a passing street sign: SDEROT SHAUL HAMELECH.

King Saul Boulevard.

37. King Saul Boulevard, Tel Aviv

MI5 had the imposing graystone solemnity of Thames House. The CIA had the glass-and-steel sprawl of Langley. The Office had King Saul Boulevard.

It was drab, featureless, and, best of all, anonymous. No emblem hung over its entrance, no brass lettering proclaimed its occupant. In fact, there was nothing at all to suggest it was the headquarters of one of the world's most feared and respected intelligence services. A closer inspection of the structure would have revealed the existence of a building within a building, one with its own power supply, its own water and sewer lines, and its own highly secure communications system. Employees carried two keys: one opened an unmarked door in the lobby, the other operated the elevator. Those who committed the unpardonable sin of losing one or both of their keys were banished to the Judean Wilderness, never to be seen or heard from again.

Gabriel had come through the lobby just once, the day after his first encounter with Shamron. From that point forward, he had only entered the building 'black' through the underground garage. He did so again now, with Shamron at his side. Amos Sharret, the director, was waiting in the foyer with Uzi Navot at his side. Gabriel's relations with Amos were cool at best, but none of that mattered now. Gabriel's wife, an Office agent, was missing and presumed to be in the hands of a proven murderer who had sworn vengeance. After expressing his condolences, Amos made it clear the complete arsenal of the Office, both human and technical, was now at Gabriel's disposal. Then he led Gabriel into a waiting elevator, followed by Shamron and Navot.

'I've cleared an office for you on the top floor,' Amos said. 'You can work from there.'

'Where's my team?'

'The usual place.'

'Then why would I work on the top floor?'

Amos stabbed at a button on the control panel. The elevator headed down.

For many years it had been a dumping ground for obsolete computers and worn-out furniture, often used by officers of the night staff as a place for romantic trysts. Now Room 456C, a cramped subterranean chamber three levels beneath the lobby, was known as Gabriel's Lair. Affixed to the door was a faded paper sign: TEMPORARY COMMITTEE FOR THE STUDY OF TERROR THREATS IN WESTERN EUROPE. Gabriel tore it away, then punched the code into the electronic combination lock.

The room they entered was littered with the debris of operations past and, some claimed, haunted by their ghosts. Seated at the communal worktables were the members of Gabriel's team: Dina and Rimona, Yaakov and Yossi, Eli Lavon and Mikhail. They had been joined by five additional officers: a pair of all-purpose field operatives, Oded and Mordecai, and three young geniuses from Technical who specialized in covert cyberops. They were the same three men who had raided Ivan's bank accounts in the days after his wife's defection. For the past several days, their frightening collection of skills had been focused on the financial holdings of another Russian oligarch: Viktor Orlov.

Gabriel stood at the head of the room and surveyed the faces before him. He saw only anger and determination. These same men and women had carried out some of the most daring and dangerous operations in Office history. At that moment, not one questioned their ability to locate Chiara and bring her home. If for some reason they failed, then tears would be shed. But not now. And not in front of Gabriel.

He stood before them in silence, his gaze moving slowly from wall to wall, over the faces of the dead: *Khaled al-Khalifa, Ahmed Bin Shafiq, Zizi al-Bakari, Yusuf Ramadan . . .* There were many more, of course, almost too many to recall. They were murderers all, and each deserved the death sentence that Gabriel had administered. He should have killed Ivan as well. Now Ivan had taken Gabriel's wife. Regardless of the outcome, Ivan would spend the rest of his life a hunted man. So, too, would anyone remotely connected to the affair. They stood no chance of survival. Gabriel would find them all, no matter how long it took. And he would kill each and every one of them.

For now, though, punishing the guilty would have to wait. Finding Chiara was all that mattered. They would start the search by locating the man who had planned and executed her abduction. The man who had introduced himself to Irina Bulganova as Anatoly, friend of Viktor Orlov. The man who had just made the biggest mistake of his professional career. Gabriel hung his photograph now in the gallery of the dead. And then he told his team a story.

*

There is a memorial not far from King Saul Boulevard. It is dedicated to those who have served, and fallen, in secret. It is fashioned from smooth sandstone and shaped like a brain because Israel's founders believed only the brain would keep their small country safe from those who wished to destroy it. The walls of the memorial are engraved with the names of the dead and the dates on which they perished. Other details about their lives and careers are kept locked away in the File Room. More than five hundred intelligence officers from Israel's various services are honored there. Seventy-five are Office. Two names would be added in the coming days – two good boys who died because Gabriel had tried to keep a promise. Chiara Zolli, he said, would not be the third name.

The Italian police were now engaged in a frantic effort to find her. Gabriel, his voice calm and unemotional, said the Italian effort would not prove successful. In all likelihood, Chiara had been removed from Italian soil even before the search had begun. At this moment, she could be anywhere. She might be heading eastward across the former lands of the Soviet empire that the Russians referred to as the 'near abroad.' Or perhaps she was already somewhere in Russia. 'Or perhaps she's not in Russia at all,' Gabriel added. 'Ivan controls one of the world's largest shipping and air freight companies. Ivan has the capability to conceal Chiara anywhere on earth. Ivan has the capability to put her in motion and keep her in motion in perpetuity.' That meant Ivan had an unfair advantage. But they had leverage, too. Ivan had not taken Chiara simply to kill her. Surely, Ivan wanted something else. It gave them time and room to maneuver. Not much time, Gabriel said. And very little room.

They would start by trying to find the man Ivan had used as his tool of vengeance. For now, he was but a few lines of charcoal on an otherwise blank canvas. They were going to complete the picture. He did not materialize out of thin air, this man. He had a name and a past. He had a family. He lived somewhere. He existed. Everything about him suggested he was former KGB, a man who specialized in finding people who wished not to be found. A man who could make people disappear without a trace. A man who now worked for wealthy Russians like Ivan Kharkov.

A man like that did not exist in a vacuum. People had to know about him in order to retain his services. They were going to find such a person. And they would start their search in the city where the affair began: the Russian city sometimes referred to as London.

Though Gabriel had no way of knowing it, he was correct about at least one thing: Chiara had not remained on Italian soil for long. In fact, within hours of her abduction, she had been moved eastward across the country to a fishing village in the region known as Le Marche. There she was placed aboard a trawler and taken out to sea for what appeared to be a night of work in the Adriatic. At 2:15 a.m., as officers of the Polizia di Stato were standing watch at Italy's border crossings, she was transferred to a private motor yacht called the *Anastasia*. By dawn, the yacht had returned to a sleepy port along the coast of Montenegro, the newly independent former Yugoslav Republic that was now home to thousands of Russian expatriates and an important base of operations for the Russian mafia. She would not stay in that country for long, either. By midmorning, as Gabriel's flight was touching down at Ben-Gurion, she was being loaded onto a cargo plane at an airfield outside the Montenegrin capital. According to documents on board, the aircraft was owned by a Bahamian-based shipping company called LukoTranz. What the documents did not say was that LukoTranz was actually a corporate shell controlled by none other than Ivan Kharkov. Not that it would have mattered to the Montenegrin customs officials. The bribe they received for not inspecting the plane or its contents was more than triple their monthly government salaries.

Chiara knew none of this. Indeed, her last clear memory was of the nightmare at the gate of Villa dei Fiori. It had been dark when they arrived. Exhausted by the operation in Como, Chiara had dozed intermittently during the long drive and woke as Lior was easing up to the security gate. To open it required the correct six-digit code. Lior was entering it into the keypad when the men with black hoods emerged from the trees. Their weapons dispensed death with little more than a whisper. Motti had been hit first, Lior second. Chiara had been reaching for her Beretta when she was given a single disabling blow to the side of her head. Then she had felt a stab in her right thigh, an injection of sedative that made her head spin and turned her limbs to deadweight. The last thing she remembered was the face of a woman looking down at her. *Behave and we might let you live*, the woman said in Russian-accented English. Then the woman's face turned to water, and Chiara lost consciousness.

Now she was adrift in a world that was part dream, part memory. For hours she wandered lost through the streets of her native Venice as the floodwaters of the *acqua alta* swirled round her knees. In a church in Cannaregio she found Gabriel seated atop a work platform, conversing softly with Saint Christopher and Saint Jerome. She took him to a canal house near the old Jewish ghetto and made love to him in sheets soaked with blood, while Leah, his wife, watched from her wheelchair in the shadows. A parade of other images filed past, some nightmarish in their depiction, others rendered accurately. She relived the day Gabriel told her he could never marry her. And the day, not two years later, when he threw her a surprise wedding on Shamron's terrace overlooking the Sea of Galilee. She walked with Gabriel through the snow-covered killing grounds of Treblinka and knelt over his broken body in a sodden English pasture, pleading with him not to die.

Finally, she saw Gabriel in a garden in Umbria, surrounded by walls of Etruscan stone. He was playing with a child — not the child he had lost in Vienna but the child Chiara had given to him. *The child now growing inside her.* She had been a fool to lie to Gabriel. If only she had told him the truth, he would have never gone to London to keep his promise to Grigori Bulganov. And Chiara would not be the prisoner of a Russian woman.

A woman who was now standing over her. Syringe in hand.

She had milk-white skin and eyes of translucent blue, and appeared to be having difficulty maintaining her balance. This was neither dream nor hallucination. At that moment, Chiara and the woman were caught in a sudden squall in the middle of the Adriatic. Chiara did not know this, of course. She only knew that the woman nearly toppled while giving her an injection of sedative, inserting the needle with far more force than was necessary. Slipping once more into unconsciousness, Chiara returned again to the garden in Umbria. Gabriel was bidding farewell to the child. It wandered into a field of sunflowers and disappeared.

Chiara woke once more during the journey, this time by the drone of an aircraft in flight and the stench of her own vomit. The woman was standing over her again, another loaded syringe in hand. Chiara promised to behave, but the woman shook her head and inserted the needle. As the drug took effect, Chiara found herself wandering frantically through the field of sunflowers, searching for the child. Then night fell like a curtain, and she was weeping hysterically with no one to console her.

When next she regained consciousness, it was to the sensation of intense cold. For a moment she thought it was another hallucination. Then she realized she was on her feet and somehow walking through snow. Her hands were cuffed and secured to her body by nylon tape, her ankles shackled. The chains of the shackles abbreviated her stride to little more than a shuffle. The two men holding her arms seemed not to mind. They seemed to have all the time in the world. So did the woman with milk-white skin.

She was walking a few paces ahead, toward a small cottage surrounded by birch trees. Parked outside were a pair of Mercedes sedans. Judging from their low profile, they had armor plating and bulletproof windows. Leaning against the hood of one was a man: black leather coat, silver hair, head like a tank turret. Chiara had never met him in person but had seen the face many times in surveillance photographs. His powerful aftershave hung like an invisible fog on the brittle air. Sandalwood and smoke. The smell of power. The smell of the devil.

The devil smiled seductively and touched her face. Chiara recoiled, instantly nauseated. At the devil's command, the two men led her into the cottage and down a flight of narrow wooden stairs. At the bottom was a heavy metal door with a thick horizontal latch. Behind it was a small room with a concrete floor and whitewashed walls. They forced her inside and slammed the door. Chiara lay motionless, weeping softly, shivering with the unbearable cold. A moment later, when her eyes had adjusted to the darkness, she realized she was not alone. Propped in one corner, hands and feet bound, was a man. Despite the poor light, Chiara could see he had not shaved in many days. She could also see he had been beaten savagely.

'I'm so sorry to see you,' he said softly. 'You must be Gabriel's wife.'

'Who are you?'

'My name is Grigori Bulganov. Don't say another word. Ivan is listening.'

39. King Saul Boulevard, Tel Aviv

The Office prided itself on its ability to respond quickly in times of crisis, but even battle-hardened veterans of the service would later shake their heads in wonder at the speed with which Gabriel's team sprang into action. They berated the analysts of Research to have another look at their files and hounded the gathering officers of Collections to squeeze their sources for the smallest threads of information. They robbed Banking of a quarter million euros and put Housekeeping on notice that secure accommodations would be required with little or no advance warning. And finally they pre-positioned enough electronics and weaponry in Europe to start a small war. But then, that was their intention.

Fortunately for Gabriel, he would not go to war alone. He had two powerful allies with great influence and global reach, one in Washington, the other in London. From Adrian Carter, he borrowed a single asset, a female officer who had recently been sent to Europe on temporary duty. Of Graham Seymour he requested a night raid. The target would be an individual, a man who once boasted he knew more about what was taking place inside Russia than the Russian president himself. Seymour would handle the legwork and logistics. Olga Sukhova would serve as the sharp end of the sword.

It was a role long reserved for Shamron. Now he had no

task other than to pace the floors with worry or to make a general nuisance of himself. He looked over shoulders, whispered into ears, and, on several occasions, pulled Uzi and Gabriel into the hall and jabbed at them with his stubby forefinger. Time and again, he heard the same response. *Yes, Ari, we know. We've thought of that.* And, truth be told, they *had* thought of it. Because Shamron had trained them. Because they were the best of the best. Because they were like his sons. And because they could now do this job without the help of an old man.

And so he spent much of that terrible day roaming the upper floors of his beloved King Saul Boulevard, poking his head through doorways, renewing old friendships, making peace with old rivals. There was a pall hanging over the place; it reminded Shamron too much of Vienna. Restless, he requested permission from Amos to go to Ben-Gurion to receive the bodies of Lior and Motti. They were returned to Israel in secret, just as they had served it, with only Shamron and their parents present. He gave them a famous shoulder to cry on but could tell them nothing about how their sons had died. The experience left him deeply shaken, and he returned to King Saul Boulevard feeling abnormally depressed. His mood improved slightly when he entered Room 456C to find Gabriel's team hard at work. Gabriel, however, was not there. He was on his way to Jerusalem, city of believers.

A steady snow was falling as Gabriel pulled into the drive of Mount Herzl Psychiatric Hospital. A sign at the entrance said visiting hours were now over; Gabriel ignored it and went inside. Under an agreement with the hospital's administration, he was allowed to come whenever he wanted. In fact, he rarely came when the family and friends of other patients were around. Israel, a country of just over five million people, was in many ways an extended family. Even Gabriel, who conducted his affairs in anonymity, found it difficult to go anywhere without bumping into an acquaintance from Bezalel or the army.

Leah's doctor was waiting in the lobby. A rotund figure with a rabbinical beard, he updated Gabriel on Leah's condition as they walked together along a quiet corridor. Gabriel was not surprised to hear it had changed little since his last visit. Leah suffered from a particularly acute combination of psychotic depression and post-traumatic stress syndrome. The bombing in Vienna played ceaselessly in her mind like a loop of videotape. From time to time, she experienced flashes of lucidity, but for the most part she lived only in the past, trapped in a body that no longer functioned, guilt-ridden over her failure to save her son's life.

'Does she recognize anyone?'

'Only Gilah Shamron. She comes once a week. Sometimes more.'

'Where is she now?'

'In the recreation room. We've closed it so you can see her in private.'

She was seated in a wheelchair near the window, gazing sightlessly into the garden where snow was collecting on the limbs of the olive trees. Her hair, once long and black, was short and gray. Her hands, twisted and scarred by fire, were folded in her lap. When Gabriel sat next to her, she seemed not to notice. Then her head turned slowly, and a spark of recognition flickered in her eyes.

'Is it really you, Gabriel?'

'Yes, Leah. It's me.'

'They said you might be coming. I was afraid you'd forgotten about me.'

'No, Leah. I've never forgotten you. Not for a minute.'

'You've been crying, Gabriel. I can see it in your eyes. Is something wrong?'

'No, Leah, everything's fine.'

She gazed into the garden again. 'Look at the snow, Gabriel. Isn't it . . .'

She left the thought unfinished. A brief look of horror flashed in her eyes; Gabriel knew she had returned to Vienna. He took hold of her ruined hands and talked. About the painting he was restoring. About the villa where he had been living in Italy. About Gilah and Ari Shamron. Anything but Vienna. Anything but Chiara. Finally, her gaze fell upon him once more. She was back.

'Is it really you, Gabriel?'

'Yes, Leah. It's me.'

'I was afraid you'd—'

'Never, Leah.'

'You look tired.'

'I've been working very hard.'

'And you're too thin. Do you want something to eat?'

'I'm fine, Leah.'

'How long can you stay, my love?'

'Not long.'

'How is your wife?'

'She's well, Leah.'

'Is she pretty?'

'She's very pretty.'

'Are you taking good care of her?'

His eyes filled with tears. 'I'm trying my best.'

She looked away. 'Look at the snow, Gabriel. Isn't it beautiful?'

'Yes, Leah, it's beautiful.'

'The snow absolves Vienna of its sins. Snow falls on Vienna while the missiles rain on Tel Aviv.' She looked at him again. 'Make sure Dani is buckled into his seat tightly. The streets are slippery.'

'He's fine, Leah.'

'Give me a kiss.'

Gabriel pressed his lips against her scarred cheek.

Leah whispered, 'One last kiss.'

There exists in Tel Aviv and its suburbs a constellation of Office safe flats known as jump sites. They are places where, by doctrine and tradition, operatives spend their final night before departing Israel for missions abroad. Neither Gabriel nor any member of his team bothered to go to their assigned site that night. There wasn't time. In fact, they worked straight through the night and were so late arriving at Ben-Gurion that El Al officials had to slip them through the usual gauntlet of security procedures. In another break with tradition, the entire team traveled aboard the same aircraft: El Al Flight 315 to London. Only Gabriel had a role to play that evening; he separated from the others at Heathrow and made his way to Cheyne Walk in Chelsea. A few minutes after six, he rounded the corner into Cheyne Gardens and rapped his knuckle twice on the back of an unmarked black van. Graham Seymour opened the door and beckoned him inside. The target was in place. The sword was ready. The night raid was about to begin.

40. Chelsea, London

It was said of Viktor Orlov that he divided people into two categories: those willing to be used and those too stupid to realize they were being used. There were some who would have added a third: those willing to let Viktor steal their money. He made no secret of the fact he was a predator and a robber baron. Indeed, he wore these labels proudly, along with his ten-thousand-dollar Italian suits and his trademark striped shirts, specially made by a man in Hong Kong. The dramatic collapse of Communism had presented Orlov with the opportunity to earn a great deal of money in a brief period of time, and he had taken it. Orlov rarely apologized for anything, least of all the manner in which he had become rich. 'Had I been born an Englishman, my money might have come to me cleanly,' he told a British interviewer shortly after taking up residence in London. 'But I was born a Russian. And I earned a Russian fortune.'

Blessed with a natural facility for numbers, Orlov had been working as a physicist in the Soviet nuclear weapons program when the empire finally collapsed. While most of his colleagues continued to work without pay, Orlov decided to go into business and soon earned a small fortune importing computers, appliances, and other Western goods for the nascent Russian market. But his true riches would come later, after he acquired Russia's largest steel company and Ruzoil, the Siberian oil giant. *Fortune* magazine declared

Viktor Orlov Russia's richest man and one of the world's most influential businessmen. Not bad for a former government physicist who once had to share a communal apartment with two other Soviet families.

In the rough-and-tumble world of Russia's robber baron capitalism, a fortune like Orlov's could also be a dangerous thing. Quickly made, it could vanish in the blink of an eye. And it could make the holder and his family targets of envy and, sometimes, violence. Orlov had survived at least three attempts on his life and was rumored to have ordered several men killed in retaliation. But the greatest threat to his fortune would come not from those who wished to kill him but from the Kremlin. The current Russian president believed men like Orlov had stolen the country's most valuable assets, and it was his intention to steal them back. Shortly after taking control, he summoned Orlov to the Kremlin and demanded two things: his steel company and Ruzoil. 'And keep your nose out of politics,' he added. 'Otherwise, I'm going to cut it off.' Orlov agreed to relinquish his steel interests but not his oil company. The president was not amused. He immediately ordered his prosecutors to open a fraud-and-bribery investigation, and within a week a warrant was issued for Orlov's arrest. Orlov wisely fled to London. The target of a Russian extradition request, he still maintained nominal control of his shares in Ruzoil, now valued at twelve billion dollars. But they remained legally icebound, beyond the reach of both Orlov and the man who wanted them back, the Russian president.

Early in Orlov's exile, the press had hung on his every word. A reliable source of incendiary copy about Kremlin skullduggery, he could fill a room with reporters with an hour's notice. But the British press had tired of Viktor, just as the British people had grown weary of Russians in general. Few cared what he had to say anymore, and fewer still had the time or patience to sit through one of his lengthy tirades against his archrival, the Russian president. And so it came as no surprise to Gabriel and his team when Orlov readily accepted a request for an interview from one Olga Sukhova, former crusading reporter from *Moskovskaya Gazeta*, now an exile herself. Due to concerns over her security, she asked to see Orlov in his home and at night. Orlov, a bachelor and relentless womanizer, suggested she come at seven. 'And please come alone,' he added before ringing off.

She did indeed come at seven, though she was hardly alone. A maid took her coat and escorted her to the second-floor study, where Orlov greeted her lavishly in Russian. Gabriel and Graham Seymour, headphones over their ears, listened to the simultaneous translation.

'It's so lovely to see you again after all these years, Olga. Can I get you some tea or something stronger?'

41. Chelsea, London

Tea would be fine, thank you.'

Orlov could not conceal his disappointment. No doubt he had been hoping to impress Olga with a bottle or two of the Château Pétrus he drank like tap water. He ordered tea and savories from the maid, then watched with obvious satisfaction as Olga pretended to admire the vast office. It was rumored Orlov had been so impressed by his first visit to Buckingham Palace he had instructed his army of interior decorators to re-create its atmosphere at Cheyne Walk. The room, which was three times the size of Olga's old Moscow apartment, had reportedly been inspired by the queen's private study.

As Olga endured a tedious tour, she could not help but reflect upon how different her life was from Viktor's. Freed from Communism's yoke, Viktor had gone in search of money while Olga had set out to find truth. She had spent the better part of her career investigating the misdeeds of men like Viktor Orlov and believed such men bore much of the blame for the death of freedom and democracy in her country. Orlov's greed had helped to create the unique set of circumstances that had allowed the Kremlin to return the country to the authoritarianism of the past. Indeed, were it not for men like Viktor Orlov, the Russian president might still be a low-level functionary in the St Petersburg city government. Instead, he ruled the world's largest country with an iron fist and was thought to be one of Europe's richest men. Richer, even, than Orlov himself.

The tea arrived. They sat on opposite ends of the long brocade couch, facing a window hung with rich floor-to-ceiling drapery. It might have been possible to see Chelsea Embankment and the Thames had the curtains not been tightly drawn as a precaution against snipers – ironic, since Orlov had spent several million pounds acquiring one of London's best views. He was wearing a dark blue suit and a shirt with stripes the color of cranberries. One arm was flung along the back of the couch toward Olga, revealing a diamond-and-gold wristwatch of inestimable worth. The other lay along the armrest. He was twirling his spectacles restlessly. Veteran Orlov watchers would have recognized the tic. Orlov was perpetually in motion, even when he was sitting still.

'Please, Olga. Remind me when it was we last met.'

Orlov watchers would have recognized this, too. Viktor was not the sort to blurt 'I never forget a face.' He actually made a habit of *pretending* to forget people. It was a negotiating tactic. It said to opponents they were unmemorable. Insignificant. Without merit or consequence. Olga cared little about what Orlov thought of her, so she answered the question honestly. They had met just once, she reminded him. The encounter had taken place in Moscow, shortly before he fled to London.

'Ah, yes, I remember it now! If I recall, I became very angry at you because you were not interested in some valuable information I had for you.'

'If I had written the story you wanted me to write, I would have been killed.'

'The fearless Olga Sukhova was afraid? That never stopped you before. From what I hear, you're lucky to be alive. The Kremlin never said what happened in that stairwell last summer, but I know the truth. You were investigating Ivan Kharkov, and Ivan tried to silence you. Permanently.'

Olga made no reply.

'So you don't deny that's what happened?'

'Your sources have always been impeccable, Viktor.'

He acknowledged the compliment with a twirl of his eyewear. 'It's a shame we haven't had the opportunity to meet again until now. As you might expect, I followed your case with great interest. I tried to find some way of making contact with you after your defection was made public, but you were quite difficult to locate. I asked my friends in British intelligence to pass a message to you, but they refused.'

'Why didn't you just ask Grigori where I was?'

The spectacles went still, just for a few seconds. 'I did, but he refused to tell me. I know you two are friends. I suppose he doesn't want to share you.'

Olga took note of the tense: *I know you two are friends* . . . He didn't seem to know about Grigori's absence – unless he was lying, which was a distinct possibility. Viktor Orlov was genetically incapable of telling the truth.

'The old Viktor wouldn't have bothered to ask Grigori where I was hiding. He would have just had him followed.'

'Don't think it didn't cross my mind.'

'But you never did?'

'Follow Grigori?' He shook his head. 'The British give my bodyguards a good deal of latitude, but they would never tolerate private surveillance operations. Remember, I am still a Russian citizen. I am also the target of a formal extradition request. I try not to do anything to make my British hosts too angry.'

'Other than criticize the Kremlin whenever you feel like it.'

'They can't expect me to remain mute. When I see injustice, I am compelled to speak. It's my nature. That's why Grigori and I get along so well.' He paused, then asked, 'How is he, by the way?'

'Grigori?' She sipped her tea, and said she hadn't spoken to him for several weeks. 'You?'

'Actually, I had one of my assistants put a call to him the other day. We never heard back. I assume he's very busy on his book.' Orlov gave her a conspiratorial glance. 'Some of my people have been working with Grigori in secret. As you might expect, I want this book to be a big success.'

'Why am I not surprised, Viktor?'

'It's my nature. I enjoy helping others. Which is why I'm so pleased you're here. Tell me about the story you're working on. Tell me how I can be of service.'

'It's a story about a defector. A defector who disappeared without a trace.'

'Does the defector have a name?'

'Grigori Nikolaevich Bulganov.'

In the surveillance van, Graham Seymour removed his headphones and looked at Gabriel.

'Very nicely played.'

'She's good, Graham. Very good.'

'Can I have her when you're done?'

235

Gabriel raised a finger to his lips. Viktor Orlov was speaking again. They heard a burst of rapid Russian, followed by the voice of the translator.

'Tell me what you know, Olga. Tell me everything.'

42. Chelsea, London

Orlov was suddenly in motion in several places at once. The spectacles were twirling, the fingers were drumming on the back of the brocade couch, and the left eye was twitching anxiously. When he was a child, the twitch had made him the target of merciless teasing and bullying. It had made him burn with hatred, and that hatred had driven him to succeed. Viktor Orlov wanted to beat everyone. And it was all because of the twitch in his left eye.

'Are you sure he's missing?'

'I'm sure.'

'When did he disappear?'

'January the tenth. Six-twelve in the evening. On his way to chess.'

'How do you know this?'

'I'm Olga Sukhova. I know everything.'

'Do the British know?'

'Of course.'

'What do they think happened?'

'They believe he redefected. They think he's now back at Lubyanka telling his superiors everything he learned about your operation while he was working for you.'

The eye was now blinking involuntarily like the shutter of a high-speed automatic camera.

'Why didn't they tell me?'

'I'm not sure you were their first concern, Viktor. But don't worry. It's not true about Grigori. He didn't redefect. He was kidnapped.' She let it sink in, then added, 'By Ivan Kharkov.'

'How do you know this?'

'I'm Olga Sukhova.'

'And you know everything.'

'Not quite everything. But perhaps you can help me fill in some of the missing pieces. I don't know the identity of the man Ivan hired to handle the kidnapping. All I know is that this man is very good. He's a professional.' She paused. 'The kind of man *you* used to hire in Moscow – in the bad old days, Viktor, when you had a problem that just wouldn't go away.'

'Be careful, Ms. Sukhova.'

'I'm always careful. I never had to print a single retraction in all the years I worked for the *Gazeta*. Not one.'

'That's because you never wrote a story about me.'

'If I had, it would have been airtight and completely accurate.'

'So you say.'

'I know a great deal about the way you made your money, Viktor. I did you a favor by never publishing that information in the *Gazeta*. And now you're going to do one for me. You're going to help me find the man who kidnapped my friend. And if you don't, I'm going to pour everything I have in my notebooks into the most unflattering exposé ever written about you.'

'And I'll take you to court.'

'*Court?* Do you really think I'm afraid of a British court?'

She reached into her handbag and withdrew a photograph: a man standing in the arrivals hall of Heathrow Airport. Orlov slipped on his spectacles. The eye twitched nervously. He pressed a button on the side table, and the maid materialized.

'Bring me a bottle of the Pétrus. *Now*.'

He tried to slip out of the noose, of course, but Olga was having none of it. She calmly recited a couple of names, a date, and the details of a certain transaction involving a company Viktor once owned – just enough to let him know her threats were not idle. Viktor drank his first glass of Pétrus quickly and poured another.

Olga had never seen Viktor show fear before, but he was clearly afraid now. An experienced reporter, she recognized the manifestations of that fear in the behavior that came next: the exclamations of disbelief, the attempts at misdirection, the effort to foist blame onto others. Viktor tended to blame all his problems on Russia. So it came as no surprise to Olga when he did so now.

'You have to remember what it was like in the nineties. We tried to snap our fingers and turn Russia into a normal capitalist country overnight. It wasn't possible. It was utopian thinking, just like Communism.'

'I remember, Viktor. I was there, too.'

'Then you surely recall what it was like for people like me who were able to make a bit of money. Everyone wanted a piece of it. Our lives were in constant danger, along with the lives of our families. There was the mafia, of course, but sometimes our competitors were just as dangerous. Everyone hired private armies to protect themselves and to wage war on their rivals. It was the Wild East.'

Orlov held the goblet of wine up to the light. Heavy and rich, it glowed like freshly spilled blood.

'There was no shortage of soldiers. No one wanted to work for the government anymore, not when there was real money to be made in the private sector. Officers were leaving the Russian security services in droves. Some didn't bother to quit their jobs. They just put in an hour or two at the office and moonlighted.'

Olga had once written an exposé about this practice – a story about a pair of FSB officers who investigated the Russian mafia by day and killed for them by night. The FSB men had vehemently denied the story. Then they had threatened to kill her.

'Some of these men weren't very talented,' Orlov continued. 'They could handle simple jobs, street killings and the like. But there were others who were highly trained professionals.' Orlov studied the photograph. 'This man fell into the second category.'

'You've met him?'

He hesitated, then nodded. 'It was in Moscow, in another lifetime. I'm not going to discuss the nature or circumstances of this meeting.'

'I don't care about the meeting, Viktor. I only want to know about the man in that photograph.'

He drank some more of the wine and relented. 'His KGB code name was Comrade Zhirlov. He specialized in assassinations, abductions, and finding men who wished not to be found. He was also supposed to be very good with poisons and toxins. He put those skills to good use when he went into private practice. He did the kind of jobs others might refuse because they were too dangerous. It made him rich. He worked inside Russia for a few years, then broadened his horizons.'

'Where did he go?'

'Western Europe. He speaks several languages and has many passports from his days with the KGB.'

'Where does he live?'

'Who knows? And I doubt even the famous Olga Sukhova will be able to find him. In fact, I highly recommend you forget about trying. You'll only get yourself killed.'

'Obviously, he's still selling his services on the open market.'

'That is what I've heard. I've also heard his prices have increased dramatically. Only men like Ivan Kharkov can afford to hire him any longer.'

'And *you*, Viktor.'

'I've never engaged in such things.'

'And no one is making that accusation. But let us suppose one required the services of a man like this. How would one make contact with him? Where would one go?'

Viktor lapsed into silence. He was a Russian – and like all Russians, he suspected someone was always listening. In this case, he happened to be correct. For a moment, the two men seated in the back of the MI5 surveillance van feared their source was unwilling to take the final step. Then they heard a single word that required no translation.

Geneva.

There was a man there, Orlov said. A security consultant to wealthy Russians. A broker. A middleman.

'I believe his name is Chernov. Yes, I'm sure of it now. Chernov.'

'Does he have a first name?'

'It might be Vladimir.'

'Do you happen to know where he keeps his office?'

'Just off the rue du Mont-Blanc. I believe I might have the address.'

'You wouldn't have a telephone number, would you?'

'Actually, I might have his mobile.'

Under normal circumstances, Gabriel would never have bothered to write down the name and telephone number. Now, with his wife in Ivan's hands, he did not trust his usually flawless memory. By the time he had finished jotting down the information, Olga was slipping through Viktor's wrought-iron gate. A taxi collected her and brought her around the corner to Cheyne Gardens. Gabriel climbed in next to her and headed to London City Airport, where an American-supplied Gulfstream G500 was waiting. The rest of his team was already on board, along with its newest addition, Sarah Bancroft. The tower log would later show the plane departed at 10:18 p.m. For reasons never explained, its destination was not recorded.

43. King Saul Boulevard, Tel Aviv

It might not have seemed like much – a name, a business address, a pair of phone numbers – but in the hands of an intelligence service like the Office it was enough to open a man up stem to stern. Shamron gave the information to the bloodhounds of Research and shot it across the Atlantic to Langley as well. Then, with Rami at his side, he headed home to Tiberias.

It was after midnight when he arrived. He undressed in darkness and crept into bed quietly so as not to wake Gilah. He didn't bother to close his eyes. Sleep came rarely, and never under circumstances like these. Rather than try, he relived each minute of the past two days and explored the remotest regions of his past. And he wondered when he might be given the chance to do something of value, something other than making a nuisance of himself or taking in a message from London. And he wrestled with two questions: Where was Ivan? And why hadn't they heard from him?

Oddly enough, Shamron was focused on that very thought when the telephone at his bedside rang at 4:13 a.m. He knew the exact time because, out of habit, he glanced at his wristwatch before answering. Fearful he was about to be informed of yet another death, he held the receiver to his ear for a moment before grumbling his name. The voice that responded was instantly familiar. It was the voice of an old rival. The voice of an occasional ally. He wanted a word with Shamron in private. He was wondering whether Shamron was free to come to Paris. In fact, said the voice, it would be wise for Shamron to find some way of getting on the nine o'clock flight out of Ben-Gurion. Yes, said the voice, it was urgent. No, it couldn't wait. Shamron hung up the phone and switched on the bedside lamp. Gilah rose and went to make the coffee.

Ivan had chosen his envoy with care. There were few people who had been in the trade longer than Ari Shamron, but Sergei Korovin was one of them. After spending the 1950s in Eastern Europe, the KGB taught him to speak Arabic and sent him off to make mischief in the Middle East. He went first to Baghdad, then Damascus, then Tripoli, and finally Cairo. It was in the tense summer of 1973 that Korovin and Shamron first crossed paths. Operation Wrath of God was in full swing in Europe, the terrorists of Black September were killing Israelis wherever they could be found, and Shamron alone was convinced the Egyptians were preparing for war. He had a spy in Cairo who was telling him so – a spy who was then arrested by the Egyptian secret service. With his execution just hours away, Shamron had reached out to Korovin and asked him to intercede. After weeks of negotiations, Shamron's spy was allowed to stagger across the Israeli lines in the Sinai. He had been severely beaten and tortured, but he was alive. One month later, as Israel was preparing for Yom Kippur, the Egyptians staged a surprise attack.

By the mid-1970s, Sergei Korovin was back in Moscow, working his way steadily up the ranks of the KGB. Promoted to general, he was placed in charge of Department 18, which dealt with the Arab world, and was later given command of Directorate R, which handled operational planning and analysis. In 1984 he took control of the entire First Chief Directorate, a position he held until the KGB was disbanded by Boris Yeltsin. If given the chance, Sergei Korovin would have probably killed the Russian president himself. Instead, he burned his most sensitive files and went quietly into retirement. But Shamron knew better than anyone there was really no such thing, especially for Russians. There was a saying within the brotherhood of the sword and the shield: once a KGB officer, always a KGB officer. Only in death was one truly free. And, sometimes, not even then.

Shamron and Korovin had maintained contact over the years. They had met to swap stories, share information, and do each other the occasional favor. It would have been wrong to describe them as friends, more like kindred spirits. They knew the rules of the game and shared a healthy cynicism for the men they served. Korovin was also one of the few people in the world who could keep pace with Shamron's tobacco intake. And like Shamron, he had little patience for trivial matters, such as food, fashion, or even money. 'It's a shame Sergei wasn't born an Israeli,' Shamron once told Gabriel. 'I would have enjoyed having him on our side.'

Shamron knew time could be hard on Russian men. They tended to age in the blink of an eye – young and virile one minute, wrinkled paper the next. But the man who entered the salon of the Hôtel de Crillon shortly after three that afternoon was still the tall, erect figure Shamron had first met many years earlier. Two bodyguards trailed slowly behind him; two others had arrived an hour earlier and were seated not far from Shamron. They were drinking tea; Shamron, mineral water. Rami had delivered the bottle himself after instructing the bartender not to remove the cap and twice requesting clean glasses. Even so, Shamron had yet to touch it. He was wearing his dark suit and silver tie: Shamron the shady businessman who played baccarat well.

Like Shamron, Sergei Korovin could discuss matters of import in many different languages. Most of their meetings had been conducted in German, and it was German they spoke now. Korovin, after settling himself into a chair, immediately thumbed open his silver cigarette case. Shamron had to remind him smoking was no longer permitted in Paris. Korovin frowned.

'Do they still let you drink vodka?'

'If you ask nicely.'

'I'm like you, Ari. I don't *ask* for anything.' He ordered a vodka, then looked at Shamron. 'It was reassuring to hear your voice last night. I was afraid you might be dead. It's the hardest thing about growing old, the death of one's friends.'

'I never knew you had any.'

'Friends? A couple.' He gave a faint smile. 'You always played the game well, Ari. You had many admirers at Yasenevo. We studied your operations. We even learned a thing or two.'

Yasenevo was the old headquarters of the First Chief Directorate, sometimes referred to as Moscow Center. It was now headquarters of the SVR.

'Where's my file?' Shamron asked.

'Locked away where it belongs. For a time, I feared all our dirty laundry would be made public. Thankfully, the new regime put an end to that. Our president understands that he who controls history controls the future. He lauds the achievements of the Soviet Union while minimizing its so-called crimes and abuses.'

'And you approve?'

'Of course. Russia has no democratic tradition. To have democracy in Russia would be tantamount to imposing Islamic law in Israel. Do you see my point, Ari?'

'I believe I do, Sergei.'

The waiter presented the vodka with great ceremony and withdrew. Korovin drank without hesitation.

'So, Ari, now that we're alone—'

'Are we alone, Sergei?'

'No one but my security.' He paused. 'And you, Ari?'

Shamron glanced at Rami, who was seated near the entrance of the ornate salon, pretending to read the *Herald Tribune*.

'Just one?'

'Trust me, Sergei, one is all I need.'

'That's not what I hear. I'm told a couple of your boys got themselves killed the other night, and the Italians are trying to keep it quiet for you. It won't work, by the way. My sources tell me the story is going to blow up in your face tomorrow morning in one of the big Italian dailies.'

'Really? And what's the story going to say?'

'That two Office agents were killed during a drive through the Italian countryside.'

'But nothing about an agent being kidnapped?'

'No.'

'And the perpetrators?'

'There will be speculation it was an Iranian job.' He paused, then said, 'But we both know that's not true.'

Korovin drank more of his vodka. The topic had been broached. Now both men would have to proceed carefully. Shamron knew that Korovin was in a position to admit little. It didn't matter. The Russian could say more with a raised eyebrow than most men managed during an hour-long lecture. Shamron made the next move.

'We've always been honest with each other, Sergei.'

'As honest as two men can be in this business.'

'So let me be honest with you now. We believe our agent was taken by Ivan Kharkov. We believe it was in retaliation for an operation we ran against him last fall.'

'I know all about your operation, Ari. The whole world does. But Ivan Kharkov had absolutely nothing to do with the disappearance of this woman.'

Shamron ignored everything about Korovin's response except for a single word: *woman*. It was all he needed to know. The Russian had just laid his bona fides upon the table. The negotiation could now begin. It would follow a set of carefully prescribed guidelines and be conducted mainly with falsehoods and half-truths. Nothing would be admitted and no demands would ever be stated. It wasn't necessary. Shamron and Korovin both spoke the language of lies.

'Are you sure, Sergei? Are you sure Ivan's hands are clean?'

'I've spoken to representatives of Ivan personally.'

Another pause, then, 'Have you heard anything about the condition of the woman?'

'Only that she's alive and being well cared for.'

'That's good to know, Sergei. If that could continue, we would be most grateful.'

'I'll see what I can do. As you know, Ivan is very upset about his current circumstances.'

'He has no one to blame but himself.'

'Ivan doesn't see it that way. He believes these charges and accusations in the West are all lies and fabrications. He would have never been so foolish as to enter into a deal to supply our missiles to al-Qaeda. In fact, he assures me he's not even involved in the arms business.'

'I'll make sure to pass that along to the Americans.'

'There's something else you should pass along.'

'Anything, Sergei.'

'Ivan believes his children were taken from him illegally in France last summer. Ivan wants them back.'

Shamron shrugged his shoulders, feigning surprise. 'I never knew the Americans had them.'

'We believe this to be the case, despite the official statements to the contrary. Perhaps someone could put in a good word with the Americans on Ivan's behalf.' Now it was Korovin's turn to shrug. 'I couldn't say for certain, but I believe it would go a long way toward helping you recover your missing agent.'

Korovin had just taken another step closer toward offering a quid pro quo. Shamron chose the path of prevarication.

'We're not a large service like you, Sergei. We're a small family. We want our agent back, and we're willing to do whatever we can. But I have very little sway over the Americans. If they *do* have the children, it's unlikely they would agree to hand them over to Ivan, even under circumstances such as these.'

'You give yourself too little credit, Ari. Go to the Americans. Talk some sense into them. Convince them to put Ivan's children on a plane. Once they're in Russia where they belong, I'm certain your agent will turn up.'

Korovin had laid a contract upon the table. Shamron did due diligence.

'Safe and sound?'

'Safe and sound.'

'There is one other matter, Sergei. We want Grigori Bulganov back as well.'

'Grigori Bulganov is none of your concern.'

Shamron conceded the point. 'And if I'm able to convince the Americans to surrender the children? How long would we have to make the arrangements?'

'I couldn't say for certain, but not terribly long.'

'I need to know, Sergei.'

'My response would only be hypothetical in nature.'

'All right, hypothetically speaking, how long do we have?'

Korovin sipped his vodka and said, 'Seventy-two hours.'

'That's not long, Sergei.'

'It is what it is.'

'How do I contact you?'

'You don't. We'll meet again on Tuesday at four in the afternoon. As one friend to another, I would strongly advise you to have an answer by then.'

'Where shall we meet?'

'Is one still permitted to smoke in the Jardin des Tuileries?'

'For now.'

'Then let's meet there. The benches near the Jeu de Paume.'

'Four o'clock?'

Korovin nodded. Four o'clock.

44. Hotel Bristol, Geneva

The news from Paris was quickly flashed to several points around the globe: to the Operations Desk at King Saul Boulevard, to Thames House in London, and to CIA Headquarters in Langley. And to the stately Hotel Bristol in Geneva, temporary home of Gabriel and his team. Though they were deeply relieved to hear Chiara was indeed alive, there was nothing resembling celebration. Ivan's terms were, of course, unacceptable. They were unacceptable to Shamron. Unacceptable to the Americans. And especially unacceptable to Gabriel. No one was prepared to ask Elena Kharkov to sacrifice her children, least of all a man who had once lost one of his own. Ivan's offer did serve one valuable purpose, though. It gave them a bit of time and some additional room to maneuver. Not much time, just seventy-two hours, and very little room. They were going to pursue Chiara and Grigori along parallel paths. One was the path of negotiation; the other, the path of violence. Gabriel would have to move quickly, and he would be forced to take chances. For now, he had just one man in his sights: Vladimir Chernov.

'Everything Viktor Orlov said checks out,' Navot told Gabriel late that afternoon over coffee in the piano bar. 'We're monitoring his phones and keeping watch on his office and apartment. King Saul Boulevard is making headway on getting into his computers. He's got good security software, but it won't keep the cyberboys out long.'

'How much do we know about his past?'

'He was definitely KGB. He worked in the Ninth Directorate, the division that protected Soviet leaders and the Kremlin. Apparently, Chernov was assigned to Gorbachev's detail at the end.'

'And when the KGB disbanded?'

'He wasted very little time going into private practice. He formed a security company in Moscow and advised the newly rich on how to keep themselves and their valuables safe. He did quite well for himself.'

'When did he set up shop here?'

'Five years ago. Langley's had concerns about him for some time. The Americans won't shed a tear if he has a mishap.'

'Age?'

'Forty-six.'

'Physically fit, I take it?'

'He's built like Lenin's Tomb, and he keeps in shape.'

Navot handed Gabriel his PDA. On the screen was a surveillance photograph shot earlier that afternoon. It showed Chernov entering his office building. He was a big man, over six feet tall, with deeply receded hair and small eyes set in a round, fleshy face.

'Does he have a security detail of his own?'

'Rides around town in a big Audi sedan. The windows are clearly bulletproof. So is the guy who sits at his side. I'd say that both the bodyguard and the driver are extremely well armed.'

'Family?'

'The ex-wife and children are back in Moscow. He's got a girlfriend here in Geneva.'

'Swiss?'

'Russian. A kid from the provinces. Sells gloves around the corner from Chernov's office.'

'Does the kid have a name?'

'Ludmila Akulova. They're having dinner out tonight. A restaurant called Les Armures.'

Gabriel knew it. It was in the Old Town, near the Hôtel de Ville.

'What time?'

'Eight-thirty.'

'How far is Vladimir's apartment from Les Armures?'

'Not far. He lives near the cathedral.'

'What's the building like?'

'Small and traditional. There's an intercom with a keypad at the street entrance. Tenants can use their keys or punch in the code. We had a look inside earlier this afternoon. There's an elevator, but Vladimir's flat is just one floor up.'

'And the street?'

'Even in the middle of the day it's quiet. At night . . .' Navot's voice trailed off. 'Dead.'

'Ever eaten at Les Armures?'

'Can't say I've had the pleasure.'

'If they sit down to dinner at 8:30, it's going to be late by the time they get to that apartment. We'll take him then.'

'You're assuming Ludmila will be accompanying him?'

'Yes, Uzi, I'm assuming that.'

'What are we going to do with her?'

'Scare the daylights out of her and leave her behind.'

'What about the driver and the bodyguard?'

'I'm going to need them to make a point.'

'We're going to require a diversion of some sort.'

'Your diversion is upstairs in Room 702. She's registered under the name Irene Moore. Her real name is Sarah Bancroft.'

'Where do you want to take them?'

'Somewhere on the other side of the border. Somewhere isolated. Tell Housekeeping we're going to need maid service. Tell them it's going to be messy.'

There are many sophisticates who dismiss Geneva as dull and provincial, a Calvinist handmaiden too frigid to loosen her blouse. But they have not heard the peal of her church bells on a cold winter's night or watched snowflakes settling gently over her cobblestoned streets. And they have not dined at a quiet corner table at Les Armures in the company of a beautiful Russian woman. The salads were crisp, the veal superb, and the wine, a 2006 Bâtard-Montrachet by Joseph Drouhin, was delivered at the perfect temperature by the attentive sommelier. They took their time with their cognac, customary on a snowy February night in Geneva, and at eleven o'clock were holding hands as they climbed into the back of the Mercedes sedan parked outside the old Arsenal. All signs pointed to a night of passion at the apartment near the cathedral. That indeed might have been the case were it not for the woman waiting outside the entrance in the snow.

She had skin like alabaster and was wearing a leather jacket and fishnet stockings. Had her makeup not been smeared from a night of weeping, she might have been very pretty. The couple who emerged from the back of the

Mercedes initially paid her little attention. A waif, they must have thought. A working girl. Maybe a drug addict. Certainly no threat to a man like Vladimir Chernov. After all, Chernov had once served as bodyguard to the last leader of the Soviet Union. Chernov could handle anything. Or so he thought.

Her voice was plaintive at first, childlike. She referred to Chernov by his first name, clearly a shock, and accused him of many crimes of the heart. He had made declarations of love, she said. He had made promises about the future. He had pledged financial support for the child she was now caring for alone. With Ludmila now seething, Chernov tried to tell the woman she had obviously mistaken him for someone else. This earned him a hard slap across the face, which had the effect of drawing the bodyguards from the car.

The mêlée that ensued lasted precisely twenty-seven seconds. A video recording of it exists and is used for training purposes to this day. It must be said that, at the outset, Chernov's Russian bodyguards acted with admirable restraint. Confronted with a young woman who was clearly disturbed and delusional, they tried to bring her gently under control and remove her from the immediate area. Her reaction, two hard kicks to their shins, served only to escalate matters. The situation intensified with the arrival of four gentlemen who just happened to be walking along the quiet street. The largest of the four, a heavy-shouldered man with strawberry blond hair, went in first, followed by a dark-haired man with a pockmarked face. Words were exchanged, threats were made, and, finally, punches were thrown. These were not the wild, undisciplined blows thrown by amateurs. They were tight and brutal, the kind that were capable of inflicting permanent damage. Under the right circumstances, they could even cause instant death.

But instant death was not their goal, and the four gentlemen tempered their assault to make certain it only rendered their victims unconscious. Once the men were incapacitated, two parked cars came suddenly to life. Vladimir Chernov was thrown into one, his bodyguards into the other. As for Ludmila Akulova, she escaped with only a verbal warning, delivered in fluent Russian by a man with a bloodless face and eyes the color of glacial ice. 'If you say a word about this, we will kill you. And then we'll kill your parents. And then we'll kill every member of your family.' As the cars sped away, Gabriel found himself unable to look away from Ludmila's stricken face. He believed in the women. The women, he said, were Russia's only hope.

45. Haute-Savoie, France

The house stood in the Haute-Savoie region of France, in an isolated valley above the shores of Lake Annecy. Neat and tidy, with a steeply pitched roof, it was more than a kilometer from its nearest neighbor. Yossi had moved in the previous evening, posing as a British writer of mysteries, and had carefully prepared the premises for the interrogation that was to come. He was standing outside as the two cars made their way slowly up the winding road, snow falling through the beams of their headlamps.

Gabriel emerged alone from the front passenger seat of the first car, a Renault station wagon, and followed Yossi into the sitting room of the house. The furniture was piled in one corner, the tile floor covered entirely in plastic drop cloths. In the open hearth burned a large fire, just as Gabriel had ordered. He added two more logs, then headed outside again. A third car had pulled into the drive. Eli Lavon was leaning against the hood.

'Were we followed?' Gabriel asked.

Lavon shook his head.

'You're sure, Eli?'

'I'm sure.'

'Take Yossi. Go back to Geneva. Wait there with the others. We won't be long.'

'I'm staying here with you.'

'You're a watcher, Eli. The best there ever was. This isn't for you.'

'Maybe it isn't for you, either.'

Gabriel ignored the remark and glanced at Navot, who was behind the wheel of the Renault. A moment later, three Russians, sedated and trussed, were wobbling drunkenly toward the entrance of the house. Lavon placed a hand on Gabriel's shoulder.

'Be careful in there, Gabriel. If you're not, you might lose more than another wife.'

Lavon climbed behind the wheel of the car without another word and headed down the valley. Gabriel watched the red taillights disappear behind a veil of snow, then turned and headed into the house.

They stripped them to their underwear and secured them to a trio of metal outdoor chairs. Gabriel gave each of the three men a shot of stimulant, small doses for the bodyguard and driver, a larger one for Vladimir Chernov. His head rose slowly from his chest, and, blinking rapidly, he surveyed his surroundings. His two men were seated directly in front of him, eyes wide with terror. Standing in a line behind them were Yaakov, Mikhail, Navot, and Gabriel. In Gabriel's left hand was a .45 caliber Glock with a suppressor screwed onto the end of the barrel. In his right was a photograph: a man standing in the arrivals hall of Heathrow Airport. Gabriel glanced at Yaakov, who tore away the packing tape wrapped around the lower portion of Chernov's head. Now missing a good deal of hair, Chernov screamed in pain. Gabriel hit him hard across the brow with the Glock and told him to shut his mouth. Chernov, blood streaming into his left eye, obeyed.

'Do you know who I am, Vladimir?'

'I've never seen you before in my life. Please, whoever you are, this is all some sort—'

'It's no mistake, Vladimir. Take a good look at my face. You've seen it before, I'm sure.'

'No, never.'

'We're getting off to a bad start, you and I. You're lying to me. And if you continue to lie to me, you'll never leave this place. Tell me the truth, Vladimir, and you and your men will be allowed to live.'

'I *am* telling you the truth! I've never seen your face before!'

'Not even in photographs? Surely they must have given you a photo of me.'

'Who?'

'The men who came to you when they wanted to hire Comrade Zhirlov to find me.'

'I've never heard of this man. I am a legitimate security consultant. I demand you release me and my men at once. Otherwise—'

'Otherwise what, Vladimir?'

Chernov fell silent.

'You have a narrow window of opportunity, Vladimir. A *very* narrow window. I am going to ask you a question, and you are going to tell me the truth.' Gabriel held the photograph in front of Chernov's face. 'Tell me where I can find this man.'

'I've never seen him before in my life.'

'Are you sure that's the answer you want to give me, Vladimir?'

'It is the truth!'

Gabriel shook his head sadly and walked behind Chernov's driver. Gabriel had been told his name. He had already forgotten it. His name didn't matter. He didn't need a name where he was going. Chernov, judging by his insolent expression, clearly thought Gabriel was bluffing. Obviously, the Russian had never heard of Ari Shamron's twelfth commandment: *We do not wave our guns around like gangsters and make idle threats. We draw our weapons in the field for one reason and one reason only.* Gabriel placed the gun to the back of the man's head and tilted the angle slightly downward. Then, with his eyes boring into Chernov's face, he squeezed the trigger.

46. Haute-Savoie, France

There is a popular misconception about suppressors. They do not actually silence a weapon, especially when that weapon is a .45 caliber Glock. The hollow-tipped round entered the driver's skull with a rather loud thump and exited through his mouth, taking much of his jaw and chin with it. Had the gun been level at the time of firing, the projectile might have continued into Vladimir Chernov. Instead, it slammed harmlessly into the floor. Chernov didn't escape completely unscathed, though. His muscular torso was now splattered with blood, brain tissue, and bone fragments. A few seconds later came the contents of his own stomach: the fine meal he had shared with Ludmila Akulova a few hours earlier at Les Armures. It was a good sign. Chernov may have trafficked in death and violence, but the sight of a little blood made him sick. With luck, he might break soon. Gabriel held the photograph in front of his face again and posed the same question: 'Who is this man, and where can I find him?' Unfortunately, Chernov's response was the same.

'I'm sure you've heard of waterboarding, Vladimir. We have a different technique we use when we need information quickly.' Gabriel gazed into the fire for a moment. 'We call it fireboarding.' He looked at Chernov again. 'Have you ever seen a man fireboarded before, Vladimir?'

When Chernov made no response, Gabriel shot a glance

at the others. Navot and Yaakov seized hold of the second bodyguard and, still attached to the chair, rammed him face-first into the fire. They left him in no more than ten seconds. Even so, when he emerged his hair was smoking and his face blackened and blistered. He was also screaming in agony.

They set him directly in front of Chernov, so that the Russian could see the horrible result of his intransigence. Then Gabriel placed the Glock against the back of the bodyguard's head and ended his suffering. Chernov, now drenched in blood, gazed in horror at the two dead men before him. Mikhail covered his mouth with duct tape and gave him a hard backhand across the cheek. Gabriel placed the photograph in his lap and said he would be back in five minutes.

He returned at the fifty-ninth second of the fourth minute and ripped the duct tape from Chernov's mouth. Then he gave him a stark choice. They could have a pleasant conversation, one professional to another, or Chernov could go into the fire like his now-deceased bodyguard. It wouldn't be a quick sear, Gabriel warned. It would be a slow roast. One limb at a time. And there would be no bullet to the back of the head to quell the pain.

Gabriel did not have to wait long for his answer. Ten seconds. No more. Chernov said he wanted to talk. Chernov said he was sorry. Chernov said he wanted to help.

47. Haute-Savoie, France

They gave him clothing to wear and a dose of alprazolam to take the edge off his anxiety. He was permitted to sit in a proper chair with his hands unrestrained, though the chair was turned in such a way that he could not help but see his two dead employees, grim reminders of the fate that awaited him if he retreated once again into claims of ignorance. Within a few hours, the corpses would vanish from the face of the earth. Vladimir Chernov would vanish with them. Whether he met his death painlessly or with extreme violence depended on one thing: answering each and every one of Gabriel's questions truthfully.

The alprazolam had the added benefit of loosening Chernov's tongue, and it took only the gentlest prodding from Gabriel to get him talking. He began by paying Gabriel a compliment over the operation they had staged on his doorstep. 'The KGB could not have done it any better,' he said, without a trace of irony in his voice.

'You'll forgive me if I'm not flattered.'

'You've just killed two men in cold blood, Allon. You have no right to quibble about comparisons to my old service.'

'You know my name.'

Chernov managed a weak smile. 'Would it be possible to have a cigarette?'

'Cigarettes are bad for your health.'

'Is it not a tradition to give the condemned a cigarette?'

'Keep talking, Vladimir, and I'll let you live.'

'After what I've seen tonight? Do you take me for a fool, Allon?'

'Not a fool, Vladimir – just an ex-KGB hood who somehow managed to claw his way out of the gutter. But let's keep this civil, shall we? You were just about to tell me when you first met the man in that photograph.' A pause, then, 'The man known as Comrade Zhirlov.'

The cocktail of narcotics coursing through Chernov's bloodstream left him unable to mount another campaign of denial. Nor was he able to conceal his surprise over the fact that Gabriel knew the code name of one of the KGB's most secretive black operators.

'It was 'ninety-five or 'ninety-six. I had a small security company. I didn't land the likes of Ivan Kharkov and Viktor Orlov, but I was doing quite nicely for myself. Comrade Zhirlov approached me with a lucrative offer. He'd acquired a reputation in Moscow. It was getting much too dangerous for him to be in direct contact with his customers. He needed someone to act as a middleman – a booking agent, if you will. Otherwise, he wasn't going to live to enjoy the fruits of his labor.'

'And you volunteered to be that person – for a commission, of course.'

'Ten percent. When someone needed a job done, they came to me, and I took the proposal to him. If he felt like doing it, he would name a price. Then I would go back to the client and negotiate the final deal. All money flowed through me. I laundered it through my consulting business and paid Comrade Zhirlov a fee for services rendered. You might find this hard to believe, but he actually paid taxes on income he earned killing and kidnapping people.'

'Only in Russia.'

'They were crazy times, Allon. It's easy to sit in judgment of us, but you've never seen your country and your money disappear in the blink of an eye. People did what they had to do in order to survive. It was the law of the jungle. Truly.'

'Spare me the sad story, Vladimir. It wouldn't have been a jungle if not for you and your fellow travelers in the Russian mafia. But I digress. You were telling me about Comrade Zhirlov. In fact, you were about to tell me his real name.'

'I'd like a cigarette.'

'You are in no position to make demands.'

'Please, Allon. I had a pack in the pocket of my overcoat last night. If it wouldn't be too much trouble, I would like one now. I swear I won't try anything.'

Gabriel glanced at Yaakov. The cigarette, when it came, was already lit. Chernov took a long pull, then told Gabriel the name he wanted to hear. It was Petrov. Anton Dmitrievich Petrov.

Not that it mattered, Chernov added quickly. Petrov hadn't used the name in years. The son of a KGB colonel assigned to the East Berlin *rezidentura*, he had been born in the German Democratic Republic during the darkest days of the Cold War. An only child, he had been permitted to play with German children and was completely bilingual at an early age. Indeed, Petrov's German was so good he was able to pass himself off as a native on the streets of East Berlin. The KGB quietly encouraged Petrov's linguistic skills by allowing him to remain in the DDR for his schooling rather than return to the Soviet Union. After graduating with honors from a gymnasium in East Berlin, he attended the prestigious University of Leipzig, where he earned a degree in chemistry. Petrov briefly considered pursuing an advanced degree or even a career in medicine. Moscow Center, however, had other plans.

Within days of graduation, he was summoned to Moscow and offered a job with the KGB. Few young men were foolish enough to refuse such an offer, and Petrov, a member of the KGB's extended family, entertained no such thoughts. After undergoing two years of training at the KGB's Red Banner Institute at Yasenevo, he was given the code name Comrade Zhirlov and sent back to East Berlin. A month later, with the help of a Soviet spy inside the West German intelligence service, he slipped through the Iron Curtain and established himself as an 'illegal' agent in the West German city of Hamburg.

Petrov's very existence was known only to a select group of senior generals inside the First Chief Directorate. His assignment was not to conduct espionage against America and its NATO allies but to wage war on dissidents, defectors, and other assorted troublemakers who dared to challenge the authority of the Soviet state. Armed with a half dozen false passports and a limitless supply of money, he hunted his quarry and meticulously planned their demise. He specialized in the use of poisons and other deadly toxins, some that produced near-instantaneous death, others that took weeks or months to prove lethal. Because he was a chemist, Petrov was able to assist in the design of his poisons and the weapons that delivered them. His favorite device was a ring, worn on his right hand, that injected the victim with a small dose of a deadly nerve toxin. One handshake, one clap on the back, was all it took to kill.

'As you might expect, Petrov didn't take the fall of the Soviet Union well. He never had any qualms about killing dissidents and traitors. He was a believer.'

'What happened to all his KGB-issued passports?'

'He kept them. They came in handy when he moved to the West.'

'And you came with him?'

'Actually, I came first. Petrov followed a month or two later, and our partnership resumed. Business was brisk. Russians were pouring into Western Europe, and they brought the old ways with them. Within a few months, we had more clients than we could handle.'

'And one of these clients was Ivan Kharkov?'

The Russian hesitated, then nodded his head. 'Ivan trusted him. Their fathers were both KGB, and *they* were both KGB.'

'Did you deal with Ivan directly?'

'Never. Only with Arkady Medvedev.'

'And after Arkady was killed?'

'Ivan sent someone else. Called himself Malensky.'

'Do you remember the date?'

'It was sometime last October.'

'After Ivan's missile deal was made public?'

'Definitely after.'

'Did you meet in Geneva?'

'He was afraid I was being watched in Geneva. He insisted I come to Vienna.'

'He had a job offer?'

'*Two* jobs, actually. Serious jobs. Serious money.'

'The first was Grigori Bulganov?'

'Correct.'

'And the second was me?'

'No, not *you*, Allon. The second job was your wife.'

48. Haute-Savoie, France

Gabriel felt a wave of anger break over him. He wanted to drive his fist through the Russian's face. He wanted to hit him so hard he would never get up again. Instead, he sat calmly, Glock in his hand, dead men over his shoulder, and asked Chernov to describe the genesis of the operation to kidnap Grigori.

'It was the challenge of a lifetime – at least, that's how Petrov viewed it. Ivan wanted Bulganov taken from London and brought back to Russia. What's more, it had to look as if Bulganov came home voluntarily. Otherwise, Ivan's backers in the Kremlin wouldn't give him the green light. They didn't want another battle with the British like the one that followed Litvinenko's poisoning.'

'How much?'

'Twenty million plus expenses, which were going to be substantial. Petrov had done jobs like this when he was with the KGB. He assembled a team of experienced operatives and put together a plan. Everything hinged on getting Bulganov into the car quietly. It couldn't be a muscle job, not with the CCTV cameras looking over his shoulder. So he tricked Bulganov's ex-wife into helping him.'

'Tell me about the people who work for him.'

'They're all ex-KGB. And, like Petrov, they're all very good.'

'Who pays them?'

'Petrov takes care of them out of his cut. I hear he's very generous. He's never had any trouble with his employees.'

Chernov had smoked the cigarette to the filter. He drew a last lungful and looked for a place to put the butt. Yaakov took it from Chernov's fingers and tossed it into the fire. Gabriel refused a request for another cigarette and resumed the questioning.

'Someone took a wild shot at a Russian journalist the other night in Oxford.'

'You're referring to Olga Sukhova?'

'I am. And I don't suppose Petrov was there that night.'

'If he had been, Olga wouldn't have survived. It was a rush job. He sent a couple of associates to handle it for him.'

'Where was Petrov?'

'He was in Italy preparing to kidnap your wife.'

Gabriel felt another wave of anger. He suppressed it and posed his next question.

'How did he find us?'

'He didn't. The SVR did. They heard rumors you were in hiding in Italy and started leaning on their sources inside the Italian services. Eventually, one of them sold you out.'

'Do you know who?'

'Absolutely not.'

Gabriel didn't make another run at him. He believed the Russian was telling the truth.

'What kind of information were you given about me?'

'Your name and the location of the estate where you were living.'

'Why did you wait so long to act?'

'Client's instructions. The operation against your wife

would go forward only if Bulganov's abduction went smoothly — and only if the client gave a final order to proceed.'

'When did you receive such an order?'

'A week after Bulganov was taken.'

'Did it come from Malensky?'

'No, it was from the man himself. Ivan called my office in Geneva. In so many words, he made it clear Petrov was to move against the second target.' Chernov paused. 'I saw a photograph of your wife, Allon. She's a remarkably beautiful woman. I'm sorry we had to take her, but business is—'

Gabriel struck Chernov hard across the face with the Glock, reopening the gash over his eye.

'Where's Petrov now?'

'I don't know.'

Gabriel gazed at the fire. 'Remember our agreement, Vladimir.'

'You could peel the flesh from my bones, Allon, and I wouldn't be able to tell you where he is. I don't know where he lives, and I don't know where he is at any given time.'

'How do you make contact with him?'

'I don't. He contacts me.'

'How?'

'Telephone. But don't think about trying to track him. He switches phones constantly and never keeps one for long.'

'What are your financial arrangements?'

'Same as the old days in Moscow. The client pays me. I pay him.'

'Do you launder it through Regency Security?'

'The Europeans are too sophisticated for that. Here he's paid in cash.'

'Where do you deliver the money?'

'We share several numbered accounts in Switzerland. I leave the cash in safe-deposit boxes, and he collects it when he feels like it.'

'When was the last time you filled a box?'

Chernov lapsed into silence. Gabriel gazed into the fire and repeated the question.

'I left five million euros in Zurich the day before yesterday.'

'What time?'

'Just before closing. I like to go when the bank is empty.'

'What's the name of the bank?'

'Becker and Puhl.'

Gabriel knew it. He also happened to know the address. He asked for it now, just to make certain Chernov wasn't lying. The Russian answered correctly. Becker & Puhl was located at Talstrasse 26.

'Account number?'

'Nine-seven-three-eight-three-six-two-four.'

'Repeat it.'

Chernov did. No mistakes.

'Password?'

'Balzac.'

'How poetic.'

'It was Petrov's choice. He likes to read. I've never had time for it myself.' The Russian looked at the gun in Gabriel's hand. 'I suppose I never will.'

*

There was one final gunshot in the villa above Lake Annecy. Gabriel did not hear it. At the moment it was fired, he was seated next to Uzi Navot in the Renault station wagon, heading quickly down the valley through the gray light of morning. They stopped in Geneva long enough to collect Sarah Bancroft from the Hotel Bristol, then set out for Zurich.

The room in the cellar of the little dacha was not entirely cut off from the outside world. High in one corner was a tiny window, covered in a century of grime and, on the outside, by a snowbank. For a few moments each day, when the angle of the sun was just right, the snow would turn scarlet and fill the room with a faint light. They assumed it was sunrise but could not be certain. Along with their freedom, Ivan had robbed them of time.

Chiara cherished each second of the light, even if it meant she had no choice but to gaze directly into Grigori's battered face. The cuts, the bruises, the disfiguring swelling: there were moments he scarcely looked human at all. She cared for him as best she could, and once, bravely, she asked Ivan's guards for bandages and something for the pain. The guards found her request amusing. They had gone to a good deal of trouble getting Grigori into his present condition and weren't about to let the new prisoner undo all their hard work with gauze and ointment.

Their hands were cuffed at all times, their legs shackled. They were given no pillows or blankets and, even during the bitter cold of night, no heat. Twice each day they were given a bit of food – coarse bread, a few slices of fatty sausage, weak tea in paper cups – and twice each day they were taken to a darkened, fetid toilet. Nights were passed side by side on the cold concrete floor. On the first night,

Chiara dreamed she was searching for a child in an endless birch forest covered in snow. Forcing herself to wake, she found Grigori trying gently to comfort her. The next night she was awakened by a rush of warm fluid between her legs. This time, nothing he did could console her. She had just lost Gabriel's child.

Mindful of Ivan's microphones, they spoke of nothing of consequence. Finally, during the brief period of light on their third day together, Grigori asked about the circumstances of Chiara's capture. She thought a moment before answering, then gave a carefully calibrated version of the truth. She told him she had been taken from a road in Italy and that two young men, good boys with bright futures, had been killed trying to protect her. She failed to mention, however, that for three days prior to her capture she had been in Lake Como participating in the interrogation of Grigori's former wife, Irina. Or that she knew how Ivan's operatives had deceived Irina into taking part in Grigori's capture. Or that Gabriel's team had loved Irina so much that sending her back to Russia after the debriefing had broken their hearts. Chiara wanted to tell Grigori these things but could not. Ivan was listening.

When it came time for Grigori to describe his ordeal, he made no such omissions. The story he told was the same one Chiara had heard in Lake Como a few days earlier, but from the other side of the looking glass. He had been on his way to a chess match against a man named Simon Finch, a devout Marxist who wanted to inflict Russia's suffering on the West. During a brief stop at the Waterside Café, he had noticed he was being followed by a man and a woman. He assumed they were watchers from MI5 and that it was safe to continue. His opinion changed a few moments later when he noticed another man, a Russian, shadowing him along Harrow Road. Then he saw a woman walking toward him – a woman who carried no umbrella and was hatless in the rain – and realized he had seen her a few minutes before. He feared he was about to be killed and briefly considered making a mad dash across Harrow Road. Then a Mercedes sedan had appeared. And its door had swung open . . .

'I recognized the man holding the gun to my former wife's head. His name is Petrov. Most people who encounter this man do not survive. I was told Irina would be an exception if I cooperated. I did everything they asked. But a few days into my captivity, while I was being interrogated in the cellars of Lubyanka, a man who had once been my friend told me Irina was dead. He said Ivan had killed her and buried her in an unmarked grave. He said I was next.'

Just then, the color retreated from the snowbank over the window, and the room was plunged once more into darkness. Chiara wept silently. She wanted desperately to tell Grigori his wife was still alive. She could not. Ivan was listening.

50. Zurich

Later, Shamron would refer to Konrad Becker as Gabriel's one and only bit of good luck. Everything else Gabriel earned the hard way, or with blood. But not Becker. Becker was delivered to him gift-wrapped and tied with a bow.

His bank was not one of the cathedrals of Swiss finance that loom over the Paradeplatz or line the graceful curve of the Bahnhofstrasse. It was a private chapel, a place where clients were free to worship or confess their sins in secret. Swiss law forbids such banks from soliciting deposits. They are free to refer to themselves as banks if they wish but are not required to do so. Some employ several dozen officers and investment specialists; others, only a handful.

Becker & Puhl fell into the second category. It was located on the ground floor of a leaden old office building, on a quiet block of the Talstrasse. The entrance was marked only by a small brass plaque and was easy to miss, which was Konrad Becker's intention. He was waiting in the gloomy vestibule at 7 a.m., a small bald figure with the pallor of one who spends his days beneath ground. As usual, he was wearing a somber dark suit and a pallbearer's gray tie. His eyes, sensitive to light, were concealed behind a pair of tinted glasses. The brevity of the handshake was a calculated insult.

'What an unpleasant surprise. What brings you to Zurich, Herr Allon?'

'Business.'

'Well, you've come to the right place.'

He turned without another word and led Gabriel down a thickly carpeted passage. The office they entered was of modest size and poorly lit. Becker walked slowly around his desk and settled himself tentatively in the executive leather chair, as though trying it out for the first time. He regarded Gabriel nervously for a moment, then started turning over the papers on his desk.

'I was assured by Herr Shamron that there would be no further contact between us. I fulfilled my end of our agreement, and I expect you to honor your word.'

'I need your help, Konrad.'

'And what sort of *help* do you require from me, Herr Allon? Would you like me to assist in a raid against Hamas targets in the Gaza Strip? Or perhaps you would like me to help you destroy the nuclear facilities of Iran?'

'Don't be melodramatic.'

'Who's being melodramatic? I'm lucky to be alive.' Becker folded his tiny hands and placed them carefully on the desk. 'I am a man of weak physical and emotional constitution, Herr Allon. I am not ashamed to admit it. Nor am I ashamed to say that I still have nightmares about our last little adventure together in Vienna.'

For the first time since Chiara's abduction, Gabriel was tempted to smile. Even he had trouble believing the little Swiss banker had played an operational role in one of the greatest coups the Office had ever engineered: the capture of Nazi war criminal Erich Radek. Technically, Becker's actions had been a violation of Switzerland's sacrosanct banking-secrecy laws. Indeed, if his role in

Radek's capture ever became public, he faced the distinct possibility of prosecution, or, even worse, financial ruin. All of which explained why Gabriel was confident that Becker, after a predictable protest, would agree to help. He had no choice.

'It has come to our attention you are the holder of a numbered account that is of interest to us. A safe-deposit box associated with this account is linked to a matter of extreme urgency. It is not an exaggeration to say it is a matter of life and death.'

'As you know, it would be a crime under Swiss banking law for me to reveal that information to you.'

Gabriel sighed heavily. 'It would be a shame, Konrad.'

'What's that, Herr Allon?'

'If our past work together ever become public.'

'You are a cheap extortionist, Herr Allon.'

'An extortionist but not cheap.'

'And the trouble with paying money to an extortionist is that he always comes back for more.'

'Can I give you the account number, Konrad?'

'If you must.'

Gabriel recited it rapidly. Becker didn't bother to write it down.

'Password?' he asked.

'Balzac.'

'And the name associated with the account?'

'Vladimir Chernov of Regency Security Services, Geneva. We're not sure if he's the primary account holder or merely a signatory.'

The banker made no movement.

'Don't you need to go check your records, Konrad?'

He didn't. 'Vladimir Chernov is the primary name on the account. One other person has access to the safe-deposit box.'

Gabriel held up the photograph of Anton Petrov. 'This man?'

Becker nodded.

'If he has access, I assume you have a name on file.'

'I have a name. Whether it is accurate . . .'

'May I have it, please?'

'He calls himself Wolfe. Otto Wolfe.'

'German speaker?'

'Fluent.'

'Accent?'

'He doesn't talk a great deal, but I'd say he came originally from the East.'

'Do you have an address and telephone number on file?'

'I do. But I don't believe they're accurate, either.'

'But you give him access to a safe-deposit box anyway?'

Becker made no response. Gabriel put away the photo.

'It is my understanding Vladimir Chernov left something in the box two days ago.'

'To be precise, Herr Chernov accessed the box two days ago. Whether he added something or removed something, I cannot say. Clients are given complete privacy when they're in the vault room.'

'Except when you're watching them with your concealed cameras. He left cash in the box, didn't he?'

'A great deal of cash, actually.'

'Has Wolfe collected it?'

'Not yet.'

Gabriel's heart gave a sideways lurch.

'How long does he usually wait after Chernov fills the box?'

'I would expect him today. Tomorrow at the latest. He's not the kind of man to leave money sitting around.'

'I'd like to see the vault room.'

'I'm afraid that's not possible.'

'Konrad, please. We don't have much time.'

The outer door was stainless steel and had a circular latch the size of a captain's wheel. Inside was a second door, also stainless steel, with a small window of reinforced glass. The outer door was closed only at night, explained Becker, while the interior door was used during business hours.

'Tell me the procedures when a customer wants access to a box.'

'After being admitted through the front door on the Talstrasse, the client checks in with the receptionist. The receptionist then sends the client to my secretary. I'm the only one who deals with numbered accounts. The client must provide two pieces of information.'

'The number and corresponding password?'

Becker nodded his bald head. 'In most cases, it's a formality, since I know virtually all our clients on sight. I make an entry in the logbook, then escort the client into the vault room. It takes two keys to open the box, mine and the client's. Generally, I remove the box and place it on the table. At which point I depart.'

'Closing the door behind you?'

'Of course.'

'And locking it?'

'Absolutely.'

'Do you and the client enter the vault alone?'

'Never. I'm always accompanied by our security guard.'

'Does the guard leave the room, too?'

'Yes.'

'What happens when the client is ready to depart?'

'He summons the guard by pressing the buzzer.'

'Is there any other way out of the bank besides the Talstrasse?'

'There's a service door leading to a back alleyway and parking spaces. We share them with the other tenants in the building. They're all assigned.'

Gabriel looked around at the gleaming stainless steel boxes, then at Becker. The tinted lenses of his spectacles shone with the reflection of the bright fluorescent lights, rendering his small dark eyes invisible.

'I'm going to need a favor from you, Konrad. A very big favor.'

'Since I would like to keep my bank, Herr Allon, how can I help?'

'Call your security guard and your secretary. Tell them to take the next couple of days off.'

'I assume you're going to replace them?'

'I wouldn't want to leave you in the lurch, Konrad.'

'Anyone I know?'

'The secretary will be new to you. But you may recall the security guard from another life.'

'Herr Lange, I take it?'

'You *do* have a good memory, Konrad.'

'That's true. But then a man like Oskar Lange is not so easy to forget.'

51. Zurich

Gabriel left the bank shortly after eight and walked to a busy café on the Bahnhofstrasse. Seated at a cramped table in the back, surrounded by depressed-looking Swiss money-men, were Sarah and Uzi Navot. Sarah was drinking coffee; Navot was working his way through a plate of scrambled eggs and toast. The smell of the food turned Gabriel's stomach as he lowered himself into an empty chair. It was going to be a long time before he felt like eating again.

'The maids arrived an hour after we left,' Navot murmured in Hebrew. 'The bodies have been removed, and they're giving the entire house a good scrubbing.'

'Tell them to make sure those bodies never turn up. I don't want Ivan to know Chernov has been taken out of circulation.'

'Ivan won't know a thing. And neither will Petrov.' Navot put a forkful of eggs on his toast and switched from Hebrew to German, which he spoke with a slight Viennese accent. 'How's my old friend Herr Becker?'

'He sends his best.'

'Is he willing to help?'

'*Willing* might be too strong a word, but we're in.'

In rapid German, Gabriel described the procedures for client access to safe-deposit boxes at Becker & Puhl. The briefing complete, he signaled the waiter and asked for coffee. Then he requested that Navot's dishes be removed.

Navot snatched a last morsel of toast as the plate floated away.

'Which girl gets the secretary job?'

'She has to speak English, German, and French. That leaves only one candidate.'

Navot looked briefly at Sarah. 'I'd feel better about getting Langley's approval before sending her in there.'

'Carter gave me the authority to use her in whatever capacity I needed. Besides, I used her in an operational role last night in Geneva.'

'And all she had to do was play the jilted lover for a few seconds. Now you're talking about placing her in close proximity to a former KGB assassin.'

Sarah spoke for the first time. 'I can handle it, Uzi.'

'You're forgetting that Ivan has pictures of you from his house in Saint-Tropez last summer. And it's possible he's shown those pictures to his friend Petrov.'

'I packed a dark wig and fake glasses. When I put them on, I barely recognize myself. And no one else will, either, especially if they've never met me in person.'

Navot was still skeptical. 'There is one other thing to consider, Gabriel.'

'What's that?'

'Her weapons training. More to the point, her *lack* of weapons training.'

'I trained her. So did the Agency.'

'No, you gave her very basic training. And the Agency prepared her for a desk job in the Counterterrorism Center. There's not a lot of gunfire on a typical day at Langley.'

Sarah spoke up in her own defense. 'I can handle a gun, Uzi.'

'Not like Dina and Rimona. They both served in the army. And if something goes wrong in there . . .'

'They won't hesitate?'

Navot made no response.

'I won't hesitate either, Uzi.'

'You sure about that?'

'I'm sure.'

The waiter delivered Gabriel's coffee. Navot handed him a packet of sugar.

'I suppose the secretary job is now filled.'

'It is.'

'Who do you have in mind for the security guard?'

'The language requirements are the same: English, French, and German. He also needs a bit of muscle.'

'That narrows the field considerably: you and me. And since there's no doubt whatsoever that Petrov knows your face, it means you can't go anywhere near that bank.'

'If you don't—'

'I'll do it,' Navot said quickly. 'I'll take care of it.'

'You're the strongest person I know, Uzi.'

'Not strong enough to stop Russian poison.'

'Just don't shake hands with him. And remember, you won't be alone. The instant you let Petrov into the vault, Sarah will signal us and we'll enter the bank. When you open the door again to let Petrov out, he'll be confronted by several men.'

'Where do we take him?'

'Out the back door and into the van. We'll hit him with a little something to keep him comfortable during the drive.'

Navot made a show of examining his clothing. Like Gabriel, he was wearing a sweater and a leather coat.

'I need something a little more presentable.' He ran his hand over his chin. 'I could also use a shave.'

'You can go shopping here on the Bahnhofstrasse. But hurry, Uzi. I wouldn't want you to be late for your first day of work.'

The old hands like to say that the life of an Office field agent is one of constant travel and mind-numbing boredom, broken by interludes of sheer terror. And then there is the waiting. Waiting for a plane or a train. Waiting for a source. Waiting for the sun to rise after a night of killing. And waiting for a Russian assassin to collect five million dollars from a safe-deposit box in Zurich. For Gabriel, the waiting was made worse by the images that flashed through his thoughts like paintings in a gallery. The images robbed him of his natural patience. They made him restless. They made him terrified. And they stripped him of the emotional coldness that Shamron had found so appealing when Gabriel was a boy of twenty-two. *Don't hate them*, Shamron had said of the Black September terrorists. *Just kill them, so they can't kill again*. Gabriel had obeyed. He tried to obey now but could not. He hated Ivan. He hated Ivan as he had never hated before.

The interminable day of watching was not without its lighter moments. They were supplied almost exclusively by the pair of transmitters Navot planted inside Becker & Puhl within minutes of his arrival. The team listened while Miss Irene Moore, an attractive young American sent by a Zurich temp agency, fetched Herr Becker's coffee. And took Herr Becker's dictation. And answered Herr Becker's telephone. And accepted Herr Becker's many compliments about her appearance. And deftly declined an invitation to dine with Herr Becker at a restaurant overlooking the Zürichsee. And they listened, too, while Herr Becker and Oskar Lange spent several uncomfortable moments getting reacquainted. And while Herr Becker instructed Herr Lange on the intricacies of opening and closing a vault. And, in late afternoon, they heard Herr Becker berating Herr Lange for failing to open the vault quickly enough when Mr. al-Hamdali of Jeddah wanted access to his safe-deposit box. Unwilling to let a good opportunity go to waste, they instructed Miss Moore to copy the contents of Mr. al-Hamdali's file. Then, for good measure, they snapped several photographs of the same Mr. al-Hamdali as he exited the bank.

Thirty minutes later, Becker & Puhl drew its shades and switched off its lights. The security guard and secretary bade Herr Becker good night and went their separate ways, Herr Lange heading left toward the Barengasse, Miss Moore right toward the Bleicherweg. Gabriel, who was with Lavon in a parked car, didn't bother to hide his disappointment. 'We'll come back tomorrow,' Lavon said, doing his best to console him. 'And the day after if we have to.' But Lavon, like Gabriel, knew their time was limited. Ivan had given them just seventy-two hours. It was time enough for just one more day in Zurich.

Gabriel instructed the team to return to their hotel rooms and rest. Though desperately in need of sleep himself, he neglected to heed his own advice and instead slipped quietly into the back of a surveillance van parked along the Talstrasse. There he spent the night alone, his gaze fixed on the entrance of Becker & Puhl, waiting for Ivan's assassin.

Ivan's brother from the KGB. Ivan's old friend from Moscow in the nineties, the bad old days when there was no law and nothing to prevent Ivan from killing his way to the top. A man like that might know where Ivan liked to do his blood work. Who knows? A man like that might have killed there himself.

A few minutes before nine the next morning, Sarah and Navot arrived for work. Yossi relieved Gabriel in the van, and it all started again. The watching. The waiting. *Always the waiting* . . . Shortly after four that afternoon, Gabriel found himself paired with Mikhail in a café overlooking the Paradeplatz. Mikhail ordered Gabriel something to eat. 'And don't try to say no. You look like hell. Besides, you're going to need your strength when we take down Petrov.'

'I'm starting to think he's not going to come.'

'And leave five million euros on the table? He'll come, Gabriel. Eventually, he'll come.'

'What makes you so sure?'

'Chernov came at the end of the day, and Petrov will come at the end of the day. These Russian thugs don't do anything when it's light out. They prefer the night. Trust me, Gabriel, I know them better than you. I grew up with these bastards.'

They were seated side by side along a high counter in the window. Outside, streetlamps were coming on in the busy square, and the trams were snaking up and down the Bahnhofstrasse. Mikhail was drumming his fingers nervously.

'You're giving me a headache, Mikhail.'

'Sorry, boss.' The fingers went still.

'Something bothering you?'

'Other than the fact we're waiting for a Russian killer to collect the proceeds for kidnapping your wife? No, Gabriel, nothing's bothering me at all.'

'Do you disagree with my decision to send Sarah into that bank?'

'Of course not. She's perfect for the job.'

'Because if you disagreed with one of my decisions, you would tell me, wouldn't you, Mikhail? That's always been the way the team works. We talk about everything.'

'I would have said something if I'd disagreed.'

'Good, Mikhail, because I would hate to think something has changed because you're involved with Sarah.'

Mikhail sipped his coffee, a play for time.

'Listen, Gabriel, I was going to say something, but—'

'But what?'

'I thought you'd be angry.'

'Why?'

'Come on, Gabriel, don't make me say this now. It's not the time.'

'It's the perfect time.'

Mikhail placed his coffee on the counter. 'It was obvious to all of us from the minute we recruited Sarah for the al-Bakari operation that she had feelings for you. And frankly—'

'Frankly what?'

'We thought you might have felt the same way.'

'That's not true. It's never been true.'

'Okay, Gabriel, whatever you say.'

A waitress placed a sandwich in front of Gabriel. He immediately pushed it aside.

'Eat it, Gabriel. You have to eat.'

Gabriel tore a corner from the sandwich. 'Are you in love with her, Mikhail?'

'What answer do you want to hear?'

'The truth would be nice.'

'Yes, Gabriel. I love her very much. *Too* much.'

'There's no such thing. Just do me a favor, Mikhail. Take good care of her. Go live in America. Get out of this business as soon as you can. Get out before . . .'

He left the thought unfinished. Mikhail began drumming his fingers again.

'Do you think he'll come?'

'He'll come.'

'Two days of waiting. I can't stand the waiting anymore.'

'You won't have to wait much longer, Mikhail.'

'How can you be so certain?'

'Because Anton Petrov just walked past us.'

52. Zurich

He wore a dark toggle coat, a gray scarf, large wire-framed glasses, and a flat cap pulled low. Oddly enough, the crude disguise threw the advantage over to Gabriel. He had spent countless hours staring at the surveillance photographs from Heathrow Airport, the fragmentary glimpses of a sturdy-jawed man wearing glasses and a fedora. It was this man who walked past the café overlooking the Paradeplatz, carrying a pair of mismatched attaché cases. And it was this man who was now rounding the corner into the Talstrasse. Gabriel raised his wrist mic carefully to his lips and informed Sarah and Navot that Petrov was headed their way. By the time the transmission was complete, Mikhail was on his feet, moving toward the door. Gabriel left a wad of money on the table and followed after him. 'You forgot to pay the bill,' he said. 'The Swiss get very angry when you run out on a check.'

Petrov walked past the bank twice before finally presenting himself at the entrance just three minutes before closing. Pressing the buzzer, he identified himself as Herr Otto Wolfe and was admitted without delay. The receptionist immediately telephoned Miss Irene Moore, Herr Becker's temporary secretary, and was instructed to send the client back straightaway. Outside, on the Talstrasse, two pairs of men moved quietly into place: Yaakov and Oded at one end, Gabriel and Mikhail at the other. Mikhail was calmly humming to himself. Gabriel didn't hear it. He was focused only on the voice in his ear, the voice of Sarah Bancroft, bidding a pleasant evening to one of the world's most dangerous men. *'Why don't you have a seat, Herr Wolfe,'* she said in perfect German. *'Herr Becker will be with you in just a moment.'*

He placed the attaché cases on the floor next to the chair, unbuttoned his coat, and removed his leather gloves. The fingers of the left hand were absent any rings. On the third finger of the right hand, the one where an ordinary Russian would have worn a wedding band, was a heavy ring with a dark stone. In America, it would have been mistaken for a class ring or the ring of a military unit. Sarah, seated at her desk, forced herself not to look at it.

'May I take your coat?'

'No.'

'Something to drink? Coffee or tea?'

He shook his head, and sat without removing his over-coat or hat. 'You're not Herr Becker's usual secretary.'

'She's sick.'

'Nothing serious, I hope.'

'Just a virus.'

'There's a lot going around. I've never seen you here before.'

'I'm a temp.'

'You're not Swiss.'

'American, actually.'

'Your German is very good. It even has a bit of a Swiss accent.'

'I went to school here for a few years when I was young.'

'Which one?'

Sarah's answer was interrupted by the appearance of Becker in the door of his office. Petrov stood.

'Your secretary was just telling me the name of the school she attended in Switzerland.'

'It was the International School of Geneva.'

'It has an excellent reputation.' He extended his right hand. 'It was a pleasure to meet you, Miss . . .' His voice trailed off.

'Moore.' Sarah grasped the hand firmly. 'Irene Moore.'

Petrov released Sarah's hand and entered Becker's office. Thirty seconds later, the formalities complete, the two men emerged and set off together toward the vault room. Sarah passed that information to Gabriel over the microphone concealed on her desk, then reached beneath the desk and unzipped her handbag. The gun was there, barrel pointed downward, grip exposed. She glanced at the clock and waited for the sound of the front buzzer. Her hand was beginning to itch on the spot where Petrov's ring had touched her. It was nothing, she told herself. Just her mind playing tricks.

Uzi Navot was waiting outside the entrance to the vault room when Becker appeared, followed by Anton Petrov. The Heathrow surveillance photos had not done justice to the Russian's size. He was well over six feet, broad shouldered, and well built. He was also clearly uneasy. Staring directly at Navot, he asked of Becker, 'Where's the usual security guard?'

The banker answered without hesitation. 'We had to fire

him. I'm afraid I can't go into the details. You may rest assured that no client assets were involved, including yours.'

'I'm relieved.' His eyes were still on Navot. 'Quite a coincidence, though. A new secretary *and* a new guard.'

Again, Becker managed a swift response. 'I'm afraid the only constant is change, even in Switzerland.'

Navot opened the secondary door to the vault room and stepped aside. The Russian remained frozen in place, his gaze flickering back and forth between the banker and the security guard. Petrov was obviously suspicious and reluctant to enter. Navot wondered whether five million euros in cash might be enough to tempt him. He didn't have to wait long for the answer.

'I'm sorry to trouble you, Herr Becker, but I've changed my mind. I'll see to my business another time.'

Becker seemed taken aback. For an instant, Navot feared he might improvise and ask the Russian to reconsider his decision. Instead, he stepped aside with the curtness of a headwaiter and gestured toward the exit.

'As you wish.'

Petrov fixed Navot with a cautionary stare, then turned and started down the corridor. Navot quickly considered his options. If the Russian managed to make it out of the bank, the team would be left with two choices: snatch him off a busy Zurich street – hardly optimal – or follow him to his next destination. Better to take him here, inside the premises of Becker & Puhl, even if it meant doing it alone.

Navot had one brief advantage – the fact Petrov's back was turned – and he took it. Moving Becker aside with one sweep of his left hand, he delivered a knifelike strike to the Russian's neck with his right. The blow might have killed a normal man, but Petrov merely stumbled. Regaining his balance, he quickly released the two attaché cases and reached beneath his coat with his left hand. As he turned to face Navot, the gun was already on its way out. Navot grabbed the Russian's left wrist and slammed it hard to the wall. Then he turned his head and frantically searched for the right hand. It wasn't hard to find. Fingers splayed, killing ring exposed, it was reaching for Navot's neck. Navot grabbed another wrist and held on. *You won't be alone*, Gabriel had said. Funny how things never seemed to go according to plan.

Sarah heard two noises in rapid succession: a man grunting in pain, followed by a heavy thump. Then, a few seconds later, she heard a third sound: the intercom buzzer. Gabriel and the others were waiting outside the entrance of the bank. It would take at least thirty seconds for them to be admitted and make their way to the vault room. Thirty seconds that Uzi would be fighting for his life alone with a professional Russian assassin.

I won't hesitate either, Uzi.

You sure about that?

I'm sure.

Sarah reached beneath her desk and drew the gun from her handbag. Chambering the first round, she got to her feet and headed into the corridor.

On the third ring, the receptionist finally answered.

'May I help you?'

'My name is Heinrich Kiever. Herr Becker is expecting me.'

'One moment, please.'

The moment seemed to last an eternity.

'Herr Kiever?'

'Ycs?'

'I'm afraid no one is answering Hcrr Bccker's line. Can you wait another moment, please?'

'Would it be possible for us to wait inside? It's a bit chilly out here.'

'I'm afraid it's against policy. I'm sure Herr Becker will be with you in a moment.'

'Thank you.'

Gabriel glanced at Mikhail. 'I think we might have a problem in there.'

'What do we do?'

'Unless you can think of some way to break into a Zurich bank, we wait.'

No amount of firearms training could have possibly prepared Sarah for the sight that greeted her as she entered the corridor leading to the vault room: one Swiss banker huddled in fear, two large men trying very hard to kill each other. Navot had managed to pin Petrov to the wall and was struggling to control the Russian's arms. In Petrov's left hand was a gun. His right was empty, but the fingers were spread wide, and he appeared to be trying to grab Navot's neck.

The ring!

One touch of the stylus was all it would take. One touch, and Navot would be dead within minutes.

Gun in her outstretched hands, Sarah sidestepped Becker and moved toward the two struggling men. Petrov imme-diately took note of her approach and attempted to aim his own weapon in her direction. Navot reacted quickly, twisting the Russian's arm and slamming it to the wall so the barrel was pointed toward the ceiling.

'Shoot him, Sarah! Shoot him, damn it!'

Sarah took two steps forward and pressed the gun against Petrov's left hip. *I won't hesitate either, Uzi* . . . She didn't. Not for an instant. The round shattered the Russian's hip joint and caused his leg to buckle. Somehow, the left hand managed to maintain its grip on the gun. The right was still inching toward Navot's neck.

'Again, Sarah! Shoot him again!'

This time, she placed the gun against Petrov's left shoulder and pulled the trigger. As the Russian's arm went limp, she quickly tore the gun from his grasp. Free to use his own right hand, Navot balled it into a massive fist and gave Petrov three sledgehammer blows to the face. The final two were unnecessary. The Russian was out on his feet after the first.

53. Bargen, Switzerland

Three miles from the German border, at the end of a narrow logging valley, stands little Bargen, famous in Switzerland because it is the country's northernmost town. It has little to offer other than a gas station and a small market frequented by travelers on their way somewhere else. No one seemed to take note of the two men waiting outside in the parking lot in an Audi sedan. One had thinning flyaway hair and was drinking coffee from a paper cup. The other had eyes of emerald and was watching the traffic speeding along the motorway, white lights headed toward Zurich, red lights streaming toward the German border. *The waiting . . . Always the waiting . . .* Waiting for a plane or a train. Waiting for a source. Waiting for the sun to rise after a night of killing. And waiting for a van carrying a wounded Russian assassin.

'There's going to be hell to pay at that bank,' said Eli Lavon.

'Becker will keep it quiet. He has no choice.'

'And if he can't?'

'Then we'll clean up the mess later.'

'Good thing the Swiss joined the modern world and took down their border posts. Remember the old days, Gabriel? They would get us coming and going.'

'I remember, Eli.'

'I can't tell you how many times I had to sit there while

those smug Swiss boys searched my trunk. Now they barely look at you. This will be our fourth Russian in three days, and no one will be the wiser.'

'We're doing them a favor.'

'If we keep going at this rate, there won't be any Russians left in Switzerland.'

'My point exactly.'

Just then a van turned into the lot. Gabriel climbed out of the Audi and walked over. Pulling open the rear door, he saw Sarah and Navot sitting on the floor of the cargo hold. Petrov was stretched between them.

'How is he?'

'Still unconscious.'

'Pulse?'

'Okay.'

'How's the blood loss?'

'Not too bad. I think the rounds cauterized the vessels.'

'King Saul Boulevard is sending a doctor to the interrogation site. Can he make it?'

'He'll be fine.' Navot handed Gabriel a small ziplock plastic bag. 'Here's a souvenir.'

Inside was Petrov's ring. Gabriel carefully slipped the bag into his coat pocket and gestured for Sarah to get out of the van. He helped her into the backseat of the Audi, then climbed behind the wheel. Five minutes later, both vehicles were safely over the invisible border and heading north into Germany. Sarah managed to keep her emotions in check for a few minutes longer. Then she leaned her head against the window and began to weep.

'You did the right thing, Sarah. You saved Uzi's life.'

'I've never shot anyone before.'

'Really?'

'Don't make jokes, Gabriel. I don't feel so well.'

'You will.'

'When?'

'Eventually.'

'I think I'm going to be sick.'

'Should I pull over?'

'No, keep going.'

'Are you sure?'

'I don't know.'

'I'll stop just in case.'

'Maybe you should.'

Gabriel pulled to the side of the motorway and crouched at Sarah's side as her body retched.

'I did it for you, Gabriel.'

'I know, Sarah.'

'I did it for Chiara.'

'I know.'

'How long am I going to feel this way?'

'Not long.'

'How long, Gabriel?'

He rubbed Sarah's back as her body convulsed again.

Not long, he thought. *Only forever*.

PART FOUR
Resurrection Gate

54. Northern Germany

For every safe house, there is a story. A salesman who lives out of a suitcase and rarely sees home. A couple with too much money to be tied to one place for long. An adventurous soul who travels to faraway lands to take pictures and scale mountains. These are the tales told to neighbors and landlords. These are the lies that explain short-term tenants and guests who arrive in the middle of the night with keys in their pockets.

The villa near the Danish border had a story, too, though some of it happened to be true. Before the Second World War, it had been owned by a family called Rosenthal. All but one member, a young girl, perished in the Holocaust, and after emigrating to Israel in the mid-1950s she bequeathed her family home to the Office. Known as Site 22XB, the property was the jewel in Housekeeping's crown, reserved for only the most sensitive and important operations. Gabriel believed a Russian assassin with two bullet wounds and a head filled with vital secrets certainly fell into that category. Housekeeping had agreed. They had given him the keys and made certain the pantry was well provisioned.

The house stood a hundred yards from a quiet farm road, a lonely outpost on the stark, flat plain of western Jutland. Time had taken its toll. The stucco needed a good scrubbing, the shutters were broken and peeling for want of paint, and the roof leaked when the big storms swept in from the North Sea. Inside was a similar story: dust and cobwebs, rooms not quite furnished, fixtures and appliances from a bygone era.

Indeed, to wander the halls was to step back in time, especially for Gabriel and Eli Lavon. Known to Office veterans as Château Shamron, the house had served as a planning base during Operation Wrath of God. Men had been condemned to death here, fates had been sealed. On the second floor was the room Lavon and Gabriel had shared. Now, as then, it contained nothing but a pair of narrow beds separated by a chipped nightstand. As Gabriel stood in the doorway, an image flashed in his memory: the watcher and the executioner lying awake in the darkness, one made sleepless by stress, the other by visions of blood. The ancient transistor radio that had filled the empty hours still stood on the table. It had been their link to the outside world. It had told them about wars won and lost, about an American president who resigned in disgrace; and, sometimes, on summer nights, it played music for them. The music normal boys were listening to. Boys who weren't killing terrorists for Ari Shamron.

Gabriel tossed his bag onto his old bed – the one nearest the window – and headed downstairs to the cellar. Anton Petrov lay supine across a bare stone floor, Navot, Yaakov, and Mikhail standing over him. His hands and feet were secured, though at this point it was scarcely necessary. Petrov's skin was ghostly white, his forehead damp with perspiration, his jaw distorted from swelling at the spot where Navot had hit him. The Russian was in desperate need of medical attention. He would get it only if he talked.

If not, Gabriel would allow the rounds still lodged in his pelvis and shoulder to poison his body with sepsis. The death would be slow, feverish, and agonizing. It was the death he deserved, and Gabriel was more than prepared to grant it. He crouched at the Russian's side and spoke to him in German.

'I believe this is yours.'

He reached into his coat pocket and removed the plastic bag Navot had given him at the Swiss border. Petrov's ring was still inside. Gabriel removed it and pressed firmly on the stone. From the base emerged a small stylus, not much larger than a phonograph needle. Gabriel made a show of examining it, then moved it suddenly toward Petrov's face. The Russian recoiled in fear, twisting his head violently to the right.

'What's wrong, Anton? It's just a ring.'

Gabriel inched it closer to the soft skin of Petrov's neck. The Russian was now writhing in terror. Gabriel pressed the stone again, and the needle retreated safely into the base of the ring. He slipped it back into the plastic bag and handed it carefully to Navot.

'In the interest of full disclosure, we worked on a similar device. But to be honest with you, I've never really cared for poisons. They're for cheap hoods like you, Anton. I've always preferred to do my killing with one of these.'

Gabriel removed the .45 caliber Glock from the waistband of his trousers and pointed it at Petrov's face. The suppressor was no longer screwed into the end of the barrel. It wasn't necessary here.

'One meter, Anton. That's how I prefer to kill. One meter. That way I can see my enemy's eyes before he dies.

Vyshaya mera: the highest measure of punishment.' Gabriel pressed the barrel of the gun against the base of the Russian's chin. 'A grave without a marker. A corpse without a face.'

Gabriel used the barrel of the gun to open the front of Petrov's shirt. The shoulder wound didn't look good: bone fragments, threads of clothing. No doubt the hip was just as bad. Gabriel closed the shirt and looked directly into Petrov's eyes.

'You're here because your friend Vladimir Chernov betrayed you. We didn't have to hurt him. In fact, we didn't even have to threaten him. We just gave him a bit of money, and he told us everything we needed to know. Now it's your turn, Anton. If you cooperate, you will be given medical attention and treated humanely. If not . . .'

Gabriel placed the barrel against Petrov's shoulder and corkscrewed it into the wound. Petrov's screams echoed off the stone walls of the cellar. Gabriel stopped before the Russian could pass out.

'Do you understand, Anton?'

The Russian nodded.

'If I stay in your presence much longer, I'm going to beat you to death with my bare hands.' He glanced at Navot. 'I'm going to let my friend handle the questioning. Since you tried to kill him with your ring back in Zurich, it only seems fair. Wouldn't you agree, Anton?'

The Russian was silent.

Gabriel stood and headed upstairs without another word. The rest of the team was sprawled in the sitting room in various states of exhaustion. Gabriel's gaze immediately settled on the newest member of the group, a doctor who had been dispatched by King Saul Boulevard to treat Petrov's injuries. In the lexicon of the Office, he was a *sayan*, a volunteer helper. Gabriel recognized him. He was a Jew from Paris who had once treated Gabriel for a severe gash to his hand.

'How's the patient?' the doctor asked in French.

'He's not a patient,' Gabriel responded in the same language. 'He's a KGB hood.'

'He's still a human being.'

'I'd withhold judgment until you have a chance to meet him.'

'When will that be?'

'I'm not sure.'

'Tell me about the wounds.'

Gabriel did.

'When were they inflicted?'

Gabriel glanced at his watch. 'Nearly eight hours ago.'

'Those bullets need to come out. Otherwise—'

'They come out when I say they come out.'

'I swore an oath, monsieur. I will not forsake that oath because I am performing a service for you.'

'I swore an oath, too. And tonight, my oath trumps yours.'

Gabriel turned and went upstairs to his room. He stretched out on the bed, but each time he closed his eyes he saw only blood. Unable to drive the image from his thoughts, he reached out and turned the familiar dial of the radio. A German woman with a sultry voice bade him a good evening and began reading the news. The chancellor was proposing a new era of dialogue and cooperation between Europe and Russia. She planned to unveil her proposal at the upcoming emergency G-8 summit in Moscow.

Like a night fever, Petrov broke at dawn. He did not walk a straight line during his journey to the truth, but then Gabriel had not expected he would. Petrov was a professional. He led them into culs-de-sac of illusion and down dead-end roads of deception. And though he had worked only for money, he tried admirably to keep faith with Russia and his patron saint, Ivan Kharkov. Navot had been patient but firm. It was not necessary to inflict additional pain or even threaten it. Petrov was in enough pain already. All they had to do was keep him conscious. The two bullet wounds and broken jaw did the rest.

Finally, exhausted and shaking from the onset of infection, the Russian capitulated. He said there was a dacha northeast of Moscow, in Vladimirskaya Oblast. It was isolated, hidden, protected. There were four streams converging into a great marsh. There was a vast birch forest. It was the place where Ivan did his blood work. It was Ivan's prison. Ivan's hell on earth. Navot located the parcel of land using ordinary commercial-grade software. The image on his screen matched Petrov's description perfectly. He sent for the doctor and headed upstairs to brief Gabriel.

He was lying in darkness, fingers interlaced at the back of his neck, ankles crossed. Hearing the news, he sat up and swung his feet to the floor. Then he used his secure PDA to send a secure flash transmission to three points around the globe: King Saul Boulevard, Thames House, and Langley. An hour after sunrise, he set out alone for Hamburg. At 2 p.m., he boarded British Airways Flight 969, and by 3:15 he was seated in the back of an MI5 sedan, heading toward the center of London.

55. Mayfair, London

In the dark days after the attacks of 9/11, the American Embassy at Grosvenor Square was transformed into a high-security eyesore. Almost overnight, barricades and blast walls sprouted along the perimeter, and, much to the ire of Londoners, a busy street along one side of the embassy was permanently closed to traffic. But there were other changes the public could not see, including the construction of a secret CIA annex far beneath the square itself. Linked to the Global Ops Center in Langley, the annex served as a forward command post for operations in Europe and the Middle East and was so secret only a handful of British ministers and intelligence officials knew of its existence. During a visit the previous summer, Graham Seymour had been depressed to find it dwarfed the primary ops rooms of both MI5 and MI6. It was typical of the Americans, he thought. Confronted by the threat of Islamic terrorism, they had dug a deep hole for themselves and filled it with high-tech toys. And they wondered why they were losing.

Seymour arrived shortly after eight that evening and was escorted to the 'fishbowl,' a secure conference room with walls of soundproof glass. Gabriel and Ari Shamron were seated along one flank of the table; Adrian Carter was standing at the head of the room, a laser pointer in hand. On the projection screen was an image, captured by an

American spy satellite, that provided coverage of western Russia. It showed a small dacha, located precisely one hundred twenty-eight miles northeast of the Kremlin's Trinity Tower. Carter's red dot was focused on a pair of Range Rovers parked outside the house. Two men stood next to them.

'Our photo analysts believe there are more security guards posted on the back side of the dacha' – the red dot moved three times – 'here, here, and here. They also say it's clear those Range Rovers are coming and going. Two days ago, the area received several inches of snowfall. But this image shows fresh tire tracks.'

'When was it taken?'

'Midday. The analysts can see tracks going in both directions.'

'Shift changes?'

'I suppose so. Or reinforcements.'

'What about communications?'

'The dacha is electrified, but NSA is having trouble locating a landline telephone. They're certain someone in there is using a sat phone. They're also picking up cellular transmissions.'

'Can they get to them?'

'They're working on it.'

'What do we know about the property itself?'

'It's controlled by a holding company based in Moscow.'

'Who controls the holding company?'

'Who do you think?'

'Ivan Kharkov?'

'But of course,' said Carter.

'When did he buy the land?'

'Early nineties, not long after the fall of the Soviet Union.'

'Why in God's name did Ivan buy a parcel of birch trees and swampland a hundred miles outside Moscow?'

'He was probably able to get it for a couple of kopeks and a song.'

'He was a rich man by then. Why this place?'

'CIA and NSA have many capabilities, Gabriel, but reading Ivan's mind isn't one of them.'

'How big is the property?'

'Several hundred acres.'

'What's he doing with it?'

'Apparently nothing.'

Gabriel rose from his seat and walked over to the screen. He stood before it in silence, hand pressed to his chin, head tilted to one side, as if inspecting a canvas. His gaze was focused on a section of the woods about two hundred yards from the dacha. Though the woods were covered in snow, the aerial view showed the presence of three parallel depressions in the topography, each precisely the same length. They were too uniform to have occurred naturally. Carter anticipated Gabriel's next question.

'The analysts haven't been able to figure out what those are. The working assumption is that they were caused by some kind of construction project. They found several more a short distance away.'

'Is there a photo?'

Carter pressed a button on the console. The next photo showed a similar pattern: three parallel depressions, overgrown by birch trees. Gabriel cast a long glance at Shamron and returned to his seat. Carter switched off his laser pointer and laid it on the table.

'It's clear from the vehicles and the presence of so many guards that someone important is staying at that dacha. Whether it is Chiara and Grigori . . .' Carter's voice trailed off. 'I suppose the only way to know for certain is to put eyes on the ground. The question is, are you willing to go in there based on the word of a Russian assassin and master kidnapper?' Carter's eyes moved from face to face. 'I don't suppose any of you would like to go into a little more detail about how you were able to track down Petrov so quickly?'

The question was greeted by a heavy silence. Carter turned to Gabriel.

'Should I assume Sarah took part in the commission of a crime of some sort?'

'Several.'

'Where is she now?'

'I'm not at liberty to say.'

'With Petrov, I take it?'

Gabriel nodded.

'I'd like her back. As for Petrov, I'd like him, too – when you're finished with him, of course. He might be able to help us close a couple of outstanding cases.'

Carter returned to the satellite photo. 'It seems to me you have two options. Option number one: go to the Kremlin, give the Russians the evidence of Ivan's involvement, and ask them to intervene.'

It was Shamron who answered. 'The Russians have made it abundantly clear they have no intention of helping us. Besides, going to the Kremlin is the same as going to Ivan. If we raise this matter with the Russian president—'

' – the Russian president will tell Ivan,' Gabriel interjected. 'And Ivan will respond by killing Grigori and my wife.'

Carter nodded in agreement. 'I suppose that leaves option two: going into Russia and bringing them out yourself. Frankly, the president and I anticipated that would be your choice. And he's prepared to offer a substantial amount of help.'

Shamron spoke two words: '*Kachol v'lavan.*'

Carter gave a faint smile. 'Forgive me, Ari. I speak nearly as many languages as you, but I'm afraid Hebrew isn't one of them.'

'*Kachol v'lavan,*' Gabriel repeated. 'It means "blue and white," the colors of the Israeli flag. But for dinosaurs like Ari, it means much more. It means we do things for ourselves, and we don't rely on others to help us with problems of our own making.'

'But this problem really isn't of your own making. You went after Ivan because *we* asked you to. The president feels we bear some responsibility for what's happened. And the president believes in taking care of his friends.'

'What kind of help is the president offering?'

'For understandable reasons, we won't be able to help you execute the actual rescue. Since the United States and Russia still have several thousand nuclear missiles pointed at each other, it might not be wise for us to be shooting at each other on Russian soil. But we *can* help in other ways. For starters, we can get you into the country in a way that doesn't land you back in the cellars of Lubyanka.'

'And?'

'We can get you out again. Along with the hostages, of course.'

'How?'

Carter dealt an American passport onto the table. It was

burgundy colored rather than blue and stamped with the word OFFICIAL.

'It's one step below a diplomatic passport. You won't have complete immunity, but it will definitely make the Russians think twice before laying a finger on you.'

Gabriel opened the cover. For now, the information page contained no photograph, only a name: AARON DAVIS.

'What does Mr. Davis do?'

'He works for the White House Office of Presidential Advance. As you probably know, the president will be in Moscow on Thursday and Friday for the emergency G-8 summit. Most of the White House advance team is already on the ground. I've arranged for a late addition to the team.'

'Aaron Davis?'

Carter nodded.

'How's he going in?'

'The car plane.'

'I beg your pardon?'

'It's the unofficial name of the C-17 Globemaster that brings the presidential limousine. It also carries a large detail of Secret Service agents. Aaron Davis will board the plane during a refueling stop in Shannon, Ireland. Six hours after that, he'll land at Sheremetyevo Airport. A U.S. Embassy vehicle will then take him to the Hotel Metropol.'

'And the escape hatch?'

'Same route, opposite direction. On Friday evening, after the final session of the summit, the Russian president will be hosting a gala dinner. The president is scheduled to return to Washington at the conclusion, along with the rest of his delegation and the traveling White House press corps. The buses depart the Metropol at 10 p.m. sharp.

They'll go straight onto the tarmac at Sheremetyevo and board the planes. We'll have false passports for Chiara and Grigori just in case. But in reality, the Russians probably won't be checking passports.'

'When will I arrive in Moscow?'

'The car plane is due to land at Sheremetyevo a few minutes after 4 a.m. Thursday. By my calculation, that leaves you forty-two hours on the ground in Russia. All you have to do is find some way of getting Chiara and Grigori out of that dacha and back to the Metropol by 10 p.m. Friday.'

'Without being arrested or killed by Ivan's army of thugs.'

'I'm afraid I can't help with that. You also have a more immediate problem. Ivan's emissary is expecting a reply to his demands tomorrow afternoon in Paris. Unless you can convince him to push back the deadline by several days . . .'

Carter didn't have the nerve to finish the thought. Gabriel did it for him.

'This entire conversation is academic.'

'I'm afraid that's correct.'

Gabriel stared at the satellite photo of the dacha in the trees. Then at the time zone clocks arrayed along the wall. Then he closed his eyes. And he saw it all.

It appeared to him as a cycle of vast paintings, oil on canvas, rendered by the hand of Tintoretto. The paintings lined the nave of a small church in Venice and were darkened by yellowed varnish. Gabriel, in his thoughts, drifted slowly past them now with Chiara at his side, her breast pressing against his elbow, her long hair brushing the side of his neck. Even with Carter's help, getting her and Grigori out of the dacha alive would be an operational and logistical nightmare. Ivan would be playing on his home turf. All the advantages would be his. Unless Gabriel could somehow turn the tables. *By way of deception* . . .

Gabriel had to get Ivan to let down his guard. He had to keep Ivan occupied at the time of the raid. And, more pressing, he had to convince Ivan not to kill Chiara and Grigori for another four days. In order to do that, he needed one more thing from Adrian Carter. Not *one*, actually, but *two*.

He blinked away the vision of Venice and gazed once again at the photograph of the dacha in the trees. Yes, he thought again, he needed two more things from Adrian Carter, but they were not Carter's to give. Only a mother could surrender them. And so, with Carter's blessing, he entered an unoccupied office in the far corner of the annex and quietly closed the door. He dialed the isolated compound in the Adirondack Mountains. And he asked Elena Kharkov if he could borrow the only two things in the world she had left.

56. Paris

In the aftermath, during the inevitable postmortem and deconstruction that follows an affair of this magnitude, there was spirited debate over who among its far-flung cast of characters bore the most responsibility for its outcome. One participant was not asked for an opinion and would surely not have ventured one if he had been. He was a man of few words, a man who stood a lonely post. His name was Rami, and his job was to keep watch over a national treasure, the Memuneh. Rami had been at the Old Man's side for the better part of twenty years. He was Shamron's *other* son, the one who stayed at home while Gabriel and Navot were running around the world playing the hero. He was the one who snuck the Old Man cigarettes and kept his Zippo filled with lighter fluid. The one who sat up nights on the terrace in Tiberias, listening to the Old Man's stories for the thousandth time and pretending it was still the first. And he was the one who was walking exactly twenty paces behind the Old Man's back, at four the following afternoon, as he entered the Jardin des Tuileries in Paris.

Shamron found Sergei Korovin where he said he would be, seated ramrod straight on a wooden bench near the Jeu de Paume. He was wearing a heavy woolen scarf beneath his overcoat and smoking the stub of a cigarette that left no doubt about his nationality. As Shamron sat down, Korovin raised his left arm slowly and pondered his wristwatch.

'You're two minutes late, Ari. That's not like you.'

'The walk took me longer than expected.'

'Bullshit.' Korovin lowered his arm. 'You should know that patience isn't one of Ivan's strong suits. That's why he was never selected to work in the First Chief Directorate. He was deemed too impetuous for pure espionage. We had to assign him to the Fifth, where his temper could be put to good use.'

'Breaking heads, you mean?'

Korovin gave a noncommittal shrug. 'Someone had to do it.'

'He must have been a great disappointment to his father.'

'Ivan? He was an only child. He was . . . *indulged.*'

'It shows.'

Shamron removed a silver case from the pocket of his overcoat and took his time lighting a cigarette. Korovin, annoyed, gave his wristwatch another distracted glance.

'Perhaps I should have made something clear to you, Ari. This deadline was more than hypothetical. Ivan is expecting to hear from me. If he doesn't, chances are your agent will turn up somewhere with a bullet in the back of her head.'

'That would be rather foolish, Sergei. You see, if Ivan kills my agent, he'll lose his only chance of getting his children back.'

Korovin's head turned sharply in Shamron's direction. 'What are you saying, Ari? Are you telling me the Americans have agreed to return Ivan's children to Russia?'

'No, Sergei, not the Americans. It was Elena's decision. As you might expect, it's torn her to pieces, but she wants no more blood shed because of her husband.' Shamron paused. 'And she also knows her children well enough to realize that they'll leave Russia the moment they're old enough and come back to her.'

Age seemed to have taken a toll on Korovin's ability to dissemble. He exhaled a cloud of smoke into the Parisian dusk and did a very poor job of concealing his surprise at the development.

'What's wrong, Sergei? You told me Ivan wanted his children.' Shamron watched the Russian carefully. 'It makes me think your offer wasn't a serious one.'

'Don't be ridiculous, Ari. I'm just stunned you were actually able to pull it off.'

'I thought you learned a long time ago never to underestimate me.'

The gardens were receding into the gathering darkness. Shamron glanced around, then settled his gaze on Korovin.

'Are we alone, Sergei?'

'We're alone.'

'Anyone listening?'

'No one.'

'You're sure?'

'No one would dare. I might be old, but I'm still *Korovin*.'

'And I'm still Shamron. So listen carefully, because I'm not going to say this twice. On Thursday afternoon at two o'clock Washington time, the Russian ambassador to the United States is to present himself at the main gate of Andrews Air Force Base. He will be met there by base security and a team of officers from the CIA and the State Department. They will take him to a VIP lounge, where he will be allowed to spend a few minutes with Anna and Nikolai Kharkov.' Shamron paused. 'Are you with me, Sergei?'

'Two p.m. Thursday, Andrews Air Force Base.'

'When the meeting is over, the children will be placed aboard a C-32, the military's version of a Boeing 757. It will land in Russia at precisely nine a.m. Friday morning. The Americans want to use the airfield outside Konakovo. Do you know the one I'm talking about, Sergei? It's the old air base that was converted to civilian use when your air force couldn't figure out how to fly planes anymore.'

Korovin lit another of his Russian cigarettes and slowly waved out the match. 'Nine o'clock. The airfield outside Konakovo.'

'Elena doesn't want the children walking off the plane into the arms of some stranger. She insists Ivan come to the airport and greet them. If Ivan isn't there, the children don't get off that plane. Are we clear on that, Sergei?'

'No Ivan, no children.'

'At 9:05, the aircraft will be parked with its doors opened. If my agent is standing outside the entrance of the Israeli Embassy in Moscow, the children will walk off that plane. If she's not there, the crew will fire up those engines and take off again. And don't get any ideas about playing rough with that aircraft. It's American soil. And at 9 a.m. on Friday morning, the American president will be sitting down with the Russian president and the other Group of Eight leaders for a working breakfast at the Kremlin. We wouldn't want anything to spoil the mood, would we, Sergei?'

'Say what you like about our president, Ari, but he is a man who respects international law.'

'If that's true, then why does your president allow Ivan to flood the most volatile corners of the world with Russian weapons? And why did he allow Ivan to kidnap one of my officers and use her as barter to get his children back?'

Greeted by silence, Shamron said, 'I suppose it all comes down to money, doesn't it, Sergei? How much money did your president demand of Ivan? How much did Ivan have to pay for the privilege of kidnapping Grigori and my agent?'

'Our president is a servant of the people. These stories of his personal wealth are lies and Western propaganda designed to discredit Russia and keep it weak.'

'You're showing your age, Sergei.'

Korovin ignored the remark. 'As for your missing agent, Ivan had absolutely nothing to do with her disappearance. I thought I made that clear during our first meeting.'

'Oh, yes, I remember. But let *me* make something clear to you now. If my agent isn't returned, safe and sound, at nine o'clock Friday morning, I'm going to assume that you and your client were acting in bad faith. And it's going to make me very angry.'

'Ivan isn't my client. I'm just a messenger.'

'No, you're not. You're *Korovin*.' Shamron watched the traffic hurtling round the Place de la Concorde. 'Do you know the identity of the agent Ivan is holding?'

'I know very little.'

Shamron gave a disappointed smile. 'You used to be a better poker player, Sergei. You know exactly who she is. And you know exactly who her husband is. And that means you know what's going to happen if she isn't released.'

Shamron dropped the end of his cigarette onto the gravel footpath. 'But just so there are no misunderstandings, I'm going to spell it out for you. If Ivan kills her, I'm going to hold the Kremlin responsible. And then I'm going

324

to unleash my service on yours. No Russian intelligence officer anywhere in the world will be able to walk the streets without feeling our breath on the back of his neck.' Shamron placed his hand on Korovin's forearm. 'Are we clear, Sergei?'

'We're clear, Ari.'

'Good. And there's one other thing. I want Grigori Bulganov. And don't tell me he's none of my concern.'

Korovin hesitated, then said, 'We'll see.'

'Two p.m. Thursday, Andrews Air Force Base. Nine a.m. Friday, the airfield at Konakovo. Nine a.m. Friday, my agent outside our embassy in Moscow. Don't disappointment me, Sergei. Many lives will be lost if you do.'

Shamron rose without another word and headed toward the Louvre with Rami now walking vigilantly at his side. The bodyguard had not been able to hear what had just transpired but was certain of one thing. The Old Man was still the one in charge. And he had just put the fear of God in Sergei Korovin.

57. Shannon Airport, Ireland

The name Aaron Davis of the White House Office of Presidential Advance was unfamiliar to them. Their orders, however, were unambiguous. They were to pick him up during the Shannon refueling stop and get him into Moscow without a hitch. *And don't try to talk to him during the flight. He's not the talkative sort.* They didn't ask why. They were Secret Service.

They were never told his real name or the country of his birth. They never knew that their mysterious passenger was a legend, or that he had spent the previous forty-eight hours in London engaged in advance work of quite another kind, shuttling between Grosvenor Square and the Israeli Embassy in Kensington. Though he was visibly fatigued and on edge, all those who encountered Gabriel during this period would later remember his extraordinary composure. Not once did he lose his temper, they said. Not once did he show the strain. His team, physically worn after two weeks in the field, responded with lightning speed to his calm but relentless pressure. Just twelve hours after the call to Elena Kharkov, half were on the ground in Moscow, credentials around their necks, covers intact. The rest joined them later that night, including the chief of Special Ops, Uzi Navot. No other service in the world would have put so senior a man on the ground in so hostile a land. But then no other service was quite like the Office.

Shamron remained at Gabriel's side for all but a few hours, when he returned to Paris to hold the hand of Sergei Korovin. Ivan was getting nervous. Ivan was dubious about the entire thing. Ivan didn't understand why he had to wait until Friday to get his children back. 'He wants to do it now,' Korovin said. 'He wants it over and done with.' Shamron did not tell his old friend that he already knew this – or that the NSA had been kind enough to share the original recording, along with a transcript. Instead, he assured the Russian there was no need to worry. Elena just needed some time to prepare the children, and herself, for the pending separation. 'Surely even a monster like Ivan can understand how difficult this is going to be on her.' As for the schedule, Shamron made it clear there would be no changes: 2 p.m. at Andrews, 9 a.m. at Konakovo, 9 a.m. at the Israeli Embassy in Moscow. No Ivan, no children. No Chiara, no safe place for any Russian intelligence officer on earth. 'And don't forget, Sergei – we want Grigori back, too.'

Though he tried not to show it, the meeting in Paris left Shamron deeply shaken. Gabriel's gambit had clearly thrown Ivan off balance. But it had also made him suspicious of a trap. Gabriel's opening would be brief, a few minutes, no more. They would have to move swiftly and decisively. These were the words Shamron spoke to Gabriel late Wednesday night as they sat together in the back of a CIA car on the rain-lashed tarmac of Shannon Airport.

Gabriel's bag was on the seat between them, his eyes focused on the massive C-17 Globemaster that would soon deliver him to Moscow. Shamron was smoking – despite the fact that the CIA driver had asked him repeatedly not to – and running through the entire operation one more time. Gabriel, though exhausted, listened patiently. The briefing was more for Shamron's benefit than his. The Memuneh would spend the next forty-eight hours watching helplessly from the CIA annex. This was his last chance to whisper directly into Gabriel's ear, and he took it without apology. And Gabriel indulged him because he needed to hear the sound of the Old Man's voice one more time before getting on that plane. He drew courage from the voice. Faith. It made him believe the operation might actually work, even though everything else told him it was doomed to failure.

'Once you get them into the car, don't stop. Kill anyone you need to kill. And I mean *any*one. We'll clean up the mess later. We always do.'

Just then, there was a knock at the window. It was the CIA escort, saying the plane was ready. Gabriel kissed Shamron's cheek and told him not to smoke too much. Then he climbed out of the car and headed toward the C-17 through the rain.

For now, he was an American, even if he couldn't quite speak like one. He carried an American suitcase filled with American clothes. An American cell phone filled with American numbers. An American BlackBerry filled with American e-mails. He also carried a second PDA with features not available on ordinary models, but that belonged to someone else. A boy from the Valley of Jezreel. A boy who would have been an artist if not for a band of Palestinian terrorists known as Black September. Tonight, that boy did not exist. He was a painting lost to time. He was now Aaron Davis of the White House Office of Presidential

Advance, and he had a pocketful of credentials to prove it. He thought American thoughts, dreamed American dreams. He was an American, even if he couldn't quite speak like one. And even if he couldn't quite walk like one, either.

As it turned out, there was not one presidential limousine on the plane but two, along with a trio of armored SUVs. The chief of the Secret Service detail was a woman; she escorted Gabriel to a seat near the center of the aircraft and gave him a parka to wear against the sharp cold. Much to his surprise, he was able to get a bit of badly needed sleep, though one agent would later note that he seemed to stir at the precise instant the plane crossed into Russian airspace. He woke with a start fifteen minutes before landing, and as the plane descended toward Sheremetyevo he thought of Chiara. How had she returned to Russia? Had she been bound and gagged? Had she been conscious? Had she been drugged? As the wheels touched down, he forced such questions from his mind. There *was* no Chiara, he told himself. There *was* no Ivan. There was only Aaron Davis, servant of the American president, dreamer of American dreams, who was now just minutes away from his first encounter with Russian authorities.

They were waiting on the darkened tarmac, stamping their feet against the bitter cold, as Gabriel and the Secret Service detail filed down the rear cargo ramp. Standing next to the Russian delegation was a pair of officials from the U.S. Embassy, one of whom was an undeclared CIA officer with diplomatic cover. The Russians greeted Gabriel with warm handshakes and smiles, then gave his passport a cursory glance before stamping it. In return, Gabriel gave each a small token of American goodwill: White House cuff links. Five minutes later, he was seated in the back of an embassy car, speeding down Leningradsky Prospekt toward the city center.

Size has always mattered to the Russians, and to spend any time there is to discover nearly everything is the biggest: the biggest country, the biggest bell, the biggest swimming pool. If the Leningradsky was not the biggest street in the world, it was certainly among the ugliest – a hodgepodge of crumbling apartment houses and Stalinist monstrosities, lit by countless neon signs and piss-yellow streetlamps. Capitalism and Communism had collided violently on the prospekt, and the result was an urban nightmare. The G-8 banners the Russians had so carefully hung looked more like warning flags of the fate that awaited them all if they didn't put their financial houses in order.

Gabriel felt his stomach tighten by degrees as the car drew closer to the Kremlin. As they passed Dinamo Stadium, the CIA man handed him a satellite photograph of the dacha in the birch forest. There were three Range Rovers instead of two, and four men were clearly visible outside. Once again, Gabriel's eye was drawn to the parallel depressions in the woods near the house. It appeared there had been a change since the last pass. At the end of one depression was a dark patch, as if the snow cover had recently been disturbed.

By the time Gabriel returned the photo to the CIA man, the car was traveling along Tverskaya Street. Directly before them rose the Kremlin's Corner Arsenal Tower, its red star looking oddly like the symbol of a certain Dutch beer that now flowed freely in the watering holes of Moscow. The darkened offices of Galaxy Travel flashed by Gabriel's window, then the little side street where Anatoly, friend of Viktor Orlov, had been waiting to take Irina to dinner.

A hundred yards beyond Irina's office, Tverskaya Street emptied into the twelve lanes of Okhotny Ryad Street. They turned left and sped past the Duma, the House of Unions, and the Bolshoi Theatre. The next landmark Gabriel saw was a floodlit fortress of yellow stone looming directly ahead over Lubyanka Square – the former head-quarters of the KGB, now home to its domestic successor, the FSB. In any other country, the building would have been blown to bits and its horrors exposed to the healing light of day. But not Russia. They had simply hung a new sign, and buried its terrible secrets where they couldn't be found.

Just down the hill from Lubyanka, in Teatralnyy Prospekt, was the famed Hotel Metropol. Bag in hand, Gabriel sailed through the art deco entrance as if he owned the place, which is how Americans always seemed to enter hotels. The lobby, empty and silent, had been faithfully restored to its original décor – indeed, Gabriel could almost imagine Lenin and his disciples plotting the Red Terror over tea and cakes. The check-in counter was absent any customers; even so, Gabriel had to wait an eternity before Khrushchev's doppelgänger beckoned him forward. After filling out the lengthy registration form, Gabriel refused a bellman's indifferent offer of assistance and made his way upstairs to his room alone. It was now approaching five o'clock. He stood in the window, hand to his chin, head tilted to one side, and waited for the sun to rise over Red Square.

58. Moscow

Though the global financial crisis had caused economic pain across the industrialized world, few countries had fallen further or faster than Russia. Fueled by skyrocketing oil prices, Russia's economy had grown at dizzying speed in the first years of the new millennium, only to come crashing back to earth again with oil's sharp decline. Her stock market was a shambles, her banking system in ruins, and her once-docile population was now clamoring for relief. Inside the foreign ministries and intelligence services of the West, there was fear Russia's weakening economy might provoke the Kremlin to retreat even deeper into a Cold War posture – a sentiment shared by several key European leaders, who were becoming increasingly dependent on Russia for their supplies of natural gas. It was this concern that had prompted them to hold the emergency G-8 summit in Moscow in the dead of winter. Show the bully respect, they reckoned, and he might be encouraged to change his behavior. At least, that was the hope.

Had the summit taken place in any other G-8 country, the arrival of the leaders and their delegations would scarcely have been a blip on the local media's radar. But the summit was being held in Russia, and Russia, despite protests to the contrary, was not yet a normal country. Its media was either owned by the state or controlled by it, and its television networks went live as each presidential or prime ministerial aircraft sunk out of the iron-gray sky over Sheremetyevo. To hear the Russian reporters explain it, the Western leaders were coming to Moscow because they had been personally summoned by the Russian president. The world was in turmoil, the reporters warned, and only Russia could save it.

Inevitably, the American president suffered in comparison. The moment his plane appeared above the horizon, a number of Russian officials and commentators paraded before the cameras to denounce him and all he stood for. The global economic crisis was America's fault, they howled. America had been brought low by greed and hubris, and she was threatening to take the rest of the world down with her. The sun was setting on America. And good riddance.

Gabriel found little disagreement in the salons and restaurants of the Hotel Metropol. By midmorning, it was overrun with reporters and bureaucrats, all proudly wearing their official G-8 credentials as if a piece of plastic dangling from a strand of nylon gave them entrée to the inner sanctums of power and prestige. Gabriel's credentials were blue, which signified he had access mere mortals did not. They were hanging around his neck as he took a light breakfast beneath the vaulted stained-glass ceiling in the famed Metropol restaurant, wielding his BlackBerry throughout the meal like a shield. Leaving the restaurant, he was cornered by a group of French reporters who demanded to know his opinion of the new American stimulus plan. Though Gabriel evaded their questions, the French were clearly impressed by the fact he addressed them fluently in their native language.

In the lobby, Gabriel noticed several American reporters clustered around the Teatralnyy Prospekt entrance and quickly slipped out the back door into Revolution Square. In summer, the esplanade was crowded with market stalls where it was possible to buy anything from fur hats and nesting dolls to busts of the murderers Lenin and Stalin. Now, in the depths of winter, only the bravest dared to venture there. Remarkably, it was clear of snow and ice. When the wind briefly subsided, Gabriel caught a whiff of the de-icer the Russians used to achieve this result. He remembered stories Mikhail had told him about the powerful chemicals Russians poured onto their streets and sidewalks. The stuff could destroy a pair of shoes in a matter of days. Even the dogs refused to walk on it. In springtime, the streetcars used to burst into flames because their wiring had been eaten away by months of exposure. That was how Mikhail had celebrated the arrival of spring as a child in Russia – with the burning of the trams.

Gabriel spotted him a moment later, standing next to Eli Lavon just outside Resurrection Gate. Lavon was holding a briefcase in his right hand, meaning Gabriel had not been followed leaving the Metropol. *Moscow Rules* . . . Gabriel headed left through the shadowed archway of the gate and entered the vast expanse of Red Square. Standing at the foot of Savior Tower, wearing a heavy overcoat and fur hat, was Uzi Navot. The tower's gold-and-black clock face read 11:23. Navot pretended to set his watch by it.

'How was the entry at Sheremetyevo?'

'No problem.'

'And the hotel?'

'No problem.'

'Good.' Navot shoved his hands into his pocket. 'Let's take a walk, Mr. Davis. It's better if we walk.'

They headed toward St Basil's, heads down, shoulders hunched against the biting wind: the Moscow shuffle. Navot wished to spend as little time as possible in Gabriel's presence. He wasted no time getting down to business.

'We went onto the property last night to have a look around.'

'Who's we?'

'Mikhail and Shmuel Peled from Moscow Station.' He paused, then added, 'And me.'

Gabriel gave him a sideways glance. 'You're here to supervise, Uzi. Shamron made it clear he didn't want you involved in any direct operational way. You're too senior to get arrested.'

'Let me see if I understand this correctly. It's all right for me to tangle with a Russian assassin in a Swiss bank, but it's verboten for me to take a walk in the woods?'

'Is that what it was, Uzi? A walk in the woods?'

'Not quite. The dacha is set a kilometer back from the road. The track leading to it is bordered by birch forest on both sides. It's tight. Only one vehicle can get through at a time.'

'Is there a gate?'

'No gate, but the track is always blocked by security guards in a Range Rover.'

'How close were you able to get to the dacha?'

'Close enough to see that Ivan makes two poor bastards stand outside all the time. And close enough to plant a wireless camera.'

'How's the signal?'

'Not bad. We'll be fine as long as we don't get six feet of snow tonight. We can see the front door, which means we can see if anyone's coming or going.'

'Who's monitoring the shot?'

'Shmuel and a girl from Moscow Station.'

'Where are they?'

'Holed up in a crummy little hotel in the nearest town. They're pretending to be lovers. Apparently, the girl's husband likes to knock her around. Shmuel wants to take her away and start a new life. You know the story, Gabriel.'

'The satellite photos show guards behind the house.'

'We saw them, too. They keep at least three men back there at all times. They're static, spaced about a hundred yards apart. With night-vision goggles, we had no trouble seeing them. In daylight' – Navot shrugged his heavy shoulders – 'they'll go down like targets in a shooting gallery. We'll just have to go in while it's still dark, and try not to freeze to death before nine o'clock.'

They had passed St Basil's and were nearing the southeast corner of the Kremlin. Directly before them was the Moscow River, frozen and covered by gray-white snow. Navot nudged Gabriel to the right and led him along the embankment. The wind was now at their backs. After they passed a pair of bored-looking Moscow militiamen, Gabriel asked whether Navot had seen anything at the dacha to warrant a change in plan. Navot shook his head.

'What about the guns?'

'The weapons room at the embassy has everything. Just tell me what you want.'

'A Beretta 92 and a Mini-Uzi, both with suppressors.'

'You sure the Mini will do?'

'It's going to be tight inside the dacha.'

They passed another pair of militiamen. To their right, floating above the red walls of the ancient citadel, was the ornate yellow-and-white façade of the Great Kremlin Palace, where the G-8 summit was now under way.

'What's the status of the Range Rover?'

'We took delivery of it last night.'

'Black?'

'Of course. Ivan's boys only drive black Range Rovers.'

'Where did you get it?'

'A dealership in north Moscow. Shamron's going to blow a gasket when he sees the price tag.'

'License plates?'

'Taken care of.'

'How long is the drive from the Metropol?'

'In a normal country, it would be two and a half hours tops. Here . . . Mikhail wants to pick you up at 2 a.m., just to make sure there are no problems.'

They had reached the southwestern corner of the Kremlin. On the other side of the river stood a colossal gray apartment building crowned by a revolving Mercedes-Benz star. Known as the House on the Embankment, it had been built by Stalin in 1931 as a palace of Soviet privilege for the most elite members of the *nomenklatura*. During the Great Terror, he had turned it into a house of horrors. Nearly eight hundred people, one-third of the building's residents, had been hauled out of their beds and murdered at one of the killing sites that ringed Moscow. Their punishment was virtually always the same: a night of beatings, a bullet in the back of the head, a hasty burial in a mass grave. Despite its blood-soaked history, the House on the Embankment was now considered one of Moscow's most exclusive addresses. Ivan Kharkov owned a luxury apartment on the ninth floor. It was among his most prized possessions.

Gabriel looked at Navot and noticed he was staring at the sad little park across the street from the apartment building: Bolotnaya Square, scene of perhaps the most famous argument in Office history.

'I should have broken your arm that night. None of this would have happened if I'd dragged you into the car and pulled you out of Moscow with the rest of the team.'

'That's true, Uzi. None of it would have happened. We would have never found Ivan's missiles. And Elena Kharkov would be dead.'

Navot ignored the remark. 'I can't believe we're back here. I swore to myself I would never set foot in this town again.' He glanced at Gabriel. 'Why in God's name would Ivan want to keep an apartment in a place like that? It's haunted, that building. You can almost hear the screaming.'

'Elena once told me that her husband was a devout Stalinist. Ivan's house in Zhukovka was built on a plot of land once owned by Stalin's daughter. And when he was looking for a pied-à-terre near the Kremlin, he bought the flat in the House on the Embankment. The original owner of Ivan's apartment was a senior man in the Foreign Ministry. Stalin's henchmen suspected him of being a spy for the Germans. They took him to Butovo and put a bullet in the back of his head. Apparently, Ivan loves to tell the story.'

Navot shook his head slowly. 'Some people go for nice kitchens and good views. But when Ivan is looking at a place, he demands a bloody past.'

'He's unique, our Ivan.'

'Maybe that explains why he bought several hundred acres of worthless birch forests and swampland outside Moscow.'

Yes, thought Gabriel. Maybe it did. He looked back down the Kremlin Embankment and saw Eli Lavon approaching, briefcase still in his right hand. As Lavon walked past, he gave Gabriel a little jab in the small of the back. It meant the meeting had gone on long enough. Navot removed his glove and extended his hand.

'Go back to the Metropol. Keep your head down. And try not to worry. We'll get her back.'

Gabriel shook Navot's hand, then turned and headed back toward Resurrection Gate.

Though Navot did not know it, Gabriel disobeyed the order to return to his room at the Hotel Metropol and made his way to Tverskaya Street instead. Pausing outside the office building at No. 6, he stared at the posters in the window of Galaxy Travel. One showed a Russian couple sharing a champagne lunch along the ski slopes of Courchevel; the other, a pair of Russian nymphs tanning themselves on the beaches of the Côte d'Azur. The irony seemed lost on Irina Bulganova, former wife of the defector Grigori Bulganov, who was seated primly at her desk, telephone to her ear. There were many things Gabriel wanted to tell her but couldn't. Not yet. And so he stood there alone, watching her through the frosted glass. Reality is a state of mind, he thought. Reality can be whatever you want it to be.

59. Grosvenor Square, London

If Gabriel earned high marks for his grace under pressure during the final hours before the operation, the same, unfortunately, could not be said of Ari Shamron. Upon his return to London, he made a base camp for himself inside the Israeli Embassy in Kensington and used it to launch raids on targets stretching from Tel Aviv to Langley. The officers on the Ops Desk at King Saul Boulevard grew so weary of Shamron's outbursts, they drew lots to determine who would have the misfortune of taking his calls. Only Adrian Carter managed not to lose patience with him. As a grounded fieldman himself, he knew the feeling of utter helplessness Shamron was experiencing. The extraction plan was Gabriel's; Shamron could only operate the levers and pull the strings. And even then, he was heavily dependent on Carter and the Agency. It violated Shamron's core faith in the principles of *kachol v'lavan*. Left to his own devices, the Old Man would have walked into Ivan's dacha in the woods and done the job himself. And only a fool would have bet against him. 'He's done things none of us can imagine,' Carter said in Shamron's defense. 'And he's got the scars to prove it.'

At 6 p.m. that evening, Shamron headed to the American Embassy in Mayfair for the opening act. A young CIA officer, a fresh-faced girl who looked as though she had just finished her junior year abroad, greeted him in Upper

Brook Street. She escorted him past the Marine Guard, then into a secure elevator that bore him downward into the bowels of the annex. Adrian Carter and Graham Seymour were already there, seated on the top deck of the amphitheater-shaped Ops Center. Shamron took a seat at Carter's right and looked at one of the large screens at the front of the room. It showed two aircraft sitting on tarmac outside Washington, D.C. Both belonged to the 89th Airlift Wing based at Andrews Air Force Base. Both were fueled and ready for departure.

At 7 p.m., Carter's telephone rang. He brought the receiver swiftly to his ear, listened in silence for a few seconds, then hung up.

'He's pulling up to the gate. It looks like we're on, gentlemen.'

There was a time in Washington when everyone in government and journalism could recite the name of the Soviet ambassador to the United States. But these days few people outside Foggy Bottom and the State Department press corps had ever heard of Konstantin Tretyakov. Though fluent in English, the Russian Federation's ambassador rarely appeared on television and never threw parties anyone would bother to attend. He was a forgotten man in a city where Moscow's envoy had once been treated almost like a head of state. Tretyakov was the worst thing a person could be in Washington. He was irrelevant.

The ambassador's official CV described him as an 'America expert' and career diplomat who had served in many important Western posts. It left out the fact his career had nearly been derailed in Oslo when he was caught with his hand in the embassy's petty-cash drawer. Nor did it mention that he occasionally drank too much. Or that he had one brother who worked as a spy for the SVR and another who was part of the Russian president's inner circle of *siloviki* at the Kremlin. All this unflattering material, however, was contained in the CIA's dossier, a copy of which had been given to Ed Fielding to assist in his preparation for the Andrews end of the operation. The CIA security man had found the file highly entertaining. He had joined the Agency in the darkest days of the Cold War and had spent several decades fighting the Soviets and their proxies on secret battlefields around the globe. A glance at the ambassador's file reassured Fielding his career had not been in vain.

He was standing beneath the crest of the 89th Airlift Wing when Tretyakov's motorcade drew to a halt outside the passenger terminal. Despite the fact the ambassador was now inside one of the most secure facilities in the national capital region, he was protected by three layers of security: his own Russian bodyguards, a detail of Diplomatic Security agents, and several officers from Andrews base security. Fielding had no trouble picking out the ambassador when he emerged from the back of his limousine – the dossier had contained a copy of Tretyakov's official portrait along with several surveillance photos – but Fielding covered his preparation by approaching the ambassador's factotum instead. The aide corrected Fielding by pointing to Tretya-kov, who now had a superior smile on his face as if amused by American incompetence. Fielding pumped the ambassador's hand and introduced himself as Tom Harris. Apparently, Mr. Harris had no title or reason for being at Andrews other than to shake the ambassador's hand.

'As you can probably guess, Mr. Ambassador, the Kharkov children are a little nervous. Mrs. Kharkov would like you to see them alone, without aides or security.'

'Why would the children be nervous, Mr. Harris? They're going back to Russia where they belong.'

'Are you saying you refuse to meet Anna and Nikolai without aides or bodyguards, Mr. Ambassador? Because if that's the case, the deal is off.'

The ambassador raised his chin a bit. 'No, Mr. Harris, that is not the case.'

'Wise decision. I would hate to think what would happen if Ivan Kharkov ever found out you personally blew the deal to get his children back over some silly question of protocol.'

'Watch your tone, Mr. Harris.'

Fielding had no intention of watching his tone. In fact, he was just getting started.

'I take it you've seen photographs of the Kharkov children?'

The ambassador nodded.

'You're confident you can identify them by sight?'

'Very.'

'That's good. Because under no circumstances are you to approach or touch the children. You may ask them two questions, no more. Are these conditions acceptable to you, Mr. Ambassador?'

'What choice do I have?'

'None whatsoever.'

'That's what I thought.'

'Please extend your arms straight out from your sides and spread your feet.'

'Why on earth would I do that?'

'Because I have to search you before letting you anywhere near those children.'

'This is outrageous.'

'I would hate for Ivan Kharkov to find out you—'

The ambassador extended his arms and spread his feet. Fielding took his time with the search and made sure it was as invasive and mortifying as possible. When the search was over, he squirted liquid desanitizer on his hands.

'Two questions, no touching. Are we clear, Mr. Ambassador?'

'We're clear, Mr. Harris.'

'Follow me, please.'

It was a small room, hung with photographs of the installation's storied past: presidents departing on historic journeys, POWs returning from years of captivity, flag-draped coffins coming home for burial in American soil. Had photographers been present that afternoon, they would have captured an image of great sadness: a mother holding her children, possibly for the last time. But there were no photographers, of course, because the mother and children were not there – at least, not officially. As for the two flights that would soon tear this family apart, they did not exist, either, and no records of them would ever find their way into the control tower's logbook.

They were huddled together along a couch of black vinyl. Elena, dressed in blue jeans and a shearling coat, was seated in the center, an arm around each child. Their faces were buried in her collar, and they remained that way long after the Russian ambassador entered the room. Elena refused to look at him. Her lips were pressed to Anna's forehead, her gaze focused on the pale gray carpet.

'Good afternoon, Mrs. Kharkov,' the ambassador said in Russian.

Elena made no response. The ambassador looked at Fielding. In English, he said, 'I need to see their faces. Otherwise, I cannot confirm that these are indeed the children of Ivan Kharkov.'

'You have two questions, Mr. Ambassador. Ask them to lift their faces. But make certain you ask them nicely. Otherwise, I might get upset.'

The ambassador looked at the distraught family seated before him. In Russian, he asked, 'Please, children, lift your faces so I can see them.'

The children remained motionless.

'Try speaking to them in English,' said Fielding.

Tretyakov did as Fielding suggested. This time, the children raised their faces and stared at the ambassador with undisguised hostility. Tretyakov appeared satisfied the children were indeed Anna and Nikolai Kharkov.

'Your father is looking forward to seeing you. Are you excited about going home?'

'No,' said Anna.

'No,' repeated Nikolai. 'We want to stay here with our mother.'

'Perhaps your mother should come home, too.'

Elena looked at Tretyakov for the first time. Then her gaze moved to Fielding. 'Please take him away, Mr. Harris. His presence is beginning to make me ill.'

Fielding escorted the ambassador next door to the Base Ops building. They were standing together on the observation deck when Elena and the children emerged from the passenger terminal, accompanied by several security officers. The group moved slowly across the tarmac and climbed the passenger-boarding stairs to the doorway of a C-32. Elena Kharkov emerged ten minutes later without the children, visibly shaken. Clinging to the arm of an Air Force officer, she walked over to a Gulfstream and disappeared into the cabin.

'You must be very proud, Mr. Ambassador,' Fielding said.

'You had no right to take them from their father in the first place.'

The cabin door of the C-32 was now closed. The boarding stairs moved away, followed by the fuel and catering trucks. Five minutes after that, the plane was rising over the Maryland suburbs of Washington. Fielding watched it disappear into the clouds, then looked contemptuously at the ambassador.

'Nine a.m. at the Konakovo airfield. Remember, no Ivan, no children. Are we clear, Mr. Ambassador?'

'He'll be there.'

'You're free to leave. You'll forgive me if I don't shake your hand. I'm feeling a bit ill myself.'

Ed Fielding remained on the observation deck until the ambassador and his entourage were safely off base, then boarded the waiting Gulfstream. Elena Kharkov was buckled into her seat, eyes fixed on the deserted tarmac.

'How long do we have to wait?'

'Not long, Elena. Are you going to be all right?'

'I'll be fine, Ed. Let's go home.'

60. Hotel Metropol, Moscow

Gabriel was notified of the plane's departure at 10:45 p.m. Moscow time while standing in the window of his room at the Metropol. He had been there, on and off, since returning from his foray into Tverskaya Street. Ten hours with nothing to do but pace the floor and make himself sick with worry. Ten hours with nothing to do but picture the operation from beginning to end a thousand times. Ten hours with nothing to do but think about Ivan. He wondered how his enemy would spend this night. Would he spend it quietly with his child bride? Or perhaps a celebration was in order: a *blowout*. That was the word Ivan and his cohorts used to describe the parties thrown at the conclusion of a major arms deal. The bigger the deal, the bigger the blowout.

With the children's plane now bound for Russia, Gabriel felt his nerves turn to piano wire. He tried to slow his racing heart, but his body refused his commands. He tried to close his eyes, but saw only satellite photos of the little dacha in the birch forest. And the room where Chiara and Grigori were surely being kept chained and bound. And the four streams that converged in a great marshland. And the parallel depressions in the woods.

My husband is a devout Stalinist . . . His love of Stalin has influenced his real estate purchases.

The secure PDA helped pass the time. It told him that

Navot, Yaakov, and Oded were proceeding to the target. It told him that the concealed camera had detected no change at the dacha or in the disposition of Ivan's forces. It told him that God had granted them a heavy ground fog over the marshes to help conceal their approach. And finally, at 1:48 a.m., it told him that it was nearly time to leave.

Gabriel had dressed long ago and was sweating beneath layer upon layer of protective clothing. He forced himself to remain in the room a few minutes longer, then switched off the lights and slipped quietly into the corridor. As the clock in the lobby tolled 2 a.m., he stepped from the elevator and passed Khrushchev's doppelgänger with a curt nod. The Range Rover was waiting in Teatralnyy Prospekt, engine running. Mikhail drummed his fingers nervously as they swept up the hill toward FSB Headquarters.

'You okay, Mikhail?'

'I'm fine, boss.'

'You're not nervous, are you?'

'Why would I be nervous? I love being around Lubyanka. The KGB kept my father in there for six months when I was a kid. Did I ever tell you that, Gabriel?'

He had.

'Do you have the guns?'

'Plenty.'

'Radios?'

'Of course.'

'Sat phone?'

'Gabriel, please.'

'Coffee?'

'Two thermoses. One for us, one for them.'

'What about the bolt cutters?'

'A pair for each of us. Just in case.'

'In case of what?'

'One of us goes down.'

'Nobody's going down except Ivan's guards.'

'Whatever you say, boss.'

Mikhail resumed his tapping.

'You're not going to do that all the way?'

'I'll try not to.'

'That's good. Because you're giving me a headache.'

Moscow refused to relinquish its grip on them without a fight. It took thirty minutes just to get from Lubyanka to the MKAD outer ring road: thirty minutes of traffic jams, broken signal lights, sinkholes, crime scenes, and unexplained militia roadblocks. 'And it's two in the morning,' Mikhail said in exasperation. 'Imagine what it's like during the evening rush, when half of Moscow is trying to get home at the same time.'

'If it continues like this, we won't have to imagine.'

Once beyond the city, the massive apartment houses began to gradually disappear only to be replaced by mile after mile of smoking rail yards and factories. They were, of course, the biggest factories Gabriel had ever seen – behemoths with towering smokestacks and scarcely a light burning anywhere. A freight train rattled by heading in the opposite direction. It seemed to take an eternity to pass. It was five miles long, thought Gabriel. Or perhaps it was a hundred. Surely it was the world's longest.

They were driving on the M7. It ran eastward into Russia's vast middle, all the way through Tatarstan. And if you were feeling really adventurous, Mikhail explained, you could hit the Trans-Siberian in Ufa and drive to Mongolia and China. '*China*, Gabriel! Can you imagine driving to *China*?'

Actually, Gabriel could. The sheer scale of the place made anything possible: the endless black sky filled with hard white stars, the vast frozen plains dotted with slumbering towns and villages, the unbearable cold. In some of the villages he could see onion domes shining in the bright moonlight. Ivan's hero had been hard on the churches of Russia. He'd ordered Kaganovich to dynamite Moscow's Cathedral of Christ the Savior in 1931 – supposedly because it blocked the view from the windows of his Kremlin apartment – and in the countryside he'd turned the churches into barns and grain silos. Some were now being restored. Others, like the villages they once served, were in ruins. It was Russia's dirty little secret. The glitz and glamour of Moscow was matched only by the poverty and deprivation of the countryside. Moscow got the money, the villages got absentee governors and the occasional visit from some Kremlin flunky. They were the places you left behind to make your fortune in the big city. They were for the losers. In the villages, you did nothing but drink and curse the rich bastards in Moscow.

They flashed through a string of towns, each more desolate than the last: Lakinsk, Demidovo, Vorsha. Ahead lay Vladimir, capital of the oblast. Its five-domed Cathedral of the Assumption had been the model for all the cathedrals of Russia – the cathedrals Stalin had destroyed or turned into pigpens. Mikhail explained that people had been living in and around Vladimir for twenty-five thousand years, an impressive statistic even for a boy from the Valley of Jezreel. *Twenty-five thousand years*, Gabriel thought, gazing out at the broken factories on the city's western outskirts. Why had they come? Why had they *stayed*?

Reclining his seat, he saw an image of his last late-night drive through the Russian countryside: Olga and Elena sleeping in the backseat, Grigori behind the wheel. *Promise me one thing, Gabriel* . . . At least then they had been driving *out* of Russia, not directly into the belly of the beast. Mikhail found a news bulletin on the radio and provided simultaneous translation while he drove. The first day of the G-8 summit had gone well, at least from the point of view of the Russian president, which was the only one that mattered. Then, by some miracle of atmospheric conditions, Mikhail found a BBC bulletin in English. There had been an important political development in Zimbabwe. A fatal plane crash in South Korea. And in Afghanistan, Taliban forces had carried out a major raid in Kabul. With Ivan's guns, no doubt.

'Is it possible to drive to Afghanistan from here?'

'Sure,' said Mikhail. He then proceeded to recite the road numbers and the distances while Vladimir, center of human habitation for twenty-five millennia, receded once more into the darkness.

They listened to the BBC until the signal became too faint to hear. Then Mikhail switched off the radio and again began drumming his fingers on the steering wheel.

'Something bothering you, Mikhail?'

'Maybe we should talk about it. I'd feel better if we ran through it a couple of hundred times.'

'That's not like you. I need you to be confident.'

'It's your wife in there, Gabriel. I'd hate to think that something I did—'

'You're going to be just fine. But if you want to run through it a couple of hundred times . . .' Gabriel's voice trailed off as he looked out at the limitless frozen landscape. 'It's not as if we have anything better to do.'

Mikhail's voice dropped in pitch slightly as he began to speak about the operation. The key to everything, he said, would be speed. They had to overwhelm them quickly. A sentry will always hesitate for an instant, even when confronted with someone he doesn't know. That instant would be their opening. They would take it swiftly and decisively. 'And no gunfights,' Mikhail said. 'Gunfights are for cowboys and gangsters.'

Mikhail was neither. He was Sayeret Matkal, the most elite unit on earth. The Sayeret had pulled off operations other units could only dream of. It had done Entebbe and Sabena and jobs much harder that no one would ever read about. Mikhail had dispensed death to the terror masterminds of Hamas, Islamic Jihad, and the al-Aksa Martyrs' Brigade. He had even crossed into Lebanon and killed members of Hezbollah. They had been hellish operations, carried out in crowded cities and refugee camps. Not one had failed. Not a single terrorist targeted by Mikhail was still walking the earth. A dacha in a birch forest was nothing for a man like him. Ivan's guards were special forces themselves: Alpha Group and OMON. Even so, Mikhail spoke of them only in the past tense. As far as he was concerned, they were already dead. Silence, speed, and timing would be the key.

Silence, speed, timing . . . Shamron's holy trinity.

Unlike Mikhail, Gabriel had never carried out assassinations in the West Bank or Gaza, and, for the most part, had managed to avoid operating in Arab countries. One notable exception was Abu Jihad, the nom de guerre of Khalil al-Wazir, the second-highest-ranking figure in the PLO after Yasir Arafat. Like all Sayeret recruits, Mikhail had studied every aspect of the operation during his training, but he had never asked Gabriel about that night. He did so now as they thundered along the deserted highway. And Gabriel obliged him, though he would regret it later.

Abu Jihad . . . Even now, the sound of his name put ice at the back of Gabriel's neck. In April of 1988, this symbol of Palestinian suffering was living in splendid exile in Tunis, in a large villa near the beach. Gabriel had personally surveilled the house and the surrounding district and had overseen the construction of a duplicate in the Negev, where they had rehearsed for several weeks prior to the operation. On the night of the hit, he had come ashore in a rubber boat and climbed into a waiting van. In a matter of minutes, it was over. There had been a guard outside the house, dozing behind the wheel of a Mercedes. Gabriel had shot him through the ear with a silenced Beretta. Then, with the help of his Sayeret escorts, he had blown the front door off the hinges with a special explosive that emitted little more sound than a handclap. After killing a second guard in the front entrance hall, Gabriel had crept quietly up the stairs to Abu Jihad's study. So silent was Gabriel's approach that the PLO mastermind never heard a thing. He died at his desk while watching a videotape of the intifada.

Silence, speed, timing . . . Shamron's holy trinity.

'And afterward?' Mikhail asked softly.

Afterward . . . A scene from Gabriel's nightmares.

Leaving the study, he had run straight into Abu Jihad's wife. She was clutching a small boy to her breast in terror and clinging to the arm of her teenage daughter. Gabriel looked at the woman and in Arabic shouted: 'Go back to your room!' Then he had said calmly to the girl: 'Go and take care of your mother.'

Go and take care of your mother . . .

There were few nights when he did not see the face of that child. And he saw it now, as they turned off the highway and headed into the northernmost reaches of the oblast. Sometimes, Gabriel wondered whether he would have pulled the trigger had he known the girl was standing at his back. And sometimes, in his darker moments, he wondered whether everything that had befallen him since was not God's punishment for killing a man in front of his family. Now, as he had done countless times before, he nudged the child gently from his thoughts and watched as Mikhail made another turn, this time into a dense stand of pine and fir. The headlamps went dark, the engine silent.

'How far is the property?'

'Two miles.'

'How long to make the drive?'

'Five minutes. We'll take it nice and slow.'

'You're sure, Mikhail? Timing is everything.'

'I've done it twice. I'm sure.'

Mikhail began drumming his fingers on the console. Gabriel ignored him and looked at the clock: 6:25. *The waiting* . . . Waiting for the sun to rise before a morning of killing. Waiting to hold Chiara in his arms. Waiting for the child of Abu Jihad to forgive him. He poured himself a cup of coffee and loaded his weapons.

6:26 . . . 6:27 . . . 6:28 . . .

*

The sun set fire to the snowbank. Chiara did not know whether it was sunrise or sunset. But as the light fell upon Grigori's sleeping face, she had a premonition of death, so clear that it seemed a stone had been laid over her heart. She heard the sound of the latch and watched as the woman with milk-white skin and translucent eyes entered the cell. The woman had food: stale bread, cold sausage, tea in paper cups. Whether it was breakfast or dinner, Chiara was not certain. The woman withdrew, locking the door behind her. Chiara held her tea between shackled hands and looked at the burning snowbank. As usual, the light remained only a few minutes. Then the fire was extinguished, and the room plunged once more into pitch-blackness.

61. Konakovo, Russia

Like Russia itself, the airfield at Konakovo had been a two-time loser. Abandoned by the air force shortly after the fall of the Soviet Union, it was allowed to crumble into a state of ruin before finally being taken over by a consortium of businessmen and civic leaders. For a brief period, it experienced modest success as a commercial cargo facility, only to see its fortunes plummet a second time with the price of Russian crude. The airfield now handled fewer than a dozen flights a week and was used mainly as a rest home for decaying Antonovs, Ilyushins, and Tupolevs. But its runway, at twelve thousand feet, was still one of the longest in the region, and its landing lights and radar systems functioned well by Russian standards, which is to say they worked most of the time.

All systems were in good working order that Friday morning, and great effort had been made to plow and treat the runway and tarmac. And with good reason. The control tower had been informed by the Kremlin that an American Air Force C-32 would be landing at Konakovo at 9 a.m. sharp. What's more, a delegation of hotshots from the Foreign Ministry and customs would be on hand to greet the aircraft and expedite arrival procedures. Airport authorities had not been told the identity of the arriving passengers, and they knew far better than to press the matter. One didn't ask too many questions when the

Kremlin was involved. Not unless one wanted the FSB knocking on one's door.

The Moscow delegation arrived shortly after eight and was waiting at the edge of the windswept tarmac when a string of lights appeared against the overcast sky to the south. A few of the officials initially mistook the lights for the American plane, which was not possible since the C-32 was still a hundred miles out and would be landing from the west, not the southeast. As the lights drew closer, the brittle air was filled with the beating of rotors. There were three helicopters in all, and even from a long way off it was clear they were not of Russian manufacture. Someone in the control tower identified them as custom-fitted Bell 427s. Someone in the delegation said that would make sense. Ivan Kharkov might be willing to put a load of weapons on a Russian rust bucket, but when it came to his family he only flew American.

The helicopters settled onto the tarmac and, one by one, killed their engines. From the two flanking aircraft emerged a security detail fit for a Russian president: big boys, well groomed, heavily armed, hard as nails. After establishing a perimeter around the third helicopter, one guard stepped forward and opened the cabin door. For a long moment, no one appeared. Then came a flash of lustrous blond hair, framing a face of Slavic youth and perfection. The features were instantly recognizable to the control tower as well as the members of the Moscow delegation. The woman had appeared on countless magazine covers and billboards, usually with far less clothing than she was wearing now. Her name had once been Yekaterina Mazurov. Now she was known as Yekaterina Kharkov. Though meticulously coiffed and painted, she was clearly on edge. Immediately after placing an elegant boot on the tarmac, she gave one of the bodyguards a good tongue-lashing, which, unfortunately, could not be heard. Someone in the Moscow delegation pointed out that Yekaterina's anxiety was to be forgiven. She was about to become a mother of two and was still little more than a child herself.

The second person to emerge from the helicopter was a trim man in a dark overcoat with a face that hinted of ancestors from deep in Russia's interior. He was holding a cell phone to his ear and appeared to be engaged in a conversation of great import. No one in the control tower or the Moscow delegation recognized him, which was hardly surprising. Unlike the ravishing Yekaterina, this man's photograph never appeared in the papers, and few people outside the insular world of the *siloviki* and the oligarchs knew his name. He was Oleg Rudenko, a former colonel in the KGB who now served as chief of Ivan Kharkov's personal security service. Even Rudenko was the first to admit the title was merely an honorific. Ivan called all the shots; Rudenko just made the trains run on time. Thus the cell phone pressed tightly to his ear and the grim expression on his face.

The interval between Rudenko and the emergence of the third passenger was eighty-four long seconds, as timed by the control tower staff. He was an immensely powerful-looking figure, somewhat short in stature, with angular cheekbones, a pugalist's broad forehead, and coarse hair the color of steel wool. One of the officials briefly confused him for a bodyguard, which was a common mistake and one he secretly enjoyed. But any inclination to such thinking was immediately dispelled by the cut of his magnificent English overcoat. And by the manner in which his trousers broke across his handmade English shoes. And by the way his own bodyguards seemed to fear his very presence. And by the sundial-sized gold watch on his left wrist. *Look at him*, murmured someone in the Moscow delegation. *Look at Ivan Borisovich!* The controversy, the arrest warrants, the indictments in the West: any one of them would have gladly accepted it all, just to live like Ivan Borisovich for a day. Just to ride in his helicopters and his limousines. And just to climb into bed one time with Yekaterina. *But why the frown, Ivan Borisovich? Today is a joyous occasion. Today is the day your children are coming home from America.*

He strode across the tarmac, Yekaterina on one side, Rudenko on the other, bodyguards all around. The head of the delegation, deputy foreign minister so-and-so of department such-and-such, met him halfway. Their conversation was brief and, by all appearances, unpleasant. Afterward, each retreated to his respective corner. When asked to recount what Ivan had said, the deputy refused. It couldn't be repeated in polite company.

Look at him! Look at Ivan Borisovich! The fancy American helicopter, the beautiful young wife, the mountain of money. And underneath it all, he was still a KGB hood. A KGB hood in a fancy English suit.

Like Oleg Rudenko, Adrian Carter was at that moment holding a telephone to his ear, a secure landline device connected directly to the Global Ops Center at Langley. Shamron had a phone to his ear as well, though his was connected to the Operations Desk at King Saul Boulevard.

He was staring at the clock while at the same time battling a crippling craving for nicotine. Smoking was strictly forbidden in the annex. So, apparently, was speaking because Carter had not uttered a word in several minutes.

'Well, Adrian? Is he there or not?'

Carter nodded his head vigorously. 'The spotter just confirmed it. Ivan's birds are on the ground.'

'How long until the plane gets there?'

'Seven minutes.'

Shamron looked at the Moscow clock: *8:53.*

'Cutting it a little close, aren't they?'

'We're fine, Ari.'

'Just make sure they switch on those jammers at 9:05, Adrian. Not a second sooner, not a second later.'

'Don't worry, Ari. No phone calls for Ivan. No phone calls for anyone.'

Shamron looked at the clock: *8:54.*

Silence, speed, timing . . .

All they needed now was a bit of luck.

Had Uzi Navot been privy to Shamron's thoughts, he would have surely recited the Office maxim that luck is always earned, never bestowed. He would have done so because at that moment he was lying on his face in the snow, one hundred yards behind the dacha, a weapon bearing his name cradled in his arms. Fifty yards to his right, in precisely the same position, was Yaakov. And fifty yards to his left was Oded. Standing directly in front of each of them was a Russian. It had been five hours since Navot and the others had crept into position through the birch forest. In that time, two shifts of guards had come and gone. There had been no relief, of course, for the visiting team. Navot, though properly outfitted for such an operation, was trembling with cold. He assumed Yaakov and Oded were suffering as well, though he had not spoken to either man in several hours. Radio silence was the order of the morning.

Navot was tempted to feel sorry for himself, but his mind would not allow it. Whenever the cold started to eat at his bones, he thought about the camps and the ghettos and terrible winters his people had endured during the Shoah. Like Gabriel, Navot owed his very existence to someone who had summoned the courage, the will, to survive those winters – a paternal grandfather who had spent five years toiling in the Nazi labor camps. Five years living on starvation rations. Five years sleeping in the cold. It was because of his grandfather that Navot had joined the Office. And it was because of his grandfather that he was lying in the snow, one hundred yards behind a dacha, surrounded by birch trees. The Russian standing before him would soon be dead. Though Navot was not an expert like Gabriel and Mikhail, he had done his obligatory time in the army and had undergone extensive weapons training at the Academy. So, too, had Yaakov and Oded. For them, fifty yards was nothing, even with frozen hands, even with suppressors. And there would be no going for the comfort zone of the torso. Only head shots. No dying calls on the radio.

Navot rolled his left wrist toward him a few degrees and glanced at his digital watch: *8:59*. Six more minutes to contend with the cold. He flexed his fingers and waited for the sound of Gabriel's voice in his miniature earpiece.

*

The second and final session of the emergency G-8 summit convened at the stroke of nine in the ornate St George's Hall of the Great Kremlin Palace. As always, the American president arrived precisely on time and settled into his place at the breakfast table. As luck would have it, the British prime minister had been placed to his right. The Russian president was seated opposite between the German chancellor and the Italian prime minister, his two closest allies in Western Europe. His attention, however, was clearly focused on the Anglo-American side of the table. Indeed, he had fixed both English-speaking leaders with his trademark stare, the one he always adopted when he was trying to look tough and decisive to the Russian people.

'Do you think he knows?' asked the British prime minister.

'Are you kidding? He knows everything.'

'Will it work?'

'We'll know soon enough.'

'I only hope no harm comes to that woman.'

The president sipped his coffee. 'What woman?'

Stalin was never quite able to get his hands on Zamoskvorechye. The streets of this pleasant old quarter just south of the Kremlin were largely spared the horror of Soviet replanning and are still lined with grand imperial houses and onion-domed churches. The district is also home to the embassy of the State of Israel, which stands at Bolshaya Ordynka 56. Rimona was waiting just inside the security gate, flanked by a pair of Shin Bet embassy guards. Like Uzi Navot, she was watching a single object: an S-Class Mercedes sedan, which had pulled to the curb outside the embassy at the stroke of nine.

The car was crouched low over its wheels, weighed down by armor plating and bulletproof windows. The glass was also blacked out, which made it impossible for Rimona to see into the passenger seats. All she could make out was the driver's chin, and a pair of hands resting calmly on the wheel.

Rimona raised her secure cell phone to her ear and heard the cacophony of the Ops Desk at King Saul Boulevard. Then the voice of a desk officer, pleading for information. *'The plane is on the ground. Tell us if she's there. Tell us what you see.'* Rimona complied with the order. She saw a Mercedes car with blacked-out windows. And she saw a pair of hands resting on the wheel. And then, in her mind, she saw a pair of angels sitting in a Range Rover. A pair of angels who would create hell on earth unless Chiara got out of that car.

62. Grosvenor Square, London

There were no pictures, only distant voices on secure phones and words that flashed and blinked on the billboard-sized communications screens. At 9:00 a.m. Moscow time, the screens told Shamron that the children's plane was safely on the ground. At 9:01, that the plane was taxiing toward the control tower. At 9:03, that the plane was being approached by ground crew and motorized passenger-boarding stairs. A few seconds later, he was informed by telephone transmission from King Saul Boulevard that 'Joshua' was proceeding to the target – Joshua being the Office code name for Gabriel and Mikhail. And finally, at 9:04, he was notified by Adrian Carter that the forward cabin door was now open.

'Where's Ivan?'

'Approaching the plane.'

'Is he alone?'

'Full entourage. The wife, the muscle, the thug.'

'By that you mean Oleg Rudenko?'

Carter nodded. 'He's on his cell.'

'He'd better not be for long.'

'Don't worry, Ari.'

Shamron looked at the clock: *9:04:17.* Squeezing the telephone to his ear, he asked King Saul Boulevard for an update on the car parked outside the embassy gate. The desk officer reported no change.

'Perhaps we should force the issue,' Shamron said.

'How, boss?'

'That's my niece standing out there. Tell her to improvise.'

Shamron listened while the desk officer relayed the order. Then he looked at the message flashing on the screen:

AIRCRAFT DOOR OPEN . . . ADVISE . . .

Be careful, Rimona. Be very careful.

'The Memuneh wants you to force the issue.'

'Does the Memuneh have any suggestions?'

'He suggests you improvise.'

'Really?'

Thank you, Uncle Ari.

Rimona stared at the Mercedes. Same chin. Same hands on the wheel. But now the fingers were in motion. Tapping a nervous rhythm.

He suggests you improvise . . .

But how? During the pre-op briefings, Uzi Navot had been resolute on one key point: under no circumstances were they going to give Ivan the opportunity to kidnap another Office agent, especially another woman. Rimona was to remain on embassy grounds at all times because, technically, the grounds were Israeli soil. Unfortunately, there was no way to force the issue in fifteen seconds by remaining behind the safety of the gate. Only by approaching the car could she do that. And to approach the car she had to leave Israel and enter Russia. She glanced at her watch, then turned to one of the Shin Bet security guards.

'Open the gate.'

'We were ordered to keep it closed.'

'Do you know who my uncle is?'

'Everyone knows who your uncle is, Rimona.'

'So what are you waiting for?'

The guard did as he was told and followed Rimona into Bolshaya Ordynka, gun drawn in violation of all diplomatic protocol, written and unwritten. Rimona went without hesitation to the rear passenger door of the Mercedes and rapped on the heavy bulletproof glass. Receiving no response, she gave the window two more firm knocks. This time, the glass slid down. No Chiara, only a well-dressed Russian in his late twenties wearing sunglasses in spite of the overcast weather. He was holding two things: a Makarov pistol and an envelope. He used the gun to keep the Shin Bet security guard at bay. The envelope he handed to Rimona. As the window rose, the Russian was smiling. Then the car lurched forward, tires spinning over icy pavement, and disappeared around the corner.

Rimona's first instinct was to let the envelope fall to the ground. Instead, after giving it a cursory inspection, she tore open the flap. Inside was a gold ring. Rimona recognized it. She had been standing at Gabriel's side when he purchased it from a jeweler in Tel Aviv. And she had been standing on her uncle's terrace overlooking the Sea of Galilee when Gabriel placed it on Chiara's finger. She brought her secure cell to her ear and told the Operations Desk what had just happened. Then, after retreating once again to the Israeli side of the security gate, she read the inscription on the wedding band, tears streaming down her face.

FOREVER, GABRIEL.

*

The news from the embassy confirmed what they always suspected: that Ivan had never intended to release Chiara. Shamron immediately spoke four words calmly in Hebrew: 'Send Joshua to Canaan.' Then he turned to Adrian Carter. 'It's time.'

Carter snatched up his phone. 'Switch on the jammers. And give Ivan the note.'

Shamron gazed at the message still winking at him from the display screens. His command had unleashed a torrent of noise and activity at King Saul Boulevard. Now, amid the pandemonium, he heard two familiar voices, both calm and unemotional. The first was Uzi Navot's, reporting that the sentries at the back of the dacha appeared restless. The next voice was Gabriel's. Joshua was thirty seconds away from the target, he said. Joshua would soon be knocking on the devil's door.

Though neither Gabriel nor Shamron could see it, the devil was rapidly running out of patience. He was standing at the base of the passenger-boarding stairs, his malletlike hands resting on his hips, his weight shifting forward to aft. Veteran Kharkov watchers would have recognized the curious pose as one of many he had taken from his hero, Stalin. They would have also suggested that now might be a good time to take cover, because when Ivan started rocking heel to toe it usually meant an eruption was coming.

The source of his rising anger was the door of the American C-32. For more than a minute, there had been no activity there, other than the appearance of two heavily armed men in black. His anger scaled new heights shortly after 9:05 when Oleg Rudenko, who was standing at Ivan's right hand, reported that his cell phone no longer appeared to be functioning. He blamed it on interference from the plane's communications system, which was partially correct. Ivan, however, was clearly dubious.

At this point, he briefly attempted to take matters into his own hands. Pushing past one of his bodyguards, he mounted the passenger stairs and started toward the cabin door. He froze on the third step when one of the CIA paramilitaries leveled a compact submachine gun and, in excellent Russian, instructed him to stay back. On the tarmac, hands reached beneath overcoats, and the control tower staff later claimed to have spotted the flash of a weapon or two. Ivan, furious and humiliated, did as he was told and retreated to the base of the stairs.

And there he remained for two more tense minutes, hands on his hips, eyes fixed on the two men with machine guns standing shoulder to shoulder in the doorway of the C-32. When finally the CIA men parted, it was not his children Ivan saw but the pilot. He was holding a note. Using only hand signals, he summoned a member of the Russian ground crew and instructed him to deliver the note to the enraged-looking man in the English overcoat. By the time the note had reached Ivan, the aircraft's door was closed and the twin Pratt & Whitney engines were roaring. As the plane began to taxi, those on board were treated to the extraordinary sight of Ivan Kharkov – oligarch, arms dealer, murderer, and father of two – wadding the paper into a ball and hurling it to the ground in disgust.

Another man might have conceded defeat at this point.

But not Ivan. Indeed, the last thing the crew saw was Ivan seizing hold of Oleg Rudenko's cell phone and hurling it at the aircraft. It bounced harmlessly off the belly of the fuselage and shattered into a hundred pieces on the tarmac. A few of the crew laughed. Those who knew what was coming next did not. Blood was going to flow. And men were going to die.

As it turned out, the wash from the C-32's engines blew the note across the tarmac toward the Moscow delegation, and, eventually, to the feet of the deputy minister himself. For a moment he considered allowing it to continue on its journey into oblivion, but his bureaucratic upbringing would not allow it. After all, the letter *was* an official document of sorts.

Ivan's mighty fist had compressed the sheet of paper into a wad the size of a golf ball, and it took the deputy several seconds to pry it open and flatten it out again. Across the top of the paper was the official letterhead of the 89th Airlift Wing. Beneath it were a few lines of English script, clearly written by the hand of a child under emotional stress. Glancing at the first line, the deputy considered reading no further. Once again, duty demanded otherwise.

We do not want to live in Russia.
We do not want to be with Yekaterina.
We want to go home to America.
We want to be with our mother.
We hate you.
Good-bye.

The deputy looked up in time to see Ivan boarding his

helicopter. *Look at him! Look at Ivan Borisovich!* He had everything in the world: a mountain of money, a supermodel for a wife. Everything but the love of his children. *Look at him! You are nothing, Ivan Borisovich! Nothing!*

63. Vladimirskaya Oblast, Russia

The warning sign at the entrance was Soviet era. The birch trees on either side had been there since the time of the tsars. Forty yards along the narrow track was a Range Rover, two Russian guards in the front seat. Mikhail flashed his lights. The Range Rover made no move.

Mikhail opened his door and climbed out. He was wearing a heavy gray parka zipped to the chin and a dark woolen hat pulled low. For now, he was just another Russian. Another one of Ivan's boys. An Alpha Group veteran with a bad attitude. The sort who didn't like having to get out of the car when it was ten below zero.

Hands shoved into his pockets, head down, he went to the driver's side of the Range Rover. The window slid down. Mikhail's gun came out.

Six bright flashes. Scarcely a sound.

Gabriel murmured a few words into his lip mic. Mikhail reached across the lifeless driver, turned the wheel hard to the right, moved the shift from PARK to DRIVE. The Range Rover eased clear of the track and came to rest against a birch tree. Mikhail switched off the engine and threw the keys into the woods. A few seconds later, he was next to Gabriel again, speeding toward the front of the dacha.

*

At that same instant, on the back side of the dacha, three men acquired three targets. Then, on Navot's mark, three men fired three shots.

Three bright flashes. Scarcely a sound.

They crept forward through the birch trees and knelt over their dead. Secured weapons. Silenced radios. Navot spoke softly into his lip mic. Targets neutralized. Rear perimeter secured.

Exactly one hundred twenty-eight miles to the east, on Moscow's Tverskaya Street, Irina Bulganova, former wife of the defector Grigori Bulganov, unlocked the door of Galaxy Travel and changed the sign from CLOSED to OPEN. *Seven minutes late*, she thought. Not that it mattered. Business had fallen off a cliff – or, in the words of Galaxy's some-times poetic general manager, it was locked up tighter than the Moscow River. The Christmas holidays had been a bust. Bookings for the spring ski season were nonexistent. These days even the oligarchs were hoarding their cash. What little they had left.

Irina settled into her desk near the window and did her utmost to appear busy. There was talk of cutbacks at Galaxy. Reduced commissions. Even firings. *Thank you, capitalism!* Perhaps Lenin had been right after all. At least he had managed to do away with the uncertainty. Under the Communists the Russians had been poor and they had stayed poor. There was something to be said for consis-tency.

The ping of the automatic entry chime interrupted Irina's thoughts. Looking up, she saw a small male figure slipping through the doorway: heavy overcoat, woolen scarf, fedora, earmuffs, briefcase in right hand. There were a thousand more just like him on Tverskaya Street, walking mounds of wool and fur, each indistinguishable from the next. Stalin himself could stroll down the street bundled in his warms, and no one would give him a second look.

The man loosened his scarf and removed his hat, revealing a head of thinning, flyaway hair. Irina immediately recognized him. He was the better angel who had convinced her to talk about the worst night of her life. And he was now walking toward her desk, hat in one hand, briefcase in the other. And, somehow, Irina was now on her feet. Smiling. Shaking his cold, tiny hand. Inviting him to sit. Asking how she might be of assistance.

'I need some help planning a trip,' he said in Russian.

'Where are you going?'

'The West.'

'Can you be more specific?'

'I'm afraid not.'

'How long will you be staying?'

'Indefinitely.'

'How many in your party?'

'That, too, is still to be determined. With luck, we're going to be a large group.'

'When are you planning to leave?'

'Late this evening.'

'So what precisely can I do?'

'You can tell your supervisor you're going out for coffee. Make sure you bring your valuables. Because you're never coming back here again. *Ever.*'

64. Vladimirskaya Oblast, Russia

A Russian dacha can be many things. A timbered palace. A toolshed surrounded by radishes and onions. The one at the end of the narrow track fell somewhere in between. It was low and stout, solid as a ship, and clearly built by Bolshevik muscle. There was no veranda or steps, just a small door in the center, reached by a well-worn groove in the snow. On either side of the door was a window of paned glass. Once upon a time, the frames had been forest green. Now they were something like gray. Thin curtains hung in both windows. The curtain on the right moved as Mikhail slid the Range Rover into PARK and killed the engine.

'Take the key.'

'You sure?'

'Take it.'

Mikhail removed the key and zipped it into a small pocket over his heart. Gabriel glanced at the two sentries. They were standing about ten feet from the dacha, guns cradled across their chests. Their positioning presented Gabriel with something of a challenge. He would have to fire at a slight upward trajectory so that the rounds didn't shatter the windows upon exiting the Russians' skulls. He made this calculation in the time it took Mikhail to pick up a cylindrical thermos flask. He had been making such calculations since he was a boy of twenty-two. Just one more decision to make. Which hand? Right or left? He had the ability to make the shot with either. Because he would be climbing out of the Rover on the passenger's side, he decided to fire with the right. That way there would be no chance of banging the suppressor against the fender on the way up.

'Are you sure you want them both, Gabriel?'

'Both.'

'Because I can take the one on the left.'

'Just get out.'

Once again, Mikhail opened the door and climbed out. This time, Gabriel did the same thing, parka unzipped, Beretta at the seam of his trousers. Mikhail approached the sentries, thermos aloft, chattering in Russian. Something about hot coffee. Something about the Moscow traffic being shit. Something about Ivan being on the warpath. Gabriel couldn't be certain. He didn't much care. He was looking at the spot, just beyond the Rover's right-front tire, where he was going to drop to one knee and end two more Russian lives.

The guards were no longer looking at Mikhail but at each other. Shoulders shrugged. Heads shook.

And Gabriel knelt on his spot.

Two more flashes. Two more Russians down.

No sound. No broken windows.

Mikhail leaned the thermos against the base of the door and quickly retreated several steps.

The birch forest trembled.

Silence no more.

On the back side of the dacha, three men rose in unison and advanced slowly through the trees. Navot reminded them to keep their heads down. There was about to be a lot of lead in the air.

Chiara sat up with a start, hands cuffed, feet shackled, dust and debris raining down on her in the pitch-darkness. From above, she could hear the hammer of footfalls against the floorboards. Then muffled gunshots. Then screams.

'Someone's coming, Grigori!'

More gunshots. More screams.

'Get on your feet, Grigori! Can you get on your feet?'

'I'm not sure.'

'You have to try.'

Chiara heard a moan.

'Too many broken bones, Chiara. Too little strength.'

She reached her cuffed hands into the darkness.

'Take my hands, Grigori. We can do it.'

A few seconds elapsed while they found each other in the gloom.

'Pull, Grigori! Pull me up.'

He moaned again in agony as he pulled on Chiara's hands. The instant her weight was centered over the balls of her feet, she straightened her legs and stood. Then, amid the gunshots, she heard another sound: the woman with milk-white skin and translucent eyes coming down the stairs in a hurry. Chiara inched closer to the door, careful not to trip over the shackles, and squeezed into the corner. She didn't know what she was going to do, but she was certain of one thing. She wasn't going to die. Not without a fight.

It turned out none of the phones were working. Yekaterina's didn't work. The built-in on board the Bell didn't work. And not one phone among the security detail worked. Not a single phone. Not until the children's plane was airborne. Then the phones worked just fine. Ivan called the Kremlin and was soon talking to a close aide of the president's. Oleg Rudenko placed several calls to his men at the dacha, none of which were answered. He glanced at his watch: *9:08*. Another shift of guards was due any minute. Rudenko dialed the number for the senior man and lifted the phone to his ear.

The combination of the concussive blast wave and the deafening thunderclap did most of the heavy lifting for them. All Mikhail and Gabriel had to do was take care of a few loose ends.

Loose end number one was the guard who had peered briefly through the window. Gabriel dispatched him with a quick burst of a Mini-Uzi seconds after entry.

Before the blast, two more guards had been enjoying a quiet breakfast. Now they were sprawled across the floor, separated from their weapons. Gabriel raked them with Uzi fire and stepped into the kitchen, where a fourth guard had been making tea. That one managed to squeeze off a single shot before taking several rounds in the chest.

The right side of the dacha was now secured.

A few feet away, Mikhail was having similar success. After following Gabriel through the blown-out doorway, he had immediately spotted two dazed guards in the dacha's central hall. Gabriel had crouched instinctively before squeezing off his first shots, thus opening a clean firing line for Mikhail. Mikhail had taken it, sending a sustained burst of gunfire down the hall just a few inches over Gabriel's head. Then he had immediately pivoted toward the sitting room. One of Ivan's men had been watching the highlights of a big football match on television when the charge went off. Now he was covered in plaster and dust and searching blindly for his weapon. Mikhail put him down with a shot to the chest.

'Where's the girl?' he asked the dying man in Russian.

'In the cellar.'

'Good boy.'

Mikhail shot him in the face. Left side of the dacha secured.

They headed to the stairs.

Squeezed into the corner of the blacked-out cell, Chiara heard three sounds in rapid succession: a padlock snapping open, a dead bolt sliding back, a latch turning. The metal door moved away with a heavy scrape, allowing a trapezoid of weak light to enter the cell and illuminate Grigori. Next came a Makarov 9mm, held by a pair of hands. *The hands of the woman who had killed Chiara's child with sedatives*. The gun moved away from Chiara a few degrees and took aim at Grigori. His battered face registered no fear. He was in too much pain to be afraid, too weary to resist death. Chiara resisted for him. Lunging forward out of the gloom, she seized the woman by the wrists and bent them backward. The gun went off; in the tiny concrete chamber, it sounded like cannon fire. Then it went off again. Then a third time. Chiara held on. For Grigori. For her baby.

For Gabriel.

*

Ivan Kharkov was a man of many secrets, many lives. No one knew this any better than Yekaterina, his former mistress turned devoted wife. Like Elena before her, she had entered into a foolish pact. In exchange for being granted her every material wish, she would ask no questions. No questions about Ivan's business. No questions about Ivan's friends and associates. No questions about why Elena had decided to hand over the children. And now, no questions about why the children had refused to leave the plane. Instead, she attempted to play the role Ivan had given her. She tried to hold his hand, but Ivan refused to be touched. Tried to soothe him with words, but Ivan refused to listen. For the moment, he had eyes only for Oleg Rudenko. The security man was shouting into his cell phone over the thudding of the rotors. Yekaterina heard words she wished she had not. *How many men do you have? How many minutes until you arrive? No blood! Do you hear me? No blood until we get there!* She summoned the courage to ask where they were going. Ivan told her she would find out soon enough. She told him she wanted to go home. Ivan told her to shut her mouth. She stared out the window of the helicopter. Somewhere down there was her old village. The village where she had lived before being discovered by the woman from the modeling agency. The village filled with drunks and losers. She closed her eyes. *Take me home, you monster. Please, take me home.*

The young aide approached the Russian president with considerable caution. Aides usually did, regardless of their age. The president leaned away from the table and allowed the aide to whisper into his ear, a rare privilege. Then the look again, chin to his chest, eyes like daggers.

'He doesn't look happy,' the British prime minister said.

'Oh, really? How can you tell?'

'I suppose things didn't go well at the airport.'

'Wait until he hears the encore.'

They had hit the stairs on the run and were halfway down when the first gunshot erupted. Mikhail was leading the way, Gabriel a step behind, his view partially obscured. Nearing the bottom, a terrible smell greeted them: the stench of humans confined in a small place for too long. The stench of death. Then another gunshot rang out. And another. *And another . . .*

Gabriel heard a scream, followed by two distinct female voices shouting in anger. They were distinct because one of the voices was shouting in Russian. And the other was shouting in Italian.

Reaching the bottom of the steps, Gabriel raced after Mikhail, listening to the sound of Chiara's voice, praying he would not hear another gunshot. Mikhail flung aside the door to the cell and entered first. Propped in one corner was a man, hands and feet shackled, face grotesquely distorted. Chiara was on her back, the Russian woman atop her. They were struggling over a gun and it was now very close to Chiara's cheek.

Mikhail grabbed the weapon and pointed it toward the wall. As it discharged twice harmlessly, Gabriel seized a fistful of the Russian woman's hair and pumped a single round through her temple. Now only one woman was screaming. Gabriel hurled the dead woman aside and fell to his knees. Chiara, in her frenzy, briefly mistook him for one of Ivan's men and recoiled. He held her face in his hands and spoke to her softly in Italian. 'It's me,' he said. 'It's Gabriel. Please, try to be calm. We have to hurry.'

65. Grosvenor Square, London

Afterward, there would be a debate as to precisely how long it took Gabriel and Mikhail to perform their assignment. Total time was three minutes and twelve seconds – an impressive feat, made more so by the fact it took well over a minute just to drive the half mile from the first guard post to the dacha itself. From entry to rescue was an astonishing twenty-two seconds. *Silence, speed, timing . . .* And courage, of course. If Chiara had not decided to stand and fight for her life, both she and Grigori would surely have been dead by the time Gabriel and Mikhail reached the cellar.

Due to the miracle of advanced secure satellite communications, King Saul Boulevard was able to hear Gabriel whispering soothingly to Chiara in Italian. No one on the Operations Desk understood what was being said. It wasn't necessary. The very fact Gabriel was speaking Italian to a hysterical woman told them everything they needed to know. The first phase of the operation had been a success. Mikhail confirmed it for them at 9:09:12 Moscow time. He also confirmed that Grigori Bulganov, though badly injured, was alive as well.

There arose in Tel Aviv a great roar as days of stress and sadness were released like steam from a valve. The cheering was so loud that ten long seconds elapsed before Shamron understood precisely what had transpired. When he broke the news to Adrian Carter and Graham Seymour, a second cheer erupted in the London annex, followed by a third at the Global Ops Center at Langley. Only Shamron refused to take part. And with good reason. The numbers told him everything he needed to know.

Five agents.

Two weakened hostages.

One thousand yards from the dacha to the road.

One hundred twenty-eight miles to Moscow.

And Ivan in the air.

Shamron twirled his old Zippo lighter between his fingertips and looked at the clock: *9:09:52.*

The numbers . . .

Unlike people, numbers never lied. And the numbers didn't look good.

Gabriel cut away the cuffs and shackles and lifted Chiara to her feet.

'Can you walk?'

'Don't leave me, Gabriel!'

'I'll never leave you.'

'Stay with me!'

'Can you walk?'

'I think so.'

He wrapped his arm around her waist and helped her up the stairs.

'You have to hurry, Chiara.'

'Don't leave me, Gabriel.'

'I'll never leave you.'

'Don't leave me here with them.'

'Everyone's gone, my love. But we have to hurry.'

They reached the top of the stairs. Navot was standing in the center hall, bodies at his feet, blood on the walls.

'Grigori's a mess,' Gabriel snapped in Hebrew. 'Bring him up.'

Gabriel helped Chiara around the bodies and headed toward the hole where the door had once been. Chiara saw more bodies. Bodies everywhere. Bodies and blood.

'Oh, God.'

'Don't look, my love. Just walk.'

'Oh, God.'

'Walk, Chiara. Walk.'

'Did you kill them, Gabriel? Did you do this?'

'Just keep walking, my love.'

Navot entered the cell and saw Grigori's face.

Bastards!

He looked at Mikhail.

'Let's get him on his feet.'

'He's in bad shape.'

'I don't care. Just get him on his feet.'

Grigori screamed in agony as Mikhail and Navot pulled him upright.

'I don't think I can walk.'

'You don't have to.'

Navot hoisted the Russian over one shoulder and nodded to Mikhail.

'Let's go.'

The back doors of the Range Rover were now open. Yaakov was standing on one side, Oded on the other. A few feet away were two Russian corpses, arms flung wide, heads surrounded by halos of blood. Gabriel led Chiara past the bodies and lifted her into the back. Then he turned and saw Navot coming out of the dacha, Grigori draped over one shoulder.

'Put him in the back with Chiara and get out of here.'

Navot eased Grigori into the car while Gabriel climbed into the front passenger seat. Mikhail dug the keys from the pocket of his parka and fired the engine. As the Rover shot forward, Gabriel glanced back a final time.

Three men. Running for the trees.

He inserted a fresh magazine into the Mini-Uzi and looked at his watch: *9:11:07*.

'Faster, Mikhail. Drive faster.'

They were doing just under a hundred along the deserted road, two black Range Rovers, both filled with former Russian special forces now employed by the private security service of Ivan Kharkov. In the front seat of the first vehicle, a cell phone trilled. It was Oleg Rudenko, calling from the helicopter.

'Where are you?'

'Close.'

'How close?'

Very . . .

For reasons that would be made clear to Gabriel in short order, the track from the dacha to the road did not run in a straight line. Viewed from an American spy satellite, it looked rather like an inverted S rendered by the hand of a young child. Viewed from the front passenger seat of a speeding Range Rover in late winter, it was a sea of white.

White snow. White birch trees. And, just around the second bend, a pair of white headlamps approaching at an alarmingly rapid rate.

Mikhail instinctively hit the brakes – in hindsight, a mistake, since it gave a slight advantage on impact to the other vehicle. The air bags spared them serious injury but left Gabriel and Mikhail too dazed to resist when the Rover was stormed by several men. Gabriel briefly glimpsed the butt of a Russian pistol arcing toward the side of his head. Then there was only white. White snow. White birch trees. Chiara floating away from him, dressed all in white.

66. Grosvenor Square, London

For Shamron, the first inkling of trouble was the sudden silence at King Saul Boulevard. Three times he asked for an explanation. Three times he received no reply.

Finally a voice. 'We've lost them.'

'What do you mean, *lost*?'

They had heard a noise of some sort. Sounded like a collision. A crash. Then voices. Russian voices.

'You're sure they were Russian?'

'We're double-checking the tapes. But we're sure.'

'Were they off Ivan's property when it happened?'

'We don't think so.'

'What about their radios?'

'Off the air.'

'Where's the rest of the team?'

'Departing as planned.' A pause. 'Unless you want to send them back in.'

Shamron hesitated. Of course he wanted to send them back. But he couldn't. Better to lose three than six. *The numbers . . .*

'Tell Uzi to keep going. And no heroics. Tell them to get the hell out of there.'

'Right.'

'Keep the line open. Let me know if you hear anything.'

Shamron closed his eyes for a few seconds, then looked at Adrian Carter and Graham Seymour. The two men had heard only Shamron's end of the conversation. It had been enough.

'What time did Ivan leave Konakovo?' Shamron asked.

'All the birds were airborne by ten past.'

'Flying time between Konakovo and the dacha?'

'One hour. Maybe a bit more if the weather's lousy.'

Shamron looked at the clock: *9:14:56*.

That would put Ivan on the ground in Vladimirskaya Oblast at approximately 10:10. It was possible he had already ordered his men to kill Gabriel and the others. *Possible*, thought Shamron, but not likely. Knowing Ivan, he would reserve that privilege for himself.

One hour. Maybe a bit more if the weather's lousy.

One hour . . .

The Office did not possess the capability to intervene in that amount of time. Neither did the Americans nor the British. At this point, only one entity did: *the Kremlin . . .* The same Kremlin that had permitted Ivan to sell his weapons to al-Qaeda in the first place. The same Kremlin that had allowed Ivan to avenge the loss of his wife and children. Sergei Korovin had all but admitted that Ivan paid the Russian president for the right to kidnap Grigori and Chiara. Perhaps Shamron could find a way to outbid Ivan. But how much were four lives worth to the Russian president, a man rumored to be one of the richest in Europe? And how much would they be worth to Ivan? Shamron had to make a move Ivan could not match. And he had to do it quickly.

He gazed at the clock, Zippo turning between his fingertips.

Two turns to the right, two turns to the left . . .

'I'm going to need a Russian oil company, gentlemen. A very large Russian oil company. And I'm going to need it within an hour.'

'Would you care to tell me where we're going to get a Russian oil company?' asked Carter.

Shamron looked at Seymour. 'Number 43 Cheyne Walk.'

Rudenko's phone rang again. He listened for several seconds, face blank, then asked, 'How many dead?'

'We're still counting.'

'*Counting?*'

'It's bad.'

'But you're sure it's him?'

'No question.'

'No blood. Do you hear me? *No* blood.'

'I hear you.'

Rudenko severed the connection. He was about to make Ivan a very happy man. He had the one thing in the world Ivan wanted even more than his children.

He had Gabriel Allon.

This time, it was the American president who was approached by an aide. And not just any aide. His chief of staff. The exchange was whispered and brief. The president's face remained expressionless throughout.

'Something wrong?' the British prime minister asked when the chief of staff departed.

'It appears we have a problem.'

'What sort of problem?'

The president looked across the table at his Russian counterpart.

'Trouble in the woods outside Moscow.'

'Anything we can do?'

'Pray.'

Graham Seymour's Jaguar limousine was parked in Upper Brook Street. It was 6:20 a.m. in London when he climbed in the back. Flanked by a pair of Met motorcycles, he headed south to Hyde Park Corner, west on Knightsbridge, then south again on Sloane Street, all the way to Royal Hospital Road. By 6:27 a.m., the car was pulling up in front of Viktor Orlov's mansion in Cheyne Walk, and, at 6:30, Seymour was entering Orlov's magnificent study, accompanied by the chiming of a gold ormolu clock. Orlov, who claimed to require only three hours of sleep a night, was seated at his desk, perfectly groomed and attired, Asian market numbers streaming across his computer screens. On the giant plasma television, a BBC reporter standing outside the Kremlin was intoning gravely about a global economy on the verge of collapse. Orlov silenced him with a flick of his remote.

'What do these idiots really know, Mr. Seymour?'

'Actually, I can say with certainty they know very little.'

'You look as if you've had a long night. Please, sit down. Tell me, Graham, how can I help you?'

It was a question Viktor Orlov would later regret asking. The conversation that followed was not recorded, at least not by MI5 or any other department of British intelligence. It was eight minutes in length, far longer than Seymour would have preferred, but this was to be expected. Seymour was asking Orlov to forever relinquish claim to something extremely valuable. In reality, this object was lost to Orlov already. Even so, he clung to it that morning, as the survivor of a bomb blast will often cling to the corpse of one less fortunate.

It was not a pleasant exchange, but this, too, was to be expected. Viktor Orlov was hardly a pleasant person, even under the best of circumstances. Voices were raised, threats issued. Orlov's household staff, though discreet to a fault, could not help but overhear. They heard words such as *duty* and *honor*. They clearly heard the word *extradition* and then, a few beats later, *arrest warrant*. They heard a pair of names, *Sukhova* and *Chernov*, and thought they heard the British visitor say something about a review of Mr. Orlov's political and business activities on British soil. And, finally, they heard the visitor say very clearly: *'Will you just do the decent thing for once in your life? My God, Viktor! Four lives are at stake! And one of them is Grigori's!'*

At which point there was a heavy silence. The British visitor emerged from the office a moment later, a tight expression on his face, his eyes focused on his wristwatch. He took the stairs two at a time and climbed into the back of his waiting Jaguar. As the car shot away from the curb, he placed a call to an emergency line at Downing Street. Two minutes after that, he was speaking directly with the prime minister, who had excused himself from the summit breakfast to take the call. It was 6:42 a.m. in London and 9:42 a.m. at the isolated dacha in the birch forest east of Moscow.

The British prime minister returned to the table.

'I believe it's time for a trilateral with our friend over there.'

'I hope you have something good to offer him.'

'I do. The only question is, will he be able to fulfill his end of the bargain?'

The sight of the two leaders rising in unison sent a murmur of anxiety through the Kremlin functionaries posted around the hall as they watched their carefully planned breakfast veering dangerously toward an unscripted moment. The only person who seemed not to be surprised was the Russian president, who was on his feet by the time the British and American leaders arrived at his side of the table.

'We need to have a word,' the prime minister said. 'In private.'

They slipped quietly into an antechamber off St George's Hall with only their closest aides present. Like the meeting that had just taken place in Viktor Orlov's study, it was not pleasant. Once again, voices were raised, though no one outside the room heard them. When the leaders emerged, the Russian president was smiling visibly, a rare occurrence. He was also holding a mobile phone to his ear.

Later, under questioning from the press, spokesmen for all three leaders would use precisely the same language to describe what had taken place. It was a routine scheduling matter, nothing more. Scheduling, perhaps, but hardly routine.

67. Lubyanka Square, Moscow

On the fourth floor of FSB Headquarters is a suite of rooms occupied by the organization's smallest and most secretive unit. Known as the Department of Coordination, its staff of veteran officers handles only cases of extreme political sensitivity. Shortly before ten that morning, its chief, Colonel Leonid Milchenko, was standing rigidly next to his Finnish-made desk, a telephone to his ear. Though Milchenko effectively worked for the Russian president, direct conversations between the two were rare. This one was brief and tense. *'Get it done, Milchenko. No fuckups. Are we clear?'* The colonel said *'Da'* several times and hung up the phone.

'Vadim!'

Vadim Strelkin, his number two, poked a bald head into the room.

'What's the problem?'

'Ivan Kharkov.'

'What now?'

Milchenko explained.

'Shit!'

'I couldn't have said it any better myself.'

'Where's the dacha?'

'Vladimirskaya Oblast.'

'How far out?'

'Far enough that we're going to need a helicopter. Tell them to drop it into the square.'

'Can't. Not today.'

'Why not?'

Strelkin nodded toward the Kremlin. 'All airspace inside the outer ring road is closed because of the summit.'

'Not anymore.'

Strelkin picked up the phone on Milchenko's desk and ordered the helicopter. 'I know about the closure, *idiot*! Just do it!'

He slammed down the phone. Milchenko was standing at the map.

'How long before it arrives?'

'Five minutes.'

Milchenko calculated the travel time.

'We can't possibly get there before Ivan.'

'Let me call Rudenko directly.'

'Who?'

'Oleg Rudenko. Ivan's security chief. He used to be one of us. Maybe he can talk some sense into Ivan.'

'Talk sense into Ivan Kharkov? Vadim, perhaps I should explain something. If you call Rudenko, the first thing Ivan will do is kill those hostages.'

'Not if we tell him the order comes from the very top.'

Milchenko thought it over, then shook his head. 'Ivan can't be trusted. He'll say they're already dead. Even if they're not.'

'Who are these people?'

'It's complicated, Vadim. Which is why the president has bestowed this great honor upon me. Suffice it to say, there is a great deal of money at stake – for Russia *and* the president.'

'How so?'

'If the hostages live, money. If not . . .'

'No money?'

'You have a bright future, Vadim.'

Strelkin joined Milchenko at the map. 'There might be another way to get some firepower out there in a hurry.'

'Let's hear it.'

'Alpha Group forces are deployed all over Moscow because of the summit. If I'm not mistaken, they're manning all the major highways leading into the city.'

'Doing what? Directing traffic?'

'Looking for Chechen terrorists.'

But of course, thought Milchenko. They were always looking for Chechens even when there were no Chechens to be found.

'Make the call, Vadim. See if there are some Alphas along the M7.'

Strelkin did. There were. A pair of helicopters could scoop them up in under ten minutes.

'Send them, Vadim.'

'On whose authority?'

'The president's, of course.'

Strelkin gave the order.

'You have a bright future, Vadim.'

Strelkin looked out the window. 'And you have a helicopter.'

'No, Vadim, *we* have a helicopter. I'm not going out there alone.'

Milchenko reached for his overcoat and headed toward the door with Strelkin at his heels. Five below and snow in the air, and he was going to Vladimirskaya Oblast to save three Jews and a Russian traitor from Ivan Kharkov. Not exactly the way he'd hoped to spend the day.

*

Though the colonel did not know it, the four people whose lives were now in his hands were at that moment seated along the four walls of the cell, one to each wall, wrists tightly trussed at their backs, legs stretched before them, feet touching. The door to the cell was ajar; two men, guns at the ready, stood just outside. The blow that felled Mikhail had opened a deep gash above his left eye. Gabriel had been struck behind the right ear, and his neck was now a river of blood. A victim of too many concussions, he was struggling to silence the bells tolling in his ears. Mikhail was looking around the interior of the cell, as if searching for a way out. Chiara was watching him, as was Grigori.

'What are you thinking?' he murmured in Russian. 'Surely you're not thinking about trying to escape?'

Mikhail glanced at the guards. 'And give those apes an excuse to kill me? I wouldn't dream of it.'

'So what's so interesting about the cell?'

'The fact that it exists at all.'

'Meaning?'

'Did you have a dacha, Grigori?'

'We had one when I was a boy.'

'Your father was Party?'

Grigori hesitated, then nodded. 'Yours?'

'For a while.'

'What happened?'

'My father and the Party went their separate ways.'

'Your father was a dissident?'

'Dissident, refusenik – you pick the word, Grigori. He just came to hate the Party and everything it stood for. That's why he ended up in your little shop of horrors.'

'Did he have a dacha?'

'Until the KGB took it from him. And I'll tell you something, Grigori. It didn't have a room in the cellar like this. In fact, it didn't have a cellar at all.'

'Neither did ours.'

'Did you have a floor?'

'A crude one.' Grigori managed a smile. 'My father wasn't a very senior Party official.'

'Do you remember all the crazy rules?'

'How could you forget them?'

'No heating allowed.'

'No dachas larger than twenty-five square meters.'

'My father got around the restrictions by adding a veranda. We used to joke that it was the biggest veranda in Russia.'

'Ours was bigger, I'm sure.'

'But no cellar, right, Grigori?'

'No cellar.'

'So why was this chap allowed to build a cellar?'

'He must have been Party.'

'That goes without saying.'

'Maybe he kept his wine down here.'

'Come on, Grigori. You can do better than that.'

'Meat? Maybe he liked meat.'

'He must have been a very senior Party official to need a meat locker this big.'

'You have another theory?'

'I used a couple of pounds of explosive to blow open the front door. If I'd placed a charge that big in front of our old dacha, it would have brought the entire place down.'

'I'm not sure I understand.'

'This place was well built. Purpose-built. Look at the

concrete, Grigori. This is the good stuff. Not the crap they gave the rest of us. The crap that used to fall away in chunks and turn to powder after one winter.'

'It's old, this place. The rot hadn't set into the system when they built it.'

'How old?'

'Thirties, I'd say.'

'Stalin's time?'

'May he rest in peace.'

Gabriel lifted his chin from his chest. In Hebrew, he asked, 'What in God's name are the two of you talking about?'

'Architecture,' Mikhail said. 'The architecture of dachas, to be precise.'

'Is there something you want to tell me, Mikhail?'

'Something's not right about this place.' Mikhail moved his foot. 'Why is there a drain in the middle of this floor, Gabriel? And what are those depressions out back?'

'You tell me, Mikhail.'

Mikhail was silent for a moment. Then he changed the subject.

'How's your head?'

'I'm still hearing things.'

'Still the bells?'

Gabriel closed his eyes and sat very still.

'No, not bells.'

Helicopters.

68. Vladimirskaya Oblast, Russia

Somewhere during his rise to wealth and power, Ivan Kharkov learned how to make an entrance. He knew how to enter a restaurant or the lobby of a luxury hotel. He knew how to enter a boardroom filled with rivals or the bed of a lover. And he certainly knew how to enter a dank cell filled with four people he intended to kill with his own hand. Intriguing was how little the performance varied from venue to venue. Indeed, to watch Ivan now was to imagine him standing at the doorway of Le Grand Joseph or Villa Romana, his old haunts in Saint-Tropez. Though he was a man with many enemies, Ivan never liked to rush things. He preferred to survey the room and allow the room to survey him in return. He liked to flaunt his clothing. And his sundial-sized wristwatch, which, for reasons known only to him, he was looking at now, as if annoyed at a maître d' for making him wait five minutes for a promised table.

Ivan lowered his arm and inserted his hand into the pocket of his overcoat. It was unbuttoned, as if he were anticipating physical exertion. His gaze drifted slowly around the cell, settling first on Grigori, then Chiara, then Gabriel, and, finally, on Mikhail. Mikhail's presence seemed to lift Ivan's spirits. Mikhail was a bonus, a windfall profit. Mikhail and Ivan had a history. Mikhail had dined with Ivan. Mikhail had been invited to Ivan's home. And Mikhail had had an affair with Ivan's wife. At least, that's what Ivan believed. Shortly before Ivan's fall, two of his thugs had given Mikhail a good thrashing at a café along the Old Port in Saint-Tropez. It was but an aperitif. Judging from Ivan's expression, a banquet of pain was being prepared. He and Mikhail were going to partake of it together.

His gaze swept slowly back and forth, a searchlight over an open field, and came to rest once more on Gabriel. Then he spoke for the first time. Gabriel had spent hours listening to recordings of Ivan's voice, but never had he heard it in person. Ivan's English, while perfect, was spoken with the accent of a Cold War propagandist on old Radio Moscow. His rich baritone caused the walls of the cell to vibrate.

'I'm so pleased I was able to reunite you with your wife, Allon. At least one of us kept up his end of the bargain.'

'And what bargain was that?'

'I release your wife, you return my children.'

'Anna and Nikolai were on the ground at Konakovo at nine o'clock this morning.'

'I didn't realize you were on a first-name basis with my children.'

Gabriel looked at Chiara, then stared directly into Ivan's iron gaze. 'If my wife had been outside the embassy at nine o'clock, your children would be with you right now. But my wife wasn't there. And so your children are heading back to America.'

'Do you take me for a fool, Allon? You never intended to let my children off that plane.'

'It was their decision, Ivan. I hear they even gave you a note.'

'It was an obvious forgery, just like that painting you sold my wife. Which reminds me: you owe me two and a half million dollars, not to mention the twenty million dollars your service stole from my bank accounts.'

'If you lend me your phone, Ivan, I'll arrange a wire transfer.'

'My phones don't seem to be working well today.' Ivan leaned his shoulder against the doorframe and ran a hand through his coarse gray hair. 'It's a pity, really.'

'What's that, Ivan?'

'My men reckon you were only ten seconds from the entrance of the property at the time of the collision. If you'd managed to make it to the road, you might have been able to get back to Moscow. I suspect you probably *would* have made it if you hadn't tried to bring the defector Bulganov with you. You would have been wise to leave him behind.'

'Is that what you would have done, Ivan?'

'Without question. You must feel rather foolish just now.'

'Why is that?'

'You and your lovely wife are going to die because you were too decent to leave behind a wounded traitor and defector. But that's always been your weakness, hasn't it, Allon? Your decency.'

'I'll trade my weaknesses for yours anytime, Ivan.'

'Something tells me you won't feel that way a few minutes from now.' Ivan gave a contemptuous smile. 'Out of curiosity, how were you able to discover where I was keeping your wife and the defector Bulganov?'

'You were betrayed.'

A word Ivan understood. He furrowed his heavy brow. 'By whom?'

'By people you thought you could trust.'

'As you might expect, Allon, I trust no one – especially people who are supposed to be close to me. But we'll discuss that topic in greater detail in a moment.' He glanced around the cell, his face perplexed, as if he were struggling over a math theorem. 'Tell me, Allon, where's the rest of your team?'

'You're looking at it.'

'Do you know how many people died here this morning?'

'If you give me a minute, I'm sure—'

'Fifteen, most of them former Alpha Group and OMON.' He looked at Mikhail. 'Not bad for a computer specialist who worked for a nonprofit human rights group. Please, Mikhail, remind me of the group's name?'

'The Dillard Center for Democracy.'

'Ah, yes, that's right. I suppose the Dillard Center believes in using brute force when necessary.' His attention shifted back to Gabriel, and he repeated his original question. 'Don't play with me, Allon. I know you and your friend Mikhail are very good, but there's no way you could have done this all on your own. Where are the rest of your men?'

Gabriel ignored the question and asked one of his own. 'What caused the depressions in the woods, Ivan?'

Ivan seemed taken aback. He recovered quickly, though, a boxer shaking off the effects of a punch.

'You'll know soon enough. But we need to talk more first. Let's do it upstairs, shall we? This place smells like shit.'

Ivan departed. Only his scent remained. Sandalwood and smoke. The smell of power. The smell of the devil.

69. Grosvenor Square, London

The message from Uzi Navot's secure PDA appeared in the London annex and King Saul Boulevard simultaneously at 10:17 Moscow time.

IVAN'S BIRDS ON THE GROUND AT DACHA . . . ADVISE
. . .

Shamron snatched up the phone to Tel Aviv.

'What does he mean, *advise*?'

'Uzi's asking if you want them to go back to the dacha.'

'I thought I made my wishes unambiguously clear.'

'Continue back to Moscow?'

'Correct.'

'But—'

'This is not a debate.'

'Right, boss.'

Shamron slammed down the phone. Adrian Carter did the same.

'The president's national security adviser just spoke with his Russian counterpart inside the Kremlin.'

'And?'

'The FSB is close. Alpha Group troops, plus two senior men from Lubyanka.'

'Estimated time of arrival?'

'They expect to be on the ground at 10:45 Moscow time.'

Shamron looked at the clock: *10:19:49.*

He slipped a cigarette between his lips. His lighter flared.

Nothing to do now but wait. And pray that Gabriel could think of some way to stay alive for another twenty-five minutes.

At that same moment, an aged Lada bearing Yaakov, Oded, and Navot was parked along the shoulder of a frozen two-lane highway. Behind them was a string of villages. Ahead was the M7 and Moscow. Oded was behind the wheel, Yaakov was huddled in the back, Navot was in the front passenger seat. The little wipers of the Lada were scraping at the snow now accumulating on the windshield. The defroster, a euphemism if there ever was one, was doing more harm than good. Navot was oblivious. He was staring at the screen of his secure PDA and watching the seconds tick away on its digital clock. Finally, at 10:20, a message. Reading it, he swore softly to himself and turned to Oded.

'The Old Man wants us to go back to Moscow.'

'What do we do?'

Navot folded his arms across his chest.

'Don't move.'

The helicopter was a reconfigured M-8, maximum speed of one hundred sixty miles per hour, a bit slower when the wind was howling out of Siberia and visibility was a half mile at best. It carried a crew of three and a passenger complement of just two: Colonel Leonid Milchenko and Major Vadim Strelkin, both of the FSB's Department of Coordination. Strelkin, a poor flier, was trying very hard not to be sick. Milchenko, headset over his ears, was listening to the cockpit chatter and peering out the window.

They had cleared the outer ring five minutes after leaving

Lubyanka and were now streaking eastward, using the M7 as a rough guide. Milchenko knew the towns well – Bezmenkovo, Chudinka, Obukhovo – and his mood darkened with each mile they moved beyond Moscow. Russia as viewed from the air was not much better than Russia on the ground. *Look at it*, Milchenko thought. It didn't happen overnight. It took centuries of tsars, general secretaries, and presidents to produce a wreck like this, and now it was Milchenko's job to hide its dirty secrets.

He keyed open his microphone and asked for an estimated arrival time. Fifteen minutes, came the reply. Twenty at most.

Twenty at most . . . But what would he find when he got there? And what would he take away? The president had made his wishes clear.

'It is imperative the Israelis leave there alive. But if Ivan needs to shed a little blood, give him your friend, Bulganov. He's a dog. Let him die a dog's death.'

But what if Ivan didn't wish to surrender his Jews? *What then, Mr. President? What then, indeed.*

Milchenko stared morosely out the window. The towns were getting farther and farther apart now. More fields of snow. More birch trees. *More places to die* . . . Milchenko was about to find himself in an unenviable position, caught between Ivan Kharkov and the Russian president. It was a fool's errand, this. And if he wasn't careful, he might die a dog's death, too.

70. Vladimirskaya Oblast, Russia

The dead were stacked like cordwood at the edge of the trees, several with neat bullet holes in their foreheads, the rest bloody messes. Ivan paid them no heed as he stepped through the ruined entrance and made his way to the side of the dacha. Gabriel, Chiara, Grigori, and Mikhail followed, hands still trussed at their backs, a bodyguard holding each arm. They were made to stand against the exterior wall, Gabriel at one end, Mikhail at the other. The snow was knee-deep and more was falling. Ivan paced slowly in it, a large Makarov pistol in his hand. The fact his costly trousers and shoes were being ruined seemed to be the only dark spot on what was an otherwise festive occasion.

Ivan's hero, Stalin, liked to toy with his victims. The doomed were showered with special privileges, comforted with promotions and with promises of new opportunities to serve their master and the Motherland. Ivan made no such pretense of compassion, no efforts to deceive the soon-to-be dead. Ivan was Fifth Directorate. A breaker of bones, a smasher of heads. After making one final pass before his prisoners, he selected his first victim.

'Did you enjoy the time you spent with my wife?' he asked Mikhail in Russian.

'Former wife,' replied Mikhail in the same language. 'And, yes, I enjoyed my time with her very much. She's a remarkable woman. You should have treated her better.'

'Is that why you took her from me?'

'I didn't have to take her. She staggered into our arms.'

Mikhail never saw the blow coming. A backhand, low at the start, high at the finish. Somehow he managed to stay on his feet. Ivan's guards, who were standing in a semicircle in the snow, found it amusing. Chiara closed her eyes and began to shake with fear. Gabriel pressed his shoulder lightly against hers. In Hebrew, he murmured, 'Try to stay calm. Mikhail's doing the right thing.'

'He's just making him angrier.'

'Exactly, my love. Exactly.'

Ivan was now rubbing the back of his hand, as if to show he had feelings, too. 'I trusted you, Mikhail. I allowed you into my home. You betrayed me.'

'It was just business, Ivan.'

'Really? Just business? Elena told me about that shitty little villa in the hills above Saint-Tropez. She told me about the lunch you had waiting. And the wine. Bandol rosé. Elena's favorite.'

'Very cold. Just the way she likes it.'

Another backhand, hard enough to send Mikhail crashing into the side of the dacha. With his hands still bound, he was unable to stand on his own. Ivan seized the front of his parka and lifted him effortlessly to his feet.

'She told me about the shitty little room where you made love. She even told me about the Monet prints hanging on the wall. Funny, don't you think? Elena had two *real* Monets of her own. And yet you took her to a room with Monet posters on the wall. Do you remember them, Mikhail?'

'Not really.'

'Why not?'

'I was too busy looking at your wife.'

This time, it was a sledgehammer fist. It opened another gash on Mikhail's face, an inch beneath the left eye. As the guards hauled him to his feet, Chiara pleaded with Ivan to stop. Ivan ignored her. Ivan was just getting started.

'Elena said you were a perfect gentleman. That you made love twice. That you wanted to make love a third time, but Elena said no. She had to be going. She had to get home to her children. Do you remember it now, Mikhail?'

'I remember, Ivan.'

'These were lies, were they not? You concocted this story of a romantic encounter in order to deceive me. You never made love to my wife in that villa. You debriefed her about my operation. Then you plotted her defection and the theft of my children.'

'No, Ivan.'

'No, what?'

'The lunch was waiting. So was the rosé. Bandol. Elena's favorite. We made love twice. Unlike you, I was a perfect gentleman.'

The knee came up. Mikhail went down. He stayed down.

Now it was Gabriel's turn.

Ivan's men had not bothered to remove Gabriel's watch. It was strapped to his left wrist, and the wrist was pinned to his kidney. In his mind, though, he could picture the digital numbers advancing. At last check it had been 9:11:07. Time had stopped with the collision, and it had started again with Ivan's arrival from Konakovo. Gabriel and Shamron had chosen the old airfield for a reason: to create space between Ivan and the dacha. To create time in the event something went wrong. Gabriel reckoned at least an hour had elapsed between the time of their capture and the time of Ivan's arrival. He knew Shamron had not spent that hour planning a funeral. Now Gabriel and Mikhail had to help their own cause by giving Shamron one thing: *time*. Oddly enough, they would have to enlist Ivan as their ally. They had to keep Ivan angry. They had to keep Ivan talking. When Ivan went silent, bad things happened. Countries tore themselves to shreds. People died.

'You were a fool to come back to Russia, Allon. I knew you would, but you were a fool regardless.'

'Why didn't you just kill me in Italy and be done with it?'

'Because there are certain things a man does himself. And thanks to you, I can't go to Italy. I can't go anywhere.'

'You don't like Russia, Ivan?'

'I love Russia.' A terse smile. 'Especially from a distance.'

'So I suppose the demand for your children was a lie – just like your agreement to return my wife unharmed.'

'I believe "safe and sound" were the words Korovin and Shamron used in Paris. And no, Allon, it was not a lie. I do want my children back.' He glanced at Chiara. 'I calculated that kidnapping your wife gave me at least an outside chance of getting them.'

'You knew Elena and the children were living in America?'

'Let us say I strongly suspected that was the case.'

'So why didn't you kidnap an American target?'

'Two reasons. First and foremost, our president wouldn't have permitted it, since it would have almost certainly caused an open rupture in our relations with Washington.'

'And the second reason?'

'It wouldn't have been a wise investment in time and resources.'

'Would you care to explain?'

'Certainly,' said Ivan, his tone suddenly convivial. 'As everyone in the world knows, the Americans have a policy against negotiating with kidnappers and terrorists. But you Israelis operate differently. Because you are a small country, life is very precious to you. That means you'll negotiate at the drop of a hat when innocent life is at stake. My God, you'll even trade dozens of proven murderers in order to retrieve the bodies of your dead soldiers. Your love of life makes you a weak people, Allon. It always has.'

'So you calculated we would bring pressure to bear on the Americans to return the children?'

'Not on the Americans,' Ivan said. 'On Elena. My former wife is rather like the Jews: devious and weak.'

'Why the pause between Grigori's abduction and Chiara's?'

'The tsar decreed it. Grigori was a test case of sorts. Our president wanted to see how the British would react to a clear provocation on their soil. When he saw only weakness, he allowed me to push the knife in deeper.'

'By kidnapping my wife and making a play for your children.'

'Correct,' said Ivan. 'As far as our president was concerned, your wife was a legitimate target. After all, Allon, you and your American friends carried out an illegal operation on Russian soil last summer – an operation that resulted in the deaths of several of my men, not to mention the theft of my family.'

'And if Elena had refused to return Nikolai and Anna?'

Ivan smiled. 'Then I was certain I would get you.'

'So now you have me, Ivan. Let the others go.'

'Mikhail and Grigori?' Ivan shook his head. 'They betrayed my trust. And you know what we do with traitors, Allon.'

'*Vyshaya mera.*'

Ivan raised his chin in a show of mock admiration.

'Very impressive, Allon. I see you've picked up a bit of Russian during your travels in our country.'

'Let them go, Ivan. Let Chiara go.'

'Chiara? Oh, no, Allon, that is not possible, either. You see, you took my wife. Now I'm going to take yours. That is justice. Just like it says in your Jewish book. Life for life, eye for eye, tooth for tooth, burn for burn, wound for wound.'

'It's called Exodus, Ivan.'

'Yes, I know. Chapter 21, if memory serves. And your laws state very clearly that I am permitted to take your wife since you took mine. Too bad you didn't have a child. I would take that, too. But the PLO already did that, didn't they? In Vienna. His name was Daniel, was it not?'

Gabriel lunged at him. Ivan stepped deftly away and allowed Gabriel to pitch headlong into the snow. The guards let him lie there a moment – a precious moment, thought Gabriel – before lifting him once more to his feet. Ivan brushed the snow from his face.

'I know things, too, Allon. I know you were there in Vienna that night. I know you watched the car explode. I know you tried to pull your wife and son out of the flames. Do you remember what your son looked like when you finally pulled him from the fire? From what I hear, it wasn't good.'

Another futile lunge. Another fall into the snow. Again the guards let him lie there, face burning with cold. And with rage.

Time . . . Precious time . . .

They lifted him upright again. This time, Ivan didn't bother removing the snow.

'But let us return to the topic of betrayal, Allon. How were you able to discover where I was keeping Grigori and your wife?'

'Anton Petrov told me.'

Ivan's face reddened. 'And how did you get to Petrov?'

'Vladimir Chernov.'

The eyes narrowed. 'And Chernov?'

'You were betrayed again, Ivan – betrayed by someone you thought was a friend.'

The blow landed in Gabriel's abdomen. Unprepared for it, he doubled over, thus leaving himself exposed to Ivan's knee. It sent him to the snow again, this time at Chiara's feet. She gazed down at him, her face a mask of terror and grief. Ivan spat and squatted at Gabriel's side.

'Don't pass out on me just yet, Allon, because I have one more question. Would you like to watch your wife die? Or would you prefer to die in front of your wife?'

'Let her go, Ivan.'

'Eye for eye, tooth for tooth, wife for wife.'

He looked at his bodyguards.

'Put this garbage on his feet.'

71. Vladimirskaya Oblast, Russia

Navot was the first to spot the helicopter. It was coming from the direction of Moscow, flying dangerously fast a couple hundred feet above the ground. Ninety seconds later, two more just like it flashed overhead.

'Go back, Oded.'

'What about our orders?'

'To hell with our orders. Go back!'

Time . . .

Time was slipping away from them. It stole silently through the forest, birch tree to birch tree. Time was now their enemy. Gabriel knew he had to seize hold of it. And for that he needed Ivan's help. *Keep him talking*, he thought. *Bad things happen when Ivan stops talking.*

For now, Ivan was wordlessly leading the procession of death along a snowy forest path, one massive hand wrapped around Chiara's arm. Flanked by bodyguards, Gabriel, Mikhail, and Grigori followed.

Keep him talking . . .

'What caused the depressions in the forest, Ivan?'

'Why are you so damn interested in those depressions?'

'They remind me of something.'

'I'm not surprised. How did you find them?'

'Satellites. They show up nicely from space. Very straight. Very even.'

'They're old, but the men who dug them did a good job. They used a bulldozer. It's still here if you'd like to have a look. It stopped working years ago.'

'So how do you open up the earth now, Ivan?'

'Same method, new machine. It's American. Say what you want about the Americans, they still make a damn good bulldozer.'

'What's in the pits, Ivan?'

'You're a smart boy, Allon. You seem to know a bit about our history. You tell me.'

'I assume they're mass graves from the Great Terror.'

'Great Terror? This is a Western slur invented by Koba's enemies.'

Koba was Stalin's Party name. Koba was Ivan's hero.

'What would you call the systematic torture and murder of three-quarters of a million people, Ivan?'

Ivan appeared to give the matter serious consideration. 'I believe I would call it a long overdue pruning of the forest. The Party had been in power for nearly twenty years. There was a great deal of deadwood that needed to be cleared away. And you know what happens when wood is chopped, Allon.'

'Splinters must fall.'

'That's right. Splinters must fall.'

Ivan translated a portion of the exchange for his Russian-speaking bodyguards. They laughed. Ivan laughed, too.

Keep him talking . . .

'How did this place work, Ivan?'

'You'll find out in a minute or two.'

'When was it in operation? 'Thirty-six? 'Thirty-seven?'

Ivan stopped walking. So did everyone else.

'It was 'thirty-seven – the summer of 'thirty-seven, to be precise. It was the time of the troikas. Do you know about the troikas, Allon?'

Gabriel did. He paid the information out slowly, deliberately. 'Stalin was getting annoyed at the slow pace of the killings. He wanted to speed things up, so he created a new way of putting the accused on trial: the troikas. One Party member, one NKVD officer, and a public prosecutor. It wasn't necessary for the accused to be present during his trial. Most were sentenced without ever knowing they were even under investigation. Most trials lasted ten minutes. Some less.'

'And appeals were not permitted,' Ivan added with a smile. 'They won't be permitted now, either.'

He nodded to the pair of bodyguards who were holding Grigori upright. The procession began moving again.

Keep him talking. Bad things happen when Ivan stops talking.

'I suppose the killing took place inside the dacha. That's why it has a cellar with a special room in it – a room with a drain in the center of the floor. And that's why the track is winding instead of straight. Stalin's henchmen wouldn't have wanted the neighbors to know what was going on here.'

'And they never did. The condemned were always picked up after midnight and brought here in black cars. They were taken straight into the dacha and given a good beating to make them easy to handle. Then it was down to the cellar. Seven grams of lead in the nape of the neck.'

'And then?'

'They were thrown into carts and brought out here to the graves.'

'Who's buried out here, Ivan?'

'By the summer of 'thirty-seven, most of the heavy cutting had already been done. Koba just had to clear away the brush.'

'The brush?'

'Mensheviks. Anarchists. Old Bolsheviks who'd been associated with Lenin. A few priests, kulaks, and aristocrats for good measure. Anyone Koba thought could possibly pose a threat was liquidated. Then their families were liquidated, too. There's a real revolutionary stew buried beneath these woods, Allon. They all sleep together. Some nights, you can almost hear them arguing about politics. And the best part is, no one even knows they're here.'

'Because you bought the land after the fall of the Soviet Union to make sure the dead stayed buried?'

Ivan stopped walking. 'Actually, I was *asked* to buy the land.'

'By whom?'

'My father, of course.'

Ivan had answered without hesitation. Annoyed by Gabriel's inquiries at first, he now actually seemed to be enjoying the exchange. Gabriel reckoned it must be easy to unburden one's secrets to a man who would soon be dead. He tried to frame another question that would keep Ivan talking, but it wasn't necessary. Ivan resumed his lecture without further prompting.

'When the Soviet Union collapsed, it was a dangerous time for the KGB. There was talk about throwing open the archives. Airing dirty laundry. Naming names. The old guard was horrified. They didn't want the KGB dragged through the mud of history. But they had other motivations for keeping the secrets, too. You see, Allon, they weren't planning to stay out of power for long. Even then, they were plotting their comeback. They succeeded, of course. The KGB, by another name, is once again running Russia.'

'And you preside over the last mass grave of the Great Terror.'

'The last? Hardly. You can't put a shovel in the soil of Russia without hitting bone. But this one is quite large. Apparently, there are seventy thousand souls buried beneath these trees. *Seventy thousand.* If it ever became public . . .' His voice trailed off, as if he were momentarily at a loss for words. 'Let us say it might cause considerable embarrassment inside the Kremlin.'

'Is that why the president is so willing to tolerate your activities?'

'He gets his cut. The tsar takes a cut of everything.'

'How much did you have to pay him for the right to kidnap my wife?'

Ivan made no response. Gabriel pressed him to see if he could provoke another outburst of anger.

'How much, Ivan? Five million? Ten? Twenty?'

Ivan wheeled around. 'I'm tired of your questions, Allon. Besides, we haven't much farther to go. Your unmarked grave awaits you.'

Gabriel looked beyond Chiara's shoulder and saw a mound of fresh earth, covered by a dusting of snow. He told her he loved her. Then he closed his eyes. He was hearing things again.

Helicopters.

72. Vladimirskaya Oblast, Russia

Colonel Leonid Milchenko could finally see the property: four frozen streams meeting in a frozen marsh, a small dacha with a hole blown in the front door, a line of people walking slowly through a birch forest.

He opened the mic on his headset.

'Do you see them?'

The pilot's helmet moved up and down rapidly.

'How close can you get?'

'Edge of the marsh.'

'That's at least three hundred meters away.'

'That's as close as I can put this thing down, Colonel.'

'What about the Alphas?'

'Fast rope insertion. Right into the trees.'

'Nobody dies.'

'Yes, Colonel.'

Nobody dies . . .

Who was he kidding? This was Russia. Someone always died.

Ten more paces through the snow. Then Ivan heard the helicopters, too. He stopped. Cocked his head, doglike. Shot a glance at Rudenko. Started walking again.

Time . . . Precious time . . .

*

Navot's message flashed across the screens of the annex.

HELICOPTERS INBOUND . . .

Carter covered his telephone and looked at Shamron.

'The FSB team confirms a line of people walking into the trees. It looks as if they're alive, Ari!'

'They won't be for long. When will those Alpha Group forces be on the ground?'

'Ninety seconds.'

Shamron closed his eyes.

Two turns to the right, two turns to the left . . .

The burial pit opened before them, a wound in the flesh of Mother Russia. The ashen sky wept snow as they filed slowly toward it, accompanied by the thumping of distant rotors. *Big rotors*, thought Gabriel. Big enough to make the forest shake. Big enough to make Ivan's men restless. Ivan, too. Suddenly he was shouting at Grigori in Russian, exhorting him to walk faster to his death. But Gabriel, in his thoughts, was pleading for Grigori to slow his pace. To stumble. To do anything possible to allow the helicopters time to arrive.

Just then, the first swept in at treetop level, leaving a temporary blizzard in its wake. Ivan was briefly lost in the whiteout. When he reemerged, his face was contorted with rage. He shoved Grigori toward the edge of the pit and began screaming at his guards in Russian. Most were no longer paying attention. A few of his mutinous legion were watching the helicopter settling at the edge of the marshland. The others had their eyes on the western sky, where two more helicopters had appeared.

Four bodyguards remained loyal to Ivan. At his command they placed the condemned in a line at the edge of the pit, heels against the edge, for Ivan had decreed that all were to be shot in the face. Gabriel was placed at one end, Mikhail at the other, Chiara and Grigori in the center. At first Grigori was positioned next to Gabriel, but apparently that wouldn't do. In a burst of rapid Russian, his gun flailing wildly, Ivan ordered the guards to quickly move Grigori and place Chiara at Gabriel's side.

As the exchange was being made, two more helicopters thundered in from the west. Unlike the first, they did not streak past but hovered directly overhead. Ropes uncoiled from their bellies, and in an instant black-suited special forces were descending rapidly through the trees. Gabriel heard the sound of weapons dropping into the snow and saw arms raising in surrender. And he glimpsed two men in overcoats running awkwardly toward them through the trees. And he saw Oleg Rudenko trying desperately to remove the Makarov from Ivan's grasp. But Ivan would not relinquish it. Ivan wanted his blood.

Ivan gave his security chief a single mighty shove in the chest that sent him tumbling into the snow. Then he pointed the Makarov directly into Gabriel's face. He did not pull the trigger. Instead, he smiled and said, 'Enjoy watching your wife die, Allon.'

The Makarov moved to the right. Gabriel hurled himself toward Ivan but could not reach him before the gun exploded with a deafening roar. As he toppled face-first into the snow, two Alpha Group men immediately leapt onto his back and pinned him to the frozen ground. For several agonizing seconds, he struggled to free himself, but the Russians refused to allow him to move or to lift his head. 'My wife!' he shouted at them. 'Did he kill my wife?' Whether they answered, he did not know. The gunshot had robbed him of the ability to hear. He was aware only of a titanic physical struggle taking place near his shoulder. Then, a moment later, he glimpsed Ivan being led away through the trees.

Only then did the Russians help Gabriel to rise. Twisting his head quickly around, he saw Chiara weeping over a fallen body. It was Grigori. Gabriel dropped to his knees and tried to console her, but she seemed unaware of his presence. 'They never killed her,' she was screaming. 'Irina is alive, Grigori! Irina is *alive*!'

PART FIVE
The Reckoning

73. Jerusalem

In the days following the conclusion of the G-8 summit in Moscow, three seemingly unconnected news stories broke in quick succession. The first concerned Russia's uncertain future; the second, its dark past. The last managed to touch upon both, and ultimately would prove to be the most controversial. But then, that was to be expected, grumbled a few of the old hands at British intelligence, since the subject of the story was none other than Grigori Bulganov.

The first story unfolded exactly one week after the summit and had for its backdrop the Russian economy – more to the point, its all-important energy industry. Because it was good news, at least from Moscow's point of view, the Russian president chose to make the announcement himself. He did so in a Kremlin news conference, flanked by several of his most senior aides, all veterans of the KGB. In a terse statement, delivered with his trademark glare, the president announced that Viktor Orlov, the dissident former oligarch now residing in London, had finally been brought to heel. All of Orlov's shares in Ruzoil, the Siberian oil giant, were to be immediately placed under the control of Gazprom, Russia's state-owned oil-and-gas monopoly. In exchange, said the president, Russian authorities had agreed to drop all criminal charges against Orlov and withdraw their request for his extradition.

In London, Downing Street hailed the Russian president's

gesture as 'statesmanlike,' while Russia hands at the Foreign Ministry and the policy institutes openly wondered whether a new wind might be blowing from the East. Viktor Orlov found such speculation hopelessly naïve, but the reporters who attended his hastily called London news conference did walk away with the sense that Viktor was not long for the fight. His decision to surrender Ruzoil, he said, was based on a realistic assessment of the facts. The Kremlin was now controlled by men who would stop at nothing to get what they wanted. When fighting such men, he conceded, victory was not possible, only death. Or perhaps something worse than death. Viktor promised not to be silenced, then promptly announced he had nothing further to say.

Two days later, Viktor Orlov was quietly awarded his first British passport during a small reception at 10 Downing Street. He was also granted a private tour of Buckingham Palace, led by the queen herself. He took many photographs of Her Majesty's private apartments and gave them to his decorator. Delivery trucks were soon spotted in Cheyne Walk, and passersby were sometimes able to catch a glimpse of Viktor working in his study. Apparently, he had finally decided it was safe to throw open his curtains and enjoy his magnificent view of the Thames.

The second story also originated in Moscow, but, unlike the first, it seemed to leave the Russian president at a loss for words. It concerned a discovery in a birch forest in Vladimirskaya Oblast: several mass graves filled with victims of Stalin's Great Terror. Preliminary estimates placed the number of bodies at some seventy thousand souls. The Russian president dismissed the find as 'of little significance' and resisted calls for him to pay a visit. Such a gesture would have been politically tricky, since Stalin, dead for more than a half century, was still among the most popular figures in the country. He reluctantly agreed to order a review of KGB and NKVD archives and granted the Russian Orthodox Church permission to construct a small memorial at the site – subject to Kremlin approval, of course. 'But let's leave the breast-beating to the Germans,' he said during his one and only comment. 'After all, we must remember that Koba carried out these repressions to help prepare the country for the coming war against the fascists.' All those present were chilled by the detached manner in which the president spoke of mass murder. Also, by the fact he referred to Stalin by his old Party nom de guerre, Koba. The circumstances surrounding the discovery of the killing ground were never revealed, nor was the owner of the property ever identified. 'It is for his own protection,' insisted a Kremlin spokesman. 'History can be a dangerous thing.'

The third story broke not in Moscow but in the Russian city sometimes referred to as London. This, too, was a story of death – not the death of thousands but of one. It seemed the body of Grigori Bulganov, the FSB defector and very public dissident, had been discovered on a deserted Thames dock, the victim of an apparent suicide. Scotland Yard and the Home Office took shelter behind claims of national security and released scant details about the case. However, they did acknowledge that Grigori was a somewhat troubled soul who had not adjusted well to a life in exile. As evidence, they pointed out that he had been trying to rekindle his relationship with his former wife – though they neglected to mention that same former wife was by then living in the United Kingdom under a new name and government protection. Also revealed was the somewhat curious fact that Grigori had failed to appear recently for the finals of the Central London Chess Club championship, a match he was expected to win easily. Simon Finch, Grigori's opponent, surfaced briefly in the press to defend his decision to accept the title by forfeit. He then used the exposure to publicize his latest cause, which was the abolition of land mines. Buckley & Hobbes, Grigori's publisher, announced that Olga Sukhova, Grigori's friend and fellow dissident, had graciously agreed to complete *Killer in the Kremlin*. She appeared briefly at Grigori's burial in Highgate Cemetery before being escorted away by several armed security men and whisked back into hiding.

Many in the British press, including reporters who had dealt with Grigori, dismissed the government's claim of suicide as hogwash. Without any other facts, however, they were left only to speculate, which they did without hesitation. Clearly, they said, Grigori had enemies in Moscow who wished him dead. And clearly, they insisted, one of those enemies must have killed him. The *Financial Times* pointed out that Grigori was quite close to Viktor Orlov and suggested the defector's death might somehow be tied to the Ruzoil affair. For his part, Viktor referred to his dead countryman as a 'true Russian patriot' and established a freedom fund in his name.

And there the story died, at least as far as the mainstream press was concerned. But on the Internet and in some of the more sensational scandal sheets, it would continue to generate copy for weeks. The wonderful thing about conspiracies is that a clever reporter can usually find a way to link any two events no matter how disparate. But none of the reporters who investigated Grigori's mysterious death ever attempted to link it to the newly discovered mass graves in Vladimirskaya Oblast. Nor did they posit a connection between the Russian defector and the heartbroken couple who by then had taken refuge in a quiet little apartment on Narkiss Street in Jerusalem. The names Gabriel Allon and Chiara Zolli were not a factor in the story. And they never would be.

They had recovered from operational trauma before, but never at the same time and never from wounds so deep. Their physical injuries healed quickly. The others refused to mend. They huddled behind locked doors, watched over by men with guns. Unable to tolerate more than a few seconds of separation, they followed each other from room to room. Their lovemaking was ravenous, as if each encounter might be the last, and rare was the moment they were not touching. Their sleep was torn by nightmares. They dreamed of watching each other die. They dreamed of the cell beneath the dacha in the woods. They dreamed of the thousands who were murdered there and the thousands who lay beneath the birch trees in graves with no markers. And, of course, they dreamed of Ivan. Indeed, it was Ivan whom Gabriel saw most. Ivan roamed Gabriel's subconscious at all hours, dressed in his fine English clothing, carrying his Makarov pistol. Sometimes he was accompanied by Yekaterina and his bodyguards. Usually he was alone. Always he was pointing his gun in Gabriel's face.

Enjoy watching your wife die, Allon . . .

Chiara was not eager to speak of her ordeal, and Gabriel did not press her. As the child of a woman who had survived the horrors of the Birkenau death camp, he knew Chiara was suffering an acute form of guilt – *survivor's* guilt, which is its own special kind of hell. Chiara had lived and Grigori had died. And he had died because he had stepped in front of a bullet meant for her. This was the image Chiara saw most in her dreams: Grigori, battered and barely able to move, summoning the strength to place himself in front of Ivan's gun. Chiara had been baptized in Grigori's blood. And she was alive because of Grigori's sacrifice.

The rest of it came out in bits and pieces and sometimes at the oddest moments. Over dinner one evening, she described in detail for Gabriel the moment of her capture and the deaths of Lior and Motti. Two days later, while doing the dishes, she recounted what it was like to spend all those hours in the dark. And how once each day, just for a few moments, the sun would set fire to the snowbank outside the tiny window. And finally, while folding laundry one afternoon, she tearfully confessed that she had lied to Gabriel about the pregnancy. She was eight weeks gone at the time of the abduction and lost the child in Ivan's cell. 'It was the drugs,' she explained. 'They killed my child. They killed *your* child.'

'Why didn't you tell me the truth? I would never have gone after Grigori.'

'I was afraid you would be mad at me.'

'For what?'

'For getting pregnant.'

Gabriel collapsed into Chiara's lap, tears flowing down

his face. They were tears of guilt but also tears of rage. Though Ivan did not know it, he *had* managed to kill Gabriel's child. His unborn child but his child nonetheless.

'Who gave you the shots?' he asked.

'It was the woman. I see her death every night. It's the one memory I don't run from.' She wiped away his tears. 'I need you to make me three promises, Gabriel.'

'Anything.'

'Promise me we'll have a baby.'

'I promise.'

'Promise me we'll never be apart.'

'Never.'

'And promise me you'll kill them all.'

The next day, these two human wrecks presented themselves at King Saul Boulevard. Along with Mikhail, they were subjected to rigorous physical and psychological evaluations. Uzi Navot reviewed the results that evening. Afterward, he telephoned Shamron at his home in Tiberias.

'How bad?' Shamron asked.

'Very.'

'When will he be ready to work again?'

'It's going to be a while.'

'How long, Uzi?'

'Maybe never.'

'And Mikhail?'

'He's a mess, Ari. They're all a mess.'

Shamron fell silent. 'The worst thing we can do is let him sit around. He needs to get back on the horse.'

'I take it you have an idea?'

'How's the interrogation of Petrov coming along?'

'He's putting up a good fight.'

'Go down to the Negev, Uzi. Light a fire under the interrogators.'

'What do you want?'

'I want the names. All of them.'

74. Jerusalem

By then it was late March. The cold winter rains had come and gone, and the spring weather was warm and fine. At the suggestion of the doctors, they tried to get out of the apartment at least once a day. They reveled in the mundane: a trip to the bustling Makhane Yehuda Market, a stroll through the narrow streets of the Old City, a quiet lunch in one of their favorite restaurants. At Shamron's insistence, they were accompanied always by a pair of bodyguards, young boys with cropped hair and sunglasses who reminded them both too much of Lior and Motti. Chiara said she wanted to visit the memorial north of Tel Aviv. Seeing the bodyguards' names engraved in stone left her so distraught Gabriel had to practically carry her back to the car. Two days later, on the Mount of Olives, it was his turn to collapse in grief. Lior and Motti had been buried only a few yards from his son.

Gabriel felt an unusually strong desire to spend time with Leah, and Chiara, unable to bear his absence, had no choice but to go with him. They would sit with Leah for hours in the garden of the hospital and listen patiently while she wandered through time, now in the present, now in the past. With each visit she grew more comfortable in Chiara's company, and, in moments of lucidity, the two women compared notes on what it was like to live with Gabriel Allon. They talked about his idiosyncrasies and his mood swings, and his need for absolute silence while he was working. And when they were feeling generous, they talked about his incredible gifts. Then the light would go out in Leah's eyes, and she would return once more to her own private hell. And sometimes Gabriel and Chiara would return to theirs. Leah's doctor seemed to sense something was amiss. During a visit in early April, he pulled Gabriel and Chiara aside and quietly asked whether they needed professional help.

'You both look as if you haven't slept in weeks.'

'We haven't,' said Gabriel.

'Do you want to talk to someone?'

'We're not allowed.'

'Trouble at work?'

'Something like that.'

'Can I give you something to help you sleep?'

'We have a pharmacy in our medicine cabinet.'

'I don't want to see you back here for at least a week. Take a trip. Get some sun. You look like ghosts.'

The next morning, shadowed by bodyguards, they drove to Eilat. For three days, they managed not to speak about Russia, or Ivan, or Grigori, or the birch forest outside Moscow. They spent their time sunning themselves on the beach or snorkeling amid the coral reefs of the Red Sea. They ate too much food, drank too much wine, and made love until they were overcome by exhaustion. On their last night, they talked about the future, about the promise Gabriel had made to leave the Office, and about where they might live. For the moment, they had no choice but to remain in Israel. To leave the country and the protective cocoon of the Office was not possible so long as Ivan was still walking the face of the earth.

'And if he wasn't?' asked Chiara.

'We can live wherever we like – within reason, of course.'

'Then I suppose you'll just have to kill him.'

They left Eilat the next morning and set out for Jerusalem. While crossing the Negev, Gabriel decided quite spontaneously to make a brief detour near Beersheba. His destination was a prison and interrogation center, located in the center of a restricted military zone. It housed only a handful of inmates, the so-called worst of the worst. Included in this select group was Prisoner 6754, also known as Anton Petrov, the man Ivan had hired to kidnap Grigori and Chiara. The commander of the facility arranged for Petrov to be brought to the exercise yard so Gabriel and Chiara could see him. He wore a blue-and-white tracksuit. His muscle was gone, along with most of his hair. He walked with a heavy limp.

'Too bad you didn't kill him,' Chiara said.

'Don't think it didn't cross my mind.'

'How long will we keep him?'

'As long as we need to.'

'And then?'

'The Americans would like a word with him.'

'Someone needs to make sure he has an accident.'

'We'll see.'

It was dark when they arrived in Narkiss Street. Gabriel could tell by the abundance of bodyguards they had a visitor waiting upstairs in the apartment. Uzi Navot was seated in the living room. He had a dossier. He had names. Eleven names. All former KGB. All living well in Western Europe on Ivan's money. Navot left the folder with Gabriel and said he would wait to hear from him. Gabriel allowed Chiara to make the decision.

'Kill them all,' she said.

'It's going to take time.'

'Take as much time as you need.'

'You won't be able to come.'

'I know.'

'You'll go to Tiberias. Gilah will look after you.'

They convened the next morning in Room 456C of King Saul Boulevard: Yaakov and Yossi, Dina and Rimona, Oded and Mordecai, Mikhail and Eli Lavon. Gabriel arrived last and tacked eleven photographs to the bulletin board at the front of the room. Eleven photographs of eleven Russians. Eleven Russians who would not survive the summer. The meeting did not take long. The order of death was established, the assignments were made. Travel saw to the flights, Identity to the passports and visas. Housekeeping opened many doors. Banking gave them a blank check.

They left Tel Aviv in waves, traveled in pairs, and reconvened two weeks later in Barcelona. There, on a quiet street in the Gothic Quarter, Gabriel and Mikhail killed the man who had been walking behind Grigori on Harrow Road the evening of his abduction. For his sins he was shot at close range with .22 caliber Berettas. As he lay dying in the gutter, Gabriel whispered two words into his ear.

For Grigori . . .

A week later, in the Bairro Alto of Lisbon, he whispered the same two words to the woman who had been walking toward Grigori, the woman who had carried no umbrella and had been hatless in the rain. Two weeks after that, in Biarritz, it was the turn of her partner, the man who had been walking next to her on Westbourne Terrace Road Bridge. He heard the two words while taking a midnight stroll along La Grande Plage. They were spoken to his back. When he turned, he saw Gabriel and Mikhail, arms extended, guns in their hands.

For Grigori . . .

After that, news of the killings began to circulate among those still to die. To prevent the survivors from fleeing to Russia, the Office planted false stories that it was Ivan, not the Israelis, who was responsible. *Ivan had launched a Great Terror*, according to the rumors. *Ivan was pruning the forest. Anyone foolish enough to set foot in Russia would be killed the Russian way, with great pain and extreme violence.* And so the guilty stayed in the West, close to ground, below radar. Or so they thought. But one by one they were targeted. And one by one they died.

The driver of the Mercedes that took Irina to her 'reunion' with Grigori was killed in Amsterdam in the arms of a prostitute. The driver of the van that carried Grigori on the first leg of his journey back to Russia was killed while leaving a pub in Copenhagen. The two flunkies sent to kill Olga Sukhova in Oxford were next. One died in Munich, the other in Prague.

It was then Sergei Korovin made a frantic attempt to intervene. 'The SVR and FSB are getting itchy,' Korovin told Shamron. 'If this continues, who knows where it might lead?' In a page taken from Ivan's playbook, Shamron professed ignorance. Then he warned Korovin that the Russian services had better watch their step. Otherwise, they were next. By that evening, Office stations across Europe detected a notable increase in security around Russian embassies and known Russian intelligence officers. It was unnecessary, of course. Gabriel and his team had no interest in targeting the innocent. Only the guilty.

At that point, just four names remained. Four operatives who had carried out the abduction of Chiara in Umbria. Four operatives who had Office blood on their hands. They knew they were being stalked and tried not to remain in one place long. Fear made them sloppy. Fear made them easy pickings. They were killed in a series of lightning-strike operations: Warsaw, Budapest, Athens, Istanbul. While dying, they heard four words instead of two.

For Lior and Motti.

By then it was nearly August. It was time to go home again.

75. Tiberias, Israel

But what of Ivan? For many weeks after the nightmare in the birch forest outside Moscow, he stayed out of sight. There were rumors he had been arrested. Rumors he had fled the country. Rumors, even, that he had been taken away by the FSB and killed. They were false, of course. Ivan was just observing another great Russian tradition, the tradition of internal exile. For Ivan, it was not marked by backbreaking labor or starvation rations. Ivan's gulag was his fortresslike mansion in Zhukovka, the secret city of the oligarchs east of Moscow. And he had Yekaterina to soothe his wounds.

Though Ivan's name was never publicly linked to the killing site in Vladimirskaya Oblast, its exposure seemed to do harm to his standing inside the Kremlin. In certain circles, much was made of the fact that Ivan's development firm lost out on an important construction project. And that his nightclub was suddenly out of fashion with the *siloviki* and the other Moscow well connected. And that his luxury-car dealership saw a sudden sharp decrease in sales. These were false readings, though, more symptomatic of Russia's troubled economy than any real decline in Ivan's fortunes. What's more, his arms dealings continued apace, weapons sales being one of the few bright spots in an otherwise bleak global financial climate. Indeed, British, American, and French intelligence all noticed a sharp spike in the number of Kharkov-owned aircraft touching down on isolated landing strips from the Middle East to Africa and beyond. And the Russian president continued to take his cut. The tsar, as Ivan liked to say, *always* took his cut.

NSA surveillance revealed that Ivan was aware of the systematic liquidation of Anton Petrov's operatives and that it troubled him not at all. In Ivan's mind, they had betrayed him and thus deserved the fate that befell them. In fact, throughout that long summer of retribution, he seemed obsessed by only two questions. Had his children been aboard the American jet that landed in Konakovo? And had they truly composed the letter of hatred handed to him by the pilot?

The children and their mother knew the answer, of course, along with the American president and a handful of his most senior officials. So, too, did the small band of Israeli intelligence officers who convened at sunset on the first Friday of August north of the ancient city of Tiberias. The occasion was Shabbat; the setting was Shamron's honey-colored villa overlooking the Sea of Galilee. The entire team was present, along with Sarah Bancroft, who had decided to spend her August holiday with Mikhail in Israel. There were spouses Gabriel had never met and children he had only seen in photographs. The presence of so many children was difficult for Chiara, especially when she saw their faces lit by the glow of the Shabbat candles. As Gilah recited the blessing, Chiara took Gabriel's hand and held it tightly. Gabriel kissed her cheek and heard again the words she had spoken to him in Umbria. *We mourn the dead and keep them in our hearts. But we live our lives.*

The summer spent by the lake had done wonders for Chiara's appearance. Her skin was deeply tanned, and her riotous dark hair was aglow with gold and auburn highlights. She smiled easily throughout the meal and even burst into laughter when Bella scolded Uzi for taking a second portion of Gilah's famous chicken with Moroccan spice. Watching her, Gabriel could almost imagine none of it had actually happened. That it had only been a dream from which they both had finally awakened. It wasn't true, of course, and no amount of time would ever fully heal the wounds Ivan had inflicted. Chiara was like a newly restored painting, retouched and shimmering with a fresh coat of varnish but still damaged. She would have to be handled with great care.

Gabriel had feared the gathering would be an occasion to relive the dreadful details of the affair, but it was mentioned only once, when Shamron spoke about the importance of what they had achieved. As Jews, they all had relatives whose earthly remains were turned to smoke by the crematoria or were buried in mass graves in the Baltics or the Ukraine. Their memories were kept by commemorative flames and by the index cards stored in the Hall of Names at Yad Vashem. But there were no graves to visit, no headstones upon which to shed tears. By their actions in Russia, Gabriel's team had given such a place to the relatives of the seventy thousand murdered at the killing ground in Vladimirskaya Oblast. They had paid a terrible price, and Grigori had not survived, but with their sacrifice they had given a kind of justice, perhaps even peace, to seventy thousand restless souls.

For the remainder of the meal, Shamron regaled them

with stories of the past. He was never happier than when surrounded by his family and friends, and his good mood seemed to soften the deep cracks and fissures in his aged face. But there was sadness there, too. The operation had been traumatic for all of them, but in many ways it had been hardest on Shamron. With his cool, creative thinking, he had saved all their lives. But for more than an hour that terrible morning, he had feared that three officers, two of whom he loved as children, were about to suffer a horrible death. There was an emotional price to be paid for an operation like that – and Shamron paid it, later that evening, when he invited Gabriel to join him on the terrace for a private chat. They sat together on the spot where Gabriel and Chiara were married, Shamron smoking quietly, Gabriel gazing at the blue-black sky above the Golan.

'Your wife looks radiant this evening. Almost like new.'

'Looks can be deceiving, Ari, but she does look wonderful. I suppose I have Gilah to thank. She obviously took good care of her while I was gone.'

'Gilah is good at putting people back together again, even when she's not sure how they ended up broken in the first place. I must say, we enjoyed having Chiara for the summer. If only my own children would come more often.'

'Maybe they would if you didn't smoke so much.'

Shamron took a final pull at his cigarette and crushed it out slowly. 'You actually looked as if you were enjoying yourself, too. Or were you just deceiving me?'

'It was a wonderful evening, Ari. In fact, it was exactly what we all needed.'

'Your team adores you, Gabriel. They would do anything for you.'

'They have, Ari. Just ask Mikhail.'

'Do you think he's actually going to marry this American girl?'

'Her name is Sarah. Surely, as a Jew from Tiberias, you should have no trouble remembering that name.'

'Answer my question.'

'He'd be a fool not to marry her. She's a remarkable woman.'

'But she's not Jewish.'

'She might as well be.'

'Do you think the CIA will let her stay on if she marries one of us?'

'If they don't, you should hire her. If it weren't for Sarah, Anton Petrov might have killed Uzi in Zurich.'

Shamron made no response other than to light another cigarette.

'How is he?' Gabriel asked.

'Petrov?' Shamron pulled his lips into an indifferent frown. 'Not so good.'

'What's wrong?'

'Apparently, he managed to escape the detention and interrogation facility. A group of Bedouin found his body out in the Negev, about fifty miles south of Beersheba. The vultures had got to him by then. I hear it wasn't pretty.'

'I'm sorry I didn't get to have a final word with him.'

'Don't be. While you were in Europe, we were able to wring one more confession out of him. He admitted to killing those two journalists from *Moskovskaya Gazeta* last year on Ivan's orders. But given the rather sensitive circumstances of his admission, we're in no position to forward the information to the French and Italian authorities. For now both cases will remain officially unsolved.'

'What did you do with the five million euros Petrov left in Becker and Puhl?'

'We made him sign it over to Konrad Becker to cover the costs of the mess you made in his bank. He sends his best, by the way. But he would be most grateful if you did your private banking elsewhere.'

'Were you forced to clean up any other messes?'

'Not really. Our disinformation campaign managed to deflect all suspicion from us onto Ivan. Besides, these were not exactly fine, upstanding citizens whom you killed. They were former KGB hoods who traded in murder, kidnapping, and extortion. As far as the European police and security services are concerned, we did them a favor.'

Shamron looked at Gabriel for a moment in silence. 'Did it help?'

'What?'

'Killing them?'

Gabriel gazed out at the black waters of the lake. 'I did terrible things in order to get Chiara back, Ari. I did things I never want to do again.'

'But?'

'Yes, it did help.'

'Eleven,' Shamron said. 'Ironic, don't you think?'

'How so?'

'Your first assignment came about because Black September killed eleven Israelis in Munich. And for your final assignment, you and Mikhail killed eleven Russians who were responsible for Chiara's abduction and Grigori Bulganov's death.'

A heavy silence settled between them, broken only by the sound of laughter at the dinner table.

'My final assignment? I thought you and the prime minister had decided it was my time to take over the Office.'

'Have you seen your fitness reports?' Shamron shook his head slowly. 'You're in no condition to take on the responsibility of running the Office now. Not when we have a confrontation with the Iranians looming. And not when your wife needs your attention.'

'What are you saying, Ari?'

'I'm saying that you are released from the promise you made in Paris. I'm telling you that you're *fired*, Gabriel. You have a new mission now. Get your wife pregnant again as quickly as possible. You're not so young, my son. You need to have another child quickly.'

'Are you sure, Ari? Are you really prepared to let me go?'

'I'm sure we'll always find something for you to do. But it's not going to be sitting behind the desk in the director's suite. We're going to inflict that chore on someone else.'

'Do you have a candidate in mind?'

'Actually, we've already settled on one. It's going to be announced next month when Amos steps down.'

'Who is it?'

'Me,' said Uzi Navot.

Gabriel turned and saw Navot standing on the terrace, his heavy arms folded across his chest. In the half-light, he looked shockingly like Shamron in his youth.

'Brilliant choice, don't you think?'

'I'm speechless.'

'For once.' Navot came forward and placed his hand on Gabriel's shoulder. 'We have a wonderful system, you and I. You turn a job down, then they give it to me.'

'But the right man got the job in both cases, Uzi. I would have been a terrible director. *Mazel tov.*'

'Do you mean that, Gabriel?'

'The Office is going to be in good hands for years to come.' Gabriel cocked his head toward Shamron. 'Now, if we can just get the Old Man to let go of the bicycle seat.'

Shamron grimaced. 'Let's not get carried away. But let us also be clear about one thing. Uzi is not going to be my pawn. He'll be his own man. But obviously I'll always be here to offer advice.'

'Whether he wants it or not.'

'Be careful, my son. Otherwise, I'll advise him to deal with you harshly.'

Navot walked over and leaned against the balustrade.

'What are we going to do with him, Ari?'

'In my opinion, he should be locked in a room with his wife and kept there until she is pregnant again.'

'Done.' Navot looked at Gabriel. 'It's an order. And you're not going to disobey another one of my orders, are you, Gabriel?'

'No, sir.'

'So what *are* you going to do with all this spare time?'

'Rest. After that . . .' Gabriel gave a noncommittal shrug. 'To be honest, I haven't a clue.'

'Just don't get any ideas about leaving the country,' Shamron said. 'For the time being, your address is No. 16 Narkiss Street.'

'I need to work.'

'So we'll find you some paintings to clean.'

'The paintings are in Europe.'

'You can't go to Europe,' Shamron said. 'Not yet.'

'When?'

'When we've dealt with Ivan. Then you can leave.'

76. Jerusalem

Gabriel and Chiara made a determined effort to follow Navot's order to the letter. They found little reason to leave the apartment; a furnacelike August heat had settled over Jerusalem, and the daylight hours were intolerably hot. They ventured out only after dark, and even then only briefly. For the first time in many years, Gabriel felt a strong desire to produce original work. His subject matter, of course, was Chiara. In just three days he painted a stunning nude that, when finished, he propped against the wall at the foot of their bed. Sometimes, when the room was in darkness and he was intoxicated with Chiara's kisses, it was almost possible to confuse canvas with reality. It was during one such hallucination that the bedside telephone rang quite unexpectedly. With Chiara astride his hips, he was tempted not to answer. Reluctantly he brought the receiver to his ear.

'We need to talk,' said Adrian Carter.

'I'm listening.'

'Not over the phone.'

'Where?'

They met for breakfast two days later on the terrace of the King David Hotel. When Gabriel arrived, he found Carter wearing a wrinkled poplin suit and reading the *International Herald Tribune*. It had been many months since they had seen each other. Indeed, their last encounter had occurred at Shannon Airport in Ireland, the morning after the G-8 summit. Under the agreement reached with the Russian president, Gabriel, Chiara, Mikhail, and Irina Bulganova had been allowed to leave Moscow the same way Gabriel had arrived: surrounded by Secret Service agents, aboard the so-called car plane. They had disembarked during a refueling stop and had gone their separate ways. Irina had accompanied Graham Seymour to Britain, while Gabriel, Chiara, and Mikhail had flown home to Israel with Shamron. Carter had been so overcome by emotion that morning that he had neglected to ask Gabriel for the official American passport he had used to enter Russia. He did so now, a moment after retaking his seat. Gabriel tossed it onto the table, emblem down.

'I hope you didn't use this during your little European holiday this summer.'

'I haven't left Israel since I got back from Russia.'

'Nice try, Gabriel. But we have it on very good authority that you and your team spent the summer killing Anton Petrov's friends and associates. And you did a damn good job of it.'

'It wasn't us, Adrian. It was Ivan.'

'My European station chiefs heard those rumors, too.'

Carter opened the passport and began leafing through the pages.

'Don't worry, Adrian. You won't find any new visas in there. I wouldn't do that to you *or* the president. My wife is alive because of you. And I'll never be able to repay you.'

'I believe the balance of our account is still weighted heavily in your favor.' Carter sipped his coffee and changed the subject. 'We hear there's about to be a change at the helm of King Saul Boulevard. Needless to say, Langley is pleased by the choice. I've always been fond of Uzi.'

'But?'

'Obviously, we were hoping the next chief would be you. We understand why that's not going to be possible. And we wholeheartedly support your decision.'

'I can't tell you how relieved I am to know I have the support of Langley, Adrian.'

'Do try to control that caustic Israeli wit of yours.' Carter dabbed his lips with his napkin. 'Have you given any thought to your future plans?'

'For the moment, Chiara and I will have to stay here.' Gabriel nodded toward the pair of bodyguards seated two tables away. 'Protected by children with guns.'

'You *could* come to America. Elena says you're welcome anytime. In fact, she says she'd be willing to build a house for you and Chiara on the estate. If I were in your shoes, I'd be tempted to take her up on the offer.'

'That's because you grew up in New England and you're used to the winters. I'm from the Valley of Jezreel.'

'She's not joking, Gabriel.'

'Please thank Elena and tell her I do appreciate the offer. But I can't accept it.'

'Her children are going to be very disappointed.' Carter handed Gabriel an envelope. 'They wrote you a letter. Actually, it's addressed to you *and* Chiara.'

'What is it?'

'A letter of apology. They want you to know how sorry they are for what their father did.'

Gabriel removed the letter and read it in silence.

'It's beautiful, Adrian, but tell the children they have no

450

need to feel guilty about their father's actions. Besides, we would never have been able to get Chiara back without their help.'

'Apparently, they put on quite a performance at Andrews. Fielding says it was one for the books. The Russian ambassador never suspected a thing.'

Gabriel returned the letter to the envelope and smiled. Though the Russian ambassador did not realize it, he had been a bit player in an elaborate deception. It was true that Anna and Nikolai had boarded the U.S. Air Force C-32 at Andrews, but at Gabriel's insistence they had been kept far from Russian airspace. Indeed, within seconds after passing through the cabin door, they walked straight into the hold of a hydraulic catering vehicle, where Sarah Bancroft was waiting. Ten minutes after the ambassador departed, they joined their mother aboard the Gulfstream and returned to the Adirondacks. Only the note was genuine. It had been written by the children at Andrews and handed over to the pilot. According to Elena, they had meant every word of it.

'My director bumped into the Russian ambassador at a White House reception a couple of months back. He's still fuming about what happened. Apparently, he lives in fear of Ivan's wrath. He spends as little time in Russia as possible.'

Gabriel slipped the letter into his shirt pocket. Surely Carter hadn't come all the way to Jerusalem to recover a passport and deliver a letter, but he seemed in no hurry to get around to the real reason for his visit. He was now reading his newspaper. He folded it in quarters and handed it across to Gabriel.

'You see this?' he asked, tapping a headline.

It was a story about the new memorial at the killing ground in Vladimirskaya Oblast. Though understated and small, it had already attracted tens of thousands of visitors, much to the chagrin of the Kremlin. Many of the visitors were relatives of those killed there, but most were ordinary Russians who came to see something of their dark past. Since the memorial's opening, Stalin had seen a precipitous slide in his standing. So, too, had the current regime. Indeed, more and more Russians were beginning to voice their discontent. The reporter for the *Herald Tribune* wondered whether Russians might be so willing to accept an authoritarian future if they spoke more openly about their totalitarian past. Gabriel wasn't so sure. He remembered something Olga Sukhova had once said while walking through Novodevichy Cemetery. Russians had never known true democracy. And, in all likelihood, they never would.

'It says here the Russian president still hasn't paid a visit.'

'He's a very busy man,' said Carter.

'Do you think he's regretting the decision to make it public?'

'I'm afraid he had no choice. We agreed to keep everything about the affair quiet and to cover up Grigori's death with that ridiculous story about suicide. But the graves weren't part of the deal. In fact, we made it clear to the Kremlin that if they didn't tell the Russian people the truth, we would do it for them.'

Gabriel folded the newspaper and tried to return it to Carter.

'Look at the story below it.'

The subject was a new round of bloodletting in the

Congo that had left more than a hundred thousand people dead. It was accompanied by a photo of a distraught mother holding the body of her dead child.

'And guess who's helping to fan the flames?' Carter asked.

'Ivan?'

Carter nodded his head. 'He put two planeloads of weapons on the ground there last month. Mortars, RPGs, AKs, and several million rounds of ammunition. And what do you think the Russian president said when we asked him to intervene?'

'Ivan who?'

'Words to that effect. It's clear no amount of cajoling or sweet talk is ever going to convince the Kremlin to shut down Ivan's operation. If we ever want to put him out of business, we're going to have to do it ourselves.'

'As long as Ivan is in Russia, he's untouchable.'

'That's true, as long as he stays in Russia. But if he were to leave . . .'

'He won't leave, Adrian. Not with an Interpol Red Notice hanging over his head.'

'One would think. But Ivan can be impulsive.' Carter bunched his hands beneath his chin and gazed at the walls of the Old City. 'By our count, you and your team killed eleven Russians in Europe this summer. We were wondering whether you might be interested in going after one more target.'

Gabriel felt his heart banging against his ribs. His next words were spoken with far more calm than he was feeling.

'Where's he going?'

Carter told him.

'Isn't he still under indictment there?'

'Langley is of the opinion the country in question has no real desire to go after him.'

'Why not?'

'Politics, of course. And oil. This country wants to improve its ties with Moscow. It believes that arresting and prosecuting a personal friend of the Russian president would only lead to Kremlin retaliation.'

'Does the intelligence service of the country in question know Ivan is headed their way?'

'Given our concerns about their politicians, we've chosen not to inform their spies. Also, it will make other options more difficult to execute.'

'What other options?'

'It seems to me we have three.'

'Number one?'

'Let him enjoy his holiday and forget about it.'

'Bad idea. Number two?'

'Arrest him ourselves and bring him to American soil for trial.'

'Too messy. Besides, it would cause a crisis between the United States and an important European ally.'

'Our thoughts exactly. In fact, we feel we are precluded from taking any action on the soil of this country.' Carter paused, then added, 'Which brings us to the third option.'

'What's that?'

'Kachol v'lavan.'

'How certain are you that Ivan will be there?'

Carter handed over the dossier.

'Dead certain.'

77. Saint-Tropez, France

Appropriately enough, the boat was called *Mischief*: one hundred seventy-eight feet of American-built, Bahamian-registered luxury, owned and operated by one Maxim Simonov, better known as Mad Maxim, king of Russia's lucrative nickel industry, friend and playmate of the Russian president, and former guest at Villa Soleil, Ivan Kharkov's now-vacant palace by the sea in Saint-Tropez. Though Maxim owned a villa worth twenty million dollars on Spain's Costa del Sol, he preferred the privacy and mobility of his yacht. He'd toured the North African coast in June and had spent July island-hopping through Greece. On the final leg of the excursion, he had ordered his crew to make a brief detour to the Turkish coast, and there, on the morning of August the ninth, he had taken aboard two more passengers: a sturdy-looking man called Alexei Budanov and his ravishing young wife, Zoya. Though childless, the couple had vast quantities of luggage — so much, in fact, they required a second stateroom just for storage. Mad Maxim seemed not to mind. His friends had endured a horrible year. And Mad Maxim, a generous soul if ever there was, had taken it upon himself to see they at least had a proper summer holiday.

The host had earned his nickname not through his business acumen but through his leisure activities. His parties were notoriously wild affairs that seldom ended without violence or arrests. Indeed, several years earlier, Maxim was briefly detained after allegedly importing a planeload of Russian prostitutes to entertain guests at his château outside Paris. The French police later agreed to drop all charges after the billionaire managed to convince them the girls were simply part of a modern-dance troupe. The outrageous but somewhat comical affair did nothing to harm Maxim's standing at home. In fact, the Moscow papers hailed him as the perfect example of the New Russian. Mad Maxim had money and he was not afraid to flaunt it, even if it meant getting into a scrape every now and again with the French police.

The pace of his partying did not slow at sea. If anything, freed from the constraints of meddlesome authorities and complaining neighbors, it reached new levels of intensity. That summer had already produced many notable evenings of debauchery, but new heights were achieved with the arrival of Alexei and Zoya Budanov. Looked after by a crew of thirty, the entourage spent the voyage eating, drinking, and fornicating their way across the Mediterranean, before finally arriving in the fabled Old Port of Saint-Tropez on the afternoon of August the twentieth. Though exhausted and deeply hungover from the previous evening's adventures, the passengers immediately boarded *Mischief*'s dinghies and headed for shore. All but the man known as Alexei Budanov, who remained on the aft deck, hands resting on the railing, staring at Saint-Tropez as if it were his forbidden city. And though Mr. Budanov did not know it, he was already being watched by a man standing at the base of the lighthouse at the end of the Quai d'Estienne d'Orves.

The man wore khaki shorts, a white pullover, a bucket

hat, and wraparound sunglasses. Several months earlier, in a birch forest outside Moscow, Mr. Budanov had tried to kill his wife. Now the man planned to kill Mr. Budanov. But, for that, he needed one thing. He needed him to leave the ship. He was confident Mr. Budanov would not stay there long. The Russian was addicted to money, women, and Saint-Tropez. The French resort had been the backdrop for his downfall, and it would be the setting for his death. The man of medium height and build was sure of this. He simply had to be patient. He had to let Mr. Budanov come to him. And then he would put him down.

Fortunately, he would not have to wait alone. He had eight associates to keep him company. Under different names and speaking different languages, they had spent most of the summer on a tour of Europe quite unlike any other. This would be the last stop on their itinerary. Then it would be over.

They lived together under one roof, in a villa located in the hills above the city. It had pale blue shutters and a large swimming pool with views of the distant sea. They spent little time in the pool, just enough to deceive the neighbors. Indeed, most of their time was spent on the streets of Saint-Tropez, watching, shadowing, listening. A friend at the CIA made their task easier by sending transcripts and recordings of all telephone calls made from the yacht or by its passengers. The intercepts gave them advance warning whenever Mad Maxim or a member of his party was coming to town. They knew ahead of time where they planned to have lunch each day, where they planned to have dinner, and which exclusive nightclub they planned to wreck sometime after midnight. The intercepts also allowed them to hear the voice of Alexei Budanov himself. Nearly all his calls were to Moscow. Not once did he identify himself or utter his own name.

Nor did he set foot off the *Mischief*. Even when the others dined at Le Grand Joseph, his favorite lunch spot, he remained a prisoner of the yacht. And the man of medium height and build passed the time a short distance away, at the foot of his lighthouse. To help fill the empty hours, he dreamed of making love to his wife. And he restored imaginary paintings. And he remembered in vivid detail the nightmare in the birch forest. For the most part, though, he kept his eyes focused on the yacht. And he waited. *Always the waiting* . . . Waiting for a plane or a train. Waiting for a source. Waiting for the sun to rise after a night of killing. And waiting for Ivan Kharkov to finally make his return to Saint-Tropez.

Late in the afternoon of the twenty-ninth, while watching *Mischief*'s dinghies returning to the mother ship, Gabriel received a call on his secure cell phone. The voice he heard was Eli Lavon's.

'You'd better get up here right away.'

In the end, it was not American technology that would be Ivan's undoing but Israeli cunning. While walking along the Chemin des Conquettes, a residential street south of Saint-Tropez's bustling *centre ville*, Lavon had noticed a new sign on the door of the restaurant known as Villa Romana. Written in English, French, and Russian, it stated that, regrettably, the famous Saint-Tropez eatery and party spot would be closed two nights hence for a private affair. Posing as a paparazzi in search of movie stars, Lavon had tossed a bit of money around the waitstaff to see if he could learn the identity of the individual who had booked the establishment. From one despondent bartender he learned it was going to be an all-Russian affair. A busboy confided it was going to be a blowout – his word, a *blowout*. And finally, from the stunning hostess, he was able to obtain the name of the man who would be throwing the party and footing the bill: Mad Maxim Simonov, the nickel king of Russia. 'No movie stars,' the girl said. 'Just drunk Russians and their girlfriends. Every year they celebrate the last night of the season. It should be a night to remember.' It would be, Lavon thought. A very memorable night, indeed.

Gabriel placed a wager, one he was confident would pay handsomely. He wagered that Ivan Kharkov could not possibly come all the way to the Côte d'Azur and resist the gravitational pull of Villa Romana, a restaurant where he had once had a regular table. He would take reasonable precautions, perhaps even wear a crude disguise of some sort, but he would come. And Gabriel would be waiting. Whether he pulled the trigger would be contingent on two factors. He would shed no innocent blood, other than that of armed bodyguards, and he would not sink to Ivan's level by killing him in front of his young wife. Lavon came up with a plan of action. They called it fun with phones.

It *was* a night to remember, and, just as Gabriel predicted, Ivan was unable to resist attending the party. The techno-pop music was deafening, the women were barely clad, and the champagne flowed like a swollen river. Ivan kept a low profile, though he wore no disguise since not one of the invited guests would have dared to report his presence. As for the possibility he might have been in any physical danger, this, too, seemed to have been discounted. The two bodyguards that Mad Maxim had brought along for protection were standing like doormen outside Villa Romana's entrance. And if either one of them so much as twitched, they would die there at two a.m. Two a.m., because Ivan's defenses would be weakened by fatigue and alcohol. Two a.m., because that is the hour the Chemin des Conquettes finally goes quiet on a warm summer night. Two a.m., because that is when Ivan would receive the telephone call that would draw him into the street. The call that would signal that the end was finally near.

For their staging point, Gabriel and Mikhail chose the edge of a small playground at the northern end of the Chemin des Conquettes. They did this because they thought it was just and because the entrance of Villa Romana was only fifty yards away. They sat astride their motorbikes in a dark patch between the streetlamps and listened to the voices in their miniature earpieces. No one gave them a second look. Sitting idly on a motorbike at two in the morning is what one does on a warm summer night in Saint-Tropez, especially when the first crack of autumn thunder is only days away.

It was not thunder that caused them to start their engines but a quiet voice. It told them the call had just gone through to Ivan's phone. It told them the time was nearly at hand. Gabriel touched the .45 caliber Glock at the small of his back – the Glock loaded with highly destructive hollow-tipped rounds – and made a slight modification in its position. Then he lowered the visor on his helmet and waited for the signal.

It was Oleg Rudenko calling from Moscow – at least, that's what Ivan was led to believe. He couldn't quite be certain. He never would be. The connection was too tenuous, the music too loud. Ivan knew three things: the caller spoke Russian, had the direct number for his mobile, and said it was extremely urgent. That was enough to put him on his feet and send him marching into the quiet of the street, phone to one ear, hand over the other. If Ivan heard the approaching motorbikes, he gave no sign of it. In fact, he was shouting in Russian, his back turned, at the instant Gabriel brought his motorbike to a stop. The bodyguards at the front door immediately sensed trouble and foolishly reached into their blazers. Mikhail shot each through the heart before they managed to touch their weapons. Seeing the guards go down, Ivan whirled around in terror, only to find himself staring down the suppressor at the end of the Glock. Gabriel lifted the visor of his helmet and smiled. Then he pulled the trigger, and Ivan's face vanished. *For Grigori*, he thought, as he drove off into the darkness. *For Chiara.*

Author's Note

The Defector is a work of entertainment. The names, characters, places, and incidents portrayed in this novel are the product of the author's imagination or have been used fictitiously. Any resemblance to actual persons, living or dead, businesses, companies, events, or locales is entirely coincidental.

The Siberian oil giant Ruzoil does not exist, nor does the *Moskovskaya Gazeta* or Galaxy Travel of Tverskaya Street. Viktor Orlov, Olga Sukhova, and Grigori Bulganov are in no way meant to be construed as fictitious renderings of real people.

The headquarters of the Israeli secret service is no longer located on King Saul Boulevard in Tel Aviv. I have chosen to keep the headquarters of my fictitious service there in part because I have always liked the name. I have tinkered with airline schedules to make them fit my story. Anyone trying to reach London from Moscow will search in vain for Aeroflot Flight 247. There is no private bank in Zurich called Becker & Puhl. Its internal operating procedures were invented by the author. The Office of Presidential Advance has been accurately portrayed, but, to the best of my knowledge, it has never been used to provide cover for an Israeli spy.

There is no airfield at Konakovo, at least not one I am aware of; nor is there a division of the FSB known as the

Department of Coordination. A chess club does indeed meet on Tuesday evenings in the Lower Vestry House of St George's Church in Bloomsbury. It is called the Greater London Chess Club, not the Central London Chess Club, and its members are charming and gracious to a fault. Deepest apologies to the management of Villa Romana in Saint-Tropez for carrying out an assassination on their doorstep, but I'm afraid it had to be done. Also, apologies to the residents of the lovely Bristol Mews in Maida Vale for placing a Russian defector in their midst. Were the author ever to go into hiding in London, it would certainly be there. Readers should not go looking for Gabriel Allon at No. 16 Narkiss Street in Jerusalem or for Viktor Orlov at No. 43 Cheyne Walk in Chelsea. Nor should they read too much into my use of a poison-dispensing ring, though I suspect the KGB and its successors probably have one.

The Great Terror killing ground discovered at the climax of *The Defector* is fictitious, but, sadly, the historical circumstances that could have created such a place are not. Precisely how many people were shot to death during the brutal repressions lasting from 1936 to 1938 may never be known. Estimates range from approximately seven hundred thousand to well over a million. Suffice it to say the number of those executed is but one measure of the suffering Stalin inflicted on Russia during the time of the Great Terror. Historian Robert Conquest estimates that the purges and Stalin-induced famines probably claimed between eleven million and thirteen million lives. Other historians place the number even higher. And still opinion polls consistently find that Stalin remains highly popular among Russians to this day.

One of the few sites where Russians can mourn Stalin's victims is Butovo, just south of Moscow. There, from August 1937 to October 1938, an estimated twenty thousand people were shot in the back of the head and buried in long mass graves. I visited the recently opened memorial at Butovo with my family in the summer of 2007 while researching *Moscow Rules*, and in large measure it inspired *The Defector*. One question haunted me as I walked slowly past the burial trenches, accompanied by weeping Russian citizens. Why are there not more places like this? Places where ordinary Russians can see evidence of Stalin's unimaginable crimes with their own eyes. The answer, of course, is that the rulers of the New Russia are not terribly interested in exposing the sins of the Soviet past. On the contrary, they are engaged in a carefully orchestrated endeavor to airbrush away its most repulsive aspects while celebrating its achievements. One can understand their motives. The NKVD, which carried out the Great Terror at Stalin's behest, was the forerunner of the KGB. And former officers of the KGB, including Vladimir Putin himself, are now running Russia.

There is a danger to such historical myopia, of course: the danger that it might happen again. In smaller, far more subtle ways, it already is. Since coming to power in 1999, Vladimir Putin, Russia's former president and now prime minister, has overseen a wide-ranging curtailment of press and civic freedoms. And in December 2008 the government introduced new legislation that would greatly expand the definition of 'state treason.' Human rights activists, already on shaky ground, fear the laws could be used to jail anyone who dares to criticize the regime. Andrei Lugovoi, the former KGB officer accused by British authorities of the November 2006 poisoning of the dissident defector Alexander Litvinenko, apparently feels the new law does not go far enough. Now a member of parliament, and a hero to many Russians, he told the Spanish newspaper *El País* that anyone who dares to criticize Russia 'should be exterminated.'

Lugovoi went on to say: 'Do I think someone should have killed Litvinenko in the interests of the Russian state? If you're talking about the interests of the Russian state, in the purest sense of the word, I myself would have given that order.' This from the man wanted by British authorities for the very same murder of which he speaks.

For those who dare to question the Kremlin and Russia's powerful elite, arrest and prosecution are sometimes the least of their worries. Too many have simply been killed in cold blood. Witness the case of Stanislav Markelov, the crusading human rights lawyer and social justice activist, gunned down on a central Moscow street in January 2009 as he was leaving a news conference. Also killed was Anastasia Baburova, a freelance journalist for *Novaya Gazeta* – tragically, the same publication that employed Anna Politkovskaya, who was shot to death in the elevator of her Moscow apartment house in October 2006.

According to the New York-based Committee to Protect Journalists, forty-nine media professionals have been killed in Russia since 1992. Only in Iraq and Algeria have more died in the line of duty during the same period. This, too, is a Russian tragedy.

Acknowledgements

As always, I am deeply indebted to my dear friend David Bull, who truly is among the finest art restorers in the world. Each year, David gives up many hours of his extremely valuable time to peer over my shoulder, and Gabriel's, to make certain we are doing our jobs correctly. His wisdom is exceeded only by the pleasure of his company.

I consulted hundreds of books, newspaper and magazine articles, and websites while preparing this manuscript, far too many to name here, but I would be remiss if I did not mention several important works: *The Terminal Spy* by Alan S. Cowell, *The New Cold War* by Edward Lucas, *Stalin: A Biography* by Robert Service, *Stalin* by Edvard Radzinsky, and *Comrade J* by Pete Earley.

Several Israeli and American intelligence officers spoke to me on background while I was preparing this manuscript, and I thank them now in anonymity, which is how they would prefer it. Aaron Nutter generously shared stories of his time at the White House Office of Presidential Advance and, along with the other members of Peloton One, was great company on Saturday and Sunday mornings. The eminent Washington orthopedist Dr. Benjamin Shaffer advised me on bullet wounds and infection. Dr. Andrew Pate, the renowned anesthesiologist of Charleston, South Carolina, explained the harmful effects of sedatives on pregnant women.

My dear friend Louis Toscano has been improving my writing since we worked together at the venerable United Press International late in the last century, and *The Defector* was made far better by his sure hand. My copy editors, Tony Davis and Kathy Crosby, spared me much embarrassment, while Olga Gardner Galvin scrutinized my use of Russian words. Obviously, responsibility for any mistakes or typographical errors that find their way into the finished book falls on my shoulders, not theirs.

A heartfelt thanks to my remarkable publishing team, especially John Makinson, David Shanks, Marilyn Ducksworth, Neil Nyren, Leslie Gelbman, Kara Welsh, Kate Stark, Dick Heffernan, Norman Lidofsky, Alex Clarke, and Putnam's president, Ivan Held. Since Ivan Kharkov is now dead, Ivan Held can once again have his name to himself. Also, I wish to extend my thanks to the members of the best publicity team in the business: Stephanie Sorensen, Katie McKee, Victoria Comella, Stephany Perez, Samantha Wolf, and Eliisa Frazier.

We are blessed with many friends who fill our lives with love and laughter at critical junctures during the writing year, especially Linda Rappaport and Len Chazen, Roger and Laura Cressey, Jane and Rob Lynch, Sue and Fred Kobak and their amazing family, and Joy and Jim Zorn. Jeff Zucker, Ron Meyer, and Michael Gendler offered friendship and support, while Rabbi David J. Wolpe, author of *Why Faith Matters*, helped me through a particularly difficult day of writing with his humor and grace. A special thanks to Sloan Harris for his professionalism, enthusiasm, and insightful suggestions, and to Marisa Ryan for casting her gifted eye over *The Defector*'s cover.

In the course of writing twelve novels, I have found I lean hardest on those at home. This book truly could not have been written without the assistance of my children, Nicholas and Lily. Not only did they help assemble the final manuscript, but they gave me unconditional love and support while I was struggling to make my deadline. Finally, I must thank my wife, Jamie Gangel. In addition to managing my business, running our household, and raising two remarkable children, she also found time to brilliantly edit each of my drafts. Were it not for her forbearance, support, and attention to detail, *The Defector* would not have been completed. My debt to her is immeasurable, as is my love.

DANIEL SILVA

THE SECRET SERVANT

In Amsterdam, an Israeli terrorism analyst is murdered. The police believe the killer is a deranged Muslim extremist, but Israeli intelligence knows better. Art-restorer, assassin and spy Gabriel Allon is dispatched to investigate, uncovering a major terrorist operation in London.

Gabriel arrives too late to prevent the kidnapping of the daughter of the US ambassador. With time running out, Allon has no choice but to plunge into a desperate search, both for the woman and for those responsible, but the truth, when he finds it, is more terrible than he could expect. It will endanger his life and shake him to the core.

'Shootouts, kidnappings and international terror plots follow Allon wherever he goes'
USA Today

'Frightening: reads like a prediction of continuing terrorism in Europe'
Wall Street Journal

DANIEL SILVA

MOSCOW RULES

The violent death of a journalist leads secret agent Gabriel Allon to Russia. Not to the grim Moscow of Soviet times, but a modern Moscow, awash in oil wealth and in thrall to a new generation of rich Stalinists plotting to challenge an old enemy: the United States.

One such man is Ivan Kharkov, a former KGB colonel, whose global empire is built on a lucrative and deadly business. Kharkov is an arms dealer – and he's about to sell Russia's most dangerous weapon to al-Qaeda. Unless Allon can learn the time and place of delivery, the world will suffer its deadliest terror attack since 9/11.

The countdown to Armageddon has begun . . .

'Shootouts, kidnappings and international terror plots follow Gabriel Allon wherever he goes' *USA Today*